Praise for *Trust No One*

"*Trust No One* is Debra Webb at her finest. Political intrigue and dark family secrets will keep readers feverishly turning pages to uncover all the twists in this stunning thriller."
— Melinda Leigh, #1 Wall Street Journal bestselling author of
Cross Her Heart

"A wild, twisting crime thriller filled with secrets, betrayals, and complex characters that will keep you up until you reach the last darkly satisfying page. A five-star beginning to Debra Webb's explosive series!"
— Allison Brennan, *New York Times* bestselling author

"Debra Webb once again delivers with *Trust No One*, a twisty and gritty page-turning procedural with a cast of complex characters and a compelling con heroine in Detective Kerri Devlin. I look forward to seeing m
lling author of
In the Deep

"*Trust No One* is a gritty and exciting ride. Webb skillfully weaves together a mystery filled with twists and turns. I was riveted as each layer of the past peeled away, revealing dark secrets. An intriguing cast of complicated characters, led by the compelling Detective Kerri Devlin, had me holding my breath until the last page."
— Brianna Labuskes, *Washington Post* bestselling author of
Girls of Glass

"Debra Webb's name says it all."
— Karen Rose, *New York Times* bestselling author

TRUST
NO
ONE

TRUST NO ONE

DEBRA WEBB

THOMAS & MERCER

Text copyright © 2020 by Debra Webb
All rights reserved.

Published by Thomas & Mercer, Seattle

www.apub.com

Amazon, the Amazon logo, and Thomas & Mercer are trademarks of Amazon.com, Inc., or its affiliates.

ISBN-13: 9781542018098
ISBN-10: 1542018099

Cover design by Shasti O'Leary Soudant

Printed in the United States of America

I cannot thank Megha Parekh enough for giving me this amazing opportunity. I am so excited about this new journey with Thomas & Mercer. Writing a novel isn't as easy as simply sitting down at your computer and allowing the magic to flow from your fingertips. It is sometimes hard, mentally exhausting work. Other times the words flow like a river. And once you've completed the manuscript, there is more work. Much more work. To create the best story possible, this part requires a team effort. I want to thank every member of the team who helped me bring this story to life. Thanks so much to Megha Parekh, Charlotte Herscher, and all the copy editors and proofreaders who touched these pages. You are brilliant!

What the eye doesn't see, the heart doesn't grieve . . .

—Unknown

1

TODAY

Saturday, June 16

7:15 a.m.

"Just tell me where she is, and we can take this down a notch." Kerri took a breath, let it out slowly. "I'll lower my weapon. You have my word. All I want is your cooperation."

Her palms were sweating. Arms shaking from maintaining the firing stance for so long. She didn't trust this bastard, but she damned sure hadn't followed him here to do *this*.

Now she had a situation.

The lieutenant would say desperation had driven her over the edge, and he wouldn't be wrong. Her new partner would shake his head and wonder how she ever dared to judge him.

Kerri blinked. She had gone too far. She knew this. Too late to change that now. Swallowing the lump of uncertainty rising in her throat, she stared at the man in her crosshairs. *Way too late.*

He laughed. Blood trickled from his swollen, no doubt broken nose. She'd punched him hard. As if to underscore the thought, her right hand throbbed mercilessly. Anger tightened her lips. Not hard enough, or he wouldn't be so smug right now. The son of a bitch.

"You should know by now, Detective Devlin, that you can't touch me. I will ruin you," he warned, the words nasally sounding. He swiped at the blood spatter staining his pale-blue polo. "Your career with the Birmingham Police Department is *over*."

Like she needed anyone to point out that glaringly obvious detail. With every fiber of her being, she wanted to kill him. The urge simmered in the deepest part of her soul. She knew what this bastard had done. She had evidence, by God. Maybe not enough for a trial conviction, but it was something. For now, that could wait. *This* was far more important . . . more urgent.

She was the one who laughed this time. "Can't you tell by now I don't care? As long as I take you all the way down first, I can live with whatever comes second."

He smiled at her, the expression incongruent with his bleeding and damaged face. "But you do care about that sweet little daughter of yours, don't you? I would hate to see her have to pay for your mistakes, Detective."

Kerri flinched. A new rush of fury lashed through her, more at her reaction than at his threat. "Just fucking tell me what I need to know." She twitched the barrel of her Glock .40 cal. "Or I swear to God I will put a bullet right between your eyes."

He stared at her for one, two, three beats; then he said, "Go ahead. Shoot me."

Shit.

Maybe he'd seen her arms shake or spotted that goddamned flinch. Either way, he'd called her bluff.

No turning back now.

Her hand tightened on the grip. Forefinger curled around the trigger. "You think I won't?"

He lunged at her.

She instinctively twisted to the right.

His body crashed into her left shoulder, sending her off balance.

She slammed backward onto the floor. The weight of his body landing on top of her forced the air from her lungs.

Weapon?

Adrenaline roaring, she locked the fingers of her right hand tighter around the butt of the Glock.

She still had her weapon. Relief trickled through her.

With every ounce of might she possessed, she punched with her left fist, aiming for the throat. He stretched his upper body to one side, ensuring the blow jammed impotently into his shoulder.

She yanked her arm back, aimed again . . . he backhanded her.

Blocking out the pain, she rammed her knee toward his groin. He dodged the move. Grabbed at the Glock with one hand and her hair with the other.

No. No. No!

She twisted her right arm, fought to wrench the barrel of the weapon from his desperate grasp. His grip tightened. His face distorted with rage. She bucked and rotated her body, used her free hand to clutch at his throat, his eyes, whatever she could reach. He slammed her head against the floor. Again. And again.

The room spun. She felt her wrist crack from the pressure of him trying to rip the Glock from her grasp.

She . . . could . . . not . . . allow . . . him . . . to . . . take . . . it . . .

Her head hit the floor again, harder this time.

Her eyes rolled back. She blinked. Shook herself. His weight ground into her waist.

Another thwack of her head . . .

The blast of a bullet discharging from her weapon exploded in the room.

She gasped.

Darkness clawed at her.

3

She fought to stay conscious. Tried to rise up.

Where was he . . . ?

The room shifted out of focus. Started to spin. She closed her eyes to slow the whirling sensation.

The darkness swallowed her, dragging her down . . . down . . . down . . .

There was sound.

She stopped falling . . . fought against the darkness still swaddling her.

The sound came again. Rattling . . . vibrating.

There was pain.

Kerri tried to open her eyes once more.

More of that vibrating.

Her eyes cracked open, and pain exploded behind them. She squeezed them shut and groaned.

That damned rattling started again, and this time she recognized it was her phone. She opened her eyes and turned her head despite the pain and stared at the black device lying on the wood floor. A moment was required before her brain got the message through to her arm that she had to reach for the phone in order to answer it.

Her partner's face flashed on the screen. *Falco.* There was something . . .

Shit!

She sat up. The room spun, and her head exploded with more of that searing pain. When she dared to open her eyes again, she stared at the man slumped facedown on the floor, one of her legs trapped beneath his thighs.

"Jesus Christ." She scrambled free of his weight.

The room whirled again. She grabbed her head and closed her eyes until the spinning stopped, and the pain leveled out. Another groan hissed past her lips.

That damned vibration erupted once more. She couldn't deal with that right now. She forced her eyes open. Slowly, she crawled on all fours until she was within reach of *him*. She touched his neck, checked for a pulse.

Nothing.

He was dead.

Fuck.

Where was her weapon?

She hoisted herself to her feet, staggered around the body. Didn't see the damned thing.

"Shit. Shit. Shit."

The Glock had to be under him.

Using her right foot, she pushed, swaying drunkenly on her left, until she rolled him onto his back. The hole in his upper chest and all the blood told her the bullet had likely gone in at an upward trajectory and pierced a major artery.

He was dead.

She'd killed him.

Reaching down, she was relieved that her weapon lay just outside the widening ring of blood. She snatched it up and shoved it into her waistband.

Her phone started rattling again. This time she grabbed it and managed to hit the necessary button. "Devlin."

"Where the hell are you?" Rather than wait for her answer, Luke Falco, her partner, said, "They've found something, Devlin. Another body, possibly female. This case is busting wide open. You need to be here. You need to be here *now*."

The case. For ten days the investigation into a double homicide had been leading them deeper and deeper into the past and giving them nothing but the occasional fragment of information. Now, suddenly the dozens of scattered pieces were coming together.

She stared at the dead man on the floor. He was one of those pieces.

A new rush of cold, hard reality gushed through her.

Fuck! She touched the back of her head gingerly with her free hand. She didn't feel any blood, but it hurt like hell. She winced and drew her hand away. *Focus!* The case. Falco. Jesus Christ, this was a mess.

"Sorry." She swallowed back the rising panic. "I got caught up in something." She closed her eyes to block the body from her field of vision. "Text me the address. I'm on my way."

"Hurry, Devlin. I've got a feeling about this."

"Yeah. Okay. I'll be there soon." She ended the call and shoved the phone into her back pocket.

What the hell should she do? Call it in? If she did . . . a new kind of foreboding slunk around her chest.

She held her aching head and fought the urge to cry. Too damned late for that. He was dead.

Okay. Okay. She had killed him. Regardless of whether she had intended to do so, he was dead, and it was her bullet that had initiated the cause of death.

She needed to think. To figure this out.

She thought of her daughter. Oh God. If Kerri went to jail, Tori . . .

She banished the thought, steadied herself. "I can't do this right now."

She had to go. Falco and the search team were already at the scene. She was supposed to be there. She could deal with this later. Claim temporary insanity for leaving the scene.

She stared at her hands and checked her clothes to ensure there was no blood on her. Clean.

After turning too quickly, she stumbled and almost fell rushing to the door. She closed the door behind her and moved a little more slowly across the porch and down the steps, her hands searching her pockets for her keys. If she had to go back in there . . .

She climbed into her Wagoneer and thanked God when the keys were in the ignition.

Summoning every ounce of resolve she possessed, she started the engine and shifted into drive, only then remembering to fasten her seat belt. Considering the way her head throbbed and the need to vomit along with the loopy feeling, she probably had a concussion, but that was another of those situations she couldn't do anything about at the moment.

She held on to the steering wheel with both hands and drew in a deep breath, then another. She could straighten this out later. "It was an accident."

The words rang hollowly in the air around her.

He'd attacked her. The weapon had discharged.

Accidental shooting. Maybe even self-defense. He had threatened her and her daughter.

What the hell had she been thinking, confronting him in the first place? Had she really expected the bastard to come clean with her? She was a better cop than this. Goddamn it.

She was losing it . . . or maybe she'd already lost it.

A man was dead. Possibly an innocent man. No way. Hell no. She refused to go that far. He was guilty of at least covering up numerous crimes, possibly even murder. Her lips tightened. Oh yes. Every instinct she had honed over the years as a detective warned that he was the one.

Curve.

Her breath stalled in her lungs. She shoved her foot down on the brake.

Too late. The car spun, sliding sideways.

She missed the curve.

The ditch rose up to meet her.

2

TEN DAYS EARLIER

Wednesday, June 6

9:15 a.m.

Birmingham Police Department
First Avenue North
Major Investigations Division

"I'm not happy about this." Kerri shook her head, dug her fists deeper into her waist. "How did I draw the short straw?"

Lieutenant Dontrelle Brooks leaned far enough back in his chair that if not for the credenza behind him, he might have actually tipped over. The sharp creases in his white shirt stood at attention; his tie lay expertly knotted at his throat. He could land the coveted cover of *GQ* as the best-dressed cop in America. Too bad the look wouldn't last long. By noon his crisp white shirt would be wrinkled and his blue-and-red-striped tie loosened the slightest bit from dealing with frustrating situations, not unlike this one, that he would just as soon ignore.

"Detective Falco needs a top-notch detective to teach him the ropes." The LT flared his big hands—hands that had collared more than his fair share of perps before ending up pushing around pencils and shuffling resources. "You're the best in the division, Devlin. What's the big deal? You were once a new detective. If Boswell hadn't wanted you as a partner, you think you'd be the next in line for a promotion to sergeant at this stage in your career?"

Trent Boswell had been her partner for seven years, until he'd retired last month. He had been the best partner any detective could ask for. A good cop, a good man. Falco, on the other hand, was rumored to be a pain in the ass who had skated on the edge his entire too-short career. He had more reprimands than anyone in the Birmingham Police Department. Frankly, Kerri didn't see how the hell he'd made detective, much less found his way into Major Investigations. Being a good detective was about a lot more than passing a written exam. A cop's record, bearing, and attitude came into play with equal gravity. She assumed the guy had unearthed a dirty little secret on someone high enough up to make a difference, because he didn't have the record, the bearing, or the attitude to hold the rank—in her possibly not-so-humble and entirely unobjective opinion.

She hated that kind of double-dealing.

But she got it now. "In other words, I'm being punished for being a good cop?"

Brooks rolled his eyes. "Enough with the grief, Devlin. You know how this works."

Before she could launch her next wave of protest, he stopped her with a caveat: "Just give this arrangement a month. If you're not happy with him as your partner, then we'll consider other options."

The lie rolled glibly off his tongue, but the body language told the real story. His shoulders had slumped forward, and he immediately averted his gaze from hers. She was stuck with Falco until he quit or got himself fired or dead.

The more likely scenario was that his cocky, completely irreverent attitude would get *her* dead.

Damn it.

"Whatever you say, sir." Might as well back away from the brick wall in front of her and get on with this new arrangement. Her only option at this point was to figure out the deal with Falco and how he'd reached the rank of detective in spite of his rocky record.

Learn his secrets and gain some measure of leverage.

As exasperating as it was to be stuck with the new guy, considering all she'd heard about him, she had rank over Falco, and she had every intention of using that seniority to see that he played by *her* rules. End of story.

Brooks nodded. "You've always been a good team player, Devlin. Your flexibility is duly noted and appreciated."

Blah blah blah. She barely held her own eye roll in check.

Not trusting herself to respond, she nodded and exited the LT's office. She walked the length of the bullpen, hesitated before reaching the cubicle she and Boswell had shared. Making detective had been her goal from the day she'd decided she wanted to be a cop. Being assigned to Birmingham's brand-new Major Investigations Division had been the icing on the cake. This division was the first of its kind, encompassing not only Birmingham proper but the communities that surrounded it, like Hoover, Mountain Brook, Vestavia, and half a dozen others. The cream-of-the-crop detectives from those same communities had been selected to serve alongside BPD's finest. Crimes that rose to the level of crossing local jurisdictions fell under the purview of Major Investigations.

Day one as partners she and Boswell had adjusted their small space so that their desks faced each other, their file cabinets were out of the way, and the shared case board was front and center. Now she was rethinking that arrangement. Separate work spaces would be far more tolerable under these new circumstances. Otherwise she would be stuck face to face with Falco, every hour of every day in the office.

Thank God a good portion of their time would be in the field. Then again, partners spent a lot of hours cramped up in a vehicle together doing surveillance or tracking down leads.

She heaved a big breath. This arrangement was going to be endlessly challenging and utterly irritating. Be that as it may, it was her duty to try and make it work. *Good team player.*

"Hey, Devlin," this new partner of hers said as she approached their shared work space. "How'd things go with the boss?"

She stared at him. In light of the fact that he hadn't been here when she'd gone into the LT's office, he had obviously nosed around to learn her whereabouts. "My meeting with the *boss* was private, Falco. Do you grasp the concept of privacy?"

He held up his hands in surrender. "I got you, Devlin. I definitely didn't mean to get all up in your business or anything."

She kept to herself the first snarky response that came to mind. *Make the best of the situation.* At some point today, they should discuss his wardrobe and appearance. Worn-out jeans, wrinkled shirts, and scuffed biker boots were not appropriate attire for a detective representing the Major Investigations Division. His beard-shadowed jaw and shaggy hair didn't make the cut either. Giving him grace, she reminded herself he was new. It was her job to ensure he was properly oriented.

"Unless you got some other private business"—Falco stood and reached for his vintage lightweight leather jacket—"we just landed our first case together. A homicide."

Wait. Wait. Wait. Kerri shook her head. "How did we land anything?"

He shrugged into that beat-up jacket she decided wasn't really vintage, just abused. "No clue," he said. "Sergeant Gordon handed it off like two minutes ago."

"Sykes and Peterson are up." She'd scarcely filed her final report on the Hayden case.

"The story is," Falco explained, "Sykes and Peterson got caught up in a robbery at their Starbucks stop this morning."

Great. She grabbed the keys on her desk and the large dark-roast black coffee she'd picked up at a drive-through and hadn't yet had the chance to drink. "We'll take my vehicle."

Falco's reputation as a reckless driver preceded him. To date he had wrecked two official vehicles in his five-year career.

"Suit yourself. Did I mention this is a two for one?"

Two vics? Not good. "What's the address?"

Kerri headed for the stairwell exit. Whoever and whatever the circumstances, the double homicide had been handed off to MID. There would be a clear and undeniable reason. Cops were territorial. No one liked someone else bulldozing into their jurisdiction without justifiable cause.

"Botanical Place in Mountain Brook." He moved up beside her. "For the record, that's why I was looking for you."

She paused at the stairwell door. "Good to know. I'd hate to think you were spying on me this early in our relationship."

"Relationship." He winked. "I like the sound of that, Devlin."

God help her. She might have to kill this guy herself.

Botanical Place, Mountain Brook

There were mansions in Mountain Brook, and there were *mansions*. The Abbott home was a *mansion*. A stunning European-style estate nestled amid the majestic trees on one of the community's most prestigious streets. The property was fenced and gated with a purportedly state-of-the-art security system. Yet somehow a killer had found his way inside and murdered two people, possibly three.

Kerri grabbed shoe covers and gloves from the repurposed tissue box that sat next to her on the classic vehicle's bench seat. She shoved them into the left pocket of her jacket along with her notebook. She kept her keys in her right. Her driver's license and necessary plastic were in a thin credit card case in an interior pocket. She never bought jackets without sufficient pockets because she hated carrying handbags or anything else on the job that set her apart from the male detectives. Whatever else she needed was in her Wagoneer. Made life far less complicated.

Kerri was all about uncomplicated, particularly these days.

She hit the lock button and closed the driver's-side door. Falco rounded the hood, and they crossed the strip of grass that separated the street from the sidewalk. Yellow crime scene tape draped across the front perimeter of the property, starting where the cobblestone driveway met the street. Kerri nodded at the uniform maintaining the perimeter and showed her credentials. She squinted to see his name tag. No matter that she was still four whole years from forty, her vision was already going downhill. The optometrist would say it was time to accommodate her astigmatism rather than ignore it, but it didn't give her enough consistent trouble to bother with glasses or contacts just yet. Either one would be annoying. Maybe not as annoying as adjusting to a new partner, but then the partnership between detectives was a special bond. She glanced at Falco. Whatever her misgivings and concerns about him, he'd made the grade somehow. She should give him the benefit of the doubt. She tugged on her gloves. It was amazing what a large extrastrong black coffee could do for her attitude.

"Morning, Detective Devlin."

The uni's broad smile jogged her memory about the same time his name came into better focus. "Morning, Baker."

Baker had been first on the scene at Councilor Hayden's homicide scene three weeks ago. She remembered thinking he'd likely been teased as a kid about being a baker or a cake maker. Not such a bad nickname either way. At least he hadn't been called a devil. Sometimes Kerri wondered why she'd chosen to reclaim her maiden name after the divorce.

Oh yeah, the bastard she'd married had cheated on her. She wanted no part of him attached to her—except their daughter, Victoria, of course. Tori was the only good thing to come of that doomed fourteen-year union.

Why had it taken her so long to recognize what Nicholas Jackman was? Or maybe he was right in his accusation that she had driven him to cheat because she'd been too obsessed with work.

Of course, it couldn't possibly be his fault.

Kerri ducked under the yellow tape and resisted the urge to groan as the thought of the divorce and her cheating ex trickled down to a more recent and pressing issue: their thirteen-year-old daughter had decided she wanted to spend the summer with Daddy in New York. Really, what young girl wouldn't want to trade Birmingham, Alabama, for Manhattan? Especially since Daddy's new firm had put him in an Upper East Side apartment with amazing views of the city.

The shock Kerri had felt when Tori had broached the subject this morning reverberated through her now. Thankfully she had been so startled by the idea she'd said little, but she felt certain her daughter was aware they would be revisiting the subject very soon. No way was Tori spending the whole summer with her dad. Not in New York at his hip apartment and especially not with his beautiful young girlfriend with whom he had cheated.

Not happening.

It wasn't that she didn't want her daughter to have quality time with her father. The trouble was the games Nick liked to play. He loved nothing more than using their daughter as a way to manipulate what he wanted. Kerri hadn't figured out exactly what he was up to with this "summer" proposition, but there would be a self-serving motive. Whatever that motive turned out to be, she didn't want Tori to be the one hurt by it. There had to be a workable compromise in the situation somewhere.

Officer Baker and Kerri's new partner were still chatting as she moved toward the home's front entrance. The arched opening leading to the front door was covered in ivy, adding to that European ambiance. From the minimal but lush front lawn to the iron flower boxes on the windows, the exterior was beautifully appointed and expertly manicured. Another uniform waited at the door. Kerri recognized the officer immediately: Tanya Matthews. Kerri had worked with her numerous times. Very detail oriented. Kerri liked that about her. The young officer's attention was focused on the notepad in her hand as Kerri approached.

"Morning, Officer Matthews." Kerri showed her credentials out of respect. No matter that Matthews would recognize her as had Baker; it was SOP before entering a crime scene. "What do we have inside?"

Matthews smiled in recognition. "Detective Devlin, good morning." Her smile promptly faded. "The husband and his elderly mother-in-law were shot to death. The wife is missing. Most of the house has been ransacked to some degree. Can't really tell if anything was taken. Crime Scene Unit is five minutes out. Medical examiner is on his way."

Damn. Kerri hated cases like this. No matter how many years she worked homicides, she would never understand how anyone could hurt a child or an elderly person. There was a special place in hell for those people. "Let's have a look."

As they started in the door, Falco hustled up to join them. "What's up, Tanya?"

Matthews gave him a nod as she continued to go over the details of the scene. "The master suite is on the first level. I'm guessing the shooter hit there first."

The front door led into a spacious entry hall. The stairs were a sharp left from the door. There was a bench, a closet, and then a powder room before the hall on that side of the entry disappeared into the depths of the home's east wing. To the right, the hall meandered toward the kitchen. The main living space or great room lay directly ahead. Kerri pulled on shoe covers as she mentally inventoried the rest of the layout visible from her position.

Falco tugged on his protective gear as they moved on, hopping on one foot and then the other behind Kerri. Matthews led the way. The officer had not exaggerated when she'd stated the house appeared ransacked. Doors stood open. Shelves had been swiped clean, scattering the books, framed photos, and knickknacks over the floor; drawers were pulled out, as if the perp had been looking in every imaginable hiding place for anything of value.

Or maybe for something specific.

They passed a laundry room and a door that led to the garage before the hall ended at the entrance to the master suite on the west side of the enormous house. The metallic odor of blood trickled into Kerri's nose as they reached those towering double doors. Her muscles tightened with that old familiar mixture of dread and anticipation.

This room had been searched by the intruder or intruders as well. Closet door opened. Elegant dresser drawers dragged forward with their contents strewn over the floor.

As they approached the king-size bed on the far side of the room, near the french doors, Matthews said, "Benjamin 'Ben' Abbott, forty. He's some kind of software guru. Got megarich before he hit thirty. He started his company in San Francisco, but he's originally from Birmingham. He moved back about a year ago. His father is *the* Daniel Abbott. He's the principal reason MID has the case."

"Top of the food chain around these parts." Kerri's gaze met the other woman's.

"The very top."

Daniel Abbott's ancestors were among Birmingham founders. Old money. Powerful. Something else to look forward to in this investigation—heavy media coverage and pressure from the department hierarchy. Not unlike last month's homicide investigation of the councilor that turned out to be a suicide for hire. The councilor had hidden his mental illness his entire adult life. Not even his wife understood the demons he had fought far too often for far too long. Rather than continue suffering in silence, and not wanting his family to endure the fallout of taking his own life, Hayden had hired someone to kill him. Made for a better payout from the insurance company too.

Ultimately things had gone exactly as he'd planned, except for his one mistake: never go cheap when hiring a hit man.

Kerri considered the first victim in her new case. Ben Abbott was handsome. He looked younger than forty. Short dark hair. Fit and tanned. The hole in the center of his forehead left no question as to how he had died. His eyes were closed, his chest was bare. The sheet was folded back at his waist, as if he'd only just crawled into bed. He could be asleep if not for the damage to his forehead and the lividity along his back and the underside of his arms, which lay at his sides. No sign of a struggle.

For the moment, Kerri ignored the blood on the other side of the bed. Boswell had taught her to focus on one element at a time, absorb all the details before moving on to the next element. His number one rule had been simple: the most important aspect of a homicide scene was the body or bodies; all else was secondary.

Kerri crouched next to the bed. She manipulated the fingers of the vic's right hand and moved the arm. Fingers were rigid, but no stiffening in the larger muscles. He'd been dead only a few hours.

"Looks as if he was shot in his sleep."

Matthews nodded. "The old lady upstairs wasn't so lucky."

Kerri grimaced, her mind immediately conjuring the images of a hard-fought struggle to stay alive. She picked up the framed photograph on Abbott's nightstand. The woman in the photo had long black hair and wide gray eyes. Her smile was warm. She looked young, physically fit, and happy.

"What about the wife?" Kerri stood and looked to Matthews. Presumably the blood on the other side of the bed belonged to the woman in the photograph.

"Sela Rollins Abbott. Twenty-eight," Matthews said. "According to the housekeeper, the couple started dating about a year and a half ago. Married a few weeks later. The wife has a ton of awards showcased in the husband's home office for all the charity work she's done since moving to Birmingham. It's like a shrine to some saint or something."

Matthews shrugged as she went on. "We haven't found her body yet, but she must have been in the house when the shooter came in." She gestured to the other side of the bed, where blood had soaked into the linens. "Obviously that blood didn't come from the husband. Her glasses and cell phone are on the bedside table, robe's in the chair. And if you check the master bath, you'll find her empty retainer case next to one of the sinks."

"How can you be sure it's her retainer case? Could be the dead guy's," Falco piped up.

Kerri resisted the urge to sigh at how he phrased the query. His question was a valid one even if it did raise doubts about the ability of a good cop to analyze a scene. She made a mental note to talk to him about communication skills. MID was under close scrutiny. It was important to be seen as team players all the way but particularly when working with the local cops in each jurisdiction.

Matthews stared at him for a moment before answering. "It's pink and has a sticker on it that says *Wife*."

Kerri bit back a smile. "You're thinking the shooter took Mrs. Abbott with him."

"We haven't found her body, which suggests as much. That said, unless the forensic guys spot something with luminol that I missed, I haven't found a blood trail—not even a drop—to indicate a hemorrhaging victim was hauled out of here."

"He may have wrapped her in something." Kerri looked around. "A throw or quilt."

When she moved away from the bed, Falco crouched next to the dead husband and had a closer look. "I'm betting it was a .22," he announced. He stood and nodded toward the victim. "Hard-contact wound. Whoever did this pressed the muzzle against his skull. This was up close and personal, Devlin. By someone who knew what he was doing. He didn't hesitate, or the vic would've woke up, opened his eyes." Falco shook his head. "No hesitation at all. Our shooter walked up and tapped him without so much as a blink."

"Looks that way," Kerri agreed, "but we'll see what the crime scene folks and the ME have to say before we make any final conclusions." Investigative procedures needed to be followed for a reason. Something else she'd learned from Boswell. Never conclude anything too quickly, and leave room for adjustments; otherwise you might miss an important detail that didn't fit neatly into your initial conclusion.

"Were the french doors open when you first arrived on the scene?" Falco asked, not put off by Kerri's reminder of protocol.

Matthews nodded. "They were. No sign of forced entry, though. No alarm triggered. I checked with the company monitoring the security system, and they said the system was disarmed at five this morning. Cameras were disabled weeks ago. No one had bothered to reactivate them."

Had the wife awakened that morning, disarmed the security system, and opened the french doors only to find an intruder? Or had the wife exited through those doors after murdering her husband and mother? Had the mother wounded her in their struggle? But then how had the blood gotten on the bed down here in the master suite?

Maybe the mother-in-law hadn't been happy with her daughter's husband and had shot him, and her daughter had been injured in the ensuing struggle.

If the shooter was the wife, there was always the possibility that after the struggle with her mother, remorse had brought her back to the bed next to her husband for a few minutes, long enough to bleed on the sheets. People did strange things when they went over an edge. Even those who had no mental incapacity often suffered a moment's remorse after it was too late to change their minds.

Kerri had seen far too much in her seven years to doubt the possibility just because the missing woman was the daughter of one of the vics or because she was injured herself. People did bad things. Sometimes those people were good people—maybe even saints—who for whatever reason snapped. Life could be like that. But there were other, more probable possibilities to rule out first.

Kerri took another look around the room. "What about jewelry? Cash?"

Matthews indicated the door to the walk-in closet, which stood open. "There's a huge jewelry box—more like a small bureau—in there full of dazzling pieces. The wife's purse is lying on top of it. Credit cards and cash inside. The husband's wallet is there as well. Credit cards and cash inside, just like the wife's."

"Makes it hard to point to robbery," Falco said from where he stood near the open french doors.

Definitely, Kerri agreed. To Matthews, she said, "Let's see the second victim."

"This way." Matthews jerked her head toward the door.

Kerri followed her back to the front hall and up the stairs. By the time they arrived at the second-floor landing, Falco had caught up.

"I checked outside," he said to Kerri. "The deck off the master overlooks the backyard. Steps lead down to a stone walkway. The ground is covered with that extrathick grass and mulched landscape beds. We won't be finding any shoe prints back there."

Kerri wasn't surprised. With a property like this one, there wouldn't be any barren areas where a shoe print might be found. There were times when an ultralush landscape was not their friend.

Upstairs there was a den and three more bedrooms, each with a private en suite. The first bedroom was that of the second victim.

"This is the mother-in-law's room. Jacqueline Rollins," Matthews said, hesitating before entering the room. "Seventy years old. She moved in with the couple right after their honeymoon. She obviously had a number of health issues. There are some serious prescriptions on the bedside table. I'm no doctor, but"—Matthews gestured for Kerri to go on in—"my father died of lung cancer. I recognize some of the meds. Whatever she had, it wasn't pleasant."

Kerri stopped in the center of the room and surveyed the space. The room smelled of disinfectant, like a freshly cleaned hospital room. The walls were painted a calming hue of blue. Several watercolor prints of the beach and the ocean adorned the wall. As Matthews had said, an array of prescription bottles sat on the bedside table. A walker stood next to the bed. The covers were tousled. But there was no victim.

Kerri's gaze wandered to an open door that provided a slanted view of the en suite. "The vic in the bathroom?"

Matthews jerked her head toward the door. "In the next room."

Judging by the expression on her face, there was more to this ugly story.

Matthews led the way to the next room—a *nursery*. At the open door she pointed to the knob. "There are a couple of scratches in the paint around the knob. I'm thinking this is where she broke her nails. She was probably terrified and struggling to get the door open. Also, you can see just the tiniest bit of tissue, probably skin, on the edge of the door here." She indicated a spot several inches above the knob.

"She wasn't thinking clearly," Kerri offered. "But she wanted in this room for some reason. Tell me we don't have a missing baby too." Her gut clenched at the idea.

"Not exactly," Matthews explained. "But the missing wife is pregnant."

Oh hell.

The second victim lay on her back on the floor in the center of the room. Her gray hair was braided, and she wore a long pale-pink nightgown. The front of the gown was soaked in blood. She'd been shot twice in the chest before giving up her battle. Her face was battered where she'd been punched or kicked.

Damn. Kerri crouched next to her. Two nails on her right hand were broken. There was a minor scrape midforearm, probably where her arm had scrubbed the edge of the door. The smell of urine and feces served as an unpleasant accompaniment to the metallic odor of blood. The violent manner of death had stolen any final vestiges of dignity from the poor woman.

Kerri pushed to her feet, glanced around the room decorated in pastel pinks and bright whites. She blew out a breath. "Maybe they were planning to adopt. How do we know the wife is pregnant?"

"Prenatal vitamins in the master bath downstairs," Matthews said, "and a photo of her and her husband holding a pic of an ultrasound on the dresser over there." She nodded to the shiny white piece of furniture across the room.

This news added another layer of possibility to the case. "We could be looking at a perp who wanted nothing more than the child she carried, but there are far easier ways to handle that sort of abduction." Kerri couldn't get right with the idea. "Coming into the house and executing the family seems a bit of an overkill."

Falco touched the mobile over the crib, sending it spinning slowly around. "Or maybe the pregnant lady went off the deep end and killed everyone."

This, too, was possible. Kerri crossed to the crib and surveyed the unicorn-print bedding and mentally ticked off the info that needed to be included in the APB for Sela Abbott. To Matthews, she said, "Do we have any idea how far along she is?"

"Due date, appointments, and information on her obstetrician are in her phone," Matthews said. "She's thirty weeks."

Kerri felt sick to her stomach. Until she had reason not to, she intended to consider the missing wife a victim rather than the shooter or an accomplice of some sort. Considering the pregnancy, she couldn't see the wife putting a couple of bullets into her own mother—at least not without some serious motivation—right here in the nursery, at that. Wives and husbands killed each other all too regularly, but daughters didn't kill their mothers quite as often. Besides, a gun wasn't the typical weapon of choice for a woman when she murdered family members—poisoning was the more common route. Sometimes a knife. But then again, Kerri didn't know this woman. Maybe she'd grown up with weapons. Her father and/or brothers may have been hunters. She could have frequented the shooting range the way some women flocked to their favorite book club.

Either way, two people were dead.

"Does the wife have any other family?"

Matthews shook her head. "According to the housekeeper, the mother was her only family besides her husband."

"Anything from the neighbors?" Kerri could hope.

"We've canvassed the closest neighbors, but no one saw or heard anything."

Too bad the closest neighbor hadn't heard the gunshots, but she wasn't surprised. Kerri had worked neighborhoods like this one before. The lavish homes were basically built to be soundproof, with sufficient distance between them to provide ample privacy. Even the landscape was designed with privacy in mind.

Kerri turned all the way around in the room to take in the unsettling scene once more; then she rested her attention on Falco. "The security company says the system was disarmed at five a.m. The shooter came in and executed the husband, presumably with a silencer so as not to wake anyone else in the house. Then he went upstairs for the mother-in-law. She surprised him by being up—or maybe the shooter didn't use a silencer, and she heard the first shot—the mother-in-law struggled, tried to get away, requiring two shots to take her down. What the hell did he do with the wife—assuming she isn't our killer?"

Murder was never good or kind, but there was something particularly grotesque about it when a family member was the killer.

"I guess we won't know the answer to that until we know the why." Falco held Kerri's gaze a moment, then turned to Matthews. "Who found them? You mentioned a housekeeper."

"The housekeeper showed up at eight," Matthews explained. "She was here a few minutes before she realized something was wrong and went to the bedrooms and found the bodies."

Beyond the fact that at least two people were dead, and a pregnant woman was missing, the entire scene felt wrong to Kerri. Something was off. "Why did Ben Abbott not hear the disarming of the security system when there's a keypad in the master bedroom only a few feet from the bed? He and his wife, assuming she was in bed with him at the time, should have heard the warning tones."

"Unless they were asleep," Falco countered.

Kerri disagreed. "That wouldn't wake you up?"

"Depends on if I took a sleeping pill or had too many beers. Maybe a few glasses of wine. These look like wine people to me."

A frown worked its way across Kerri's forehead. "I would think anything either one of them drank or took at or before bedtime would have been worn off by five this morning."

Falco gave a nod. "Reasonable assessment."

"Besides," Kerri expanded on the conclusion, "the wife is pregnant; she shouldn't have been drinking."

"Doesn't mean she wasn't," Falco tossed back.

"Fair point," Kerri acquiesced.

"And why struggle to get into this room?" Falco said as he surveyed the nursery once more. "It's not like there was a baby to protect already."

Kerri considered the room in light of his question. "Maybe she thought the shooter wouldn't look for her here."

Falco walked to the closet and had a look. Kerri joined him, suddenly understanding exactly what he was looking for.

"There's an attic-access door." He crouched down and tugged the small door open. Heat from the attic immediately wafted into the closet. Her new partner looked up at her then. "Makes for a good hiding place."

"She came into the nursery to hide in a place she hoped the shooter wouldn't look," Kerri concluded.

He nodded. "Which tells us she heard the shot that killed the vic downstairs."

If their shooter hadn't used a silencer, the lab could easily confirm that when the slugs were removed from the victims. "Let's talk to the housekeeper."

When they emerged from the closet, Matthews said, "The housekeeper's downstairs in the kitchen."

Kerri nodded. Maybe the lady could shed some light on whoever might have wanted these folks dead.

Or wanted something they possessed.

Downstairs the Crime Scene Unit had arrived. Kerri gave the okay for the investigators to get started. The ME and his assistant appeared next. Falco followed those guys while Kerri headed to the kitchen with Matthews to interview the housekeeper.

Officer Matthews made the introductions. Kerri pulled out a chair and sat down across the breakfast table from the woman identified as Ilana Jenkins. According to Matthews's notes, Jenkins was sixty-seven and had worked as a housekeeper most of her adult life, the better part of that time for Ben Abbott's family. She had retired at sixty-five, but then Abbott had convinced her to come out of retirement and work for him after he moved back to Alabama until someone suitable could be found. With the news that Mrs. Abbott was expecting, Jenkins had decided to stay on for a while longer.

Kerri moved on to the harder questions. "I know this is very difficult for you, Mrs. Jenkins, and we sincerely appreciate your help. Can you think of any reason anyone would want to hurt Mr. Abbott or his family?"

Jenkins shook her head. Her eyes were red and swollen from crying. "They are—were the nicest family. Mrs. Abbott spends all her time fundraising to help others. She told me it was the least she could do after the way she had been blessed. She is the sweetest lady. I hope she's all right." Her face scrunched with grief. "I can't believe this has happened."

Kerri kept her expression neutral yet attentive. No reason to tell the woman that the missing wife could be a number of things, but all right was not one of them. She had either gone over some edge no one had noticed, or she was a hostage. Or, worse, the third homicide victim in this case.

"No marital trouble between them?"

Jenkins shook her head again. "They were madly in love. I've never seen two people more committed to each other. Ask anyone who knows them."

So, what they had here was the perfect couple with the perfect life. Unfortunately, half of that equation was dead—murdered. Murder rarely slipped so quietly into such a perfect life. Somewhere amid all the perfection was a flaw, a chink . . . some sort of rub.

"What about Mr. Abbott's work?" Kerri asked.

The magnitude of entries Falco had found in his Google search on the drive here pointed overwhelmingly to the software thing. Apparently, Abbott's programs for smartphones and other devices had put him on the map more than a decade ago. His last known financial worth listed him as one of the wealthiest men in the world. If Kerri had to hazard a guess, his power and assets would be where the trouble reared its ugly head. All too often that kind of ugliness followed a target to his home.

"No problems," the housekeeper repeated. "He traveled a lot, but there was never any mention of problems. Never. You must believe me," she urged, her voice resolute. "These are the last people on earth you expect to be hurt, much less murdered."

"What about close friends?" Kerri flipped to a new page in her notepad. "Were there any friends they socialized with more often than others? Relatives who visited on a regular basis besides Ms. Rollins?"

"They had many friends." Jenkins lifted her shoulders and let them fall. "His parents visited once in a while. Most of the time Ben and Sela would go to their house for family dinners. Otherwise, there are no other living relatives."

"Ms. Jenkins, as difficult as the task will be, it would be very helpful if you could go through the house and tell us to the best of your knowledge if anything is missing."

She nodded. "I can do that. Whatever I can do to help."

The rest of the questions garnered Kerri more of the same. Everyone adored the Abbotts. They were an admired and respected couple.

Except by the someone who had wanted one or both dead.

And no matter that the wife wasn't here—Kerri knew in her gut that unless she was involved in the murders on some level, she was dead or soon would be.

Kerri rendezvoused with the ME, Jeffrey Moore, who agreed with the theory that the husband had been killed with a single shot, probably a .22-caliber handgun, to the head while sleeping. The mother-in-law's death had been decidedly more violent since the intruder had apparently awakened her. The ME estimated time of death at between four and seven that morning, but since the security system had been disarmed at five, he suggested they go with five to seven for now.

Unless the shooter was in the house when the security system was armed the night before and then waited all night to do the deed. Of course, there was always the chance he was waiting for something. The go-ahead, a completed business transaction. Or just the courage to do what needed to be done.

Before leaving the Abbott home, Kerri caught up with the house-keeper on her tour through the house with Matthews and asked once more if anyone—besides the mother-in-law—had stayed overnight with the Abbots recently. Out-of-town guests who had stayed a few days. Anyone at all.

Jenkins considered the question for a bit before saying the Abbotts rarely had overnight company. When they did, it was generally busi-ness associates from California, but no one in the past several months. Christmas, she believed, was the last time anyone had stayed overnight.

It was conceivable that a visitor had found the code to the secu-rity system during a previous stay. Or the code had been leaked by a member of the household staff or someone who worked for the security company. Kerri asked Jenkins to make a list of friends with whom the Abbotts associated at their home, as well as any employees who visited or worked at the house and all members of the household staff.

Her next stop would be the notification of Abbott's parents—her least favorite duty. But it was necessary, and often pertinent details could be gleaned in those minutes before the devastating news was revealed. After that unpleasant task, the victim's workplace, Abbott Options, was next on the agenda.

Back on the street a couple more cruisers had arrived, and the officers were keeping the media vehicles at bay. Two—no, three—local channels had already appeared. The fourth news van Kerri didn't recog-nize. She slid behind the wheel and started the Wagoneer.

Falco dropped into the passenger seat and closed his door. "He's the one who created the software that actually works in preventing cell phones from operating when a user is driving."

Kerri reached for the gearshift. "A company that's created and mar-keted such advanced and intensely popular technology has probably made plenty of enemies."

"Don't you know it," Falco granted. "It's dog eat dog, Devlin."

Before she pulled away from the curb, her cell vibrated. She braked rather than moving out onto the street so she could check the screen. *Amelia.*

She smiled. Just over two weeks ago her niece, the new high school graduate, had started full time as an intern at York, Hammond & Goldman, Birmingham's top law firm. In the fall she was heading off to Princeton on a full scholarship. Kerri still didn't think her sister had recovered from the shock that her beautiful daughter didn't want to pursue dance as her mother had hoped. Nope. Amelia loved the law, and she wanted to use it to help others. The girl was always protesting something or working to support some cause. She'd actually started at York, Hammond & Goldman one afternoon a week after school back in January, and already she was acting more like a lawyer than a teenager.

Amelia reminded Kerri far too much of herself at that age.

Recently Tori had gone out of her way to be nothing like her mother. Kerri wondered why her own daughter suddenly believed she was the enemy in all things. Adolescence was proving far harder than Kerri had anticipated, particularly since the divorce. She desperately needed to find a way to bridge this abrupt gap between her and Tori.

She opened the text from her niece. Don't forget to order the cake for mom and dad's anniversary! Love you!

Oh hell. Kerri had forgotten about the cake. There was still plenty of time since the party wasn't until a week from Saturday. But she couldn't let it slip her mind again.

Doing that now!

Kerri hit send and tossed her phone onto the seat. She decided to drop by the bakery before going to her next stop. Otherwise she would absolutely forget again.

"You know, Devlin," Falco said. "You could take care of things like that with a simple phone call if you'd just let me drive."

"Reading my texts?" She rolled away from the Abbott home and shot her new partner a dubious glance.

She ignored the shouts from reporters and the panning of cameras as they rolled past the media blockade.

"What else am I going to do?"

She thought about it for a moment. He was right. She could save some time. "Got your pad and pen handy?"

He reached into his pocket. "What am I doing? Making a list?"

"Yes. Ten people. White cake with white buttercream frosting. *Happy Anniversary, Diana and Robby.* The words should be in yellow—that's my sister's favorite color. I need to pick it up before noon on Saturday the sixteenth. It's Dreamcakes over on Oxmoor Road. I'm sure you can find the number."

She had used that bakery for every cake she'd ordered since her daughter was born. Her sister loved the place too.

"Yes, ma'am." Falco flashed a fake smile.

Maybe he would learn not to stick his nose into her personal business in the future.

3

11:30 a.m.

Abbott Options
First Avenue South

Kerri parked in the lot at Abbott Options. The LT had called to say that the chief of police himself had gone to Ben Abbott's parents and made the notification, which was frustrating. But that part wasn't nearly as frustrating as the idea that the chief insisted the Abbotts were not to be bothered until tomorrow. In other words, Kerri couldn't interview them today. It was ludicrous. Just because the Abbotts were rich and powerful didn't give them special treatment in a homicide case.

Except that, apparently, it did. Damn it. Every surviving member of the man's family, every close friend or business associate, had to be scrutinized. No one could be set aside or overlooked. *Everyone* acquainted with the victim or victims was a potential suspect at this stage. She reminded herself to breathe and stared at the home of Ben Abbott's internationally famous business operation. The sleek concrete-and-steel building that housed Abbott Options was a close neighbor to Birmingham's iconic Sloss Furnaces. The building was relatively new, built by an interior design company only a couple of years ago. According to Falco's internet search, Abbott had flown to Birmingham early last year and made the company an offer they couldn't refuse, and they had promptly vacated the premises. Just another indication that Ben Abbott was a man unafraid to go after what he wanted—even when it wasn't on the market.

"Oh, man, Devlin," Falco said as she parked. "There's like a rooftop party room made of glass for celebrating milestones and wining and dining customers." He thrust his phone in front of her. "Check out that view of the city's skyline." He tapped the screen. "The one of Sloss is killer too. No wonder the guy wanted this place."

"Nice views," Kerri agreed. "Did you find anything that suggested bad blood between Abbott and the previous owners?"

Falco shook his head. "In fact, the wife of the previous owner and our missing vic worked on a big fundraising project together last Christmas. You know, one of those charities that helps make sure all kids get a visit from Santa."

"Add them to our interview list just the same."

"Already done."

"Thanks." Surveying the minimalist approach to landscaping and the modern architecture of the property, Kerri scooted from behind the wheel. "This is a drastic change from the Abbott home."

"I think maybe the crime scene is just temporary lodging. I sent a text to a friend of mine in property records to find out if the dead guy owns any other properties. Abbott recently purchased a residence over on Whisper Lake Circle. My contact says he filed all the paperwork for tearing down the existing house. Since the property is restricted to residential, seems to me he's planning to build a new house."

Might not be significant, but it was worth checking out. "We should take a drive there next. Have a look around. Talk to his contractor." She met Falco at the front of the Wagoneer. "Did your contact know the name of his contractor?"

"She sure did." Falco grinned, gave her a wink. "Creaseman and Collier."

Before she could respond, he said, "Added them to the interview list too."

Maybe she had misjudged the man's ability and work ethic. In this instance she had no problem at all being wrong.

Inside, a marble reception desk sat amid the steel, glass, and concrete. A young man, midtwenties maybe, rose from his ultramodern transparent chair as they approached. His gray tight-fitting suit and crisp white shirt were a sharp contrast to the narrow bright-fuchsia tie that completed the ensemble.

"Good morning. My name is Brent. Welcome to Abbott Options. How may I assist you?" He looked from Kerri to Falco and back.

Kerri showed her credentials. "I'm Detective Devlin; this is Detective Falco. We need to speak with whoever is in charge this morning."

Brent blinked as if he needed a moment to process the request or, more likely, the fact that they were cops. "Certainly." He picked up the phone and pressed a series of buttons, then announced, "I'm sending Detectives Devlin and Falco from our esteemed BPD to your office."

He placed the handset back into the cradle and gestured to his right. "The elevator will take you to the fourth floor. Marcella Gibbons will be waiting there for you."

"Thanks." Kerri strode across the sleek concrete floor to the single elevator.

When she and Falco paused in front of it, the doors opened automatically. Interesting. They stepped into the gleaming steel box. State of the art—what else would she have expected?

"I guess we don't have to tell it where to take us," Falco murmured.

He was right. There was no control panel or visible speaker. Just sleek stainless steel walls that shone to a mirror finish.

"Looks that way."

The elevator lifted and a few seconds later glided to a stop. The doors slid open, and a tall slender woman waited in the corridor.

"Hello, I'm Marcella Gibbons, Mr. Abbott's personal assistant. Please follow me."

Kerri and Falco exchanged a look and followed the woman, who was a bit older than the man who'd sent them up, but she was still young. Thirty, maybe. Also like the employee downstairs, she wore slim-fitting attire—in this case a dress—that was somehow still modest with a knee-length hemline, three-quarter sleeves, and a higher neckline. The dress was black, as was her hair, which she wore short and neatly styled in a no-nonsense bob. Her shoes were practical flats, also in black.

There was carpet on this level, but the color was very near to that of the concrete in the lobby. The offices they passed were walled with glass, giving new meaning to transparency. So far everyone they'd seen seated at a desk was twenty- or thirtyish. All were stylishly dressed and appeared very busy.

When they reached the end of the corridor, double glass doors slid open to what appeared to be a conference room. Gibbons moved through the open doors and gestured to the long glass table. "Please sit wherever you'd like."

Falco followed Kerri inside, and they sat in the first chairs they encountered. The chairs, too, were transparent, like sitting on air.

"Would you like water or coffee?" Gibbons asked. "Hot tea, perhaps?"

"No thank you," Kerri said. Falco declined as well.

Gibbons used a remote to darken the glass walls, giving them privacy from the rest of the floor. Then she settled into the chair at the head of the table.

"How may I help you, Detectives? I assume this visit is related to the public disagreement that Mr. Abbott had with Mr. Thompson. Mr. Abbott isn't here at the moment, but I'll answer your questions as best I can. I was with him when the debacle occurred."

Falco deferred to Kerri with a glance. This was the thing she had meant when she'd been irritated about not being able to make the notification to Abbott's parents. Whenever the police showed up, most people immediately blurted whatever incident they believed might be relevant to the visit. It was a defensive instinct of sorts. If there was more than one possibility, they always—always—went with the least offense.

"Why don't you tell us your version of what happened," Kerri suggested, as if they had one damned clue what she was talking about, "and we'll go from there, Ms. Gibbons."

"Certainly." She sat a little straighter. "Mr. Abbott purchased a property on Whisper Lake Circle with the intention of removing the current older home along with any other buildings or patios within the property's boundaries. His ultimate goal is to build a new, state-of-the-art smart home. When Mr. Thompson learned of the property's transfer, he and Mr. Abbott had a disagreement."

Kerri, like anyone else who lived in Birmingham, recognized the Thompson name. "Are we talking about the Mr. Theodore Thompson running for the Senate or his father, T. R., the one running for governor?"

"The son, Theo." Her voice sounded the same, but the woman's face clearly expressed her distaste for the man.

"Did your boss buy the place from Thompson?" Falco asked.

"No." Gibbons folded one hand atop the other on the table. "The house was built by the parents of Mr. Thompson's wife. After her mother passed away some years ago, Mrs. Thompson opted to sell the property. The problem arose when Mr. and Mrs. Thompson learned that Mr. Abbott had bought out the current owners and intended to remove the existing home. Apparently, Mrs. Thompson was disturbed by the plan and wanted to reacquire the property."

"When and where did this disagreement take place?" Kerri asked.

"It was at the Giving Gala last week. Mrs. Abbott wasn't feeling well, so I attended the event with Ben—Mr. Abbott—in her stead. Mr. Thompson approached him on the veranda outside the ballroom and demanded that he sell the property to him rather than destroy it. Mr.

Abbott refused, and the exchange grew quite heated. Mr. Thompson threatened to take legal action to stop the work, and then he stormed off. I don't think very many of the other guests saw or heard the exchange, but it was quite uncomfortable for several minutes."

"Have Mr. Abbott and Mr. Thompson had disagreements before? Business or personal?" Chances were, Kerri realized, the two families knew each other well. Theo Thompson was five or more years older than Ben Abbott, but their fathers were about the same age. It was highly doubtful that the two didn't know each other. If nothing else, they certainly traveled in the same social circles.

Gibbons shook her head adamantly. "Not at all. Mr. Abbott is a peacemaker. Everyone loves him. Mr. Thompson is quite a bit older than him, but the two families, the Abbotts and the Thompsons, have known each other for decades," she said, confirming Kerri's conclusion.

"My impression," Gibbons went on, "was that Mr. Thompson had been drinking excessively that evening and lost control of himself. Considering his run for his father's Senate seat, I'm surprised he behaved so badly about this, particularly in public. Has he taken some sort of legal step? Is that why you're here? He did threaten to do so, and we're fully prepared to react in kind."

Falco looked up from his cell. Kerri suspected he'd already googled the event to see if there was anything in the news about the disagreement between the two men. He prompted, "Mr. Thompson believes your boss bullied the owners into selling the property."

The woman's cheeks darkened. "He did say something to that effect, but the statement is entirely inaccurate. Mr. Abbott wanted the property, and he simply approached the owner and offered a price he couldn't refuse. There was absolutely no pressure or intimidation."

"You mean, like ten times its current value?" Falco turned the screen of his cell toward Kerri and mouthed the word *wow*. "He has a habit of doing that, doesn't he?"

"Is there a law against paying more than a property is worth?" Gibbons demanded, obviously taken aback. "Mr. Abbott would never do anything illegal. As far as Mr. Thompson's reaction to his plans, the man is being completely unreasonable. If he and his wife felt some sentimental attachment to the property, why did they sell it in the first place? I'm certain the true issue lies with the wife."

"Ms. Gibbons," Kerri said, softening her voice, "we're not here about the exchange you described or the purchase of any property. If there has been any sort of legal step taken against Mr. Abbott, we're unaware."

Her concern mounting, Gibbons looked from Kerri to Falco and back. "I don't understand."

"Did Mr. Abbott have any early appointments this morning?" Kerri asked. "Or maybe something last evening? Outside the office, I mean." Once she gave the woman the news, logical answers might be difficult to garner.

Gibbons shook her head. "His final meeting of the day was at six last evening. A conference call with the San Francisco office. He was supposed to be in at nine this morning, but he hasn't made it yet. I've called, but there's no answer." Her eyes widened. "Is everything all right? Mrs. Abbott is expecting and—"

"Does he do this often?" Kerri asked, drawing her attention back to the more pressing questions. "Come in late or do some business or personal errand before coming to the office without letting you know?"

She stared at Kerri, uncertainty creeping into her gaze. "No. Never. He's completely anal about punctuality and staying on top of things. He always keeps me informed." Her face furrowed with confusion. "What's this about?"

"Ms. Gibbons, I'm sorry to tell you this, but early this morning Ben Abbott was murdered in his home, as was his mother-in-law. His wife, Sela, is missing."

Shock claimed the other woman's face before she burst into tears.

Kerri gave her a moment to gather her composure before going on. "We need several things this morning. First, a list of any ongoing issues Mr. Abbott or his wife might have been dealing with, professional or otherwise. The names of any staff members who had access to their home or who might have had more than a business relationship with them."

"A clear picture," Falco chimed in, "of your own relationship with Mr. Abbott."

Gibbon's face froze; then her jaw dropped. "You can't be serious."

"I cannot stress enough," Kerri pressed, "how important it is that we know everything there is to know about this family. The smallest thing could help us find the person who did this horrible thing."

Gibbons managed a tight nod. "Whatever you need. But I don't see how this is possible."

"What do you mean?" Kerri asked.

"How could this happen? Mr. Abbott has no enemies. Everyone loves him."

Maybe, Kerri kept to herself. *Except for the person who put a bullet in his head.*

4

12:00 p.m.

York, Hammond & Goldman Law Firm
North Twentieth Street

The oldest and most prestigious law firm in the state. Theo Thompson stood outside the historic limestone building, the names engraved there and what they represented failing for the first time to give him comfort. How would he ever survive the shit storm that was coming? He'd spent the entire morning in meetings with his most influential supporters. They were all grumbling that his numbers weren't hitting the gold standard his father had set decades ago. His numbers were rising, damn it. But not fast enough to make those vultures happy. What was worse, he had this Abbott business to deal with. The bastard had threatened to go public. He hadn't come right out and said as much, but he'd repeatedly insinuated that he had proof of his allegations.

The part that terrified Theo the most was the idea that Abbott might just be telling the truth.

As if that in and of itself wasn't enough, his wife was warning that she intended to be done with him if Theo lost his run for his father's Senate seat. She wanted to be First Lady of the state one day, and he had better not screw up her chance. He closed his eyes and shook his head. How could he have ever loved that heartless bitch?

A weariness gushed out of him on a breath. He hadn't ever really loved her. Their marriage had basically been arranged when they were in high school. It was expected that the only Thompson heir would marry the older of the two Baldwin girls.

Here they were twenty-five years later, and Theo at times pondered if the price he'd paid had been worth it.

Not once in his life had he felt this helpless. His chest was ready to explode. But, like everything else in his life, he had no choice. Her family's support was as imperative to furthering his career as the other supporters with whom he'd met this morning. If he didn't work out this situation with Abbott, all would be lost. He would have failed, dropped the ball on the family legacy.

He couldn't allow that to happen.

Collecting his resolve, he pushed through the gold entry doors and crossed the marble-floored lobby. The receptionist looked up and smiled. She was young and beautiful, of course. York, Hammond & Goldman didn't employ ugly people. Only the most talented and the most beautiful.

"Mr. York is expecting you," she said.

Theo gave her a nod and headed for the bank of elevators on the far side of the lobby. He pressed the call button and waited. The briefcase in his hand felt as if it weighed a hundred pounds, when it weighed ten at best.

He was so damned tired of every single thing going wrong. How had he become that person? The one who made the same poor personal choices his father had? He'd intended not to be that man. His father would say the key to those choices was in not getting caught. Bastard. Things were different now than they were forty years ago. With social media and the utter ruthlessness of reporters, hiding secrets was nearly impossible.

The probability that he was completely screwed was strong.

The shiny gold doors that reflected his weary desperation slid apart, and he stepped into the richly paneled car and pressed the number eight. He leaned against the wall and waited for the upward whoosh. He looked like hell. Bags under his eyes. Even his color was too pale. He needed that time away at the beach he'd promised Jen.

Just one more promise he had no idea how he would make happen.

Another sigh slipped past his lips. Frankly, Jen was another complication he didn't need. He enjoyed being with her, and the truth was, she kept him sane to some degree. But he could never leave his wife for her—at least not as long as he had a choice in the matter. But his mistress didn't understand. She wanted more. He'd indulged himself too long with her, and now he would have a hell of a time setting her aside.

Everything was going to hell.

Above all else, he needed this Abbott situation to go away.

Despite the Thompson name, his supporters would start pulling out if Theo didn't get that jump in the polls they wanted. That would not happen if Abbott went public. In fact, there was a strong possibility that Theo could lose far more than this election if the bastard made good on his threats. Theo was counting on his friend Lewis York, a brilliant and cutthroat attorney, to help him ensure that did not happen. More importantly, if Lewis got this situation under control, Theo's father would never have to know that the apple hadn't fallen far from the tree.

The thought twisted in Theo's belly.

He did not want to be like his father. The things Theo knew about the man made him sick. But he could never tell anyone. He could only wait for him to die and hope no one ever exposed that ugly little secret.

Lewis had sent Theo a text to come straight to his office as soon as he was out of his meeting. He hoped like hell there was good news.

He needed good news.

If Lewis had good news, it would be worth the fury Jen had unleashed when he'd canceled their lunch plans. For his private pleasure, there were those he could pay without the pressure of expectations. But no one like Jennifer Whitten.

The story of his life. He always wanted what he couldn't have.

"Good afternoon, Mr. Thompson," the eighth-floor receptionist said as he stepped out of the elevator.

Theo gave her a nod and headed toward Lewis's office. His shoes sank into the carpet. Though elegant marble floors spread over the entire first floor, everything above it was carpeted in the lushest carpeting available. York, Hammond & Goldman wanted their clients comfortable. Only the very best was good enough.

He rapped once on Lewis's door and walked in.

Lewis stood and thrust out his hand. "I thought that meeting was never going to end."

Theo shook his hand and collapsed into one of the chairs in front of his desk. "You have no idea. I need a drink."

Lewis crossed the room to the mirrored bar—each of the partners had one in his or her office. There was an even larger one in the main conference room. Lewis claimed a bottle of scotch and two short glasses and strolled over to join Theo. He set his bounty on the table next to Theo and then claimed the other chair.

"A drink is exactly what we need," Lewis said. "In fact, we have reason to celebrate."

Unless Abbott had decided to let sleeping dogs lie, Theo couldn't see how that was possible. "I would love to know how you reached that conclusion." He laughed. "Outside Abbott having dropped dead, I can't see surviving this simmering crisis. Every jackass in that meeting is just waiting for an excuse to pull his support. Apparently, I simply don't have the charm my father wields."

There were those who didn't appreciate paying the devil his due. Thompsons had long held the gate key, the final say amid the power in Birmingham. Some wanted change.

"You should be careful what you wish for, Theo." Lewis sipped his scotch, his gaze never leaving Theo's.

"What does that mean?" Theo was in no mood for guessing games. He reached for his glass.

"Sometime this morning, Ben Abbott was murdered."

The glass almost slipped from Theo's hand. "Are you serious?" He hated the way anticipation soared inside him at the idea. He didn't want to find relief in the news, but he did nonetheless.

"Oh yes. I am very serious, my old friend. Ben Abbott is dead. Birmingham PD just released the news. They've been keeping it under wraps all morning."

Somehow Theo managed to lift the glass to his mouth. He downed the scotch. Lewis watched intently. He quickly poured him another, and Theo forced himself to sip it more slowly. "What . . ." He cleared his throat. "What does this mean? What about his wife and that mother of hers? The three are like an unholy trinity haunting my every waking moment."

Lewis knocked back another slug of his drink, then shook his head. "Trust me, it's over, Theo. That's all you have to know."

Theo had other questions, but he was so overcome with relief he couldn't summon the wherewithal to demand the answers. "This is . . . as demented as it sounds, good news."

Lewis nodded. "Very good news. I suggest you get accustomed to being addressed as *Senator*, my friend."

Theo lifted his glass. "To the future. It suddenly looks far brighter."

They turned up their glasses.

When the nice warm buzz had relaxed Theo sufficiently, he asked, "Do they know what happened?"

Lewis shook his head. "The investigation will take some time, but I'm guessing that a competitor had him assassinated. It happens when so much is at stake. The technology war is fierce and global."

"It's certainly a big scary world out there," Theo said, as if he actually knew. The truth was, Birmingham had always been home. Sure, he'd traveled, but he'd never lived anywhere else the way Abbott had. In fact, he'd never really had to work for anything until now. The Thompson name and his father's legacy had guaranteed everything he'd ever wanted—at least until Kyle Hunter had decided to run against him in the Senate race. Kyle had serious backing as well, and he had the support of his mother, Birmingham's esteemed mayor.

Something else Lewis was working on. Everyone had secrets. Skeletons in their closets. All he had to do was find those of Kyle Hunter and his beloved mother.

"Abbott chose a merciless industry," Lewis suggested.

Theo grunted his agreement. "And here I thought politics was ruthless." So far no one had tried to kill him. He shook his head then. "I guess today is my lucky day."

Too bad a man had to die to make that happen.

5

12:45 p.m.

The Summit
Summit Boulevard

Theo was on her shit list.

Jennifer Whitten's lips tightened in anger as she strode toward the restaurant. They were supposed to have had lunch together today, but he'd canceled at the last moment.

"Damn you, Theo Thompson."

Two years. Jen had given him two years. At thirty-eight, she didn't have that many good years to throw away. Her mother's voice echoed in her head. If she'd gone to college like she should have or if she'd waited and married a nice man, like a doctor or a lawyer.

If, if, if. If a frog had wings, he wouldn't bump his ass every time he jumped.

Jen was so damned tired of the rendezvous in out-of-the-way restaurants where they wouldn't be seen and secret encounters at cheap hotels outside town. Fear trickled through her as she reached the door to the restaurant where Diana waited. The truth was, Jen was terrified that he was lying to her about his marriage. He'd been telling her it was over all this time. Stringing her along for his own pleasure.

Why, why, why did she have to be drawn to men like Theo?

She was so grateful Diana was available for lunch. Jen needed a sounding board before she erupted and did something truly stupid . . . something she couldn't take back.

Her cell phone chirped, and she paused at the restaurant entrance to dig it from her handbag. If it was Theo texting another apology, she didn't want to hear it. She glanced at the screen, but it wasn't Theo. A text from Amelia. Despite the frustration suffocating her, Jen smiled.

Aunt Jen, can you get the balloons for the party next Saturday?
🥂

Jen quickly typed back: You can count on me, kiddo!

Diana's wedding anniversary was the sixteenth. Jen had to come up with a great gift. She tucked the phone back into her bag and hurried through the entrance. She and Diana had been best friends since they were kids. But Diana always said that Jen was not just her friend but her other sister, so she'd insisted her kids call her *Aunt Jen*. And she was Amelia's godmother. Sadly, Amelia might just be the closest thing Jen ever had to a child of her own.

Diana waved to her, and Jen smiled, bypassed the line forming at the maître d' stand, and headed for her table. Thank God her friend had arrived and gotten a table before the main lunch crowd descended.

Jen collapsed into the chair opposite Diana. "I am so glad you could come. I really, really did not want to do lunch alone."

"I ordered you a glass of chardonnay." Diana nodded to the waiter who appeared at their table. "And our favorite salads."

Jen put her hand to her chest. "Bless you." She smiled at the waiter as he placed a stemmed glass in front of her. Jen grabbed it and took a long swallow. "Mmmm. Thank you. Thank you." She gazed across the small table at her dearest friend. "Diana Swanner, will you marry me? No one else will ever be as good to me as you are."

Diana laughed, then sipped her own wine. "I would love to marry you, sweetie, but as you well know, I'm already married, and Robby might have an issue with sharing me that way."

Jen sighed. "All the good ones are."

Diana's smile turned to concern as she placed a hand on Jen's. "Tell me what's happened. I thought you had lunch with Theo today?"

Jen rolled her eyes. "He bailed at the last possible minute. I swear, I feel like he's using me . . . like, like I'm nothing."

"This is my fault." Diana shook her head. "You probably wouldn't have met him if it wasn't for me." She pressed her fingers to her eyes. "Since Kerri's divorce the whole situation has been eating at me." Diana lowered her hands to the table. "At first it didn't feel so wrong, this thing with you and Theo. His kids are away at college. His wife has no time for him. But after watching Kerri go through what she did with Nick, I can't pretend anymore."

Kerri was Diana's younger sister and a dear friend too. Jen propped her chin in her hand. "You're right. We're terrible people with our nasty secrets and our white lies."

"That's not true, Jen. You know that's not what I mean," Diana argued. "I'm saying you deserve so much better." She shook her head. "And whatever his wife is, however uncaring she is, she's still his wife. He needs to do the right thing. If not, then you should do the right thing for *you*."

Jen fiddled with her napkin, unable to meet her friend's gaze. "He says he's already spoken to his attorney. He was ready to set the divorce proceedings in motion, but then his father decided to run for governor. Theo had no choice but to run for his Senate seat—at least that's what he said. He promised he would file for divorce after the election, but . . ." Jen shook her head. "I don't think it's going to happen. And to tell you the truth, I've heard and seen things in the past couple of weeks that make me wonder if I even know him at all."

Diana frowned. "What kind of things?"

Jen moved her head from side to side again. "I'm not sure. But he's had several angry conversations with someone. They seem to be about that billionaire guy who's always in the news. The one who started some big software thing. You know the one, Abbott something or other."

"Abbott Options?" Shock flashed on Diana's face. "Are you talking about Ben Abbott?"

Jen nodded. "Yeah. That's the one. Do you know him?"

"No more than you," Diana said, "but I heard on the news as I drove over here that he was murdered this morning. His wife is missing, and her mother was murdered too."

"Oh my God." Jen's heart started to pound. Was this why Theo had suddenly canceled lunch? "That's just awful."

Diana nodded sadly. "I know." She reached across the table and took Jen's hands in hers. "We should cherish each day. We never know how many we have left. I want you to be happy, Jen. Everyone makes mistakes, but you're not a bad person. You just fell in love with the wrong guy."

"As Kerri would say"—Jen stared at her wine—"that seems to be my MO."

Diana managed a feeble smile. "Just break it off, and start over. Kerri and I will be there for you."

Jen closed her eyes and drew in a long deep breath. "You're right. That's exactly what I should do." She looked to her friend and pasted on a broad smile. "Enough about me. What's happening in your world?"

Diana rolled her eyes. "Certain mothers are driving me nuts about who'll take Amelia's place on the dance-competition team."

"Already? She hasn't even left for college yet. People can be so selfish."

The waiter arrived with their salads. Diana thanked him, and he moved on to the next table. "I'm still struggling a little with the idea that she'll be leaving in a few short weeks." She sighed, blinked rapidly in an attempt to hold back the tears shining in her eyes. "All this time, I was certain she would be going off to Juilliard and becoming a star."

Jen didn't have to say, *The way you didn't*. Diana had been an incredible dancer. She had been accepted by Juilliard; then she'd found out she was pregnant with Amelia, and everything had changed. She and Robby had married, and that was that. Jen always wondered how Diana had turned off her dream so easily. Maybe motherhood was enough to change everything.

"She's going to be amazing as an attorney," Jen assured her friend. "It's not the future you had mapped out for her, but it'll be fantastic anyway."

Diana nodded. "I know. I know. Between Robby, the twins, and the studio, I'll be too busy to even notice she's gone."

The wobble in her voice as she said the last warned that she wasn't anywhere near convinced that would happen.

"We're a mess," Jen confessed. "You and your worries about Amelia and me and my affair"—she lowered her voice—"with a married man. Kerri with her hateful ex."

"We are," Diana agreed as she picked at her salad. "But you've given him more than enough time."

"Way too much." Jen nudged the arugula with her fork. "Starting over is just so hard."

"Let's have a girls' night," Diana suggested. "You, me, and Kerri. I'll be your wingwoman. There are plenty of guys out there. We just have to find them."

"That would be fun." Jen hoped her face looked more enthusiastic than her voice sounded. At this point she really didn't want to talk about Theo anymore. "Amelia seems really happy with her internship. I have to say"—she poked at her salad with her fork—"that was a serious coup, girl. There are people who would kill to get their seniors into an internship at a firm like York, Hammond & Goldman. They select what? Like two seniors each year out of the thousands graduating in Birmingham?"

Diana put up a hand and waved it back and forth. "I can't take credit for that choice. The firm was already considering Amelia. Her academic record is excellent. She's done all the right things, volunteering in the community, joining all those clubs at school. Not to mention she's listed as one of the top competition dancers in the country for her age group. The internship was her coup, not mine. My friendship with Lewis had nothing to do with it."

"All true." Jen gave a knowing wink. "But I still think that man has a thing for you." She wondered if Diana understood that relationships— even mere friendship—with men like Lewis York and Theo Thompson was playing with fire. Jen had learned that the hard way. Maybe she should be warning Diana.

"Don't be ridiculous," Diana argued despite the telltale blush that spread across her cheeks. "I gave his daughter private dance lessons all those years. I was never anything more than just another teacher, like her violin teacher and her cotillion coach. His wife had passed away, and he needed my help." She shrugged. "You know the mothers are always the ones who ensure their daughters attend those kinds of classes. The poor man had no idea what to do."

"And he never married again." Jen sighed. "Too bad he isn't my type."

Maybe then she wouldn't have wasted all this time on Theo damned Thompson. Unfortunately for her, Jen had never been afraid of playing with fire. Sometimes she really wished she had been.

From there Diana talked about all she was getting done around the house now that the studio was closed for the summer and her ten-year-old twins were at baseball camp. Jen smiled and nodded at the appropriate times, but her mind wouldn't let go of the other thing Diana had told her. Ben Abbott had been murdered.

Jen swallowed at the bile rising in her throat even as she shoved a forkful of salad into her mouth. The last time she and Theo had been together, she'd heard what he'd said in that hushed phone conversation.

Abbott is going to cost me this election and a hell of a lot more. How the hell are we going to stop him?

Jen repressed the shudder that rose inside her. Had to be coincidence. Maybe it was a different Abbott. Theo wouldn't murder anyone . . .

The little voice she had failed her entire life to listen to screamed at her now to talk to Kerri . . . but what if she was mistaken? Then she would have spilled to Kerri about the affair for no good reason. As much as Jen knew Kerri loved her, after going through what she had with her ex, she wouldn't understand about Theo.

No. Jen couldn't talk to her.

She forced a smile at something else Diana said.

Really, the mere concept was ridiculous. Theo would never be involved with murder.

He wasn't a killer, just a cheater.

6

4:55 p.m.

Abbott Crime Scene
Botanical Place, Mountain Brook

Kerri stood on the rear deck of the Abbott home and stared at the french doors that led to the master bedroom. The security-system cameras had been turned off for weeks. The entire system had been deactivated that morning. Not a single sign of forced entry. If not for the sporadic ransacking and the blood, the home would appear as if nothing untoward had happened inside.

Except a man and his mother-in-law had been murdered. And the pregnant wife was still missing. Maybe injured. Possibly dead.

If the wife was dead, there was a reason her body had not been left with the others.

Perhaps she had gotten up early, deactivated the alarm to go outside for a walk in the gardens, and encountered the killer. Maybe she'd gone for a run and returned home to find the killer. Jenkins had said the wife liked staying in shape. Early-morning runs were a matter of routine.

Was taking her—or her body—some sort of proof the job was done or for some sort of blackmail?

A hostage for money or something else of value? She had no surviving family. Abbott's parents were still alive and lived right here in Birmingham. They had been informed about the tragic news. A more in-depth interview was scheduled for tomorrow morning. As of yet, they had not been contacted regarding a ransom, or Kerri would surely know. She felt confident Daniel Abbott was far too savvy a businessman to allow his emotions to rule him and attempt negotiating a hostage situation on his own.

Neighbors had been interviewed. No one had seen anything unusual except for the one neighbor directly across the street, who'd noted an old blue car parked at the curb on the Abbott side the previous week. Since street parking wasn't illegal, and many of those employed in the neighborhood drove "older" cars, it wasn't likely a useful lead. Those living closest to the Abbott home were happy to provide access to their security cameras, which gave Kerri nothing. The angle of the cameras didn't cover every possible access point to the Abbott property, and they'd noted nothing useful happening in those that did show some of the property. Even stranger, Ms. Jenkins had concluded that nothing was missing from the house.

A second crime scene team was making a sweep of the residence. The chief didn't want to wait until tomorrow. This was going to be a particularly high-profile investigation, and he wanted nothing left to chance.

Falco exited the french doors and walked toward her. "They're done."

With the bodies at the morgue and the evidence collectors done, there was no reason for them to stay any longer.

"Let's call it a day." She headed back into the house to find Matthews.

Matthews and Baker would see that the house was secured. Two other uniforms would babysit the place until morning, and then another team would take their place. No one was to come near this scene until further notice.

And there was always the chance the wife might have escaped death and would return to the house, perhaps in shock and half-dead from her own injuries. An APB had been issued for her. Both Abbott vehicles remained in the garage. Whatever way she'd departed the premises, it was not in one of the couple's cars. A spokesperson for the family would appear on the local evening news with an appeal for Sela's safe return. If they were lucky, she would be found in the next twenty-four hours. The idea was unlikely, but they could hope.

With Falco following, Kerri exited the crime scene and climbed into her Wagoneer. She turned the vehicle around and drove out of the gate. She waved to the officer maintaining the outer perimeter. Thankfully the reporters had decided there was nothing more to be gained by hanging out near the victim's house.

"We going back to Abbott Options tomorrow?" Falco asked.

"We are." Today's visit had gotten the ball rolling. The staff had fallen apart as the news had spread through the offices. The few who had answered questions had been so emotional it was difficult to cultivate complete responses.

The staff was smaller than Kerri had expected. From what she understood, the primary operation remained in San Francisco. The office here was more the face of the company than the research and development activities. Abbott's personal assistant, Marcella Gibbons, was pulling together the answers to many of their questions.

"While the techs were finishing up in the house, I flipped through a few of the photo albums," Falco said. "Checked the personal files—any medical records I could find—and the medicine cabinets. Besides Sela's mother, no one in the family was on any sort of prescription drugs unless the prenatal vitamins count."

Kerri felt him watching her as she drove. "Anything else?"

"After looking at those photos, I'm convinced there's no way Mrs. Abbott killed her mother or her husband." He shook his head. "No way. They looked happy. Over the moon about the baby coming. It doesn't add up."

"Whether she did or not, she's probably dead too," Kerri reminded him. "If she was still alive, anyone capable of providing whatever the perpetrator wanted in return for her release would know by now. No one in the family has heard a word. No one at the office. No ransom demand. No contact at all."

Silence filled the space between them for a few miles.

Then Falco said, "I have a kid."

She glanced at him. "You do? I thought you'd never been married. No kids. Free as a bird, single guy."

He shrugged. Stared forward. "I have no entanglements, Devlin. No wife, no mortgage, and no child that I am legally responsible for."

She frowned. "Wait, you just said you have a kid."

He nodded. "Boy. Eight years old. I gave up parental rights when he was six hours and four minutes old."

Kerri wasn't sure what she should say to that. *Why?* would be the next logical response. Not something she really wanted to know. If he was a bigger shit than his colorful reputation suggested, she would just as soon skip the conversation.

"It wasn't because I wanted to," he said before she could ask, his voice lower, softer than she'd ever heard it. "It was because it was the right thing to do. I wanted him to be safe and happy. As long as he was connected to me, he wouldn't be either."

"Wow." That was certainly unexpected. "Do you know where he is now?"

"Huntsville. She sends me pictures and notes about what he's doing and how school is going. Sometimes I drive by and see him playing in the yard or getting off the bus at his school. He played soccer this year. I even went to a game."

"Have you considered asking for visitation? Sounds like she's cooperative on some level."

He shook his head. "Her husband adopted him. He's his father. I don't want to do any harm to that relationship. It wouldn't be fair."

Maybe the guy was a little deeper than she'd given him credit for. "That has to be hard, Falco."

"Yeah, well, I made my decisions. I won't have him pay for those."

Prison? Drugs? Not possible. He likely wouldn't be a cop now if that were the case.

"There are things I can't tell you, Devlin," he announced, as if he'd read her mind.

She braked to a stop for a red light and turned to him. "What does that mean, Falco?"

"I watched you today. You're a damned good detective. I'm lucky to have you for a partner, and I know that. I don't want you to judge me on what you think you know when you don't really know me at all."

A horn blew, and she forced her attention forward. The light had changed. She shifted her foot from the brake to the accelerator. "Okay. I'll do my best not to base my assessments on rumor. I'll stick to what I see with my own eyes. Does that work for you?"

"Yeah. Thanks. Maybe tomorrow you'll even let me drive."

Kerri laughed. "Let's not get ahead of ourselves, Falco."

More of that silence settled between them; oddly this time it was a little more relaxed.

Her cell sounded off, and she grabbed it, checked the screen. She didn't recognize the number, but it was local. She hit speaker with her thumb. "Devlin," she said instead of hello.

"Detective, this is Marcella Gibbons."

"Ms. Gibbons." Kerri exchanged a glance with Falco. "Have you found something that might prove useful to our investigation?"

"I was just thinking about something Detective Falco said."

Kerri split her attention between her partner and the mounting traffic. "What's that, Ms. Gibbons?"

"When we were in Mr. Abbott's office, Detective Falco asked if the laptop on the desk was his."

"And you said it was," Falco spoke up.

"Yes," she agreed. "But I started thinking about the laptop. The one at the office is the one he used for official business. All the security software, et cetera, that we use in Abbott Options is loaded onto it. But he also has a personal laptop. You should have found that one at his home."

Another of those looks passed between Kerri and Falco before she said, "We only found a desktop computer in the home office. Two iPads and two cell phones. There was no laptop."

They'd also found household inventory sheets in the files, the sort people filled out for insurance companies. Nothing listed was unaccounted for. There was a laptop listed, but they had assumed it was the one at his office.

"If his personal laptop—and it's exactly like the one in his office—is not in his home or in his car, then it's missing."

They spoke for a few minutes more. Several reporters had camped outside the gates at Abbott Options, causing issues getting in and out. Kerri promised to send an officer to handle the situation. Ms. Gibbons agreed to come to the house tomorrow and do a walk-through with Officer Matthews to see if she noticed anything else that might be missing.

Until about three minutes ago, Kerri had been fairly convinced that the only thing missing was the pregnant wife.

It seemed that wasn't the case at all.

7

I had to do it . . .

There was never a choice.

I was aware of that undeniable detail when I started this so very long ago. I was warned. Good God, I was warned. Most of my adult life the words haunted my existence.

You can't do this. You will fail. Just like she did.

I work the rope around my wrist back and forth. The skin is raw already, but I cannot stop. I cannot fail.

My preparation was meticulous. Every single detail was in place. You see, perception is everything.

But I had not anticipated *this*.

Now, I have only one thing to lose, and I took that with me. Do I wish other things could have turned out differently? That perhaps I could have seen this one coming? Maybe there was a moment . . .

Ultimately, it wouldn't have mattered. I would have lost the part that felt *almost* real anyway. Deception, betrayal—no matter how pure the motive—is never well received. Not even by those who profess to love you.

That final image of him appears in my mind's eye. The tissue around the hole in his forehead had puckered and started to turn an ugly shade of purple. I blink the memory away, and I experience something akin to sadness. It feels strange. I can't remember the last time I experienced a true emotion other than bitterness, unless, of course, determination counts. Yet somehow I feel . . . regret.

I'm sorry.

I don't want to feel this sadness. That wasn't part of the plan. Yet I do.

When all is said and done, people will hate me. They will say bad things about me. I know this, but it is what it is.

I had to do it . . .

If she were here, she would say that despite her misgivings, I did the right thing and that, in time, I will be okay. So many times she insisted I would be okay if only I would move on. Forget the past. Never look back. But how could I do such a thing? How could I forget and pretend the past never happened?

Don't look back . . . you will be okay.

Even now I hear her voice deep inside me.

As comforting as the sound is, the one thing I am very certain about is that I will never again be okay.

It is the price I must pay to finish this, and I will not fail. I have been far too careful with my planning.

The most essential part of the plan was to never tell another living soul.

No one—*absolutely* no one—could know the first, second, third . . . or even the last step until the time was right.

I learned the importance of keeping secrets when I was a child. My mother taught me well. She had many secrets. So *many* secrets. I have kept them all . . . just as she did. Ultimately some will be revealed . . . they are essential to the steps that must come.

But the rest will go with me to my grave.

I continue rubbing the ropes on my wrists back and forth, first one and then the other. Back and forth. Then I reach down and do the same to the one on my right ankle. Back and forth. Back and forth. My skin bleeds. I do not stop. I ignore the pain. It is necessary to the final step.

The neighbors will all have expressed the same things to the police. *Such nice people. Quiet. Private. Always pleasant. Always smiling and happy.*

They have no idea they only saw what I wanted them to see. They don't know me. I'm invisible. No one knows me. Not the real me. They will hear about all the good I've done—I worked particularly hard to accomplish so much in a short time. It was essential. But they will never know about the bad.

The bad was necessary as well. It was part of the plan . . . the *promise*. There are things that must occur moving forward. Events that work as catalysts to others.

As the steps play out, there are certain players who are not completely in the dark. Those select few are well aware of *their* roles. At first each no doubt denied the idea; then the next step happened, and they were forced to see what they wanted desperately to deny. They know what I want them to know. See what I want them to see.

More importantly, they have each reacted exactly as I predicted. How easy it was to prompt the desired response at exactly the right time. Not one has or will see the finale coming until it's too late.

They will all, including the police, search and dig for truth. They will never find it . . .

But the players in this game will be forced to recognize one undeniable lesson.

They did this to themselves.

8

Thursday, June 7

7:00 a.m.

Devlin Residence
Twenty-First Avenue South

Kerri slugged down the last of her coffee. Her fingers tightened around the mug. Tori hadn't said a word when Kerri had rapped on her door and told her to come down for breakfast.

She stared at the cheese toast topped with a single pineapple ring—her daughter's favorite. How had Tori gone from her little girl to this impossible-to-make-happy teenager in the span of a few short months?

It would be easy for Kerri to blame it on her ex. The bastard had skipped out on his daughter the same as he had her. Made sense that losing a father was far more difficult at thirteen than losing a husband at thirty-six. As angry as Kerri was, her daughter was hurt. The man had lost his ability to truly hurt Kerri about a year before he left. She had stopped counting on him to be the man she had thought she married.

Then again, she wasn't exactly the woman he had married either. His accusations about her all-work-and-no-play attitude rang in her head.

She had just finished the academy when they met and married. He had already graduated from college and locked in his first big job offer. Life had been exciting and full of possibility. But the honeymoon phase didn't last long. Their careers slowly but surely took over their lives, and the beautiful baby girl they so happily brought into the world became a bone of contention. Who was taking her to school? Picking her up? PTA meetings. School plays. Parents' night. Birthday parties. Ball games. Band practice. Doctor appointments. Work was always in the way. Anger, frustration, and resentment had mired them deep in misery.

Poor Tori had been the innocent victim trapped in the slow, agonizing death of her parents' marriage.

She had a right to be angry. The two people she had depended upon most had both let her down. Kerri and Nick with their career obsessions and, more recently, his lust for a younger, more attentive woman.

"I'm not hungry."

Kerri turned at her daughter's announcement. The girl busily typed on her cell phone as she made her way to the fridge, bypassing the breakfast Kerri had prepared. It wasn't an elaborate spread, but it was an effort. Did effort no longer count? Smiles and laughter from days gone by—before hormones had invaded—whispered through Kerri's mind. She resisted the urge to sigh for fear of flipping the switch that set off another round of deafening silence from her daughter.

"You have plans for today?" Somehow Kerri managed to ask the question in a neutral, almost amiable tone. She was tired of fighting with Tori. For now, she would be thrilled for five minutes of peace between them.

"Nothing special." Tori opened the fridge door and reached for a soda. "Elise is coming over to work with me on that art project for the band fundraiser."

Kerri clenched her jaw to prevent herself from reminding her daughter that one day soon all the sugar she consumed would come back to haunt her. Instead, she offered, "Sounds like fun. You need money to order Chinese or something?"

Tori scooted onto a stool at the island. "Her mom's bringing lunch."

"Great. Oh, I may be late again. We're eyeball deep in a double homicide."

"What's new? You're always late." Same bland, indifferent tone.

Deep breath. "I'll try my best to be home by six."

"Sure. Whatever." Tori opened her soda and took a swallow—all without once taking her eyes from the screen of her cell phone.

Kerri silently counted to ten, then announced, "I'll call your dad today."

Tori's gaze shot to Kerri's, her expression hopeful. "Awesome."

Kerri poured herself another cup of coffee to buy some time for bracing before she went on: "He and I will come to some sort of agreement for when you'll visit and for how long."

Fury instantly replaced the hope that had dared to make an appearance on Tori's sweet face. How could a child emit such contempt for the person who had brought her into this world?

"I'm leaving a week from Monday, the eighteenth," she snapped. "And I won't be back until just before school starts. Dad already bought my airline tickets."

"That's not going to happen, Tori." Kerri clutched her mug of coffee. "Two weeks is long enough." She opted not to mention that it was also in the legal documents she and Tori's father had signed—a point he had conveniently forgotten.

Her daughter shot to her feet, her glare turning accusatory. "You just want me to be as miserable as you are."

Before Kerri could come up with a logical and reasonably calm response, her daughter had stamped out of the room. Kerri closed her eyes and shook her head. She wasn't trying to punish Tori. She wasn't sticking to her guns for revenge against her ex or to prove she was in charge since she had primary custody. The truth was, Kerri was terrified that if she allowed her to spend the summer with her father in his new glamorous city, the next step would be her moving there permanently. Nick would love nothing better than to entice Tori into a game of Let's Punish Mom. He'd done it so many times before. She couldn't bear to see him manipulate their daughter, particularly since the stakes were so high—much higher than ever before. In the end, he would let her down. He always had.

Still, what if Tori had a point? Kerri wasn't at home nearly as much as she should be, no matter that she'd sworn things would be different after Nick left. School was out. Tori was no doubt lonely. This was her first summer without her dad. Kerri didn't want her to be unhappy.

Before she could analyze the troubling idea any further, her cell vibrated, and she snatched the welcome distraction from the table. She checked the screen. *Nick.* She dropped onto the nearest stool. Tori had probably called him or sent him a text and complained.

Kerri steeled herself once more and accepted the call. "I'm not changing my mind," she said rather than the usual greeting of *What do you want?* He was damned lucky she didn't tack on what she really thought—*asshole.*

"You're being unreasonable, Kerri."

This was possibly true. "Think what you will, but it's my decision."

The silence that followed was not what she'd hoped for. *Fine. Whatever. You be the bad guy, then.* Those were the sorts of responses she had anticipated.

"Very well," he said on an exaggerated release of air. "You've left me no other choice. I will be contacting my attorney and pursuing primary custody."

A rusty laugh burst out of her. "Like that's going to happen." They had been down this road already. "Tori has lived in Birmingham her whole life. The judge is never going to rule in your favor. Particularly considering the circumstances of your abrupt departure from our marriage."

"She's thirteen, Kerri. Tori's testimony will carry more weight than you realize, and she's ready for a change. You're never home, and you have no one to back you up."

Outrage blasted her. "I have a sister who is always happy to back me up." If he thought the little tart he now called his fiancée was going to compete with a loving aunt who had been a part of Tori's life from the beginning, he was dead wrong.

"I guess we'll let the court settle the disagreement."

She opened her mouth to let him have it, but he ended the call before she could utter another word.

"Bastard."

She strode from the kitchen and into the hall. At the bottom of the staircase, she bit back the urge to demand that Tori come down and explain herself. Wouldn't help. It would only make bad matters worse. After a couple of deep breaths to find some sense of calm, she called out, "I'm going. Have a good day, and be safe!"

No response, of course.

After snagging her jacket from the back of a stool as she walked through the kitchen, she stopped at the back door and pulled it on. No matter how hot the summers got in Alabama, most detectives wore lightweight dress jackets to cover their shoulder holsters and to give a more professional appearance.

Everyone, she amended, except her partner.

As if the thought had conjured him, his black Charger turned into her driveway. She locked the door and shoved the key into her pocket. He rolled right up behind her Wagoneer and powered down his window.

He lowered the volume of the music vibrating his vehicle like an oversize stereo speaker and said, "Morning, Devlin. You ready to rock this case?"

"I don't recall deciding you would drive." She lingered on the stoop, considered the reality that she'd barely slept last night. Between the case and the fight with her daughter, she'd been far too keyed up to manage more than a couple of hours.

"A good partner senses the needs of his other half."

"Other half?" She shook her head and descended the two steps. "Do me a favor, Falco," she said as she walked toward his car.

"What's that?"

Kerri waited until she'd opened the door and settled into the passenger seat. "Never call me your other half again."

He grunted and shifted into reverse. "You're the boss. Where we headed first?"

"The parents." She fastened her seat belt and stared up at the window that was her daughter's as they rolled out of the driveway. "Hopefully they can tell us something more about the wife."

The APB on the wife had garnered no hits. A few calls had come in after the press release last evening, but nothing that panned out. One would think the woman had simply vanished.

Except that wasn't possible. Basic physics. Mass occupies space.

So far Abbott's staff and his parents were the only people who seemed even remotely close to the couple. None of the neighbors admitted to knowing them other than in passing and by reputation. Some folks were private that way and didn't allow anyone too close. Kerri imagined that in Abbott's line of work, enemies were difficult to see coming. Sometimes it was easier to avoid close personal connections altogether in an effort to lower or eliminate the potential for deception.

Kerri understood the concept better than ever these days. The fact of the matter was, you never really knew a person—no matter how close the connection.

Case in point, she had not seen her husband's affair coming.

Then again, maybe she just hadn't been looking.

———

Abbott Residence
Saint Charles Drive, Hoover

Ben Abbott's parents lived in a gigantic house that had to be twenty thousand square feet if it was one. A member of the household staff—quite possibly a butler—led Kerri and Falco through the vast entry hall with its marble floors and towering muraled ceiling. The interior of the house resembled a museum rather than a home. Pausing at an open set of french doors, their guide gestured for them to enter.

Beyond those classic double doors, which stood a good ten feet in height themselves, was a richly paneled den with coffered ceilings and the most elaborate molding Kerri had seen anywhere. The conversational grouping of chairs and sofas stood in the center of the room. A family area complete with all sorts of entertaining pieces—including a massive television and a sprawling bar featuring every sort of libation imaginable stored along the mirrored shelves, as well as an elegant billiard table—was only steps away from the seating area. Above the space was a second-story gallery bordered with shelves from floor to ceiling, every single one lined with books.

"Detectives."

The man who spoke was clearly Ben Abbott's father. Kerri had seen photos of Daniel Abbott in the newspaper and on the net, but even if she hadn't, the resemblance was undeniable. The shape of his face, the nose. She thought of the man in his big comfortable bed with the bullet hole in his forehead.

Kerri blinked the image away and thrust out her hand. "Mr. Abbott. I regret this interview is necessary."

Mr. Abbott gave a nod and turned to Falco and shook his hand as well. Falco offered a similar sentiment.

"Why don't we sit down?" Abbott gestured to the chairs. "My wife will be along shortly." He shook his head. "This nightmare has devastated the both of us. Every minute of every hour has been an incredible trial."

Kerri didn't want to imagine. Losing a child had to be the most painful agony any parent could face—no matter if that child was fully grown with a family of his own. "We'll try to keep our questions focused and brief so as not to drag out this painful meeting any longer than necessary."

"Is there any word on Sela?" Mr. Abbott asked, his face shadowed with worry.

"Not at this time, sir." No point in beating around the bush. Kerri understood this man would not want the facts softened or embellished in any way. Not to mention, he had friends in high places. He likely knew the answer before he asked. "I assume you've still had no ransom demand of any sort?"

He shook his head. "Nothing." He glanced around. "Well, let's get down to the reason you came this morning."

Kerri waited before doing as he asked, since Mrs. Abbott entered the room. She was a petite woman with soft blonde hair in one of those short swing styles so popular with older women. Her eyes were red and swollen. The black suit emphasized her overly pale complexion. She was grieving, and she took no measures to hide it.

Abbott rose, as did Falco. As soon as Mrs. Abbott settled on the sofa, the two resumed their seats. A handkerchief was wadded in her hand. She rolled and shifted it back and forth between her fingers while her husband made the introductions. The woman's gaze lingered on Falco for a time. No doubt she wondered how a man who looked more like he'd just crawled out of a box under the expressway bridge than he did a homicide detective could possibly find her son's killer.

Kerri glanced at her partner. She was quickly learning that this particular book could not be judged by its cover. She was glad. Strangely enough, she kind of liked Falco. A little, at least.

"I only want to know one thing," Tempest Abbott said, her voice thin, frail. Her attention now fixed solidly on Kerri.

Kerri waited for her to go on.

"What are you doing to find my grandchild?"

"We're doing everything possible," Kerri assured her, "to find Sela, as well as the person or persons who did this. We hope to have some answers very soon."

Mrs. Abbott collapsed against the back of the sofa, as if it had taken every ounce of wherewithal she possessed to hold up long enough to ask that single question.

"We have a few questions," Falco said. "Your responses could help us find the answer you want more quickly."

"Ask us anything," Mr. Abbott urged. "We want to help. We *need* to help."

The urgency in his tone tugged at Kerri's own sense of urgency. Already twenty-four hours had elapsed, and they basically had nothing.

"Are you aware of anyone who might have been holding a grudge against your son?" This question Kerri directed to the father.

He moved his head side to side. "The software industry is mercilessly competitive, no question. Everyone wants to be the creator of the next big thing—the app that will change the way we conduct our lives or react to simply living. Ben ran into his share of those who tried to undercut him or cheat him in some manner. But he always found a way to work things out. He didn't like holding grudges or living with misunderstandings. He preferred facing the problem head-on and clearing the air before he was done, then moving on."

"What about Theo Thompson?" Falco asked. "He and your son had a disagreement at an event recently. Is there bad blood between those two?"

Daniel Abbott shook his head as if the question had no merit. "Theo isn't the problem. It's his wife, Suzanne. After her mother died, nothing would satisfy her until she sold the house. She didn't want her father and his new wife living there. There didn't appear to be a problem until she learned Ben intended to tear the place down. Suzanne was suddenly insistent that Theo buy it back for her. She's a selfish woman who cares for no one but herself. Theo has his hands full, believe me."

"So in your opinion," Falco pressed, "there is nothing to investigate about the property dispute."

"You would be wasting valuable time and resources," the older man insisted.

"What about your son's wife?" Kerri asked, redirecting the focus of the conversation. "Are there any problems in her life? Has she ever mentioned any trouble? Anything out of the ordinary?"

Daniel Abbott shook his head once more. "Sela is very involved in fundraising for a wide array of charities," he explained. "She loves her work, and she's very, very good at it. In the short time she's been in Birmingham, she has raised a tremendous amount of money for several major charities, particularly those for women in jeopardy."

"Nothing in her past that gave you pause?" Kerri opened her notepad and readied her pen. She needed more than what they already had. The neighbors, the husband's staff, and every damned thing they found on the net raved about the kind and generous Sela Rollins Abbott.

"They met in San Francisco," Abbott said. "I'm sure you're aware that's where the major part of Ben's business remains."

Kerri nodded. She was well aware. A lengthy conversation with those in charge in San Francisco had given her the same thing she'd gotten from everyone else. The Abbotts were above reproach. Madly in love. Exemplary humans.

"He moved a portion of his business back here to be closer to home. After what happened he didn't want to be so far away." Abbott glanced at his wife.

This was news. "What happened?" Kerri looked from the man to his wife.

"I had a heart attack," she said. "I recovered better than expected, but there was substantial damage. Bearing in mind the possibility of another, Ben wanted to come back home and be near me. I believe that's also why he decided to marry Sela so suddenly. They had been dating for only a couple of months. My near-death experience seemed to put his life in a new light. He realized he wanted a family of his own, and Sela was . . . there."

Handy, Kerri silently finished for her. "Was there any time after the marriage that Ben perhaps felt he'd been too hasty?"

"Are you suggesting," Mr. Abbott interrupted, "that this horror has something to do with his marriage to Sela?"

"I am not, sir," Kerri explained quickly. "I'm only trying to narrow down the possibilities. You've stated that he had no business enemies. He had no problems with work. That leaves his personal life. If the property dispute with Thompson is irrelevant as you say, there must be something else."

The older couple stared at each other for a long moment.

"There was a period of time," Mrs. Abbott said finally. "About four or five months ago. I don't know what was going on, but Ben and Sela went through something. We sensed a great deal of tension, but he wouldn't discuss it. It didn't last very long. They discovered the baby was coming, and suddenly they were happy again. Ben never told us what happened."

"Lots of couples go through bumps early on." Mr. Abbott patted his wife's hands. "We certainly suffered our share."

His wife gave a single nod of agreement, and then she dabbed at her eyes with the handkerchief.

"Your son must have had friends," Falco spoke up. "Maybe an old friend from his school days. Someone he trusted that he might have talked to about any problems with his work or his wife."

"Ben learned to be inordinately private. In the world of Abbott Options, it's essential," the father reiterated. "But there is one

71

relationship he maintained over the years. Speak to Keith Bellemont. He's an attorney. He and Ben have been friends since kindergarten."

Kerri wrote the name in her pad. "Has Mr. Bellemont been in contact with you since he learned what happened?"

"He was here last night," Mrs. Abbott said. "He's devastated just as we are."

When more of that silence dragged on, Falco said, "Was there any issue with Sela's mother living in the home? Sometimes a couple can feel cramped with an extra person around."

"Jacqueline lived with them from the beginning," Mr. Abbott offered. "She has—had—many health complications of her own and no one else to care for her except her daughter."

Kerri watched Mrs. Abbott's face carefully as her husband answered the question. Her expression tightened with distaste. She didn't care for Jacqueline Rollins; that was fairly obvious.

"What sort of health problems did Ms. Rollins have?" Kerri asked.

"Ironically," Mrs. Abbott said, "only a few days after my heart surgery, Jacqueline was diagnosed with cancer. I found it rather odd that she only saw an oncologist that once—when she was diagnosed." Her lips tightened as she spoke of the other woman. "Sela insisted on taking her mother to one of those herbalists. As far as I know, the woman never saw another *real* doctor. She had all those prescriptions from the first doctor but refused to take any of it."

Her voice confirmed her dislike for the wife's mother, maybe the wife too.

"Do you remember the herbalist's name?" Kerri readied to write down the information for additional follow-up.

Mrs. Abbott shook her head. "She may have mentioned the name once, but I don't recall."

"I'm sure I can track down the name." Kerri slipped her notepad into her pocket as she rested her gaze on the father once more. "Mr. Abbott, as much as I hate to ask this next question, I really feel it's necessary."

"As I said," he reiterated, "ask anything you like. We want to help."

"Your own company, DATACO, is the largest in the state. In the top two hundred in the nation. Is it possible what happened has anything to do with your company or an enemy of yours?"

Daniel Abbott appeared taken aback by the question. "I can assure you that DATACO had nothing to do with this tragedy. We are a multifaceted company with all sorts of endeavors from publishing to manufacturing to real estate. We do not and never have had those sorts of enemies."

"I imagine," Falco said, "you were disappointed when your son chose to pursue building his own business rather than joining DATACO."

Mrs. Abbott continued to stare at the crumbling tissue in her hands, but Mr. Abbott looked straight at Falco with something that bordered on indignation. "My son, as I'm sure you're aware, had far bigger plans. DATACO will be—would have been—his one day for him to do with as he pleases. He was his own man."

DATACO was an acronym using the first letters of Mr. and Mrs. Abbotts' given names. Mr. Abbott had taken the small company he'd inherited from his father and sold it to create DATACO. Kerri supposed holding his son's decision against him would have made him a hypocrite. That said, it was an avenue that required clarification.

"I hope one or both of you will call us if you think of anything at all that might be useful to our investigation. Anyone new who had entered your son's life. Any trouble—no matter how slight—he might have mentioned. Anything at all." Kerri passed a card to the father.

"Of course," Daniel Abbott assured her.

"If we have more questions," Falco put in, "we may need to drop by again."

The Abbotts repeated their desire to help. Kerri thanked the grieving couple for their cooperation, and then the same staff member who'd led them inside showed them to the door.

As she and Falco descended the steps, he said, "We going to Abbott's office now?"

"We are." Kerri paused before opening the passenger's-side door of his Charger. "Then we're going to find this friend Keith Bellemont."

"The friend none of the neighbors seemed to know about?" Falco tossed across the roof of the car.

"That's the one."

When they drove through the gate that protected the property from the uninvited, Kerri turned to Falco. She'd watched Tempest Abbott closely during their meeting. One conclusion in particular bugged her. "Mrs. Abbott didn't like Sela's mother. There was some sort of animosity there."

"Yeah, I picked up on that too."

"I also got the impression she wasn't exactly thrilled with Sela. You notice she didn't ask about her missing daughter-in-law. Just the grandchild."

Falco sent Kerri a knowing look. "I found that a little on the strange side. But the strangest part to me was the sort of businesslike way Old Man Abbott handled the questions. I expected him to be a lot more broken up. You know? His only child is murdered. Seems to me he'd be all torn up even a day later."

Kerri nodded. "You're right. The conversation was very controlled, almost careful."

And there it was . . . the first crack in the perfect facade of the Abbott life.

9

11:00 a.m.

Law Office of Keith Bellemont
Third Avenue North

Keith Bellemont locked the bathroom door and turned to the mirror. The horror on his face would not be contained inside. He hurried to the stall, flushed the toilet, and put his hands over his face, covering his mouth so he could release the groan trapped in his throat.

Dear God, how had he not realized this could happen?

The ache burst inside him, and tears spilled down his cheeks.

He was in part responsible for this horrific tragedy.

The police had been here . . . to question him, but he couldn't talk to them.

Not yet. A groan of misery welled once more in his throat.

When Ben had come to him, he should have said no. He should have warned his lifelong friend that the war he was about to start would not end well.

Now Ben was dead.

"Dear God, dear God." Keith scrubbed at his face. *My fault. My fault.*

The possibilities of what might be happening to Sela at this very moment ripped at his guts, twisted his heart.

And the baby. He moved his head side to side, bit his lips together to hold back another howl of misery.

He thought of his own children, and the agony intensified. Someone could be watching them at this very moment. They had opened a Pandora's box, and there was no way to know what might emerge next.

His body trembling, he shuffled to the sink, washed his face, and attempted to regather his composure. Ben and his wife—dear God, and her poor mother—deserved better than him falling apart. He had to make this right. Whatever it took.

The cell in his trouser pocket vibrated. He snatched it out, peered at the screen.

Thank God it wasn't that detective again. Besides coming to his office this morning, she had called twice already. He wouldn't be able to put her and her partner off much longer. But he needed time. Time to piece together a reasonable and logical way to answer their questions . . . time to figure this out.

"Tell me you've found something," he said to the caller.

"Not yet."

Neal Ramsey's words widened the cracks in Keith's chest. "Were you able to get into the house? Was anything missing? Anything that would suggest this was the work of someone else . . . someone . . ." Besides the bastards they had poked with a big-ass stick.

"Yes, and I found nothing to suggest the home invasion was motivated by robbery."

Keith's chest tightened. Then it was true. He was the reason this nightmare had happened. He took a moment, turned over the words. Ramsey was an investigator he employed—one who had never failed him. He would trust the lives of his own children to this man, no question.

"I won't ask how you got in," he said. The police had the house guarded. He suspected it would be so until the forensic investigators finished their work. Sometimes property was kept in police custody for days or weeks due to the possibility of potential evidence that might become relevant at a later time in the investigation.

"It's better that you don't know these things," the other man said.

Keith had worked with Ramsey for many years; they understood each other. "Have we learned anything new from the inside?"

No matter that Keith trusted Ramsey implicitly; phone conversations could still be overheard, tapped into. It was extremely important that they chose their words carefully.

"I'm afraid not, Mr. Bellemont."

"And nothing at all on Sela?" The air refused to enter his lungs as he waited for something, anything that would provide hope.

"Nothing."

Keith's hopes sank. "Call me when you have more."

He ended the call before he broke down again. He had a two o'clock. He couldn't hide in his personal restroom forever.

He considered the risk of allowing this off-the-record investigation to continue. A thousand knots tied and twisted inside him. He didn't want to be responsible for another loss of life. Worry gnawed at him. But if he stopped now, the bastards would get away with what they had done.

Fury tightened his lips. He would find the truth, and he would get those sons of bitches one way or another.

He unlocked the door and readied to step back into his office.

He owed it to Ben to try and finish this.

10

1:30 p.m.

Birmingham Police Department
First Avenue North
Major Investigations Division

"Sela Abbott oversaw four major fundraisers and half a dozen smaller ones in the past year," Kerri said as she stood back and surveyed the new timeline added to the case board. "She is one busy lady."

Falco paced the length of the board, studying the new line of dates and activities they had added to the lower portion of the board. The upper part of the board was already dotted with known activities for the week prior to the murders as well as with a host of photos of persons of interest—not that they had that many. The one person who might be able to give them more insight was not available. Keith Bellemont's assistant insisted he was out of town. Kerri wasn't entirely convinced the woman was telling the truth. Either way, they were a day and a half in and still hadn't been able to interview Ben Abbott's only close friend.

Falco stopped his pacing and peered at the board. "She's damned sure made all the right connections. Look at this list of names." He tapped one after the other as he recited them. "The who's who of the Magic City. Including Mrs. Suzanne Thompson."

"I noticed," Kerri said. She shook her head. "Most fundraising professionals have a staff or at least an assistant. But not Sela Abbott. She does everything personally."

"Sounds like we should have a talk with the cohosts for these events and see what they have to say about the missing wife."

"We should divide and conquer," Kerri decided. "You hang around Bellemont's office and try to catch him, and I'll start on this list."

"Do I get to guess where you're starting?" Falco grinned.

"Any updates I should know about, Detectives?"

Kerri turned at the sound of Lieutenant Brooks's voice. The LT stood in the doorway of their cubicle and surveyed their case board.

"We interviewed the Abbotts," Kerri said. "We're working on an interview with a Keith Bellemont. Mr. Abbott named the attorney as his son's closest friend."

"We're still waiting on the lab and the ME's office," Falco mentioned.

Kerri decided to give him the one other lead they'd found, for what it was worth. "Ben Abbott's assistant stated that he and Theo Thompson had a very public disagreement over a piece of property. We're planning to follow up with Mr. Thompson."

The LT frowned. "Maybe you should hold off on Thompson until you have more than hearsay. The chief doesn't want us bringing unnecessary grief to Theo Thompson or his father. They have a lot going on right now."

Falco nodded. "Yeah, right. Political campaigns can be hell."

Kerri bit back a smile, but the LT wasn't amused.

"The media watches our every step in a high-profile case like this one, Falco. One misstep can have a ripple effect for which we do not want to be responsible."

Falco nodded. "Got it, sir."

"Keep up the good work," Brooks said to Kerri before walking away.

"I don't think he likes me," Falco said.

"It's not about you, Falco. It's politics. This department depends on a certain level of donations from the city's elite. It's a sad fact of life."

Falco grunted. "So I'm off to wait out Bellemont."

"Take me by my place to get my Wagoneer first."

"Oh yeah, I forgot you need wheels to go rattle a cage yourself." He held her gaze for a moment. "You sure you want to do that, Devlin?"

"He said not to go to Theo without more; he didn't mention his wife."

———

Theo Thompson Residence
Augusta Way

Kerri parked on the cobblestone drive in front of the Thompson home. The towering limestone structure sat on more than three acres of gorgeous landscaping. Huge windows, grand entrance doors—the place was like a palace.

Four steps led up to the veranda. Kerri paused at the door and pressed the bell. The deep bass of the chime echoed through the house. She glanced up at the camera tucked discreetly above the door. Whoever was home had likely already checked to see who had arrived.

The door opened, and the lady of the house herself stood in full regalia before Kerri. Her shoulder-length blonde hair was perfectly coiffed. Her face was without a blemish, much less a wrinkle, even as she edged closer to fifty. Her brown eyes surveyed Kerri as she flashed her badge.

"I'm Detective Kerri Devlin, and I'd like a moment of your time, ma'am."

Mrs. Thompson produced a polite smile. "I'm always happy to accommodate the BPD; however, I would very much like to know the topic of discussion before I commit."

The elegant cream-colored sheath she wore along with the matching pumps spoke of having just left an important lunch engagement or of having a significant appointment. Surely no one lounged around the house dressed so smartly.

"Of course," Kerri said, humoring her. "I'm investigating the Abbott homicide."

Thompson caught her breath. "Such a tragedy. Please do come in."

She led the way across a small foyer and down the steps into a lavish great room that soared three stories with overlooking landings from the upper two levels. The furnishings were every bit as sophisticated as the lady. Wealth exuded from every angle.

She sat on the sofa, crossed her legs, and folded her hands in her lap. Kerri chose the chair opposite her. Thompson didn't offer refreshments or ask any questions; she simply waited.

"How well do you know the victim's wife, Sela Abbott?"

"I really didn't know her," she answered, chin held high. "We met at several social engagements, which is to be expected. But I hardly knew her otherwise."

"You worked with her on a fundraising event," Kerri pointed out. "Did the two of you spend much time together during the planning and execution of the event?"

Thompson scoffed. "Heavens no. Although my name was on the event, my personal assistant handled most everything. I made an appearance at the actual function. My time is very limited."

Kerri hummed a surprised note. "So you really don't know Mrs. Abbott at all."

"I do not. Only what I hear from others." She shrugged. "Rumors, you know."

"What sort of rumors?" Kerri readied her notepad.

Thompson glanced at the notepad, then said, "Would you prefer that I be brutally honest, or shall I give you the gentler version?"

"Please be brutally honest," Kerri urged.

"Most of the other ladies in our circles believed her to be a gold digger. Ben was a bit of a strange one. Always with his head stuck in a computer. He was never very sociable. A geek or nerd, I suppose you'd say. Worked all the time, according to his mother. But Sela came along, seemingly from nowhere, and changed all that."

"Was she friendly with anyone in *your* circles?"

"Oh no. Not at all." Thompson shook her head. "But she watched us. All of us. As if she was planning our demise. It was quite unsettling."

"But you never had any personal one-on-one dealings with her?"

"Never."

"What about her husband's recent purchase of your parents' home? Did the two of you ever discuss this transaction or the Abbotts' plans for the property?"

Thompson's face turned a bright red. She tucked a strand of hair behind her ear. Her red nails lingering there, the color almost matching her cheeks. "The whole ordeal was infuriating and painful, but to answer your question, no, we did not talk about the travesty of her husband's plans. The very idea was unconscionable. It was as if they understood how deeply painful this would be for me, and they chose to do it anyway."

"Pardon my frankness, ma'am, but if you were so attached to the place, why sell it in the first place? As long as it stayed in your family, you had control."

"It was an impulsive decision. One I should never have made." She shook her head. "But the family who bought it was so happy there and seemed to be taking such wonderful care of the place that I came to the realization that it was likely for the best. My mother would have wanted someone to enjoy the home she'd loved so much. My father's new wife wanted something more manageable."

"But this wasn't really your childhood home," Kerri pushed.

"No. It wasn't. But it was the home my mother had always wanted. I helped her to decorate it, and she lived the final years of her life there. She loved it so much."

Kerri nodded. "It's difficult to see something that meant so much to someone you cared about be destroyed."

"It was her," Thompson accused. "There was something about her, Sela, I mean. Something evil, I believe. She probably killed her husband and her mother just because a plan she'd hatched up didn't go her way."

That was quite a statement. "What sort of plan?"

She huffed a breath. "I have no idea. I'm simply saying that Sela Abbott is intensely self-centered and determined to take everything she can."

"If you didn't know her very well, what makes you say so?" Her statement sounded so resolute.

"These are the things others said about her. She would do anything to get what she wanted. Anyone who had the occasion to spend time with her said the same."

So maybe the saint wasn't so saintly after all.

"Mrs. Thompson, I really need to learn all I can about Sela Abbott. If you or your friends can shed light on any part of our investigation, it would be immensely helpful. But I do need facts rather than innuendos."

"Really, I've told you all I know, and most of that was, as I said, rumor. My friends weren't involved with Sela Abbott." She glanced at the antique grandfather clock on the other side of the room. "I'm afraid I have an appointment at our offices. We're very busy with the campaign." She stood. "I hope you solve this case, Detective. I'm certain Daniel and Tempest are beside themselves with grief."

"Thank you," Kerri said as she followed her to the front door. Before leaving, she asked, "Perhaps your husband would know more about Ben and Sela Abbott."

"I'm certain he does not," she said firmly. "If you feel the need, I'm confident one of his assistants could help you. Good day, Detective."

The door closed in Kerri's face.

She walked to her Wagoneer and climbed in. Apparently Sela Abbott wasn't so popular with the wives of her husband's family and friends.

All Kerri had to do was find the real reason.

11

5:35 p.m.

Devlin Residence
Twenty-First Avenue South

Falco was waiting for Kerri when she pulled into her driveway. She glanced up to the second floor. Tori stood at her window. When she saw Kerri, she moved away. A very concise text at four thirty had declared that her friend had gone home and nothing more. Kerri supposed she should be grateful for that small gesture. It was more than some parents got, but it was so unlike her daughter.

At least she'd made it home before six as promised. She exhaled a weary sigh. Wondered if her mother had suffered through times like this with Kerri and Diana.

Her new partner sat on the front steps. Kerri climbed out and walked toward him.

"Your daughter offered to have me wait inside, but I figured it was best if I waited out here."

"Good call." Kerri sat down beside him. "I don't know you well enough to have you hanging out in my house alone with my daughter."

He turned his head to look at her. His bloodshot eyes and rusty chuckle classic Falco. "Wait. I didn't go in, because I was worried *I* would be the one in danger. The kid came to the door with a can of mace in one hand and the phone in the other with 911 already on the screen. One tap of her thumb, and I was headed for trouble."

In spite of how unproductive and frustrating this day had been, Kerri laughed. "Smart girl."

"Definitely," he agreed.

The sound of a car coming down the block drew their collective attention to the street, and they watched the minivan roll past.

"So I staked out Bellemont's office, and he never came out." He exhaled a big breath that ballooned his cheeks. "I guess his secretary or assistant, whatever, was telling the truth about him being out of town. After she left, I had a look in the window, and the place was dark."

Kerri wasn't sure what to make of the attorney just yet. He'd visited the Abbotts last night. She supposed he could have had an out-of-town appointment today. Why wasn't he here doing whatever he could to help the family in the search for Sela? She was the wife of his lifelong friend, after all. The Abbotts had offered a sizable reward for her safe return. Had he advised them to make that move? She wouldn't know, because he was too busy to meet with her.

"This Ben Abbott is just too clean, Devlin." Falco rested his forearms on his knees and leaned forward. "No enemies, few personal involvements. Nothing but his laptop stolen from the house, as far as we can tell."

Except the wife. No need to point that out.

"What's your point?" she asked.

"My point is, I think we're going at this all wrong. Maybe the vic—Ben Abbott—is dead because of something related to his past, not his present."

"You're suggesting we should shift our focus to some event that his family didn't feel the need to share?" She shook her head. "I'm not really on board with that. The man is one of the wealthiest people on the planet; that alone makes him a target. If there was something in his past that might have put him in danger, his parents would have told us." This was not necessarily true, but it was more likely than not. Still, she had to play devil's advocate.

"Unless they didn't know," Falco countered.

Okay, maybe he had a point. She couldn't argue the possibility. Ben Abbott had lived away for well over a decade. "You want a beer or something?"

He waved her off. "No thanks. I should probably get going. I just wanted to update you on Bellemont. Did you talk to Thompson's wife or anyone else on that fundraiser list?"

"I did." In fact, Kerri's head was still spinning from listening to endless and meaningless gossip. "I spoke to everyone on that list, some by phone, some in person. Every last one had something to say about each other." She made a face. "I had no idea socialites could be so heartless. But when it came to Sela Abbott, all but one recited the same old, same old. Sela Abbott is a saint, blah blah blah."

"You want me to guess who the one was?" He smirked.

Kerri rolled her eyes. "Suzanne Thompson claims she hardly knows Sela, but she really pushed the idea that she's a gold digger and an overall bad person. She insists that opinion is based on rumors she heard from the other women in her circle—except she's the only one who dished the negativity. It was clear she does not like Sela Abbott. I'm thinking she dislikes her far too much not to know her."

"You think it's worth following up?"

"Maybe. Let me process the meeting overnight, and we'll discuss it tomorrow."

He stood, and Kerri held up a hand for him to hold on a second. "Almost forgot, I got a call from Gibbons too. We met at Ben Abbott's house and did a walk-through. She didn't notice anything missing other than the laptop she mentioned."

"Damn, Devlin, you've been a busy little bee."

Kerri pushed to her feet. "And I'm exhausted."

"Get some rest. Tomorrow's another day." When he would have walked away, he hesitated. "Listen, I have a friend who keeps her thumb on the pulse of this city. She's a cop, too, but you wouldn't know her. She's spent most of her career as one of those deep-cover types." He shrugged. "Like I used to be. Anyway, she has all these killer connections. I gave her a call, and she had an interesting scrap of info about our case."

Kerri hoped this was not some friend with whom he'd doled out details he shouldn't have shared. "What sort of scrap?"

"She says that as recently as a few weeks ago, Abbott was digging around in something that happened a long time ago. Something that happened here—in Birmingham."

"Did she define this something in any way?" To say the man was digging around in the past wasn't exactly a lot of help, but it did explain how her new partner had come up with this "let's look in the past" suggestion.

Give it a rest, Kerri. At this point she couldn't afford to dismiss any sort of lead.

"She's working on it. She promised to get back to me as soon as she had something concrete. She's not the kind to play loose with theories. She wouldn't have mentioned it if there wasn't something there."

Kerri took a moment, chose her words carefully. "You're aware that we have a certain protocol when it comes to distributing information. This is particularly important in a homicide case. MID is scrutinized by all the other divisions, by the media. We can't afford to play loose. If your friend talks about your call to anyone, there could be a backlash."

His eyebrows reared up. "First, I didn't *distribute* information, Devlin. I asked questions of a source I know from personal experience casts a wide net when trolling for information. She picks up all sorts of bits and pieces about the folks in this town."

"Okay. As long as we're clear."

He held up his hands. "We're clear. You don't trust me. I get it."

Well, hell. "We've worked together for two days, Falco. It's not that I don't trust you. I just need a little time to get a feel for your methods."

"Yeah. Okay. See you tomorrow."

Feeling like a real shit, Kerri watched him drive away. She turned and trudged up the steps to where another of the humans who wasn't happy with her could be found. She unlocked the door and opened it. "I'm home," she called out. "If anyone cares," she muttered.

She walked into the kitchen and checked the fridge. She wasn't really hungry, but she knew she should eat. She grabbed a snack pack that included nuts and cheese and dried cranberries. *Close enough,* she decided. On second thought, she snagged a beer too. She went to her office and dropped into the chair at her desk.

With her feet propped on her desk and her beer handy, she surveyed the board she'd created last night. Two victims—probably four, counting the missing wife and the child she carried. Nothing stolen beyond the laptop, which could contain proprietary information. Kerri frowned. Didn't seem like the sort of mistake a software guru would make, so maybe not. No ransom demand. No indication of trouble personally or professionally—outside the disagreement over the Whisper Lake Circle property.

But there had to be something. People rarely ended up dead for no reason.

Setting her beer aside, she got up and walked over to the board. Despite her misgivings, she made a note of what Falco had told her. If something in Abbott's past had come back to haunt him, it had to be personal, and it had to be big. She added *gold digger* beneath Sela's photo and put a question mark.

They needed to look into the family's history here and then the victim's history in the other places he had lived the past ten or so years. The wife's and mother-in-law's as well.

She stared at the photo of Sela Abbott. "Where the hell are you?"

Kerri's gut told her the woman was probably dead, but deep in her chest she wanted to believe she was still out there, breathing, maybe running for her life.

Plenty of calls were coming in to the hotlines, particularly considering the sizable reward involved. None had proven useful. The two officers following up on those leads were keeping Kerri apprised.

There was always tomorrow, she reminded herself. Each case unfolded in its own time. They'd barely begun on this one.

Kerri climbed the stairs and paused at her daughter's door and listened. Tori's favorite pop song played softly on the other side. Until a few months ago, Kerri would have opened the door and gone inside to discuss Tori's day.

Now she wasn't wanted.

Rather than slide into that pity party, she headed to her room, hung up her jacket, and put her service weapon in the lockbox on her bedside table. Then she went back downstairs to make dinner and let the details of the case percolate.

Maybe her brain would spit out some brilliant scenario that would make all the difference.

The doorbell rang, and Kerri set the frozen lasagna entrée aside. Whenever she was deep in a case, frozen entrées and takeout were the mainstay of their meals. Tori had never complained before, but now Kerri couldn't help feeling like a bad mother.

She sighed and checked the security peephole. Jen and Diana waved madly. Smiling despite the exhaustion, Kerri opened the door. "What're you guys up to?"

Jen brandished the six-pack in her hand. "Since you're too busy to manage a girls' night, we decided to bring girls' night to you—sort of."

Kerri should have expected this. Both Diana and Jen had been after her for days to go out to dinner with them. But there never seemed to be time, and with her working so many hours, she needed to spend every free moment with her daughter.

Diana grabbed Kerri for a hug. "Tori told me how hard you're working on this awful, awful case."

"Really?" Kerri drew back. "My daughter is worried about me?"

Diana's expression warned that *worry* wasn't exactly the motive for the comment. "Of course. Didn't we always worry about our folks?"

Kerri laughed. "Sure. Come in, guys. I was just about to throw frozen lasagna in the oven. I'd love for you two to join us."

Jen plopped the six-pack onto the dining table. "Forget the frozen stuff. We have pizza coming."

Kerri had no sooner closed the door when the bell rang again. She opened it to find a delivery guy with his big red bag on her porch. "Kerri Devlin?"

"That's me," she said. She was glad the girls had shown up. She needed a break.

Delivery guy opened the bag and pulled out two pizza boxes. He passed them to her. "Compliments of Robby Swanner. He also said he'd give me a serious tip if I did a little dancing for you guys."

"Thanks, but no thanks." Shaking her head, she closed the door and locked it. Behind her Jen and Diana booed and hissed.

"He was kind of cute." Jen hopped on one foot and then the other to remove her impossibly high heels.

Kerri carried the pizza to the table. "And way too young for any of us," she pointed out.

"Who's too young?" Tori asked as she descended the stairs.

Diana and Jen laughed. Kerri said, "The pizza-delivery guy. Your aunts were saying he was cute."

"Eww. You guys are gross. I saw him out my window. He's like Amelia's age or something."

Kerri was the one laughing then.

Tori grabbed a soda and joined them at the table. "Didn't you marry a younger guy once, Aunt Jen?"

Diana and Kerri choked back laughter between bites of pizza.

"That was number one. He was as handsome as sin," Jen told Tori. "But he decided he didn't want commitment after only six months."

"At least you didn't give up," Tori said with all the innocence of a pubescent teen.

Kerri and Diana exchanged a wide-eyed look. If either of them had made the statement, Jen would have bitten off their heads.

"Number two was rather plain looking but reliable. He was older and an accountant who'd never had so much as a parking ticket." Jen shivered and not in a good way. "He wanted too much commitment. I'd had enough after only three months."

"You and number three were married a whole year, weren't you?" Diana dared to mention as she reached for a beer.

"We were," Jen confirmed with a pointed look. "But then he decided to go back home to his mother. Evidently I didn't take proper care of him. Mama did his laundry, cooked his meals, and kept the house neat and clean for his friends who were *always* coming over. I would probably have dumped him sooner, but turning thirty and facing yet another failed marriage was too much to deal with in the same year."

Diana laughed, her hand over her mouth to hold back the beer that no doubt would have spewed otherwise. "None of them were good enough for you, Jen. Mr. Right will come. You wait and see."

Jen grunted. "If he waits much longer, he'll have to hunt me up in the nursing home."

When the new round of amusement subsided, Tori announced, "I'm never getting married."

Kerri's heart sank at the determination on her daughter's face. "You might change your mind when you meet the right guy."

"Amelia's not getting married either," Tori said rather than respond to her mother's comment. "When I go to college, I'm moving in with her. She said I could."

Diana smiled. "That will be great fun for both of you."

Kerri forced her lips into a smile. "Did you decide what you'd like to do? Maybe you want to be an attorney like Amelia."

Tori shrugged. "Don't know yet. Thanks for the pizza." She grabbed another slice and her drink and rushed back up the stairs.

"At least she spoke to me." Kerri dropped her half-eaten slice back onto her napkin. Her appetite had abruptly gone missing.

"Is she still determined to spend the summer with her dad—in Manhattan?" Jen asked.

"Oh yes." Kerri downed another slug of beer. She had to find a way to convince Nick to be reasonable.

Diana reached out and squeezed Kerri's hand. "We should have a family dinner and find a way to talk about all the things we need to do together this summer. Maybe that would inspire her to want to stay home."

Kerri braced her hands on the table. "Nick threatened to pursue primary custody if I don't agree to the whole summer."

"What an asshole!" Jen gritted her teeth, as if she needed to keep the rest of what she wanted to say from streaming out.

Kerri got it. There was plenty she would like to say, but if Tori overheard, it would not help their relationship. Whatever else he was, Nick was her father.

"We won't let that happen," Diana insisted. "You're the mother, and this has always been her home."

"I hope you're right."

No one spoke for a minute or two. The silence weighed heavy on Kerri's chest.

"On a lighter note," Diana said, "as much as I hate to see Amelia go, I'm slowly but surely getting right with it. In fact, I'm actually working up some serious excitement for her. She's going to make an amazing attorney."

Kerri gave her a high five. "It's about time you came around."

"No kidding," Jen teased as she slapped her palm against Diana's. "Hey." Jen turned back to Kerri. "How's it going with the new partner?"

Kerri shrugged. "Better than I expected. He's a little rough around the edges, but he has good instincts."

Diana put her hand to her throat. "I should have asked already. How's your investigation going?"

"Slow," Kerri admitted. "We have lists of people to interview. A few rumors to check out, but basically we have nothing concrete yet. We're waiting on lab results, autopsies." She shrugged. "And a little good luck."

"It's just terrible—the whole thing," Diana said, her expression pinched. "Do you think the wife is alive?"

"Every hour that passes with her still missing, the likelihood of finding her alive grows dimmer," Kerri admitted. "Assuming someone took her."

"You think maybe she had something to do with the murders?" Jen asked as she picked at her barely touched slice of pizza.

"At this stage, anything is possible, and we have to look at all the potential scenarios."

"I was thinking about her—Sela Abbott—this afternoon," Diana said as she looked from Kerri to Jen and back. "I think Amelia helped with one of her fundraisers. The one back in March." She frowned, gave her head a little shake. "Spring Blitz or something like that. It was to help abused young women."

"Did Amelia see much of her or meet her at all?" Kerri would welcome any reliable insight into Sela Abbott.

"I sent her a text and asked if she remembered her. I'm sure she's heard the news by now," Diana said. "I swear, that girl is never home anymore. I'm lucky if I ever see her. She comes home after I've gone to bed, and she's gone before I get up. If not for text, I might never hear from her."

"What do you do in a case like this?" Jen wanted to know. "Look for enemies?"

Kerri took a sip of her beer and nodded. "We look for anyone with motive. Whoever killed Ben Abbott and his mother-in-law had a motive. Whatever the motive is, it involves his wife somehow, I think." She looked from Jen to Diana and back. "Otherwise we would likely have found her body by now."

"Do you think it's someone who knew the family?" Diana asked.

"That's the case more often than not," Kerri allowed. "Whoever it was, we'll keep digging until we find them."

"I sure hope the dead guy's wife is okay," Jen said as she peeled at the label on her beer bottle.

"She's pregnant." Diana shook her head. "What kind of person hurts a pregnant woman?"

Unless the pregnant woman was somehow involved in the murders, and Kerri wasn't anywhere near convinced of that scenario.

Suzanne Thompson's words echoed. *She would do anything to get what she wanted.*

But would she commit cold-blooded murder?

12

One misstep . . .

I really did try hard not to make a single one.

I was so very careful. My every move was calculated very precisely. Preparation is, after all, of the utmost importance. To minimize the potential for mistakes, I have spent years preparing for this finale. But, in the end, I am only human—though some might argue with that assessment before this is done.

While I have taken great care, there comes a point when the preparation is only as reliable as the choice made for executing any one aspect of the plan. One of those choices failed me. The *pill*. The damned things have been around for decades. I never missed a dose. But failure happened anyway.

A *baby*. At first, I was alarmed. This was not supposed to happen. And here is another reason some won't like me: my initial thought was to take care of it.

There was no baby in the plan. I had made no preparations for a baby.

I was not—am not—mother material.

As it turned out, the baby proved essential to holding the plan together as the time for a certain step arrived. He balked. I had anticipated this reaction and assumed I would need some sort of leverage. Not so difficult, considering all the secrets I had uncovered. With the unexpected pregnancy, the other leverage was not required. I merely told him about the baby, and suddenly it was all good. He wasn't even disappointed when we learned the baby is a girl.

Does that mean he really loved me?

Perhaps.

Did I love him?

I'm not certain. But I will love his child. I will do all within my power to protect her.

I already have her name picked out. I didn't tell him, though. He wouldn't have understood.

If I've unknowingly made any other missteps thus far, they have not come to light as of yet.

I work the ropes. Back and forth. Back and forth.

Only a few more days, and it will all be done. Finally.

I wonder who will break first.

Suspicion and fear will do their work. The suspicion builds and builds with each new move, each new revealed detail. Fear needles its way under the skin, expanding until it can no longer be ignored. Lines are drawn. Sides are taken.

Whatever they think they know or believe is the perfect retaliation; ultimately none of them wants to be the last man standing when this is done.

And yet, someone will.

13

Friday, June 8

8:30 a.m.

Women's Clinic
Saint Vincent's Drive

"You're aware I can't discuss a patient with you without express permission from the patient."

Kerri restrained the impatience hammering at her. "I'm aware of the rules of privilege, Dr. Boone. Detective Falco and I aren't asking you to share information that would breach those boundaries. We only need to know if there is any reason we should be concerned for the physical or mental welfare of Sela Abbott beyond her abduction. We don't need specifics. Only whether or not there are health concerns that might make her even more vulnerable under the circumstances."

Boone adjusted his eyeglasses. "I can tell you that the last time I saw Mrs. Abbott, which was one week ago, she was in excellent physical condition."

Dr. Alan Boone wasn't much taller than Kerri's five-six, but he likely outweighed her by a hundred pounds. He had a congenial face and smiled even when he obviously wasn't happy that representatives from the BPD were in his office. According to Vitals.com, the obstetrician/gynecologist was fifty-eight, had gone to med school right here in Birmingham, and had an overall 4.5-star rating among his patients. Now if only he would play nice.

"No depression problems?" Falco nudged.

Boone sent a pointed look at him. "You are pushing those boundaries, Detective. It might be best if you produced a warrant."

This was the fork in the road. The place where things could go either way. "Warrants take time, Doctor, and that's the primary thing we don't have a lot of at the moment," Kerri pressed. "Just tell us if she was depressed or if she seemed okay."

"I would call her state of mind *anxious*, like most first-time mothers. As for the rest, I witnessed no indication of any mental or physical abnormalities. This is absolutely all I will share without a warrant."

"That's all I needed to hear." Kerri stood. "Thank you, Doctor."

As she and her partner reached the door, Boone spoke again. "I sincerely hope you find her alive and well, Detectives. It's a terrible, terrible situation."

"It is," Kerri agreed. "We appreciate your cooperation."

Falco gave the man a nod and pulled the door closed behind him. "Well, that didn't give us much of anything."

"Maybe more than you think." Kerri took a right in the corridor toward the exit, bypassing the checkout counter.

When they were outside, she went on, "We now know our missing wife has no physical health concerns beyond the pregnancy. And, apparently, no obvious mental health issues."

Falco considered her conclusion for a few strides, then paused at the driver's side of his car. "So you're ready to rule out the possibility that the wife went over the edge and killed her husband and mother."

"I never thought she did, still don't. But it's a scenario we had to consider and can't completely rule out even now."

Kerri slid into the passenger seat as Falco dropped behind the wheel. When had she decided that it was okay for him to do all the driving? Just another of those situations where she let go of the tug-of-war. Maybe that was the main reason she had ended up the victim of a cheating spouse. Even when she had understood something was off with her husband, she had let it go. Ignoring the issue was easier than dealing with the constant bickering. She was far too focused on work anyway. But she could not allow that to happen with her daughter. She had to find a way to get their relationship back on track . . . even if it meant allowing her to go to Manhattan for a large portion of the summer. The thought twisted like a knife inside her. Tori didn't understand that her father was playing a game. He was still upset that Kerri had gotten primary custody, and he would have no qualms about using Tori or anyone else to prove he should have been the one.

Kerri did not want her daughter to be hurt. But maybe this was a lesson she would have to learn for herself.

Her cell vibrated, saving her from having to go any further down that path. She pulled it from her pocket. She had a voice mail. Her phone had been on silent for the meeting with the doctor. She pulled the seat belt across her lap, snapped it into place, and played the message on speaker so Falco could hear too.

"Detective Devlin, this is Martha Keller at Keith Bellemont's office. He wanted me to advise you that he's in the office today and will make himself available at whatever time is good for you. Thank you."

"Well, well," Falco said with a look in Kerri's direction. "I guess the vic's friend is finally ready to talk."

"Let's not keep the man waiting." Kerri was more than ready to hear what he had to say.

Bellemont would hopefully offer a more knowledgeable account of the Abbotts. Attorneys weren't like other people. They had a different way of looking at things and always searched for the hidden motive.

With any luck, that difference would give them a better starting place for this forty-eight-hour-old double homicide.

Law Office of Keith Bellemont
Third Avenue North

Keith Bellemont's office was in an older and less upscale part of downtown Birmingham, nestled between a floral shop overflowing with greenery and blooms and a small drugstore that had closed years ago, unable to compete with the big chains. An alley ran between the office and the floral shop. The delivery van had nosed up to a dumpster near the side entrance, allowing for easy loading.

Beyond the vintage door with Bellemont's name emblazoned across it, Martha, the attorney's office assistant according to the brass plaque on her desk, greeted them with an offer of coffee or water while they waited. A client had popped in unexpectedly, but the meeting shouldn't take more than five or ten minutes more.

Declining the offer of refreshments, Kerri sat next to Falco in the stiff upholstered chairs of the small waiting room and stared at the muted television mounted on the wall. A local talk show was discussing the Abbott case. A photo of the happy couple and another of the wife's mother served as the background. It wasn't necessary to bump up the volume to know what was being said.

BPD had nothing. No leads. No suspects. The wife remained missing.

The hotline numbers for providing anonymous information flashed on the screen. Information about the reward followed.

A commercial break featuring Senator T. R. Thompson's run for the governor's office came next. Seventy-five-year-old Theodore Roosevelt Thompson Sr. was a legend in Birmingham. Like Ben Abbott's father,

Thompson was among the founders of the Magic City. Thompsons and Abbotts had always been part of the movers and shakers in Birmingham. Kerri didn't see that changing anytime soon.

"Detectives."

Kerri shifted her attention from the screen to the woman behind the desk.

"Mr. Bellemont can see you now. Down the hall and to your left."

"Thank you." Kerri pushed to her feet and headed for the hall. When she and Falco were well past the woman's desk, Kerri asked, "Did you see anyone go out?"

She was relatively certain she wouldn't have missed a departing client crossing the small lobby.

"Nope. If there was someone in his office, that person left by another exit."

When Kerri made the left as directed, she spotted a side exit. She thought of the floral shop's side exit into the alley. She supposed some of Bellemont's clients preferred anonymity. No doubt the attorney liked a handy, quick getaway option.

"I guess we have our answer," Falco said, reading her mind.

The door to Bellemont's office stood open. He sat behind his desk, surveying the pages of a file spread open before him. Kerri paused at the door, Falco behind her. The attorney looked up, then stood.

"Please come in, and make yourselves comfortable." He gestured to the two chairs that flanked his desk.

Hopefully these chairs would be more comfortable than the ones in his lobby, not that Kerri expected she and Falco would be here long enough to get comfortable either way. For attorneys, in particular, time was money.

Kerri extended her hand across his desk. "I'm Detective Devlin, and this is my partner, Detective Falco."

Bellemont shook first her hand and then Falco's. As soon as they lowered into their chairs, he resumed his. "How can I help you,

Detectives? I presume you're here about the tragedy in the Abbott family."

"We are," Kerri said. "Mr. Abbott's father told us that you and his son were longtime friends. We hoped you might be able to help us clear up a few things."

"Ben was a good man," Bellemont said. "The best. You can dig all you want, Detective, and you will never find anything negative about this man. He was a model human being."

Falco jumped in. "Can you say the same about his wife?"

"Ben and Sela met around a year and a half ago, I believe. I can't claim to know all there is to know about her, but what I do know is good and noble. She devotes herself to helping others. No one gives as much as she does. Sela is an incredible woman."

"I'm assuming she isn't wealthy in her own right," Kerri said, moving past the part they already knew.

Bellemont blinked. His gaze shifted a bit as he considered his answer. "No. She was not. Sela has taken care of her mother—God rest her soul—for many years. There's no one else; you probably know already. And she worked a full-time job at a law firm in San Francisco, but she was far from wealthy."

The wife had worked as a paralegal before meeting and marrying Ben Abbott. To Kerri, legal work seemed considerably different than fundraising. "What do you suppose makes her so good at fundraising when she's had no experience in that world as far as we've determined?"

Then again, she amended silently, lawyers were pretty good at separating people from their money. As much as she liked her divorce attorney, he'd cost an arm and a leg.

"She has a big heart and pours all that heart into her work," Bellemont offered. "People recognize that and are drawn to her. In hardly any time at all, she's built a remarkable presence in Birmingham."

Again, as he spoke, there was that subtle shift in his gaze, a stiffening of his posture. He didn't like talking about the wife. Interesting.

"But someone didn't like her and her husband," Falco said. "So all aspects of their lives weren't perfect."

"The cash in their wallets, credit cards, jewelry—none of that was taken from the house, and there's been no ransom demand," Kerri said, expanding on Falco's point. "Obviously money wasn't the motive behind what happened, which means we have to explore other possibilities."

Bellemont leaned forward in his chair, propped his forearms on his desk. This time he looked directly at Kerri as he spoke. "I can assure you that you will not find any skeletons hidden in Ben Abbott's closet. This is a man above reproach."

"I notice you didn't include his wife and mother-in-law in that statement," Falco said in his usual irreverent tone, digging at that same itch again.

Bellemont's lips tightened. He wasn't going to say more.

"What about your wife, Mr. Bellemont?" Kerri went on. "Is she friends with Sela Abbott?"

Frustration and impatience made an appearance in his expression. "We have three small children, Detective. My wife's life is far too busy for a lot of socializing. The two know each other, of course. We've had many dinner parties to which they were invited and vice versa, but until recently there wasn't a lot of commonality between the two."

"So they weren't close friends?" Kerri pushed. "Not like you and Ben."

"That's correct."

"Really you don't know Sela very well at all, do you?" Falco followed with a push of his own. "Maybe someone from her past—or her mother's—wanted to settle a debt or dispute of some sort, which might explain why she isn't dead like the others."

Bellemont looked from Falco to Kerri and back before responding, "I can't give you something that doesn't exist." He leaned back, putting a little distance between them once more. "Everyone who knows Ben and his family is devastated. He is a dear friend of mine. I simply don't know anything negative to say. You may theorize all you wish, but you will never find what you're looking for with the path you're taking."

"Was," Kerri pointed out.

Bellemont frowned, then appeared to realize his mistake of referring to Abbott in the present tense. "I'm sorry, Detectives, but I do have other appointments. I've made myself available to answer your questions, and now I feel as if you should go out and do your job. You won't find any answers of the sort you're looking for here."

That was certainly plain enough. Kerri stood. "I assume you'll be available for additional questions if there are more we need to ask."

He pushed to his feet. "Of course. No one wants Sela found and justice for Ben and Jacqueline more than me."

When they started to go, Falco hesitated and turned back to the man. "You do realize that we're going to figure this out? Devlin here is the best homicide detective in the department. Whatever happened, she'll get to the bottom of it. Maybe if you helped us now, your friend's wife might have a chance of surviving whatever has happened to her."

"Goodbye, Detectives."

No hesitation, no additional comment. The attorney was done.

They didn't speak again until they had cleared the exit at the end of the hall. The door led into the narrow alleyway and locked once it closed behind them. Like other larger metropolitan areas, Birmingham alleys weren't that attractive. They were generally filled with garbage dumpsters and unadorned side exits from businesses. Made for hasty getaways and good parking spots for delivery vehicles.

"I think I hit a nerve, Devlin."

Kerri flashed him a deserved smile. "I think you did." As they reached the street, she ticked off the list she had been mulling over to her partner. "Let's nose around in the wife's and the mother's backgrounds a little more. See what else we can find." So far it was a lot of nothing. "I also think we should have another go at the two closest neighbors to the Abbott property. Maybe one or the other has remembered something else."

"We should follow up with the housekeeper who works for the lady directly across the street," Falco said. "You know, the one who mentioned the old car parked on the street."

"Yeah." Kerri remembered the one.

"Her housekeeper sort of gave off a vibe like she wanted to say something but was afraid to speak up in front of her employer."

"You didn't mention that part before." Kerri waited at the passenger door.

"Maybe it was nothing." He unlocked the doors. "It's just been nagging at me, that's all."

Kerri got in, fastened her seat belt. "Maybe I should talk to her this time. See if she opens up to me."

He started the engine. "I meant what I said, you know."

She watched as he fastened his seat belt. He always did that last. Got in, started the car, and then fastened his seat belt. As much as she would like to believe she knew what part he meant, she wasn't about to put words in his mouth. "Which part?"

"The part about you being the best." He checked the street and eased away from the curb.

"Flattery will get you nowhere, Falco." She fished out her cell and checked for messages or calls. "The jury is still out on you."

He laughed, and she did, too, because that statement wasn't really accurate anymore.

A text popped up on her screen.

I'm thinking I should be a cop instead of a lawyer. ☺

Amelia.

Why? You already getting your fill of how merciless lawyers can be?

Kerri thought of the attorney they'd just interviewed. The man had a good reputation, and he seemed genuinely hurt by the loss of his friend. And still, there was a deceptiveness about him. An evasiveness.

Bad day, that's all.

Kerri smiled. Her niece had no idea, but she wasn't about to be the one to burst her bubble.

Tomorrow will be better. Never forget that you can be the one who sets the new standard.

<3

Kerri sent a kiss in response to her heart emoji. Amelia was like that. She never met a stranger, and she would do for someone else before herself. She would make a difference.

That reminded her. She sent Amelia another text.

Your mom told me about that fundraiser you worked. Did you meet Sela Abbott?

Kerri watched the ellipsis moving as she waited for her niece's response.

I did! A couple of times. She's super nice! Smart too! What happened is so sad. :-(

Kerri agreed and thanked her. The whole situation was sad. Losing a child, whether an infant or an adult, was the worst kind of pain. Ben Abbott's parents were suffering.

Maybe that was the part about Suzanne Thompson's callous statements that truly nagged at Kerri. The woman had two kids in college, and yet she seemed to have no sympathy for the Abbotts' loss. She'd wanted more than anything else to express her opinion about the missing wife.

Gold digger, she had stated unequivocally. *Sela Abbott would do anything to get what she wanted.*

Maybe Thompson was the one who didn't stop until she got what she wanted.

14

12:45 p.m.

York, Hammond & Goldman Law Firm
North Twentieth Street

Today Jen had selected her best dress—the one she'd snagged on clearance and had been waiting for a very special occasion to wear. Usually, she saved her high-end name-brand steals for dates with Theo.

But she had no idea when her next outing with Theo would be. He hadn't called or even sent a text since canceling lunch on her.

This was not acceptable, by God. Not acceptable at all. It was time she demanded to know his true intentions. Lewis York was Theo's attorney. Maybe if she ran into him, she could get a sense of where her relationship with Theo was going. His attorney would surely know if he was inching toward a divorce.

For this covert operation, she'd pulled out the big guns. This white linen sleeveless sheath showed off her fabulous tan and long toned legs while giving only a glimpse of her cleavage. Sexy yet sophisticated. The white sandals with their sleek wedge heels completed the look. She wore her hair down around her shoulders and used a light hand with the cosmetics. Relaxed and elegant. She looked stunning, even if she did say so herself.

If she ran into Lewis, she had the perfect conversation starter. She wanted to thank him for taking care of her brilliant goddaughter. Maybe she should even mention that he needed to keep a closer watch on his friend. Theo seemed to be overly tense lately.

If Theo was deep in trouble somehow, Jen hoped to God it didn't involve what had happened to that Abbott man and his family.

The very idea was ridiculous to even think . . . wasn't it?

In any event, what better way to accomplish this mission than to meet Amelia for lunch? They needed to catch up anyway. She hadn't seen Amelia all week.

Jen strode across the marble floor as if she owned the place and parked herself directly in front of the receptionist. The woman behind the desk might be a decade younger than Jen, but she had nothing on her. Jen worked hard to keep her tits high and her ass tight and her face absolutely wrinkle-free.

"May I help you?" the woman asked, indifference dripping from her tone.

Other women were always jealous of Jen and rarely tried to hide it. Even the ones who worked in fancy law offices.

"My name is Jennifer Whitten. I'm meeting Amelia Swanner for lunch."

"Have a seat, Ms. Whitten." She turned her palm up and gestured toward the seating area as if she were Vanna White. "I'll let Ms. Swanner know you're here."

"Thank you."

Jen turned on her heel and strode across the lobby to the grouping of lush chairs. She settled into one facing the desk so she could watch the bank of elevators beyond it. Though she would never say the words out loud, nor would she put thought into action, she was famished.

She would starve before she allowed an extra ounce to plant itself on her body.

The receptionist picked up her phone and made a call, then replaced it and turned to the woman who had just walked up to her desk. The newcomer was obviously another employee. She held a stack of files in one arm. She, too, was young and quite attractive. She rested her designer-clad hip on the edge of the desk and chatted with the receptionist.

Jen kept her shoulders back and head held high as the seconds and minutes ticked off. When the two glanced at her and began to laugh behind their hands, fury bolted through her. Of course, she had no way of knowing if they were talking about her. By the second time they looked toward her, she was ready to walk over and demand what the hell they thought was so damned funny.

But she couldn't do that. Not and embarrass Amelia as well as herself.

She pulled out her cell and typed a text to her goddaughter. God, she wished she knew all that shorthand text stuff. It took forever to type a whole sentence, much less two.

Where are you? I'm waiting in the lobby.

Jen chastised herself for becoming impatient. She'd always had an inferiority complex. No matter how well she dressed or how carefully she controlled her diction, she felt as if others considered her white trash.

She hated that feeling.

Aunt Jen I'm so sorry! The boss just called all the interns into a meeting. Can I have a rain check???

Jen prayed the marble floor would crack open and swallow her. How would she ever walk out of here now?

Rather than wallow in self-pity and drag Amelia into it, she typed a response. Sure thing, sweet girl. Love you!

Jen stood and marched out of the lobby without once looking at the two at the desk. She was going to be someone important one day. Maybe even a senator's wife.

Maybe that was why Theo hadn't called her. He was rising in the polls. He had warned her that he would be incredibly busy making that happen.

Outside the sun was shining, and Jen took a deep breath. By the end of the year, her investment in this relationship would pay off big for her. All she had to do was hang on. Her new life would be worth the wait.

She hoped.

As she descended the steps, a dark sedan pulled to the curb, and the back door opened. A blonde woman, half her face hidden by fashionably large, upscale sunglasses, emerged from the car, her poise regal, her rose-colored suit no doubt Chanel.

The woman started up the steps as Jen reached the final few, and then she recognized her.

Suzanne Thompson. *Theo's wife.*

Before Jen could prevent the move, she had stopped. She felt herself staring at the woman, and somehow she couldn't snap from the trance. It was like driving past an accident; you just had to look.

When Suzanne reached the same step where Jen stood, she glanced briefly at her, distaste glaringly obvious, before continuing upward. Jen watched her go.

The senator's wife was so full of herself she hadn't even recognized the woman who was fucking her husband.

15

3:30 p.m.

Whisper Lake Circle

Kerri walked around to the back of the property. Falco started on the opposite side of the driveway. The estate-size lot overlooking the lake was a full one or one and a half acres. For now, the goal was to have a look at any areas scheduled for demolition. This aspect of the disagreement between Abbott and Thompson might or might not have any relevance on the case.

The preparations for demo had begun. KEEP OUT and BEWARE signs were posted. A detached garage had received the same treatment. Around behind the house the in-ground pool had been marked with a large red *X* as well. The patio, all hardscapes. Every single feature of the previous dwelling would be gone. The utilities and other services had not been disconnected; at least the electricity hadn't, since one of the lights on the back of the house was on. A large excavator stood next to the pool. Apparently, that was where the contractor was to begin as soon as the final permitting was approved. Obviously, the disconnecting of the public services was part of the holdup.

Deep into the backyard, almost to the lake's edge, Kerri paused and looked back at the house; then she surveyed the scene out over the lake. It was a beautiful place, no question. But it wasn't so unique or so beautiful that something very similar couldn't have been purchased someplace else in or around Birmingham for far less and without the hassle of demolishing the old to build the new.

Why this piece of property? Just to annoy the Thompsons? Some sort of get-even maneuver?

"What you think, Devlin?"

She turned around slowly, taking another long look. "I'm wondering why Abbott would bother. I mean, it's a great view, but I don't see anything unique about the neighborhood or this particular property."

"I checked the school rating," Falco said. "Not spectacular, and there are no private schools in the immediate area." He shook his head. "I don't get it either. Schools are usually the top concern for parents, right?"

"Definitely. We should talk to Bellemont about this." Kerri had opted not to bring it up to see if the attorney would during their one and only meeting. But he hadn't. "After seeing the place, I'm thinking there was some other reason for buying the house and tearing it down."

"Like an in-your-face to Theo Thompson?" Falco suggested.

"Exactly like that," Kerri agreed.

"Since we have to wait until tomorrow to talk to that neighbor's housekeeper," Falco said, "we should just go back and ask him."

The housekeeper Falco had mentioned, one Angie Cowart, was at work today, and her employer was having a party tonight. She wouldn't be home until around midnight. To avoid warning Cowart that they wanted to question her, Kerri had asked Jenkins to find out her schedule without mentioning the request to Cowart or anyone else. Still beside herself about the murders, Jenkins had gladly agreed to do so.

"Good idea." Kerri was annoyed that Ben Abbott's one close friend had failed to be as forthcoming as she suspected he could have been. "I don't think playing nice with the attorney worked so well."

"Does that mean I get to shake him up a little?"

"We'll wait and see how this goes." Kerri started back toward the driveway. "On the way to his office, why don't you call your friend at the property records office and find out if Abbott had actually submitted drawings for a new build here."

The posted permit for demo listed Creaseman and Collier as the contractor, but that didn't mean any more than exactly what it said.

Kerri wanted every bit of information she could scrape together about the Abbotts, particularly their recent activities.

———

Law Office of Keith Bellemont
Third Avenue North

The office was closed when they reached it. But Falco spotted Bellemont's SUV parked up the block.

"He's parked closer to the alley entrance," Kerri pointed out.

"Then we should wait for him there. He probably leaves via the side door more often than the front anyway." Falco sent her one of his suspicious looks. "You know lawyers have lots of enemies. Maybe even more than cops."

Her partner was right. She wondered if her niece had considered that point. Being a cop or an attorney wasn't just a job. It defined a person's life . . . invaded their entire existence. Kerri couldn't say as far as attorneys went, but for a cop the job became like an addiction. It didn't let go when you went home, not even when you went to sleep. You went to sleep thinking about the case and woke up that way.

As they reached the alley, Kerri gestured to the floral delivery van. "We can wait on the other side of the van."

"Right." Falco hitched his head toward the side exit of the law office. "We don't want him checking that security peephole and making a run for the front exit."

Falco's contact at the property records office had confirmed that Abbott had only requested a permit for demolition; final approval remained pending. Nothing for building had been submitted. A call to Gibbons, his assistant at Abbott Options, had confirmed that as of yet he had not hired an architect or anyone else related to building the new smart home. Kerri had a feeling there was a lot more to this story than the possibility of a new house.

She leaned against the brick wall of the floral shop and watched Bellemont's side door through the driver's window of the van. "I don't know about you, Falco, but if I had a worrisome situation going on in my life, I would confide in my closest friend."

"I've never had that many close friends," he confessed, "but it makes sense you would do that. Hell, if you can't trust your best friend, what's the point?"

"Exactly." Kerri had always been able to confide in Diana and Jen. Those relationships were an important part of maintaining her objectivity, possibly even her sanity. "Bellemont isn't telling us everything he knows. Either that or he and Abbott weren't good friends anymore."

"Maybe they had a falling-out that his daddy doesn't know about." Falco gave her a look. "Even as adults we don't always tell our parents everything."

Both Kerri's parents were gone now, but Falco was right about that. There were things she hadn't told her father, and he had been a social worker. Like her, he had fully understood how a case could take over your life. No matter that she was certain he would have understood, she'd never said a word to him about how she had wanted another child after Tori was born. The truth was, she'd been terrified that she wouldn't be so good at this mom thing.

Worry that maybe she wasn't nudged at her even now.

She blinked it away. "How about you, Falco? Your parents still around?"

He didn't meet her eyes, just stared forward. "My old man died when I was twenty-one. Good thing too. If I'd gotten home before he drove off that bridge, I would have killed him."

She gave him a minute, but when he didn't elaborate, she said, "You can't just say something like that without explaining."

"My dad beat me all the time when I was growing up. He didn't stop until I was seventeen, and he only did then because I beat the shit out of him when he tried."

"Your mother couldn't stop him or leave him?" Kerri didn't know why she bothered asking the question. Some in that situation were too terrified to seek out help. Others were simply so beaten down by their abuser they didn't have the fortitude to do what needed to be done. She had never understood it, but then she had never been treated that way. It was easy to judge someone else when you weren't walking in their shoes.

"She tried, but he always changed her mind one way or another. When he couldn't take his aggressions out on me anymore, he took them out on her. The last time he laid a hand on her, I was on my way to kill the bastard. I guess when she told him I was coming, he got scared, so the drunk-as-a-skunk dumb-ass climbed into his truck and drove away. He didn't make it far, though. Passed out behind the wheel and drove right off that damned bridge."

"That's terrible, Falco. Was she afraid to go to the cops?"

Falco exhaled a big breath. "My dad was a cop."

Now there was a revelation she hadn't expected. "I'm surprised you decided to follow in his footsteps."

He stared directly at her then. "That's the thing, Devlin. I'm not. I'm better than he was, and I intend to prove it."

Kerri resisted the urge to reach out to him in some way. She wasn't sure he would appreciate a physical display of understanding. "Is he the reason you're not involved in your child's life?"

Falco shook his head. "Nah. It's not him. It's fear."

The creak of the door across the alley was like a shotgun blast drawing her from the moment. They both moved at the same time, skirting the delivery van and blocking Bellemont's path.

"We have a few more questions for you, Bellemont," Falco announced.

The attorney looked from Falco to Kerri. "I've told you all I know."

"We can do it here or in your office," she tacked on for clarification. They weren't leaving without more answers.

"Fine." Bellemont executed an about-face and unlocked the door.

Kerri and Falco followed him inside and into his office. He dropped his briefcase on his desk and settled into the seat. "Ask whatever you wish, Detectives."

Kerri fired the first round. "Why did Ben purchase the property at Whisper Lake Circle?"

Bellemont stared at her for a long moment.

During his hesitation, Falco piped up. "We don't want some neat answer you put together with all your legalese. We want the quick and dirty. The *truth*."

Bellemont squared his shoulders. "Ben bought the place because Sela found it and fell in love with it. She wanted a home in that exact spot. Ben balked at first, but Sela could be persuasive. He purchased the property and set her dream in motion."

"Theo Thompson's wife was not happy about this," Kerri said. "She wanted her husband to take legal action against Ben."

"Whatever she wanted to do was pointless. The buy was a perfectly legal transaction, and barring any issues with the permitting office, he could do as he pleased with the property."

"But he hadn't hired anyone to build the new house," Falco said. "No architect or contractor. I checked, and Creaseman and Collier don't build; they only do demo."

"He may have a friend back in San Francisco who's doing the building plans for him. I don't know the answer to that question."

Kerri had a feeling Marcella Gibbons would have known if that were the case.

"Why would Suzanne Thompson call Sela a gold digger?" Kerri watched his expression as he digested the question.

"Well, Suzanne is like that. She is not a particularly nice person. She dislikes those who make their own way in life. If your money is too new or you married into it, she thinks you're beneath her. She is not a pleasant person, Detective."

Kerri watched him for a moment longer.

"Is there anything else? If not, I would really like to get home to my wife and children."

"Thank you for your time. I'm sure we'll have more questions." Kerri pushed to her feet.

"If your questions help find who did this, I am more than happy to oblige."

Kerri held his gaze for a moment before walking out of the man's office.

Falco had caught up with her by the time she hit the alley.

It wasn't until they reached his car that her partner said, "You let him off damned easy, Devlin. But I'm down with your strategy. What do you think he's hiding?"

Kerri stared at Falco across the top of the car. "Everything he knows."

16

8:30 p.m.

The call went to voice mail.

Neal Ramsey gritted his teeth and shoved his phone back into his pocket.

Where the hell was she? Why wasn't she answering her cell?

He sent a text message, for all the good it would do.

Call in now

Neal stared at the house. He'd parked halfway down the block and watched for the past two hours. She had not come home. His last visual on her had been early that morning.

He hadn't been so worried, since he had heard from her last night. But everything had changed today. She'd stopped responding.

His cell vibrated with an incoming call.

He checked the screen.

The boss.

Great. Reluctantly, he accepted the call. "Yeah."

"Has she contacted you yet?" Bellemont demanded.

Neal hated to pass this update along, but he had no choice at this point. "No."

A span of silence went on for too long. He knew better than to try and explain. When things went this far south, it was best just to listen and follow orders.

"Do you have any idea where she is?"

"No," he admitted. "She has evaded my surveillance since early this morning."

"Jesus Christ." Bellemont exhaled a worried breath.

Until recently Keith Bellemont had been Neal's sole employer for more than five years. He had worked for several attorneys in the Birmingham area, but Bellemont was the only one who made him want to stay on. Most of the others rubbed him the wrong way eventually.

Still, as much as he liked Bellemont, sometimes a man had to do what he had to do. As long as his boss didn't find out before it was all said and done, Neal could live with what happened after that.

"I will get eyes on her again," Neal assured him. "No need to be overly concerned for now."

"What about—"

"I will locate *her* as well. You have my word."

"This has gone to hell, Ramsey. I don't think we can find our way back from this."

"Let's not go there just yet," he suggested. "Whatever it takes, we'll get the situation back under control."

"What if we're too late?"

The absolute fear in Bellemont's voice warned that he was close to the edge. Never a good place. Not even for an attorney who had more integrity than most.

"Give me more time before you do anything that can't be undone," Ramsey advised. He did not want Bellemont going to the police. That move would ruin everything.

"You have until Monday," Bellemont warned. The connection ended.

Neal had to keep the man calm. Until this was done, Bellemont had to keep his mouth shut.

Neal's phone vibrated again. This time it was a text from his *other* boss. The new one. The one who paid the big bucks.

Meet me. You know the place.

It wasn't that he was planning to leave Bellemont in the lurch. Neal didn't have a problem going back to their exclusive arrangement when this was over. But the money for this side job was too good to pass up. Loyalty was vastly overrated and woefully underpaid.

He drove straight to the agreed-upon location. She was there already. He parked against the curb several yards behind her. This street was always poorly lit. Went with the territory. You came to this neighborhood, you didn't expect the ambience of the better areas in the city.

Emerging from his car, he scanned the area. No other vehicles. No lights in any of the run-down businesses. He walked to the passenger's side of her sedan. The door unlocked as he reached for it. He glanced inside before sliding into the seat.

The scent of her perfume immediately filled his lungs. Sent an entirely different sort of tension coiling inside him.

"We have a new development?" he asked. She didn't usually request a meeting unless there was something urgent that required his attention.

Suzanne Thompson turned her blonde head in his direction. "Theo is getting nervous. He's overreacting. How close are you to finding her?"

Theo Thompson was quickly becoming a pain in Neal's ass, and he didn't even know the man other than what he read in the papers and saw on the news, especially lately with both him and his father in pivotal political races. Well, that wasn't entirely true. He knew a few particulars from Bellemont, but those were superficial details related to Abbott's purchase of the Whisper Lake Circle property.

In this instance, Neal's business was strictly with Thompson's wife—his new temporary employer.

Frankly, he didn't know how the man survived being married to such a cutthroat bitch. He imagined that she could be a good fuck if she felt the urge. Though he doubted she depended on anyone else to please her. Most likely she took care of that herself. Still, he would be willing if the offer appeared on the table.

"I'm getting closer. I've got eyes on her contact. It won't be long now."

"What about the laptop?"

This was something else she wasn't going to like. "There was self-destruct software. Anything on the laptop is gone. Irretrievable. Keep in mind, this guy was the best." Did she really think a software genius would be that stupid? "I've already disposed of it."

"I'm paying you a tremendous amount of money, Ramsey, and so far I'm not seeing the sort of results I expected. Do better. Work faster. If you had completed your initial assignment, we wouldn't be in this position."

Assignment. Right.

Neal waited for her to meet his gaze before he spoke. As heartless and cold as the woman was, he didn't miss the frustration in her eyes. "This is not like planning a shopping trip to New York or Paris," he warned. "There are variables. Sometimes those variables go against you. The end result doesn't always happen the way you expect."

Her smooth, perfectly sculpted cheeks hardened as those surgically enhanced lips tightened into a firm line before she spoke. "I always get what I want when I want it, Mr. Ramsey. If I don't this time, you will sincerely regret ever having claimed you could handle the job."

"You'll get what you asked for, Mrs. Thompson. Just keep your husband in line until then."

Neal exited the car and walked back to his own. That was the problem with working for rich people. They never appreciated what they had. They always wanted more.

17

9:00 p.m.

Devlin Residence
Twenty-First Avenue South

The case file was scattered over the kitchen island. Kerri and Falco had gone over every page, reviewing all that they knew up to this point. "We need to hear back from the San Francisco PD," she said, frustrated.

She had read the interviews twice. There was nothing useful. Nothing that gave them anything at all. How could people live in the same neighborhood and know nothing about each other? She knew the names of each of her neighbors. Where they worked or if they were retired. The names of their kids. There was a time when she wouldn't have bothered, but once Tori was born, everything changed. Kerri had needed to be aware of those living around her child.

"A place the size of San Fran probably has a lot more to worry about than answering questions from a cop down in Birmingham, Alabama," Falco reminded her.

"At this point the only info we have on the missing wife's history," Kerri went on, ignoring his reminder, "is that her father died in a car accident when she was ten, and her mother was a secretary in her younger days. Sela went to San Diego State University. She graduated and was eventually hired by a legal firm in San Francisco, where she met Ben Abbott, and the rest is history. No other next of kin. Nothing."

"Yeah." Falco scooted over next to her and tapped the page Kerri was reviewing at the moment. "Don't you think it's kind of weird that she studied criminology and became a paralegal for that San Fran law firm?"

"Frankly, I can't see either one as the sort of thing a woman who excels at fundraising would do. I guess when she married into the Abbott family, she decided she'd rather talk other people into giving their money away than earn her own. It wasn't like she needed it as Mrs. Ben Abbott."

"We need to find out what she did after graduation," Falco said. "There's no employment record before she started with that law firm in San Fran."

Kerri frowned. "Which leaves us with a major gap we can't account for. Like two years."

"Maybe she traveled." Falco glanced at the fridge.

Could he be any more obvious? "If you want another beer, you don't have to ask."

"Thanks."

He swaggered over to the refrigerator. Kerri shook her head. Men were not born walking like that. Did they take lessons? She blinked to clear her mind, stared at the pages in front of her. The better question was, Why did she even notice? Exhaustion did that. Your mind grabbed on to the strangest things.

Beer in hand, Falco closed the fridge door. "The carrier still hasn't provided her cell phone records."

Cell phone carriers resisting and putting off responses to warrants was far too common. "I'm hoping we'll have them by tomorrow."

Though they had Sela Abbott's phone, her call and text history had been deleted. Learning whom she'd communicated with could provide additional insights into the final days before the murders and her disappearance.

"We've called every herbalist in the city," Kerri grumbled, exhaustion catching up with her way too fast. "We didn't find anyone who had Jacqueline Rollins as a client."

Though herbalists weren't legally allowed to diagnose, treat, or prescribe to patients, they could certainly provide advice on various herbs and herbal remedies to clients. It was a fine line and one not necessarily monitored as closely as it should be.

Her partner removed the top from his beer and tossed it in the trash can. "Maybe she took her mother to Huntsville or some other place." He sipped the beer.

"Mom?"

Kerri looked up to find her daughter at the door, looking startled. "I thought you were watching a movie."

"Hey there, little Devlin," Falco said as he came back to the island to lean against it. "I almost didn't recognize you without your weapon."

Tori cut him a look. "I'm not a Devlin; I'm a Jackman." Then to Kerri, she said, "It's late."

It was a few minutes past nine. It wasn't that late. "We still have more work to do. Did you need something?"

"Dad has been trying to call you." Her arms went around her waist, and her chin jutted out defensively.

Could they not have one evening without this discussion? "I'll call him back in the morning."

"Whatever." Tori spun around and disappeared.

"I'm kinda getting a complex here, Devlin," he said. "The LT doesn't like me. Now your kid doesn't like me."

"Don't feel too bad. I don't think she likes me either." Kerri shook off the intrusion and focused on the case. It was sad when a homicide investigation was more appealing than a conversation with your daughter. "Let's go over the old car thing again and that housekeeper we're going to reinterview."

"The neighbors—the Chapins—specifically the wife, noticed an old car parked next to the Abbott driveway last week. She called it a *jalopy*. Old four door. Midsize. She couldn't tell me the make or model. Just that it was old. Blue in color. Kind of rusty. Her housekeeper, Cowart, looked as if she wanted to say something but was afraid to speak up."

Oftentimes when a detective tried to follow up with neighbors, no one would be available. The longer an investigation went on, the more people would lean that way. Everyone feared being accused or somehow dragged into an investigation—even those who were smart enough to know better. Some would never shake the belief that the cops just wanted to solve the case even if they had to create a suspect.

"Maybe the car belonged to someone doing yard work or household maintenance for the Abbotts," Kerri suggested.

He shrugged. "That's very possible. Chapin didn't know. I asked if she had noticed anything unusual, and that was her answer."

"We should talk to Ms. Jenkins about this too." The Abbotts' housekeeper would surely have noticed anything odd about someone parked right outside the gate.

"Too bad none of the neighbors have security cameras that reach that particular spot." Falco sipped his beer. "For such high-end neighborhoods, they've got low-end security systems."

Having security video footage might very well have made this investigation a lot easier. Luck like that rarely happened outside television. Kerri felt her frustration rising. "We need something to give the LT tomorrow before the press conference."

"You mean besides the truth that we have nothing significant?"

"Besides that, yeah."

How could they have been at this for three days and have nothing?

"What's your daughter so upset about?"

Startled by the sudden change of subject, Kerri met his gaze, held it for a moment. Reminded herself that he was her partner. A partner whom she had decided she might actually like. "She wants to go to New York and spend the summer with her father."

He held her gaze for a long assessing moment. "You don't want her to go."

Kerri shrugged. "I'm torn. He lives with his fiancée."

"The other woman," Falco guessed.

Kerri nodded. "But the real problem is that he likes to play games. He's not good at what he perceives as losing. My having primary custody is bugging him. He will use our daughter to make himself feel better, and then who knows what will happen?"

Not exactly the sort of personal information you wanted to share. It was late. She was tired and aggravated. Running on empty.

"Damn. No wonder you've been tense."

She glowered at him. "What does that mean, Falco? I haven't been *tense*."

"Yeah, you kind of have been."

"Whatever." She started to gather the pages back into the folders. "It is late. We should call it a night."

"Sometimes you're better off without what you thought you needed."

She stopped, stared straight at him. Their working relationship had smoothed out more quickly than she'd expected, but the personal stuff was still a little touchy for her. Especially when it related to her daughter and her failed marriage. "Don't pretend to know what I need."

He shook his head. "I'm not talking about you. I'm talking about me."

Unable to keep her curiosity at bay, she surrendered and gave him her undivided attention.

"I thought I needed a wife and kids," he continued. "That's what most people want, right?" He shrugged. "But some people shouldn't have wives and kids. Some people are better off alone. They don't have the goods to make people happy. If you can't make people happy, you shouldn't tie them to you. Maybe your ex was smart to leave. Maybe he did you a favor. He couldn't make you happy, so he cut and run."

Obviously, she was too tired to be reasonable, or she would never in a million years have found logic in his words. "I'm not sure my happiness was ever his primary concern. Anyway, as soon as the press conference is over in the morning, we'll talk to Cowart and then Jenkins. See if we can find out about this jalopy and whatever the housekeeper needs to get off her chest."

He tossed his empty beer bottle into the trash. "I'll be here at seven thirty sharp."

She started to argue but decided against it. So far she had no complaints about his driving skills. As long as he continued that way, she could live with him driving. Gave her time to think about the case and to search for info.

She followed him to the door. "Good night, Falco."

On the stoop he turned back to her. "Night, Devlin." He took two steps and stopped again. "For the record, your ex is an idiot."

Kerri laughed. "Yeah, he is."

She watched Falco drive away before she closed and locked the door.

After turning out the lights, she picked up her cell and headed for the stairs. She had four missed calls from her ex.

He could wait until morning.

18

I am not afraid.

I tell myself this over and over.

But it's not entirely true. I thought this would be the easy part. But there are emotions tearing at me that I cannot afford to feel. I cannot grieve. Grief is for a loss. You cannot grieve losing something that was never really yours. You should not grieve when most of the events that have transpired are necessary to what comes next.

But not all were necessary. Fury burns through me, overriding the unexpected grief.

Even worse, I discovered that I did make another mistake. I left something important. If it has been found . . . no, I can't think that way. Not yet. I will find a way to make this right. The rest is almost ready. One by one, I work the ropes. Back and forth. Back and forth. The time is near.

I am ready for this to be done.

This place is dark, and it smells very bad, but it is the one place no one will think to look. I brought the things I would need very early that morning. A quick trip here, then back home. If he woke, he would assume I had gone for my usual morning run. At that hour there was little or no traffic. Nothing to get in the way of my careful planning.

I did not anticipate the enemy making a preemptive strike. I was forced to deviate from my plan before this place was fully prepared, before I had checked to see that nothing was forgotten. Still, I will manage.

You see, the one person who understands the relevance of this place died long ago. A strange feeling goes through me as I consider her. I am here just as she was, and that part is disturbing on so many levels. But I have no regrets.

She loved me. I do not doubt this. She loved the one who came before just as much. She was more cautious with me. I had to pull information from her. She kept much to herself until the bitter end.

She is the reason I cannot fail. I must finish this. For her. For both of them.

I have waited and prepared so long for this moment. Sometimes it overwhelms me when I look back. For that reason, I rarely look back.

No matter the unexpected twists and turns that have occurred, I will not fail.

There can be no turning back now.

19

Saturday, June 9

9:00 a.m.

Birmingham City Hall
North Twentieth Street

The press conference was held outside city hall.

Kerri was stunned that Falco had shown up in sharply pressed dress trousers and an equally well-starched button-down shirt. Though he certainly looked the part of a detective—sans the tie that most of the males wore—he also appeared incredibly uncomfortable.

A grin tugged at her lips, but she resisted the impulse. This was no time to be caught on camera smiling. This was a somber occasion. Two people were dead, possibly three, as well as an unborn child. No matter that this was day four of the investigation, they were no closer to solving the case.

And Sela Abbott remained missing.

For this press conference most of the detectives in the Major Investigations Division were present. Kerri glanced at Sykes and Peterson. If not for a holdup at Starbucks, those two would have been under the gun on this one. Lucky bastards. Maybe she would have had some time to work things out with her daughter if not for this case.

Kerri forced her attention forward. The truth was, she was glad she'd caught this one. The vics deserved the best investigators, and according to Falco, she was the best. Then again, this case might very well prove him wrong.

Besides, if she wasn't here, she would be at home, where her daughter would be refusing to speak with her again since today's early-morning phone conversation with Nick had gone so badly. The man had been married to her long enough to know that he should not call to raise hell with her before she had her first cup of coffee.

And now this—she surveyed the crowd of cops and reporters in the audience—was the kickoff to her workday.

Sometimes the tug-of-war between work and home was so closely matched there was no winning either way.

She resisted the urge to shake her head. Two things she understood for certain. Whether she had landed this case or not, she would still be working long hours. She always did. Maybe that had been her MO these past several months because she wanted to avoid confrontations with her daughter and the reality that her husband had cheated on her and left her for someone else.

The entire situation was new territory for both her and Tori. It was like finding their way through a minefield.

The LT and the chief of police took a final question, and Kerri readied to move. She wanted out of here as soon as possible. She and Falco had a double homicide to investigate. But this was the way things were done in cases like this one. Always. The chief was certain it helped keep the community calm and reassured them, seeing the detectives assigned to the case during a press conference.

Politicians were all the same, and the chief was definitely a politician.

The instant the chief walked away from the podium, the LT right behind him, Kerri elbowed Falco and moved in the opposite direction.

The reporters would follow the chief. She and Falco were halfway to where his Charger was parked when her cell vibrated in her pocket.

If it was her ex again . . .

The screen showed a number she didn't recognize. She couldn't readily identify the area code either.

"Devlin."

Falco unlocked his car, and Kerri climbed in while the male voice on the other end, a Sergeant Rossi from San Francisco PD, explained that there was no record of criminal activities or domestic disturbances for Sela Rollins Abbott or her mother, Jacqueline Rollins. The same for Ben Abbott.

Kerri thanked him and slid the phone back into her pocket.

"San Francisco PD had nothing," she told Falco as he eased away from the curb. It was a miracle his car hadn't been towed since he'd parked in a no-parking zone.

He'd mentioned as he'd rolled into the spot this morning that the last time he'd done so, a street sweeper had plowed into the official BPD cruiser he'd been using. At least that explained one of the accidents on his record.

"I guess that means we move backward to San Diego," he suggested.

Kerri nodded, her gaze on the traffic he expertly navigated. He wasn't a bad driver at all. She'd chauffeured Boswell around for so long she'd forgotten how nice it was to be a passenger. "I'll make the call." It was Saturday, but law enforcement was twenty-four seven. She turned to Falco. "We headed to talk to the housekeeper, Angie Cowart?"

"We are. She lives over on Forty-Second Avenue."

Kerri made the call to San Diego PD while Falco drove to the housekeeper's address.

The dispatcher in San Diego would leave an urgent message for the liaison officer, who would call Kerri back as soon as possible. Whatever that meant in West Coast time. She hoped the folks there worked faster than the ones in San Francisco. But given it was Saturday, the dispatcher hadn't made any promises.

"Looks like someone's home," Falco announced as he pulled in the drive behind an older-model Ford pickup.

"I guess Jenkins kept her word and didn't warn Cowart." Kerri hadn't really expected she would.

They emerged from the car, Falco slipping into his trademark leather jacket, and started for the porch.

Kerri had wondered how long he would be able to survive without it.

The Forty-Second Avenue area was shabby for sure, and the house was likely a rental whose landlord refused to maintain it properly. But it wasn't the worst neighborhood in the city by any means.

The landscape was a little overgrown, and the house badly needed a coat of paint, but the place was clean. No garbage lying around. No defunct vehicles up on blocks. On the porch two pots of blooming flowers welcomed guests. Two plastic chairs with a table between them sat at the far end of the space. Clean and charming.

Falco knocked on the screen door.

A burst of ferocious barking had them both stepping back.

The tan-colored pit bull shoved his nose against the screen and snarled as if he'd had to pause to catch his breath before launching into a second barking rant.

"Take it easy, boy," Falco offered, which prompted a round of threatening growls.

"Maybe it's the jacket," Kerri suggested. "He probably doesn't recognize that you're a cop."

"Funny, Devlin."

"May I help you?"

The hesitant voice came from deep inside the house, in the shadows well beyond the now-slobbering dog.

"Ma'am, I'm Detective Devlin, and this is my partner, Detective Falco. We need a few moments of your time."

135

The barking resumed, as if the dog wanted to warn his master that trouble was on her doorstep.

"Khaki, go!"

The dog swung his head back and looked at her but didn't make a move to obey the order.

"Go! Now!"

The muscled animal reluctantly turned the rest of his body around and trotted off.

Falco glanced at Kerri and mouthed the word *Khaki* as he made a what-the-hell face.

The dog was kind of khaki colored.

A woman, approximately midtwenties, appeared at the door. Her dark hair was pulled back into a ponytail. She wore a plain white tee and jeans. "I've already talked to you." This she directed at Falco. "I don't know anything."

A sure sign that she did. "Ms. Cowart"—Kerri stepped closer to the screen door—"we just need to go over a few details. I'm certain you've told us everything you know, but it never hurts to go over information twice. This is very important."

"Should I call for a warrant, Devlin?" Falco asked.

The younger woman gasped. Kerri turned to her partner. "I don't believe that will be necessary." She shifted her attention back to the door. "I'm sure Ms. Cowart wants to help us."

"Yes. Please. Come in. You don't need a warrant. I have nothing to hide."

She backed away from the door as Falco reached to open it. Once they were beyond the threshold, Cowart just stood in the middle of the room, wringing her hands.

"Do you mind if we sit down?" Kerri nodded to the sofa and chair facing the old console-style television set.

Head bobbing up and down, Cowart said, "Sure. Sure."

They settled around the likely inoperative television. Cowart continued to wring her hands, the fear obvious on her face.

"Mrs. Chapin mentioned an older blue car parked near the Abbotts' gate last week," Falco said. "Do you remember the one she was talking about."

Cowart stared at her hands a moment.

"Anything you can tell us," Kerri put in, "could be crucial to finding Mrs. Abbott alive."

The housekeeper's head came up, her eyes wide with fear. "It belongs to Joey. Joey Keaton. He's Ms. Jenkins's nephew. He does yard work sometimes for the Abbotts—when their regular landscaper is behind."

"Angie, may I call you Angie?"

She nodded without meeting Kerri's gaze.

"Why were you concerned about telling us this?"

Cowart stared at her hands again. "Because he . . . he's my boyfriend."

Now Kerri got the picture. The two may have been having secret rendezvous when Angie was on the Chapin clock.

Kerri said, "We'll need to speak with him, Angie. Do you have a phone number?"

She nodded. "But his minutes are out, so it's not working right now."

"How can we find him?" Falco pressed.

"He's living with Ms. Jenkins until he finds more work. His family is all gone now. His aunt is all he has left."

For the moment Kerri had no reason to be concerned that Jenkins hadn't mentioned her nephew. It wasn't as if they'd asked her about the old blue car.

"One last question." Kerri took her time, framing the question carefully. "Do you have any reason to believe Joey might know something about what happened? Maybe he saw something, and he's afraid to talk about it."

Cowart shook her head. "No. I was just afraid to say anything. I worried I would get fired."

"We have no reason to mention any of this to the Chapins," Falco assured her. "But we will need to speak with Joey. We're going over to his aunt's house now, and we need you not to call and tell him. You keep our secret, and we'll keep yours."

She nodded, her expression uncertain. "Okay."

Kerri waited until they were in Falco's car and driving away before she shared her conclusion. "I think she's telling the truth."

"I guess we'll know when we get to the aunt's house. If Joey has recently taken off, I say we come back and rattle the girl's cage again."

"Maybe. But I don't think we'll have to do that."

Montevallo Road

Ilana Jenkins was home, and so was her nephew Joey.

The thirty-year-old deadbeat sat on the sofa next to his aunt. Kerri had run the nephew's name. There was a breaking and entering when he was twenty and at least one domestic disturbance for each of his eight girlfriends over the past decade. The most recent altercation had escalated to domestic violence. According to his probation officer, Joey had an issue with his temper, which kept him unemployed most of the time. He'd gone through more jobs in the past decade than he had girlfriends. Currently he was employed by the Second Time Around Auto Salvage.

Kerri felt sorry for Jenkins. Jenkins should kick his ass out.

"He's my only sister's child," she explained. "He has no one else."

"This is why you didn't tell us about his car being at the Abbott home last week?" Falco made no effort to hide his frustration.

"She didn't know." Keaton spoke up for the first time.

Maybe the guy had one decent bone in his body after all.

"Go on," Falco ordered.

After exhaling dramatically, Keaton started to talk. "Angie and I have a thing."

Jenkins burst into a rant about how she'd told him not to get involved with anyone close to her work. Though tears shone in her eyes, she was livid.

"I know, I know." Keaton's shoulders sagged. "We've been real careful. I wasn't there to see her last week, though. I swear, Aunt Illy. Being there had nothing to do with Angie. I wouldn't do that to you."

"If you weren't in the neighborhood to see Angie or to work," Kerri said, "why were you there? Parked near the gate to the Abbott property? You have to know that your record of domestic violence puts you at the top of our suspect list."

"It's not like that. I swear!" He stared at his hands for a few seconds. Unlike his girlfriend's, his lay loosely against his jean-clad thighs. "*She* wanted to talk to me."

Kerri's instincts went on point. "Who wanted to talk to you?"

"Mrs. Abbott."

Kerri and Falco exchanged a glance. This could be the moment— the turning point in the case.

Jenkins erupted into another outraged monologue. This time the tears flowed unencumbered down her cheeks.

"Why did Mrs. Abbott want to speak with you?" Kerri was careful to keep her rising anticipation out of her tone. She didn't want this guy to shut down or, worse, lawyer up. Whatever he had seen, heard, or done, they needed it.

"She had a problem." He looked from Kerri to Falco and back. "She wouldn't really say what it was. Believe me, I asked. I told her I might not be able to help if she wasn't up front with me, but she wouldn't say."

"If she wouldn't explain what the problem was," Kerri ventured, "why did she want to speak with you?"

"She said there was something she needed to do, and she couldn't do it with her car or her husband's. She needed one that couldn't be tied to her or her husband."

"She wanted to borrow your car," Falco suggested.

Keaton wagged his head from side to side. "She wanted to buy it. I told her it wasn't for sale, but she insisted. Finally, I thought, *What the hell?* But I did warn her it wasn't that great. Just an old beater."

Now this was an interesting turn of events. "And you're sure she didn't mention why she needed it," Kerri pushed. "Anything she said might help us determine what's happened to her."

"No. Not even a hint. She just said she had something to do. She offered me ten thousand dollars, and I couldn't say no."

Jenkins was shaking her head and muttering now. Kerri couldn't determine if she was praying for or chanting a curse against her nephew.

"She gave you cash?" Falco asked.

"Ten K in one-hundred-dollar bills. I bought a killer 1987 red Porsche 944. Even had enough left over to pay for the insurance for a whole year."

Kerri pulled out her notepad. "Joey, I need you to tell me exactly what day this transaction occurred and every single detail about the car you sold Mrs. Abbott."

"It was on Friday of last week. She made the offer on Thursday, and then I came back on Friday and got the money." He listed off the relevant details of his 1996 Plymouth Breeze.

"Did you turn the car over to her on Friday?" Falco asked.

"I only gave her one of the keys and the title. She told me exactly where to leave the car parked at the Walmart over on Palisades Boulevard, so that's what I did. I left the second key under the floor mat and locked the doors, like she said. She must've picked it up, because I drove by there after I got my Porsche, and the Plymouth was gone."

Kerri's heart rate kicked into high gear. The Walmart would have surveillance cameras for the parking lot.

"Did you leave the license plate on the car?" Falco asked.

"I didn't take it off. It's possible she did."

Falco said, "I'll need the registration information."

When Keaton had produced a tag receipt, Kerri passed him her notepad and pen. "I need you to write down everything you just told us and sign it."

She wasn't going to risk this guy taking off on her or changing his story.

A full five minutes later he signed his name with a little more flair than necessary and passed the notepad and pen across the table to Kerri. "Done."

"Thank you, Joey." She stood and gave the aunt a nod. "Ms. Jenkins." Kerri pulled a card from her pocket and thrust it at Keaton. "I need to hear from you if you remember anything else about the Abbotts. Anything at all."

He nodded as he accepted the card. "Sure thing. You think she offed her husband and disappeared?"

Ms. Jenkins started to sob once more. Poor woman. She'd known Ben Abbott his whole life.

"We don't know," Kerri confessed. "That's why we need your help."

Keaton acknowledged this with a jerk of his head. "For the record, she didn't seem like the type, you know."

"Type?" Falco asked.

"To, you know, kill anybody."

"But you barely knew her," Kerri countered. "Are you sure about that?"

Keaton shrugged. "Maybe not. But I've known bad people before, and she didn't give off that kind of vibe."

Jenkins tearfully apologized repeatedly as she followed them to her porch. Kerri assured her that it was all good now.

Kerri needed to get to that Walmart.

No sooner did her seat belt click into place than Falco roared out of the driveway.

En route Kerri called dispatch and put out an APB on the blue Plymouth.

Maybe no one had taken Mrs. Abbott from the house.

There was a real possibility she'd left before the murders occurred.

But where had the blood on her side of the bed come from?

20

12:00 p.m.

Walmart
Palisades Boulevard

The parking lot surveillance at the Walmart had given them nothing. The car had been parked in the one part of the lot where the cameras didn't reach. Was Sela Abbott really so clever that she'd calculated that move? The blue car was spotted on a different camera leaving the lot later the same night Keaton had dropped it off, but it was impossible to see who the driver was.

"You realize it took some doing to figure out the exact range of the camera closest to where she parked," Falco said. "Maybe the husband isn't the only genius in the family."

Kerri understood this. Yes. "Whatever her motives, Sela Abbott planned everything very carefully. We just don't know what *everything* includes yet."

That was the problem. Had she been planning to leave her husband? Maybe she was having some sort of breakdown. Though her doctor didn't seem to think so.

Kerri got up on her knees in her seat and reached for the stack of files in the back. She slid back into her seat and rifled through them until she found the one she needed. She skimmed the bank statements she'd printed out.

"There are no big cash withdrawals over the past month." Kerri ran her finger down the column again. The larger debits from the account were payments for utilities and other services. Insurance. The house, the business, the vehicles they owned were all purchased outright. No mortgages. No loans.

"Maybe she'd been saving up over the course of several months." Falco used his thumbs to tap out a few beats on the steering wheel. "Stashing a little away here and there."

"Either that or there's a bank account we don't know about." Kerri closed the file. "With this kind of money, there are likely accounts all over the world."

"But would Ben Abbott give his new wife access to all of them?"

"No way to be certain, I suppose."

Falco tugged at the collar of his starched shirt, which had likely started to chafe. "We know she didn't register the car. She didn't want her husband or anyone else to know about it."

"The fact that she secretly bought the car only a few days before she disappeared does not lend credibility to her being a victim." Kerri felt confident Falco understood there was no way to spin this other than the way it was.

"Obviously she had access to money we can't track, and she had wheels that no one knew about," Falco agreed.

"It's time to seriously consider that Sela Abbott was either involved, or she had some plan in the works that may or may not have contributed to what happened."

"We need the results back on the blood found in the bed with the husband," Falco said. "The lab stuff is all taking way too long. Didn't the chief put a rush on all this?"

"He did," Kerri relented. "But he wants the t's crossed and the i's dotted. The lab is likely repeating all tests just to make sure there are no mistakes."

She was grateful Falco didn't point out that he'd been leaning in the direction that the wife was involved all along.

"The chief of police is keeping tabs on this," Falco said aloud— to himself, no doubt, since he was aware Kerri already understood as much. "This goes as high as you can go in Birmingham. The top of the top. The department wants no mistakes."

"Daniel Abbott's son is murdered." Kerri picked it up from there. "It's all over the news. Talk show hosts and investigative reporters are doing the same thing we are: tossing out scenarios. Did the wife do it? Did she take a big chunk of his fortune and disappear? Was she having an affair, and her lover did the killing, and then the two of them disappeared?"

"Hey." Falco glanced at her. "We didn't talk about that one."

Kerri rolled her eyes. "Because it isn't plausible. None of it is, really. She's taken the mother with her everywhere her whole life. Why kill her now? Why kill anyone? Take the money and disappear. The killing was completely unnecessary if those sorts of motives were the ones driving her."

He grinned. "Makes for a great headline, though." His lips eased down into a flat line. "Unless she was afraid of him," her partner suggested. "Maybe she knew he would hunt her down if he wasn't taken out."

"But what about his daddy? She had to know Daniel Abbott would do the same thing. He isn't going to sit idly by and allow her to get away with killing his son—his only heir. If we don't get this case solved, he'll hire private investigators to find her or whatever there is to be found." Kerri chewed at her lip. The man had been damned calm in that interview. "Maybe he already has."

"I see what you're saying, Devlin. When you get down to the nitty-gritty, this little plot was a no-win situation for her either way."

"Which would suggest she had no idea this was coming. Getaway car aside, she could be a complete innocent in the murders. Maybe dead already. What do we know about Sela Abbott since she moved here?" Kerri silently mulled over the meager details.

"She's very good at separating rich people from their money," Falco pointed out.

"For a good cause," Kerri qualified.

He nodded. "Everyone believes she's like an angel. A saint. Except maybe her mother-in-law."

"And Suzanne Thompson."

"But the mother-in-law," he countered. "Pulling one over on her would be the true measure of her ability to deceive. If we go with the scenario that the wife is somehow involved with something that accidentally prompted the murders, why would she go to the trouble to so completely fool all the other people around her," Falco ventured, "and not the woman closest to her? The one who really mattered to her new husband? Why would she let that happen? She fooled her husband, so we know she possesses the necessary skills."

Kerri turned to him. "It's far more difficult to fool a mother," she argued. "The old saying that mothers have a kind of intuition is true, I think." She mentally flipped the coin and looked at the other side. "Then again, maybe she doesn't care what Mrs. Abbott thinks of her. Maybe Sela doesn't like her either. Allowing her to see what she was doing may have been part of the fun."

"She wouldn't be the first new wife who loved sticking it to her MIL."

This was true. Kerri had never had to deal with the in-law thing. Her husband and his family weren't close at all. She'd only met them once. Even after Tori was born, there had been no relationship. Since it had always been that way, she hadn't questioned it. Maybe there was a reason Nick and his family didn't get along. Maybe she should make it a point to learn what that reason was.

"We should go to lunch," Falco decided.

Kerri's stomach rumbled. She turned to her partner. "Can we pick up Chinese or something and go to my place so I can check on Tori and bring her lunch too?"

"Sure thing, but does it have to be Chinese? Way too many MSGs or whatever. How about Mexican? There's this place I love. I swear it's to die for."

Made no difference to her. "Mexican it is."

As he drove away from the Walmart, Kerri decided that she needed to speak to Suzanne Thompson again. If Sela Abbott wanted her mother-in-law to understand things were not as they should be, she may have wanted Mrs. Thompson to be aware as well. Taking into consideration the property dispute, it made an odd kind of sense. All Kerri needed was the why. This was, of course, simply another working theory. They had several, and not a single one rose above the others, which meant they had to keep digging and turning over rocks.

By Monday she intended to talk to Theo Thompson with or without approval from the chain of command.

The one true negative they had encountered regarding Sela Abbott had come from the Thompsons. The Thompsons were angry over the property purchase.

It wasn't much, but it was all they had that actually pointed to any sort of motive.

21

2:00 p.m.

Crestwood Inn & Suites
Crestwood Boulevard

Jen leaned toward the dingy mirror and reapplied her lipstick, then used her fingers to fluff and arrange her tousled red hair. What a dump he'd chosen as their meeting place. Things with Theo were really going downhill fast.

She felt like a whore. He ignored her, canceled on her, and then he showed up for a quickie?

She was a whore, and she wasn't even getting paid.

In the mirror she watched Theo buttoning his shirt. He was using her. Why did she keep pretending otherwise? Diana was right. She should just end it and start over.

The end was bound to happen sooner or later. Why prolong the agony?

She turned to face him. "I'm sick of this." She surveyed the shabby room. "This is not what I want."

Her eyes burned, and she blinked back the tears. She would not cry for this bastard. She had cried enough over men in the past. Tears never changed a thing.

Damn Theo Thompson. He didn't deserve her tears. She turned her back on him. Couldn't bear to face him any longer.

"Sweetheart." He moved toward her.

She watched his advancement in the mirror. No matter that she wanted to be angry with him, her heart skipped a beat. He was so damned handsome. So smart and rich to boot. He was everything she had ever wanted. Her eyes closed as she thought of the way his skin smelled. She'd never been with a man who smelled as delicious as he did.

"You don't need to worry. When this election is behind me, you and I will have the life we deserve. I made that promise to you, and I'm standing firm behind it. Please don't give up on me yet."

"How can I keep believing the same story over and over?" She whirled to face him. "I want a family."

She could have bitten off her tongue for saying out loud the words she had held inside for so very long.

Too late now.

He looked as startled as she felt. "I had no idea."

A new fear crept into her heart. He didn't want this. She could hear it in his voice. He'd had his family. Raised a brilliant, overachieving son and an equally talented daughter. At forty-six why would he want to start all over?

But she hadn't had those things. Why should she give up everything she wanted just to make him happy? This relationship had been one sided from the beginning. It was time she counted as much as he did.

"It's true. I want a family. I can't have that like this. You need to make up your mind what you really want and take the necessary steps."

His arms went around her. "Don't you want to be the First Lady of the great state of Alabama one day? I will follow the same path as my father. Who knows after that? We could end up in DC, rubbing shoulders with the real movers and shakers. Going to extravagant parties and ignoring paparazzi."

As hard as she tried not to allow his words to excite her, they did just the same. "Of course I want to but . . ."

"But what?" He nipped at her cheek.

"What if you change your mind?" Was she pathetic or what?

"My kids are in college. You think I want to spend the rest of my life in the same house alone with the woman I made the mistake of marrying when I was too young to know better?"

Jen wanted to believe him. Damn her, but she did. "She's very pretty. I saw her downtown the other day."

"She spends a lot of time and money to look pretty. The sad part is that it's only superficial. The woman inside is cruel and hateful. Not like you at all."

Jen melted against him in spite of her best intentions.

Maybe she was a fool, but it was too late to change that now.

Across the shabby room his cell phone rattled against the cheap bedside table. He immediately turned away from her and rushed to answer it.

Jen closed the bathroom door and leaned against it. She stared at her reflection in the mirror and hated the weakness she saw.

"Define *significant*!"

His raised voice had Jen going still, listening more intently.

"Oh my God. Then she could know . . . *everything*."

The hollowness of the word, the utter shock in his voice, had her heart racing.

"Of course I know what this means."

Silence.

Jen hugged herself tightly.

"You do whatever necessary to make this go away."

Jen reached for the faucet and turned on the water. She didn't want him to think she'd been listening.

Jesus Christ . . . what the hell was he involved in?

22

4:00 p.m.

T. R. Thompson Residence
Briarcliff Road, Mountain Brook

Theo sat in his car for a long while just staring at the house where he had grown up. It wasn't as modern and filled with state-of-the-art amenities as his own home. Rather, it was a classic mansion laden with architectural details, antique chandeliers, and mahogany floors and cabinets. At seventeen thousand square feet it was enormous by 1960s standards. It stood on five acres, an unheard-of advantage in the area now. There was even a three-hole golf course.

Theo had been taught to play golf as soon as he'd learned to walk. Like Ben Abbott, he had been an only child. He'd been spoiled, allowed to have whatever he wanted growing up. But everything had changed when he'd finished his education. He'd returned from the prestigious University of Alabama, his father's and his grandfather's alma mater, on fire to change the world. He'd eventually married and had his children, and all had seemed right.

Until that one mistake.

The one slip had changed everything.

When it happened, he had known what he wanted. He wasn't like his father. He couldn't live that way. But his father had ensured that he stayed in his place.

T. R. Thompson had seen to it that his only son did not stray from the path assigned him before he was even born.

His gaze lit on the other sedan in the cobblestone drive. Suzanne was here. He should have known she would attempt a head start on kissing his father's ass. She had always been very good at ensuring her place was protected. Whatever happened to Theo, she would remain in the soon-to-be governor's good graces. This was a lesson she had been taught from birth. Her ancestors weren't members of Birmingham's esteemed founders, but they had come along soon after, finding their place among those powerful families. Suzanne had learned early on how important it was to make all the right connections. She had made herself invaluable to his father and to others in powerful positions. Theo never asked questions. He didn't want to know.

He despised the loathsome bitch.

He wondered how long it would be before his father was made aware of all that was at stake now. Lewis would do all within his power to avoid that end, but each day seemed to bring another stumbling block.

It was all out of control.

Deciding to get on with it, he opened the car door and climbed out. He trudged up the steps and, using his key, let himself into the house. The foyer had been his mother's most prized design feat. The marble floors and curving marble staircase—all imported from Europe. Even the railing had been forged by hand. Nothing was too good for the great T. R. Thompson.

He walked along the long entry hall, passing rooms and ignoring the voices from the past that whispered to him. His mother had died in this house when he was only twenty. His father had not remarried. But he had never gone without the pleasures associated with a relationship.

No one had known, of course. Theodore Roosevelt Thompson Sr. was above reproach. No one kept a secret better.

His father's clandestine indiscretions had caused Theo to lust for the things he shouldn't have. After all, like father, like son.

"Mr. Theo, I didn't realize you were stopping by today."

Theo paused and turned to the man who had spoken. Melvin Patterson, the same age as his father, had worked for the family for fifty years. He insisted he would retire when Mr. T. R. did. Those who knew Theo's father well called him Mr. T. R., and everyone knew T. R. would never retire. He would die, his cold, dead hands still grappling for more power.

"I had a break in my schedule," Theo lied. "I thought I'd drop by and see how his week has gone."

Patterson grinned. "He will tell you that the conservative news is making him look bad and that a two percent rise in the polls is hardly measurable."

Theo chuckled. "Well, I'll see if I can cheer him up."

"You'll find him in his study. Miss Suzanne is with him. They've been discussing the postelection celebrations for the two of you."

"Is it wise to count our chickens before they hatch?"

Patterson laughed outright. "Mr. Theo, you know who's going to win."

It was true. The odds were certainly in their favor. Theo thanked the man who had often been like a surrogate father to him and moved on to the study. He was surprised Patterson was here on a Saturday. Typically by five on Fridays Patterson and the rest of the staff were gone until Monday. His father liked having the house to himself on the weekends. Theo could only imagine the things his father did when no one else was about. He'd always had a nasty sexual appetite.

The door to the study was open, so he paused a moment and watched his father chatting with Suzanne. For a man in his midseventies, he looked damned good. He'd had an enviable gym added to the house years ago. He worked out faithfully. His gray hair remained thick and his blue eyes clear. He was not one to fall down on taking care of himself. He swore that his good looks and robust health played as vital a role as his platform in keeping him in office. Theo doubted his good looks and health or even his platform kept him in office. It was the way things were. Always had been. He was a Thompson; he would win whatever office in the state of Alabama he chose to seek.

Likewise, plenty of Alabamians would vote for Theo for no other reason than the fact that he was T. R.'s son.

Theo both appreciated and despised the idea.

Suzanne looked beautiful, of course. She spent a great deal of time and money ensuring she looked elegant and youthful. But beneath all that enhanced beauty beat a heart that was as black as the coal her daddy and his forefathers had dug out of the ground in and around Birmingham for a century.

"Well." T. R. shifted his focus from the no doubt titillating conversation. "If it's not the future senator."

"How did you get away from the office so early?" Suzanne wanted to know. A fine line had formed between her brows. She hated when anyone or anything made her frown. He could see her now, rushing home to inject a shot of Botox.

Theo walked in and settled into a chair. "After my last meeting, I needed a break. A few of my supporters are getting nervous."

T. R. leaned back in his chair. "You have nothing to worry about, son. We've won already. Our opponents know it; they just refuse to admit it. Thompsons are impossible to beat."

For a single heartbeat Theo considered telling his father that he had good reason to worry, but he kept his mouth tightly shut. Things were going to hell quickly enough without him adding fuel to the fire.

Theo produced a dim smile. "I'm sure you're right."

"Of course he's right," Suzanne purred. "When has your father ever been wrong?"

Theo clamped his jaw shut. He had no desire to go there.

"It's a shame about Daniel's boy and his family." T. R. shook his head. "I can't imagine what he's going through, having lost his only son. Have they found his wife yet?"

"They have not. It's positively awful," Suzanne agreed. "With the woman carrying their only grandchild, I'm sure Daniel and Tempest are devastated."

Theo thought of that fundraiser back in February. Sela Abbott had flirted incessantly with the old man. He'd ended up donating millions of dollars to the cause she supported. Theo couldn't even remember the name, but he remembered vividly watching his father laugh and Sela hover around him, her smiles dazzling. How could his father not have seen what Theo saw?

How could he not know what Theo had known even then?

The past was back to haunt them, and there was a very good chance that both of them were going to pay.

The election was the least of their worries.

23

5:00 p.m.

Birmingham Police Department
First Avenue North
Major Investigations Division

Kerri surveyed the board she and Falco had pieced together. The fragments of this case were coming together slowly, so damned slowly. At this point she was simply grateful for the slightest scrap of information.

The attorney for the Abbott family's personal interests had explained the way the victim's estate would be divided. One-quarter of Ben Abbott's holdings in the company would transfer to his wife. The rest would go to his father and mother. The same with all monies, stocks, what have you. All of this was contingent on there being no children. If Abbott and his wife had children, things changed dramatically in the favor of the wife and children.

"The only people who stand to benefit from the wife's death"—Falco angled his head and studied the board—"are the husband's parents."

Kerri considered Falco's unquestionable statement. "Particularly since the wife was pregnant with an heir, which shifted everything." She tapped the dry-erase marker against her cheek. "But the parents would never kill their son or grandchild. The mother-in-law, maybe. The wife, possibly."

"But if someone else killed their son—like the wife," Falco suggested, "they might work up the motivation to take her out. Maybe that's why her body hasn't shown up. They're waiting for her to have the baby and then—" He made a slicing action across his throat.

Kerri shook her head. "But why would the wife kill the husband? As we've already discussed, there's still no logical motive, and the act would only put a bigger target on her own back."

"But we do know she went all cloak-and-dagger and bought a car." Falco tapped the photo of the blue car, a frame taken from the Walmart surveillance of it leaving the parking lot. "She had a plan for that car, Devlin. Whether it was to go slumming in her free time or whatever, she didn't buy it to add to her landscaping."

Clearly.

Kerri's cell vibrated against her desktop. She twisted and picked it up. She recognized the number that popped up because she had called it about a dozen times over the past few days. "It's Bellemont."

She met Falco's gaze as she answered the call, setting it to speaker. "Devlin."

"I understand you've been trying to reach me, Detective."

"We've had a development in the case."

"Please tell me you've found Sela, and she's safe."

"Unfortunately, we haven't been so lucky. What we do have is new information regarding some rather surprising actions taken by Sela before the murders."

Silence echoed across the line for four or five seconds.

Then he asked, "What sort of actions?"

That he didn't sound startled by Kerri's announcement wasn't lost on her.

"She purchased an older-model car from the housekeeper's nephew with an exorbitant cash payment. I'm thinking this may be just the tip of the iceberg." That last part was true, just not necessarily of the wife.

"You're reaching here, Detective. There is no way Sela had anything to do with Ben's murder, much less her mother's. Whatever purpose she had for buying this car, you can believe me when I say that she must have had a very good reason, and it had nothing to do with murder."

"I wonder if the Abbotts will be so certain when they hear the news."

"Do what you must, Detective, but you will only be hurting those two grieving people without contributing any sort of positive result toward your investigation."

"You give me one good reason not to go to the Abbotts, and I won't. You have until tomorrow morning."

Kerri ended the call. She wasn't playing games with Bellemont anymore. He was hiding something, and she needed to know what that secret was and how it impacted this case.

"You told him, Devlin."

She glanced at Falco. "Would you have handled it any differently? He knows information that might help this case, but for whatever reason he's keeping it to himself."

Before her partner could answer the question, another call shimmied through her phone. She checked the screen. California area code. She hit speaker and said, "Devlin."

"Detective Devlin, this is Lieutenant Winston Brown. I'm returning your call about Jacqueline and Sela Rollins."

"Yes, Lieutenant. Thank you for calling me back. Especially on a Saturday." Kerri took a moment to explain the murders and the current status of Sela Rollins, now Abbott.

"Oh my." He cleared his throat. "I hadn't heard this news. I knew they had moved, but I had no idea where to or that there had been trouble. I really hate to hear this."

"Wait. Is this the liaison officer?" The detective sounded more like an old friend of the family.

"Lieutenant Elsworth, our liaison, brought this to me since I was the one who always handled the Rollins situation."

"Situation?" Kerri and Falco exchanged hopeful looks.

"It's a bit of a long story, and I'm not sure it's relevant to your investigation," he offered.

"Believe me, Lieutenant," Kerri assured him, "we'll take whatever you have."

"All right." He took a deep breath. "Mrs. Rollins had another daughter, Janelle Stevens. She went missing fifteen years ago. Poor woman never really recovered from the loss. Every time her younger daughter, Sela—who was thirteen, I believe, at the time—came home late or failed to call, Mrs. Rollins would dial 911 and say she was missing. It took some time to work out the trouble, but we managed to get the situation under control."

Kerri was still reeling from the news that there was an older sister. "The sister, Janelle, she disappeared in your jurisdiction fifteen years ago?"

"That's the ironic part," the detective said. "Mrs. Rollins's—Stevens is her maiden name—older daughter didn't live in San Diego when she went missing. She had moved to Alabama. Janelle Stevens disappeared in *your* jurisdiction."

Surprise radiated through Kerri. "You're certain about that?"

"I am. Sela came to visit me several times during her senior year of high school. She had decided to go into law enforcement. She wanted to make a difference. I think maybe she thought she might be able to find the truth about what happened to her sister. I sort of kept up with her over the years. She did really well at SDSU. When she and her mother moved away after her graduation, I never heard from them again until Sela landed in San Francisco. She had applied for a position at a law firm and wanted a letter of recommendation from me. She was so excited. I was a little surprised that she hadn't gone into law enforcement as she'd planned for so many years, but people change. At any rate, that was the last time I heard from her."

"Thank you, Detective." Kerri's mind reeled with questions she couldn't quite pull together in any sort of logical manner. "I may need to call you again. Is this your cell number?"

"It is. Call anytime. I'm sorry to hear about Sela and her mother."

Kerri ended the call and tossed her phone onto her desk. For a moment, she sat, stunned by the news. An older sister. One the in-laws didn't know about—one who disappeared *here*, in Birmingham. "I have to say, I didn't see that one coming."

"No kidding." Falco slid into the chair behind his desk and started pecking at the keyboard of his computer. "J-A-N-E-L-L-E S-T-E-V-E-N-S."

"Stevens is the mother's maiden name." Kerri pondered the idea for a second. "Maybe she wasn't married to Janelle's father or chose not to take his name. I'm surprised the daughter didn't. Maybe the mother never shared who the father was."

Falco grunted his agreement. He was focused on his search, but Kerri was still gobsmacked by the news. Sela had a sister. Why would anyone keep her sister a secret—particularly a sister who went missing—unless there was a damned good reason?

Kerri's cell vibrated again, this time with an incoming text. It was the LT. He'd asked her to stop by his office, but she'd gotten caught up in this. "Pull everything you can find on the Stevens case. I'll be right back." Before rushing away, she turned back once more. "Also, call the assistant, Marcella Gibbons, and find out if that law firm Sela worked for is or was in any way connected to Ben Abbott or his company out in San Francisco."

Falco glanced up. "Will do."

She hurried across the bullpen and down the hall to the LT's office. She knocked on the door, and he motioned for her to come in.

"I would have been here sooner, but we may have a break in the Abbott case."

"That would make my day, Devlin. I don't like spending my entire Saturday in this office. But how can I not be here when I have people working on cases that the chief and the mayor—among others—want to see cleared up?"

That was her cue, Kerri assumed. "Sela Abbott had an older sister, Janelle Stevens, who lived in Birmingham."

"Well, I'll be damned," he said, then frowned. "Wait, I remember that name. Janelle Stevens." He considered the name for a moment. "If I recall correctly, she disappeared, and the case was never solved." He pushed his glasses higher up his nose. "You think this might somehow play into what happened?"

"Too soon to know, but it's definitely a new angle to investigate."

"It's certainly more than we had." The frown lining his brow warned that he was attempting to pull anything about the old case from his memory banks.

The few other disjointed details Kerri and Falco were toying with, like pursuing additional info about the disagreement between Thompson and Abbott, she didn't share with the LT. He'd made it clear he didn't want to hear anything related to the Thompson name without sufficient evidence to back it up.

"I'll give you an update as soon as we have anything new." She really wanted to get back to work.

"One thing, Devlin."

She hesitated at the door. "What's that?"

"How's it going with Falco? Any problems?"

"It's going surprisingly well. No problems."

His eyebrows reared up. "Does that mean this is going to work out?"

She shrugged. "I think so." She hesitated again. "I'd like to know what all that redacted stuff in his file is about."

"I'll see what I can do, but no guarantees. I don't even know that story."

Kerri thanked him and walked back to the cubicle. Falco was pacing the small space.

"Did you find something?"

"Have a seat," he said as he pulled out his own chair and dropped into it.

Hoping this was the break they had needed, Kerri did as he asked. "I'm listening."

He turned his monitor around so that she could see it. A photo of a young woman, midtwenties, stared back at her. There was enough of a resemblance to easily guess that it was Sela's older sister.

"She moved here from San Diego and went to work—wait for it," Falco said with a quick drumroll of his fingers against his desk, "with Senator T. R. Thompson. A few months later she vanished."

A boost of adrenaline shot through Kerri. "What do you know? We have another Thompson connection. Interesting."

"Could be coincidence," Falco said, but his skeptical expression was not sufficient to override the obvious optimism in his tone.

"Definitely," she agreed with a heavy dose of sarcasm.

"You remember anything about the Stevens case?"

Kerri shook her head. "I guess I missed that one since I was away in college at the time." This unexpected twist needled at her with new verve. "If Sela was so tuned in to the case all the way through college—even choosing criminal justice as her major—why just let it go? Especially with her being *here*—where it happened—and married to a man of means?"

"Maybe she didn't. Maybe that's the part that's missing in all this."

Kerri and her partner were definitely on the same wavelength. "What about any connection between the law office where Sela worked and Abbott Options?"

Falco leaned back in his chair and clasped his hands across his abdomen. "That was a damned good call, Devlin. In fact, the law firm is very connected—as in it represented Ben Abbott personally as well as his business when he lived in Cali. Still represents his business."

"Are you serious? When I spoke to her former supervisor, he acted as if he didn't know her husband well."

Falco nodded. "That's because the firm you called is the one where she worked the first three months she lived in San Francisco. She left that firm and went to Arnold, Fox, and Patton and found her own Cinderella story."

Kerri braced her forearms on her desk. Now this was good. "Let's lay this out, Falco. Ben Abbott is a native of Birmingham—the city where Sela's sister disappeared. She spends her higher education preparing to solve her sister's case. Then she moves to San Francisco, and instead of becoming a cop, she goes to work for a law firm, eventually landing at the one that represents Ben Abbott of Birmingham. She steals his heart and, voilà, becomes Mrs. Ben Abbott. The next thing you know, they move back here."

"But there's no happily ever after because now Ben is dead, and Sela has disappeared," Falco declared.

"This is a hell of a lot of trouble to go to in hopes of solving an old case or for some sort of revenge." Kerri still had a doubt or two.

"True," Falco agreed, "but the cop from San Diego said she talked about the case a lot. So much so that he seemed damned surprised she hadn't gone into law enforcement."

Kerri's phone vibrated again. She pulled it from her pocket and checked the screen. "It's the ME." She tapped accept and set it to speaker. "Devlin. Tell me something good, Dr. Moore."

The older man chuckled. "I'm a medical examiner, Detective. Whatever I have to tell you is about the dead. How good could it be?"

Kerri laughed. "Let me rephrase that. Tell me something that might help solve my case."

"Well, I had a second look at Jacqueline Rollins. The autopsy wasn't scheduled until Monday, but I decided to move forward today. What else is an old man going to do on Saturday?"

Kerri wasn't quite as old as her esteemed colleague, but she definitely got it. "Tell me about it."

"Especially," Moore added, "when *your* chief is breathing down my neck."

She got that as well. "Join the club."

He grunted. "You stated that Ms. Rollins had been diagnosed with cancer; is that correct?"

"That's what we were told, and the meds in her room seemed to suggest that was the case."

"Unless some of the labs tell me different, I found no indication of cancer."

Kerri stared at Falco. They had both seen the medications. Listened to the Abbotts discuss the fact that Sela's mother suffered with cancer and that her daughter had to take care of her.

"Is it possible it went away or was in remission to the point you can't find it now?"

"Anything's possible, Detective, but based on the autopsy I'd have to say there was no cancer. If she had been ill for an extended period, there would be some evidence, I assure you."

A whole new scenario was forming in Kerri's head. "Did you find anything else that would suggest she had been ill?"

"I did not. Muscle tone was exceptionally good, as if she worked out regularly. The only anomaly I did find was a bit of an odd one. There are indications that blood had been drawn from the antecubitals in the crevices of both elbows. If it turns out she had some sort of health condition, I would say that was perhaps indicative of lab work. There's something off, however."

"Off how?" Falco asked.

"Well, based on my examination, the size needle used was unusual. It was at least seventeen gauge, which is typically for donating blood, not simple lab draws. Certainly, it's not impossible that a newbie used the wrong-size needle, but it's not the norm."

"Maybe she had donated blood recently," Kerri offered.

"Of course," Moore agreed. "But that goes against the idea that she was in ill health and on multitudes of medication."

Valid point.

"How long would it take," Falco asked, "to get DNA on the blood found on the sheets next to Ben Abbott's body compared to that of the mother?"

"Since I've already requested the analysis as a matter of course to confirm the blood belongs to the missing wife, it's possible I might be able to push for results as early as Monday afternoon. Bear in mind," Moore cautioned, "this is a very optimistic schedule."

"I understand," Kerri assured him. "Anything you can do to speed things up will be greatly appreciated."

"I'll do my best," Moore promised before ending the call.

"Tell you what I'm thinking, Devlin," Falco said.

She had a feeling they were on the same page.

"I'm thinking we've got ourselves a vanishing-wife act. She wants us to believe she's a victim, too, so she set the stage, only she used her mother's blood instead of her own because she's pregnant."

It was possible. Sela Abbott could be out there hiding somewhere or long gone, for that matter. She might have transferred all sorts of funds by now. People like the Abbotts had money in foreign and online accounts that forensic accountants and investigators took weeks or months to discover. This was a possibility they had already considered without the vanishing-wife element.

"I think you're right." Kerri pushed back her chair and stood. "If Sela Rollins sought out Ben Abbott . . . found a way into his life and then moved back here as his wife with the intention of solving her sister's disappearance, my guess is the true target was one or both of his parents. If he was the target, why not kill him in San Francisco? Why bother going to all the trouble of embedding herself in Birmingham?"

Obviously, Falco hadn't considered that possibility, though he tried to school his surprise before she noticed. "How would you tie Abbott's folks to this? The sister worked for Thompson."

"You're right," Kerri agreed. "The sister lived here and worked for Senator T. R. Thompson, but his son isn't the one who's dead. It's possible the sister became involved with Abbott somehow through her work with Thompson. The two families have a long history of association, at least socially. T. R. Thompson and Daniel Abbott are the same age. It's possible they attended school together."

Falco nodded. "Taking into account this new information, Detective Devlin, I think we should pay the Abbotts a visit whether we hear from Bellemont or not."

Kerri shut off the computer. "First we should both work on finding a more definitive connection between Daniel Abbott and T. R. Thompson. Beyond the fact that they're both from founding families and richer than God. We need something to throw on the table before we show our hand. We have an opportunity here to apply some pressure to a couple of key players. We have to do this right, or we lose the edge."

"We'll need pizza and plenty of beer for that."

"Not tonight, Falco. You do your research at your place, and I'll do mine at home. My daughter is feeling neglected." Not fair to Tori and not good for Kerri since her daughter was no doubt using her mother's absence as an excuse for spending the summer in New York.

"No problem." He stood and reached for his jacket. "I think we're onto something big here, Devlin."

"If we're right, Ben Abbott's father or maybe one or both of the Thompsons may be the next victim we find."

24

It's all in the details.

There are details—many, many details required in a plan of this magnitude.

The fewer people involved in the execution, the better. But there are certain things that require the participation of one or more persons.

A good example is the car—and certain other things I acquired. These things were essential. Yet it's those little things that can be traced—can create difficulties.

But I was smart. I kept contact to a bare minimum. Although the items can be traced back to who and where I was, they cannot reach who and where I am.

I am an enigma. I am well hidden.

No one will find me here. I work the ropes. Back and forth, back and forth. I no longer feel the pain. Perhaps I am too preoccupied to notice.

Even my single lifeline has no idea where I am. We communicate using disposable phones, and we only meet if absolutely necessary and never, ever anywhere near my hiding place. She, too, is keeping a low profile as a precaution. There are dangers associated with making an alliance with me. She is aware and willing, but I worry.

Of course, this arrangement might have to change if slipping out becomes too dangerous for me.

The details, every last one, are immensely important. Each one can make or break the plan.

The closer I come to the finale, the more precarious my situation grows. Because though I have carefully laid out this plan, taking great care with each detail, there is always a chance that a particularly smart person or detective can find something I overlooked or didn't conceal well enough.

Or forgot in my rush to hide.

There are certain things that are impossible to hide. Perhaps if I had thought out the plan more clearly, I would have taken an alias at the start. But I did not, which leaves my history—at least part of it—naked for anyone to see if they dig deeply enough.

Time will tell. For now, I am safe. My mother always said I was stronger than my sister, but I don't believe that to be the case. The difference between my sister and me is in the preparation.

As I prepared, I had the advantage of the old saying "Better the devil you know."

I know this devil extremely well.

Everything is progressing as planned.

25

Sunday, June 10

9:00 a.m.

Abbott Crime Scene
Botanical Place, Mountain Brook

Kerri walked through the master bedroom, searching for any place that Sela might have hidden a secret from her husband.

Falco was going through the family photo albums with an eye toward a female who looked like Janelle Stevens from the image in her fifteen-year-old case file. Any photos he might have seen on his previous search would not have drawn his attention since they hadn't known about the older sister at the time.

But they knew now.

They knew a lot of things they hadn't known this time yesterday. Kerri had discovered that Daniel Abbott and T. R. Thompson had indeed attended high school as well as the University of Alabama together. Falco had grabbed that ball and run with it and learned the two were actually roommates their freshman year. On top of all that, Abbott was a longtime supporter of the Thompsons, politically and otherwise.

The connection between the two men ran deep. Whether the chief or the LT liked the idea of the two being persons of interest in the case, they were just the same.

Kerri found nothing between the mattress and the box spring. The linens had been taken to the lab for analysis. The bed was one of those platform types, so you couldn't see anything on the floor beneath it without removing both the mattress and the box spring. With no other choice, Kerri dragged each, a piece at a time, onto a part of the floor she had already searched. The effort provided nothing but a few dust bunnies.

She rummaged through the bedside tables, even removed the lamps and turned the tables over to check beneath, as well as in and under the two drawers of each.

Then she moved on to the dresser and bureau. She should really check under stuff at her house. If she were murdered in her home, she wanted to be sure the investigators didn't find anything embarrassing. No one ever expected to be murdered—at least no one normal. Over the past seven years, she had found all sorts of things in the private spaces of murder vics. Notes from secret lovers. Dirty underwear. Sex toys. A stash of cash. Drugs. You name it, she had seen it.

Since the Abbotts had lived in this house scarcely over a year, and, apparently, Ms. Jenkins was very thorough at her job, there wasn't much in the way of dust or other unexpected items.

Kerri moved on to the walk-in closet, which was about the size of her bedroom at home. She went through clothes and shoes and moved on to purses. Sela Abbott had thirty-six handbags. But her attention to detail was commendable: she hadn't left anything—not even a tissue or a loose dime—in a single one.

The large jewelry armoire provided nothing either. Sela owned her share of jewelry but nothing overly gaudy. More the quietly elegant pieces.

The mother's room was next. Going through the same steps, Kerri found nothing there either. Lastly, she sat down on the bedside to have a closer look at the prescription bottles. Painkillers, mostly. Something for nausea. For constipation.

"Wait." She went back through the bottles, checking the date prescribed. Each one had expired and not recently either—years ago. If the mother had been ill, why would she be taking years-old medication that might have lost its effectiveness?

Because she wasn't ill, which would explain Dr. Moore's findings. "Holy shit." Kerri shook her head. There was a major cover-up going on in this family; there was no denying that at this point. And obviously the mother was as involved as the daughter. Kerri stared at the walker as she considered the ME's comments about her good muscle tone—as if she worked out regularly. The lack of evidence that she'd suffered with cancer or had been under a doctor's care. None of this added up.

"Devlin!"

She placed the prescription bottle back on the bedside table and went to the top of the staircase. "Yeah?"

"I found what we're looking for!"

She hustled down the stairs. Falco had several photo albums spread on the coffee table.

He waved one in his hand. "This one starts when Sela was ten years old."

Kerri collapsed onto the sofa next to him and thumbed through the pages of the album. Dozens of photos of the sisters over the course of several years. The last showed Sela when she was thirteen, according to the notes on the page. Her sister had graduated college. There were no photos of the sisters with their mother. Most were dated, but none had names written on the back.

"Where are the photos of the mother and father or fathers?"

Falco shook his head. "There aren't any. I noticed that in the other albums. All the photos were of Sela. The more recent ones were Sela and her husband. I didn't find anything before she was ten years old."

"Strange that the mother wouldn't have photos of Sela or her sister when they were small. You know, little kids or babies."

"Maybe those are in storage somewhere," Falco offered. "The furniture in this house belongs to the Abbotts. What happened to the mother's belongings when she moved in with her daughter and her new husband? Sold? Donated? Stored?"

All valid questions. "It's possible she sold or donated everything. Except photos or special mementos. Those she would surely keep. Maybe you're right, and her personal things are in storage somewhere."

"Unless she was like me." Falco tidied the stacks of albums. "I kept nothing of my former life."

"Why?"

He looked at her for a long moment. "Because I couldn't keep any part of that life. Why hang on to the reminders?"

Before Kerri could delve into the questions she wanted to ask, he grabbed another album. "I took a second look at this after what the detective from San Diego told us."

Kerri placed the first album he'd handed her onto the stack on the coffee table and accepted the next one. This one was from Sela's time at San Diego State University.

"Flip to the final two pages."

Kerri did as he said. There was a congratulations card that had been opened and placed on the page so that you could see the note written inside.

I expect great things from you!

The note was signed *Dr. Elizabeth Saxon, Dean of Students.*

"Maybe no one here knows the real Sela Rollins Abbott," Falco suggested, "but there are people in her past who seemed to know her pretty damn well. Like that detective."

Her partner was right. "Whenever we find what we think might be a lead, it drags us deeper into the past. Maybe we should see what else is back there."

He nodded. "That's what I'm saying. This whole thing goes way back, Devlin."

"I'm with you on that one. As a matter of fact, all those prescription bottles in the mother's room go way back too. They all expired like five years ago, and the pharmacy isn't a local one. But it's a chain we have here, which is why we didn't pick up on the irregularity."

Falco tapped the card signed by the dean of students. "We're moving in the right direction. I can feel it."

Less than ten minutes were required for Kerri to locate a number for Elizabeth Saxon and to get her on the phone. It was two hours earlier in San Diego, so thankfully she wasn't tied up in church or out for Sunday brunch with family.

Kerri couldn't remember the last time she'd done either.

"Dr. Saxon, this is Homicide Detective Kerri Devlin from Birmingham, Alabama." She had the call on speaker so Falco could listen as well. "I'd like to ask you a few questions about a former student, Sela Robbins."

"All right," Saxon said. "Let me just say first that I have not seen or heard from Sela since she graduated."

"I understand, ma'am," Kerri responded. "We're looking for information about her when you knew her."

"Very well. Certainly, I remember Sela. Hardworking. Excellent student. She had her future all mapped out."

"Can you tell me a little about the map she had planned?"

"I'm sorry, did you say *homicide detective*? Has something happened to Sela?"

"I can't share the details, Ms. Saxon, but I can tell you that Sela is missing. Her mother and her husband were murdered." All things the public already knew. "We're trying to find her. We're hoping someone from her past has heard from her or can provide some insight into where she might be."

A moment of silence. "Are you saying she killed her husband and mother?"

"No, ma'am," Kerri explained. "I'm saying she may be in hiding from whoever did this. She may not know who to trust. Or she could be the victim of an abduction."

She exchanged a look with Falco. Hopefully this tactic would work.

"Sela was very focused on building a career in law enforcement so she could dedicate her life to preventing other women from becoming statistics as her sister had. I'm sure you're aware of the Janelle Stevens case."

"I am." She was now, anyway.

"The loss of her sister had a tremendous impact on her life. She wanted more than anything to help protect others from that awful fate. As I said, I haven't heard from Sela since she graduated, but you might speak with a professor to whom she was particularly close. His name is Carlos Percy. Give me a moment, and I'll find his number for you."

Kerri muted the speaker while Saxon searched for the number. "We need to speak with the Abbotts and learn whose idea it was to move back to Birmingham. I think at this point we can safely conclude it wasn't just because Ben's mother had a heart attack."

"Here it is." Saxon recited the number.

Falco entered the number into his phone.

Kerri tapped the key to unmute the speaker and offered, "Thank you, Dr. Saxon."

"I hope you find her unharmed," Saxon offered. "Sela has been through a lot with her mother's illness. I had hoped her life would turn out well."

"Her mother's illness?" Kerri prompted.

"Poor thing, she was diagnosed with cancer just before Sela graduated."

Either the mother had been diagnosed with cancer twice—which was entirely possible—or Sela had lied about one or both times. Dr. Moore had found no indications of a recent illness. "Thank you again, Dr. Saxon. I assure you we will do all we can to find Sela."

When the call ended, Kerri entered the number her partner had saved on his screen for her. The call went to voice mail, and she left a message for Professor Percy. No sooner had she finished than the phone in her hand vibrated, snatching her attention back to it. She recognized the number. *The Abbotts.* "Devlin."

"I apologize for missing your earlier call, Detective," Mr. Abbott said. "If you still need to meet with us, we're home. Feel free to come at your leisure."

"Headed there now, sir."

Kerri had a good many questions for Abbott, and not all were about his son or the missing wife.

Daniel Abbott and T. R. Thompson had obviously been close for most of their lives. There was no way Abbott didn't know Janelle Stevens or at least about her case.

———

Abbott Residence
Saint Charles Drive, Hoover

As promised, Mr. and Mrs. Abbott were waiting when Kerri and Falco arrived. Mrs. Abbott's eyes weren't so red and swollen as they had been the last time they'd visited, but it was clear she was deeply enveloped in grief. Judging by the glazed look of her eyes, she was medicated as well.

Falco started the questioning. "How well do you know Sela's family and history? Would your son have conducted a background search before becoming involved with her?"

Mrs. Abbott simply stared at Falco. Her expression didn't change, and she said nothing.

Mr. Abbott did the talking. "Ben generally had a background check done on anyone with whom he interacted. Employees, associates, and certainly the women he dated. He didn't allow anyone close to him who hadn't been properly vetted."

"So there was a background check on Sela." Kerri was surprised Abbott's people hadn't found the connection to Janelle Stevens.

"I questioned him about her when he brought her home for the first time. My son said he knew everything there was to know about her. He trusted her. She made him happy."

"Did Sela ever mention her older sister?" Kerri popped this question to see the man's reaction. Surprise? Confusion? Those were the two she expected. Instead, his face remained clean of emotion as he shook his head in answer.

"I was under the impression Sela was an only child like Ben. He talked about that being one of the things they had in common."

So, the husband hadn't known Sela's big secret either. At least not in the beginning.

"Have you found her?"

This question came from Mrs. Abbott, and she stared at Kerri with such blankness that she wondered if the lady realized she had said the words out loud.

"No, ma'am," Kerri said, "but we are doing everything we can to change that."

Mrs. Abbott nodded and drifted back into silence.

"She had an older sister, Janelle," Kerri explained, her attention shifting back to Mr. Abbott. "She moved to Birmingham right after college and went missing. Her case is still unsolved. Are you certain Sela never mentioned this? It seems odd that she would move to Birmingham and never mention the family tragedy that happened here. Surely her mother mentioned it."

He shook his head. "She never mentioned it that I can recall, and I certainly believe I would remember such a thing. As for her mother, we rarely saw her. Sela said she suffered with a mild case of agoraphobia and didn't deal well with social activities."

"But you did see her on occasion," Falco countered.

"Of course." He shook his head, as if the continued line of questioning was immensely annoying. "But she never spoke of another daughter."

"She watched us."

All eyes turned to Mrs. Abbott.

Her head moved up and down. "She did." She turned to her husband. "She watched you most of all."

Mr. Abbott patted her hand and offered a smile to Kerri. "You'll have to forgive my wife. She is, as you've probably guessed, heavily medicated. No matter, she insisted on sitting in on this meeting."

Kerri smiled, but the older woman quickly looked away. "I can understand why." She turned her attention to Mr. Abbott once more. "I'm surprised you don't remember her sister. She worked with Mr. T. R. Thompson. The two of you attended college together. You're close friends, are you not?"

Both the surprise and the confusion made an appearance then before he quickly banished the outward reactions. "We are friends, yes. There was a time when we were closer, when we were young and determined to take over the world. If there was a sister and she worked for T. R., it's possible I met her at some point during her employment. However, you might not be aware, but T. R. had and still has a huge staff. I know very few of his employees. What did you say her name was?"

"Janelle Stevens."

He shook his head. "The name isn't familiar at all." He frowned then. "You know, there was, as we told you before, that time a few months ago just before Ben and Sela learned about the baby that there seemed to be some tension between them. I suspected it was related to Sela or her past, but Ben explained it away with the idea that they had discussed waiting a few years before beginning a family." Abbott shrugged. "But that odd tension was over very quickly. I wish I could tell you more, but honestly there is nothing negative to say. They were very happy. Devoted to each other."

Funny how that same theme kept repeating itself.

Except the wife had bought a car for some purpose she wanted to keep from her husband, and it was possible she'd planted the evidence that made it appear she had been injured the night of the murders.

26

1:30 p.m.

Swanner Residence
Twenty-Third Avenue South

Robby hadn't come home for lunch today.

Diana popped a load of bath towels in the washing machine. She added detergent and fabric softener in the appropriate slots, then closed the lid and hit the start button. She leaned against the machine as it filled with water. He rarely dropped in on weekdays but almost always on the weekends.

He worked too hard.

Today she was feeling particularly lonely. With the boys at summer camp and Amelia at a friend's, it was too quiet around here.

But Diana had her laundry.

She sighed. Five more piles of clothes lay in the hall next to their small laundry room. She would be doing laundry the rest of the day, and tomorrow it would start all over again.

It was an endless cycle.

Like making the beds in the mornings and loading and unloading the dishwasher. Figuring out meals for a family of five two and three times a day. Keeping the studio going, the dancers and their mothers happy.

It was too much some days.

But it was her life, and she loved it. A smile tugged at her lips. Every frantic, crazy minute of it.

What if she hadn't met Robby and she'd gone on to Juilliard the way she'd dreamed from the first time she slipped on a pair of toe shoes?

She closed her eyes and thought of the hours and hours of intense discipline. The music and the dancing . . . the hard work. It had been like the very air she breathed.

But if she'd gone to Juilliard, she wouldn't have had her kids.

And she wouldn't have Robby.

Memories of their young bodies entwined. Of the way he'd stared at her so reverently. The awe on his face when he'd laid eyes on Amelia when she was born. The way he had beamed when the boys were born, even though they had both been terrified they couldn't afford three kids.

And somehow they'd always managed to get by.

She wanted better for her kids, and Amelia was on the right path. She smiled and sent her sweet girl a text.

Hope to see you tonight!

Definitely!<3

A sense of happiness flooding through her, Diana decided to surprise Robby at the shop. She hurried downstairs. After a quick survey of the options in the fridge, she made him a ham-and-cheese sandwich and grabbed a bag of chips and two bottles of water. She packed it all in a neat little basket and found her keys.

She'd stopped being spontaneous two kids ago. It was time she infused some of that back into their marriage. Starting right now.

She'd reached for the door, when the bell rang. Kerri and Jen were both working today. Who in the world? She checked the security view-finder and abruptly drew back.

Lewis York?

She pressed a hand to her throat and reached for calm. He'd visited her plenty of times at the studio. At least once a week when he'd dropped off or picked up his daughter. Sometimes an assistant dropped her off or picked her up, but Lewis always did one of the two. Still, he had never been to Diana's home.

The idea that there could be some sort of issue with Amelia had her clutching at the doorknob. She drew the door open. "Lewis? Is everything okay?"

He smiled. "Everything is great. I had to drop off some papers to a client in the neighborhood, and I thought I'd stop by and tell you again how much we love having Amelia at the firm. I'm not sure I've passed that along to you since she started."

Diana's smile stretched so wide she was certain she looked a bit goofy. "Please come in." She set the basket aside. "I was on my way out, but I have some time."

He held up a hand. "I don't want to keep you."

"Don't be silly. Come in."

When he stepped inside, she closed the door behind him. He surveyed her home. She had only seen the outside of his when she'd dropped off his daughter once, but she hadn't gone inside. The man lived in a megamansion. This house likely wasn't even as nice as his garage, but it was home.

His gaze landed on the framed photos gracing the top of the table next to the door. "You have a beautiful family and a lovely home."

"Thank you." She felt herself blush, and she crossed her arms over her chest, as if that would somehow conceal how nervous she suddenly felt.

He looked around again. "Is Amelia here?"

"Oh no." Diana tucked her hair behind her ear. "She's spending every minute she's not working with friends. I can give her a message." She frowned. "I'm sure you have her cell number."

"I do." He leveled his gaze on hers. "But I don't actually need to speak with her. It's you I wanted to talk to, but I didn't want Amelia to overhear."

Her pulse jumped. "Me? Okay. Would you like to sit down?"

He glanced at the basket she'd set aside. "No, that's not necessary. I just wanted you to know that we're planning to make a sizable donation to Amelia for whatever she might need when she leaves in August."

Diana pressed a hand to her throat. "Oh my goodness, that's so generous." She shook her head. "You really shouldn't. You've done so much already."

He touched her arm, gave it a squeeze. "You and Amelia are like family to me. I want to do this."

Diana did something then that she had not done in all the years she had known this kind man. She gave him a hug as she thanked him profusely.

He smiled and gave her a nod. "Enjoy your afternoon. I'll see Amelia at the office tomorrow."

Diana watched him drive away, and she wondered how she could have been so lucky to have such a good friend. Jen was right; it was too bad Lewis wasn't her type.

———

The drive to Robby's shop took only ten minutes. The shop he'd inherited from his father was on the south end of the boulevard. The clientele had dropped off, and the place had fallen into disrepair just before Robby had taken over and turned it around. Diana had been terrified, but he'd managed. He'd worked seven days a week, like he did now, but he'd never missed an important event at the kids' schools. He'd never failed to be the great dad they all three adored.

And he was a great husband too.

Diana tightened her fingers on the steering wheel as she pulled into the shop parking lot. She didn't have to see him to know he would be hunkered over his desk, doing the accounting. Trying to keep everything in balance. He always did that on Sundays.

She used her key and let herself in, locking the door behind her. As she had known, he was at his desk. The calculator buzzed under his quick fingers. He grabbed his pencil and made a few notes, then rubbed at his chin. He looked tired and old, like her, but he also looked strong and loving. He looked like home.

"I missed you at lunch," she said, announcing her presence before she reached the open door to his office.

His head snapped up in surprise, and those wide lips slid into a smile. "You snuck up on me."

"Good thing you didn't have another woman bent over that desk."

He laughed. She did too. Robby would never ever cheat on her. He wasn't like Kerri's jerk of an ex.

She entered the office as Robby stood. Before he could say another word, she placed the basket in the chair in front of his desk, walked around to him, and slid her arms around his neck. She kissed him. She kissed him the way she used to when it was just the two of them. His arms tightened around her.

She drew back and looked into his eyes. "I love you, Robby."

"I love you, Di."

Without another word, they made love right there on his desk, uncaring of the paperwork he'd been trying to balance. They made love the way they had twenty years ago, with complete abandon. And when they were finished, they held each other for a long while, then helped each other back into their clothes.

"As much as I hate to say it"—Diana smiled as she watched him devour his lunch—"I should get going and let you get back to work. Otherwise you'll never get home."

He reached out, squeezed her hand. "Thank you for this."

"My pleasure. Before I go, is there any way I can help?"

"You already have." He grinned. "I feel like a new man."

While they gathered the scattered papers, his cell rang. He checked the screen. "I gotta take this."

To Diana's surprise he hurried out of his office and out the door to the parking lot. She could still see him since the entrance door was glass. He paced back and forth, back and forth, looking serious and perhaps a little worried. He wasn't happy about the call or with the caller. She finished tidying his papers as best she could while she split her attention between the task and watching her husband.

Now he was angry. His face had reddened, his jaw hardened, free hand planted on his hip.

What in the world?

Deciding she wasn't going to keep playing this guessing game, she wandered toward the entrance. Just as her hands came to rest on the door to push it open, he glanced her way and then ended the call.

She pushed out into the warm afternoon and watched him for a moment. "Is everything okay?"

"Yeah. Just a jerk customer." He glanced at her but immediately dropped his gaze.

"People can be jerks sometimes." She walked over to him and rubbed his shoulder, felt the tension in him.

He worked up a smile and met her gaze. "I won't be much longer."

She went up on tiptoe and kissed his cheek. "See you then." Before she turned away, she said, "Oh wait, I forgot to tell you that Lewis York dropped by the house."

The look that claimed her husband's face was something between fear and outrage. What in the world was that all about?

"What did he want?"

His words were cold and hard.

Confused, she explained, "The firm is planning to make a sizable donation to Amelia's needs going off to school." Another of those giddy smiles spread across her face despite her husband's strange reaction. "Isn't that great?"

He nodded, but the move was hardly noticeable. "Yeah. Great."

"Robby." She took his hand in hers. "Are you sure you're okay? Is there something going on that I should know about?"

"I guess I'm angry at myself since I can't do all those things for our daughter. The firm gives her a job. The firm gives her fringe benefits." He shook his head.

Diana hugged him. "Don't be silly. We worked hard to raise Amelia, and she has worked hard in school. It's not like we're accepting charity. We're reaping the benefits of hard work."

"You're right." He flashed a half-hearted smile. "See you at home."

Diana left, feeling torn. That phone call nagged at her. His reaction to Lewis's visit made her uneasy.

If Robby was in real trouble, would he tell her? Were they going to need an attorney?

At least she had an in with the best attorney in Birmingham, and God knew he had friends in high places.

27

4:30 p.m.

Law Office of Keith Bellemont
Third Avenue North

Daniel Abbott had shown up at Keith's home.

Keith's wife had called to warn him. She was concerned since the older man had seemed overly agitated. She'd apologized for telling Abbott that Keith was at work. He imagined his wife had bemoaned the fact that he worked long hours, seven days a week. Abbott had likely pretended to care.

But he didn't, not at all.

He didn't care where Keith was as long as he found him.

Keith heard him in the lobby. Martha attempted to greet him, but he ignored her. Instead, he barged past her, his footfalls heavy on the old wood floors, and appeared at Keith's door.

"Mr. Abbott." Keith rose from his chair. "Is everything all right?"

Abbott slammed the door behind him. "Of course everything is not all right. Are you mad?"

Keith let go a weary breath and gestured to the chairs in front of his desk. "Please have a seat, and let's talk about what's going on."

Obviously struggling to maintain his composure, Abbott crossed the room and sat. Keith took his seat and waited for the other man to begin. He had never felt more tired in his life.

"Those detectives came back to my house again today."

Keith pursed his lips and gave a succinct nod. "They'll likely do that from time to time until the case is closed. They have a responsibility to try their best to find Sela and the person who hurt Ben and her mother. As unpleasant as it is, sometimes it's necessary to go over information a number of times. We all want justice for Ben and a safe return for Sela."

The man had to know this would happen. Did he think he was above the law? Exempt from the steps necessary to conducting a thorough investigation? Fury detonated in Keith's belly, and he tamped it back. He couldn't afford to lose control.

"Cut the crap, Bellemont. We both know what they're going to find. And they'll find it soon. They know about the sister."

A flash of fear doused the anger. Keith wasn't innocent in all this any more than the man staring at him. Damn it! "That's unfortunate but—"

"Did you think they wouldn't find out?" Abbott blustered, cutting him off. "For God's sake, man, it was always going to come to this if things went wrong, and things are very wrong!"

"Mr. Abbott," Keith urged, "I want you to stay calm and as disengaged as possible from this aspect of the *situation*. I will handle whatever happens."

"You will handle it?" Disbelief blasted him. "You mean the way you handled the rest? My son is dead, you fool. My grandchild is God only knows where with that insane woman. We have no idea what she intends to do next. How do you propose to *handle* this?"

From the moment Keith had learned of Ben's death, he had known it would likely come to this. He had also known there was no stopping it once it started. "I'm afraid the only thing we can do at this point is spin the damage. Prevent the fallout from landing in the wrong places."

"I should have handled this personally from the beginning, but I relied on you. Obviously, that was a mistake." Abbott stood. "Just remember, *you* allowed this to happen."

The man stormed out the same way he had stormed in.

There was no point in Keith telling him what he knew for a certainty.

This was only the beginning.

28

7:30 p.m.

Birmingham Police Department
First Avenue North
Major Investigations Division

"It's Sunday, and it's late, Devlin."

If Falco reminded her once more what time it was and that it was Sunday, she was going to kick his ass.

"I'm aware of the day and time, Falco. What's your problem? You have a hot date? If so, by all means go!"

He leaned back in his chair. "I don't have a date, but you have a daughter."

Now he'd pissed her off. "Are you going to tell me how to be a good parent now?"

He held up his hands. "Simmer down, Devlin. I'm not trying to start a fight. I'm just saying we've gone over this same information a dozen times. Until we hear from the professor or one of these players starts telling the whole story, we might be banging our heads against the wall."

"FYI," Kerri informed him, "Tori is having dinner with Diana—my sister—and her family tonight. I've got all the time in the world."

"Well, all right then, partner," Falco tossed back. "Let's keep at it."

She flashed him an exaggerated smile. "Thank you. As I was saying, there are some things we do know. This case isn't about the money." Kerri had been pondering the idea that Sela Abbott stood to gain a whole lot more by staying in the marriage. "This is about revenge."

"I'm with you," Falco chimed in. "She was attempting to avenge her sister's death—assuming the sister is dead. So she put herself in the path of a good old Alabama boy. One from Birmingham—the scene of the crime."

"Not just any good old boy," Kerri argued.

"Right. Right. A rich one whose family is connected to the Thompsons."

"She inserted herself into the lives of the elite, all of whom are friends of the Abbott family. Makes a name for herself in fundraising—an unavoidable facet of life for anyone dragging in the big bucks or enjoying old family money. It makes them feel better about their abundance to donate to the less fortunate."

"But who's the mark, Devlin? We can assume Old Man Thompson, since the sister worked for him, but that might not be the case. Obviously, it's someone with money and power, or she wouldn't have had to go to all the trouble of luring in Ben Abbott for a husband. But there's a lot of rich folks in Birmingham. How do we figure out for sure which one was or is the real target? I think we can pretty much rule out the husband since he was off getting all those fancy degrees when Janelle Stevens disappeared."

Kerri stared at the photos of the players—both dead and alive—lined up on their case board. "Part of figuring out who was involved depends on the lab results. If we're right, and the blood on the bed came from the mother, we'll know the wife set up at least part of the crime scene. She bought that car. Getaway car?" Kerri shrugged. "Maybe. Makes sense. I can't think of any other reason. If she'd wanted to donate a car to some worthy cause or person, she would have been better off buying a nicer one for the ten K she spent. Giving someone a junker doesn't feel like her style."

"I think we can assume the car was for her." Falco laced his fingers behind his head, leaned back, and propped his feet on his desk. "The problem is the old Stevens case file doesn't give us a whole lot. The two detectives who worked on the case have since passed. All we know is where she worked and lived. Since she lived in an apartment building that no longer exists—it's a mall now—we haven't been able to locate any old neighbors to interview. We got nothing except that she worked for the Thompsons—who are connected to the Abbotts."

Kerri checked her phone. "Bellemont still hasn't called back."

They had called him again when they'd left the Abbotts. His vehicle hadn't been at his office when they'd driven by, so they'd gone to his home. His wife had said he was at work. Maybe work was at a client's house today. Or maybe he'd gotten smart and hidden his vehicle.

"He's putting together his story," Falco said. "That's what lawyers do. Old Man Abbott has no doubt already called and told him what we're up to. The two are probably trying to work out a story to cover their asses for not telling us this shit up front. That's what people who have something to hide do. Trust me. I know this from personal experience."

She told herself to stay out of personal territory, but she couldn't do it. He was right. It was late. It was Sunday. Well past time to go home, and she was suddenly sick of rehashing the disjointed fragments they had raked together.

"Why did you give up everything, Falco?"

He held her gaze for three seconds . . . five seconds . . . ten. By the time he spoke, she had decided he wasn't going to answer.

"Because I wasn't fit to be a part of it."

Somehow this idea of selflessness got to her. Made her want to know things. Exhaustion really was playing with her tonight. "Why weren't you fit? Because your father abused you?"

191

"That was part of it." He closed his eyes for a moment before he opened them again. "I was undercover for a long time. It was my thing. I was really, really good at it. But I had to go deeper and deeper to get what we needed." He shrugged. "I ended up in too deep. Drugs became a part of who I was. I . . ." He exhaled a big breath. "I became like them. I lived, I breathed, I killed . . . just like them."

Surprise, regret, sympathy all seared through her so quickly her heart couldn't pound fast enough to catch up. "But you came through in the end." She was certain of it. He wouldn't be sitting here otherwise. "Right?"

"Yeah, yeah. My loyalties were never in question. It was my obsession with doing what no one else had done that became the problem. With going where no one else had gone. My determination not to fail at bringing down a *legend*. To be a better cop than my father. It almost killed me. It took everything in this world that meant anything from me. Except the job. The job is all I have. It's all I am."

Legend. Headlines scrolled through her head. "Oh my God. You're talking about the Bayards case. Down in Mobile. You were there before you came here?"

The case had been national news for weeks. The Bayard brothers, Kurt and Sullivan, had been running the biggest drug operation in the history of the area. No one—and plenty had tried—had ever been able to tie the two to anything other than real estate. Big real estate, all over the Southeast. The brothers had set up a near-impenetrable cover.

"That investigation took years," she said, more to herself than to him. "Wow." She stared at him with a new kind of respect. "I can't imagine how you pulled that off."

"We can't talk about this, Devlin."

The sadness, emptiness in his eyes took her breath. She held up her hands. "I understand. I guess I thought your career in law enforcement started in Birmingham just five years ago."

He shook his head. "Try nine years before I came back here."

Shock rumbled through her as she did the math. "You went straight from the academy into undercover work?"

"Never went to the academy."

Wait. That wasn't possible. "You're yanking my chain, right?"

"I attended a special training program, and then I went straight to work. That's all I can tell you."

"You were undercover on that operation for nine years?"

Before he could or would answer, her cell vibrated. The area code was a California one. "This is probably that professor."

Falco looked more than a little relieved to be moving on.

"Devlin." She put the call on speaker.

"This is Carlos Percy. You left a message about Sela Rollins?"

Kerri explained the situation to the degree possible. "We're wondering if you may have heard from her?"

"This is terrible news, but to answer your question, no. I haven't heard from her in years. Not since she moved from San Diego. I had no idea she'd gotten married and moved to Alabama."

"Can you tell me about Sela when she was your student? We're hoping information from her past will help us with what's happening now."

"She was a very dedicated student. Keenly interested in criminal investigation."

"Is that the course you taught?"

"It is. In fact, my course focused on the lengths to which criminals will go to avoid leaving evidence. Sela was the best student I had. She became very good at planning a crime from the perpetrator's perspective. She was particularly skilled at taking a situation and figuring out a way to work around it." He laughed. "I told her she would be the best detective on whatever force she joined or a damned clever criminal."

This news was tipping the scale. "Do you have any idea where Sela went after graduating?"

He was silent for a moment. "You know, her mother had quite a number of health issues. I'll never forget how devastated Sela was when the cancer diagnosis came." He made a sound as if he were thinking back through the years. "I recall her mentioning some hospital in Mexico where they planned to go for a while. I believe it was in Mexico City. Of course, I have no idea if they actually went."

Kerri met Falco's gaze. She imagined they were both thinking the same thing. Cancer. Expired medications. Kerri suddenly wondered if Sela had ever told anyone the truth.

"I appreciate your help, Professor Percy. I may need to call you again if I have other questions."

"Don't hesitate. I'm more than happy to help. I hope the situation is resolved quickly and Sela is found safe and sound."

Kerri hoped so too. The only question was, Would they be rescuing her or arresting her? At this point, her money was on the latter.

When the call ended, her partner held up his phone. "I just ordered pizza. I've got a feeling we'll be here for a while."

"Oh yeah," Kerri agreed.

She was beginning to believe that no one really knew Sela Rollins Abbott, particularly not her husband.

29

So, so many secrets.

They will never uncover them all.

There are so very many. The vast number was essential to ultimate success. Some were simply unavoidable.

I covered my tracks extremely carefully. They will not be able to find the answers they seek in time to stop what has begun.

They will try.

The struggles to stop me will be mighty.

But they will all be too late.

My only worry is that they will do harm to the one person I have trusted completely. It's time for me to let go of my final connection to this life that is no longer mine and to her. For her safety there must be no further contact. She must move on with her life and forget about me.

I work the ropes, back and forth, back and forth.

My one misstep in my hasty escape that awful morning has been rectified. Who knew I would need the weapon for this stage? If they thought I wouldn't notice what they had done, they were so very wrong. I know exactly what they did, and it will be part of their undoing in the end.

I've even left a clue, if anyone cares to notice.

Before this is done I will have their full attention.

30

Monday, June 11

7:00 a.m.

Devlin Residence
Twenty-First Avenue South

Kerri glanced at the digital clock on the microwave as she downed her second cup of coffee. Falco would be here soon. There were forty-odd pawnshops in the greater Birmingham area. Not all sold weapons, but more than thirty did. They intended to visit each one in an effort to determine if Sela Abbott had purchased a weapon—specifically a .22 pistol. The lab had sent the ballistics report to Kerri's email at six this morning.

The .22 used to kill Jacqueline Rollins and Ben Abbott was the same weapon. There were no weapons registered to Ben or Sela. None to Jacqueline Rollins. The murder weapon had been brought into the house by the shooter. Considering Sela had purchased a potential getaway car and mentioned having a problem to Keaton, it was reasonable to follow up on the possibility that she had armed herself as well.

Kerri still wasn't all in with the theory that the wife was their shooter, but she couldn't ignore the probability that she was involved somehow. Too many of those fragments they continued to find kept pointing back to the missing wife.

Since her daughter obviously wasn't coming out of her room before Kerri left, she decided to go up and tell her to have a nice day. The silent treatment had gone on long enough. Though most teenagers slept late every chance they got, Tori was usually up by seven even on weekends.

Maybe she'd decided it was easier to ignore her mother if she stayed in her room.

Kerri topped the stairs and walked to her daughter's door. She knocked and then opened the door. "I have to go, kiddo."

The bed was empty. The covers spread smoothly and the pillows piled against the headboard. That was another thing about Tori: she always made her bed.

Kerri glanced across the hall at the open bathroom door.

Where was she?

Panic started its steady climb up her backbone. She rushed to her bedroom and checked her unmade bed and then her bathroom. No Tori.

The third-bedroom-turned-office-for-Kerri was empty.

She dashed back downstairs to see if maybe her daughter had fallen asleep on the sofa and Kerri had failed to notice. She wasn't exactly at the top of her game in the mornings until after a sufficient amount of coffee had been consumed.

No Tori in the living room.

Fear slammed into her chest. Had Nick, the bastard, dared to drive all the way here and pick her up?

Not reasonable. Think!

Kerri grabbed her cell and called Tori's. Straight to voice mail. Her heart pounding, she called Amelia.

Voice mail.

"Shit!"

Her cell rang, and a trickle of relief gave Kerri the ability to breathe again. Not Tori or Amelia.

"What?" she demanded of her partner.

"Whoa. Just calling to let you know I'm out here."

"I can't find my—" An incoming text snagged her attention. "I'll be right out," she said to Falco.

She ended the call and stared at the text from Amelia.

Sorry at work. Something wrong?

Tori is missing! Even as she typed and sent the words, Kerri's heart threatened to burst from her chest.

No! She's ok. She spent the night with me. I'm sorry. Thought you knew. Left her asleep in my bed.

Kerri leaned against the wall to brace herself. She drew in a deep breath, ordered her heart to slow.

Ok. Thanks. She and I haven't been talking much lately.

She's just confused. She loves you. I remember 13. It sucked.

Kerri managed a smile. Love you!

Ditto! <3

Pushing away from the wall, Kerri turned off the coffee maker and took a couple more deep breaths.

She had no idea how Diana survived with three kids.

On the way out the door, she made a call to Diana just to confirm that Tori was still there. Diana assured Kerri she was and promised to see that she got home safely. She reminded Kerri that Tori had come for dinner last night. Since Kerri still hadn't been home at eight, Tori had asked to spend the night, and Diana had agreed. She hadn't realized Tori had failed to inform her mom.

Kerri felt like kicking herself as she slid into the passenger seat of Falco's car. She should have remembered her daughter's plans—especially plans she had helped to make—and maybe she wouldn't have freaked out. When she'd arrived home last night at eleven o'clock, she'd stood outside Tori's door but decided not to knock since she was likely already asleep. She should have opened the door. Should have checked then.

What if Tori had been missing?

Kerri had allowed this case to take over her life. She knew better. The truth was, since the divorce it was easier that way.

Anger at her own selfish actions roared through her. How could she accuse Nick of only thinking of himself when she was doing the same thing?

"Good morning to you too, Devlin."

Dragging her attention back to the here and now, she grunted a skeptical sound and focused on slowing her pounding heart. "We'll see."

"Still no transactions on the accounts at the local banks or on the credit cards," he announced. "If our missing wife is alive, she definitely planned for all her needs, including cash. Cell carrier finally came through with her records. I skimmed those at the office this morning. Nothing except calls to her husband and other known folks listed in her contacts. No calls or texts since Tuesday night."

Kerri frowned. "You've been to the office already?"

"Couldn't sleep. Finally got up at three." He glanced at her. "I figured you wouldn't want me showing up at that hour."

"Thanks for that." She exhaled a big breath. Her nerves were still rattled. "I've looked at this upside down and sideways, Falco. From what the professor and that detective out in Cali said, she's been preparing for this for a very long time. I'm still not prepared to label her our shooter, but she's part of this or behind it somehow for sure."

Falco merged onto the interstate. "So you're leaning toward the revenge motive."

"I am. But I think something went wrong, and her husband and mother were murdered. She was either in the middle of setting up her vanishing-wife scenario and hid while the intruder did the killing, or she came in after, found the mess, and went on with her plan."

"Makes her sound damned coldhearted."

"Sometimes when you focus on something for so long, nothing else matters." She didn't look at Falco, but she was reasonably confident he got the message. Maybe they were both guilty of going down that path. Only he hadn't walked or stumbled; he'd run as hard as he could.

"Sometimes you do what you think you've gotta do," he agreed.

There was more to his story. Some reason that had prompted him to give up everything and dive into the deep water before he'd learned to swim. She pushed the thought aside. If he wanted her to know, he would tell her.

"What we need more than anything right now is to know why Sela Abbott set in motion this elaborate plan to disappear." They could no longer ignore that scenario. "Was she attempting to pin her abduction on the person or persons responsible for her sister's disappearance, and some aspect of her plan backfired?"

"Chances are," Falco said, "her rich husband would have moved mountains to find her and get to the bottom of what happened. Maybe he was supposed to solve the crime and see that the revenge she wanted so badly was carried out. All she had to do was make him want to—he loved her; they're having a baby. Bam, he's in all the way."

Kerri contemplated the scattered pieces of this puzzle that were slowly but surely coming together. "But we need evidence. The car is a start, but we need more." Kerri studied the search results on her phone. "We have six pawnshops that open at eight. We can start with those."

"Just call out the address where you want to start, and we're on our way."

Eventually she would know the rest of Sela's secrets. Kerri studied her partner. *And maybe his as well.*

31

11:00 a.m.

Swanner Auto Repair
Richard Arrington Junior Boulevard South

Jen parked in front of the shop entrance and climbed out. She did not have time for this. Today was her only day off this week, and she needed to run a dozen errands. She would rather be anywhere than at home.

Plus the idea of being stranded without her car was like a death sentence. She would never survive being stuck at home, helpless to do as she pleased.

For the first time she was glad Theo had not called. A shiver swept through her. Something was going on with him, and whatever it was, it was not good.

She pulled the entrance door open and stepped into the business side of Robby's shop. The smell of grease and cleaner made her nose twitch. She waited a few steps from the counter while Robby finished up with a customer. The elderly man thanked Robby and turned to go. The old man smiled at Jen, and she flashed her pearly whites back at him as he shuffled out the door.

"Uh-oh." Robby's expression turned dubious. "What have I done? Or not done? My anniversary is not until Saturday."

Jen laughed as she approached the counter. "If you've done something or vice versa, your wife doesn't know it yet. Not to worry, Amelia has everything under control with the anniversary party."

Robby laughed. "She sure does. She sent me a text this morning reminding me to get her mom a present."

"Make it a good one," Jen cautioned.

"You have my word it will be amazing." Robby braced his forearms on the counter. "What can I do for you, Jen?"

"That damned Chevy is acting up." She shrugged. "When I press the accelerator, there's a hesitation, and even when it kicks in, it's a little sluggish. I just want to make sure everything is okay. The thought of it breaking down is more than I can bear."

Robby rounded the end of the counter. "Come on outside, and let's have a look."

Outside she handed him her keys. He slid his tall frame behind the wheel, powered back the seat, and started the engine. "We'll take her for a spin and see if we can narrow down the problem."

She climbed into the passenger seat and buckled up. She relaxed, confident he would find the problem as he backed out of the lot and pulled away. He took a right at the next intersection and drove. When they were clear of traffic, he gunned the accelerator.

"Feel that?" she asked.

"Yep. I'm pretty sure this is no big deal."

"Thank God."

He repeated the maneuver and then slowed and turned around to head back to the shop. He drove nearly the whole way without saying a word. The quiet suddenly felt overwhelming. Jen didn't know why she felt awkward. She had brought her car to Robby dozens of times. He'd been taking care of any vehicle maintenance she or her mother needed for years.

As if he'd read her mind, he asked, "You sure Diana didn't send you to check on me?"

"I swear she did not send me." Jen glanced at him. "Is there a reason she might have been considering the idea?"

A big breath whistled out of him. "She brought me lunch yesterday."

"That was nice." How Jen wished for a relationship like theirs.

"There are things going on at the shop that I can't talk about. Diana overheard part of a phone conversation, and I don't want her worrying. I have everything under control."

Jen studied the big man. Whatever *everything* was, it had to be significant. Why else would he have brought it up? "You sure you've got whatever this is?"

He nodded. "It's a tough time right now, but I've got it. Don't mention that I brought it up, okay?"

"I won't. I promise."

"You're sure she didn't mention anything about the call?" He glanced at her.

"She hasn't said a word."

When he parked in front of the shop and shut off the engine, he said, "You go on inside and grab a soda or a bottle of water, and I'll have a look under the hood."

"Thanks, Robby. You're a prince."

He laughed. "Yeah, right."

Jen went inside and walked straight back to the small break room. It smelled of grease and gasoline, but the place was clean. She pulled out a chair from the one table and caught up on her text messages and social media. She sent Diana a text and told her she was at the shop having her car checked. Diana sent her a smiley face. Jen sent another asking Amelia what day she preferred for rescheduling their lunch.

The door opened, and Jen glanced up, hoping it was Robby. Not so lucky. Burt, his lead mechanic, gave her a nod as he sauntered over to the fridge and pulled out his lunch.

"How you doing, Jen?"

"Good. You?"

Burt was a reasonably nice-looking man. He'd been married twice, and like her he was still alone. He was attracted to her; she knew he was. Maybe she should pay him a little attention.

God help her, she was losing it. A grease monkey—no offense to Robby—was not her idea of Mr. Right.

"I'm doing real good. Just paid off my mortgage and bought a new car. I'm mighty fine." He beamed a smile.

"Wow. That's great."

"I'm thinking of celebrating."

The man had a house. Paid for. She blinked. Decided not to touch that open invitation. "I think I'll have a bottle of water." She stood and started for the fridge.

"You might have to check the freezer part. I put some in there earlier to get it cold fast. Somebody didn't remember to restock when he took the last bottle from the fridge."

Jen opened the door to the freezer compartment. Several bottles of water, a box of ice cream sandwiches, and a bag of ice took up most of the space. She reached for a water, and a box from Drake's—the high-end department store where she worked—captured her attention.

She grinned as she bypassed the water and reached for the box that had been tucked into a plastic bag. "Well, well, what do we have here?"

She shouldered the door closed and held the box in both hands. It was too large for a jewelry box, more like a perfume box set. But there could be a smaller box inside. Robby wouldn't put a perfume set in the freezer.

"Oh, you'd better put that back," Burt said. "Robby gets all out of sorts if anyone touches that box."

"I'll bet he does." Jen opened the plastic bag, which was like a large freezer bag with a zip closure.

"Don't mess with that."

The box was snatched out of her hands before she could look up at the man who had spoken.

Robby clutched the box as if it were a football and he was running toward the end zone for the winning touchdown.

"Sorry." She squared her shoulders, a little taken aback by his overreaction. "Is that Diana's anniversary present?"

"No." He tucked the box back into the freezer. "It's something else." He turned to her, plastered on a smile that didn't reach his eyes. "You're good to go. You just needed a new engine air filter."

She nodded. "Great. Thanks. I . . . I should pay you."

"You know better than that." He handed her the keys. "See you Saturday."

"Saturday. Right."

As Jen drove away, she told herself she was the one who'd overreacted. The box probably really was a gift for Diana, and he didn't want Jen telling her.

It was no big deal.

She shook off the creepy sensation.

Everything was fine.

"Fine," she muttered. "Just fine."

Except it didn't feel fine at all.

32

1:00 p.m.

Kerri slid into the passenger seat, and Falco started the engine and rolled away from the curb. Going from shop to shop and questioning owners or employees—whoever was available—was one of the most frustrating and time-consuming parts of investigative work.

"Twenty down," Falco said all cheery.

Two of those twenty had been permanently closed. Sometimes it took a while for that sort of change to show up on the internet search engines.

"There's always a chance she bought a gun from an individual." Kerri exhaled a big breath. If that was the case, they might never know. In truth, she hoped Sela hadn't bought one. Kerri wanted her to be the justice-seeking younger sister the people from her past thought she was.

Except that was looking less and less likely.

"Like Joey Keaton," Falco suggested. "He'd sell his own aunt if the price was right."

"No kidding. If we run out of pawnshops with no luck, we'll track him down and ask him," she said. He would likely lie if he had sold Sela a handgun. Two people were dead. It wouldn't be smart to admit to selling the potential shooter a weapon.

"Can we take him out in the middle of nowhere and play with him first?"

Kerri laughed. "I wish."

Falco answered a call on his cell, and Kerri checked her own. She sent Tori a text to see how she was doing but wasn't expecting much of a reply. She hadn't heard from Nick, which was likely a bad sign. As desperately as she hated to put her daughter through how it would likely end, Tori needed to see that Nick's plan was not about making her happy; it was about Nick manipulating.

God, Kerri wished she was wrong about that.

To her surprise Tori sent her a pic of the kitchen. She'd cleaned up. Kerri sent her a *wow* and several happy faces. Maybe things were turning around.

"You ready for lunch?"

She turned to Falco. "Sure."

"Good. That was my contact. Our friend Bellemont has an investigator who freelances for him. If the lawyer is in deep on anything, Ramsey is his go-to guy. We need to talk to him, and right now he's having lunch at Pop's over on Twentieth."

"Great hot dogs." Kerri had eaten there a number of times. "You know anything about this guy?"

Falco shook his head. "Name's Neal Ramsey. Former Army Special Forces. Now he's doing private work."

Kerri entered his name into a search box and scanned the results. "At least we know what he looks like." She turned the image on her screen toward her partner. "Tall, blond buzz cut. Midforties."

Falco made the turn that would take them to Twentieth. "Looks like the hard-ass type."

"I doubt he'll be inclined to play with us." She put her phone away.

Falco pulled to the curb down the block from the vintage diner. "I guess we'll just have to ask him what we want to know."

"The trick will be getting him to answer," Kerri pointed out.

"Touché."

Every single table in the diner was occupied. Neal Ramsey sat alone at the back, facing the front of the establishment. He seemed to be multitasking like most folks these days, scrolling on his phone while mindlessly devouring his lunch.

She and Falco walked straight back to his table and pulled out the two empty chairs across the expanse of Formica from Ramsey.

"You don't mind company, do you?" Kerri asked with a glance around the place.

Ramsey wiped his mouth with a paper napkin. "No problem, Detectives."

She and Falco exchanged a smile.

"You psychic or something?" Falco asked.

"I know cops when I see them." Ramsey reached for the bottle of water next to his plate.

"Oh." Falco nodded, his gaze glued to his phone; then he looked up at Ramsey. "You probably saw that big news conference on Saturday. We're investigating the murders at the Abbott home."

"We're concerned that his missing wife may be in danger." Kerri took it from there. "We've spoken to Abbott's friend Keith Bellemont. We're hoping you might be able to help as well."

Ramsey tossed his napkin onto the table. "Why would I be able to help?"

"You work for Bellemont," Falco said. He slid his phone into his jacket pocket. "You must know his closest friend, Ben Abbott." He nodded to the remaining hot dog on the man's plate. "You going to eat that?"

Ramsey stared at him, his expression as clean as a freshly washed window. "I've lost my appetite."

Falco pulled the plate to his side of the table. He sent a questioning look at Kerri. She shook her head.

While Falco wolfed down the rest of the man's lunch, she extended her hand across the table. "I'm Detective Kerri Devlin, and this is my partner, Detective Luke Falco."

Ramsey gave her hand a brief shake. "I watch the news. I read the paper and scan online reports. So of course I'm aware of the Abbott case, but I know nothing about the family. If Abbott and Bellemont are— were—close friends, that's news to me. I've worked for Mr. Bellemont for a number of years, but it has always been strictly business. I don't have private relationships with any of the people with whom I work."

"That's strange." Falco wiped his mouth with the back of his hand. "I was under the impression you did a couple of small jobs for Abbott Options—on referral from Mr. Bellemont, of course. I'm sure you know his assistant, Marcella Gibbons, *privately.*"

Kerri's gaze swung to Falco before she could stop the startled reaction. What the hell was he talking about? She quickly shifted her attention back to Ramsey.

The private investigator stared directly at Falco, his expression still clean of tells. "The two small jobs, as you say related to Abbott Options, were at the behest of another client, and I'm afraid I cannot divulge that client's name. As you can well imagine, it's a competitor."

"Is that right?" Falco asked.

Ramsey smiled. "That is correct." He pushed back his chair. "Enjoy your lunch, Detectives."

Kerri watched him walk away before turning to her partner. "What the hell was that, Falco? You might have told me this before we walked in to meet the guy."

He nodded as he watched Ramsey stride out of the diner. "Just got another text as we walked in here. Evidently, Ramsey was banging Ms. Gibbons, and that's how he got the info he wanted—whatever that was."

Kerri held up her hands. "Who the hell told you this? Who is this contact?"

"My go-to girl. The one I told you about." His gaze landed on Kerri. "She knows people. She has ways of finding out shit like nobody you've ever seen."

Contacts, informants, they were useful tools to a cop, no doubt. Kerri had her share, but it wasn't always possible to trust all the intel. More often than not, you had to sift through it for the good stuff. "You're certain you can trust this information?"

"I'd bet my life." His gaze held hers, the certainty there underscoring his words.

"I guess we need to have a chat with Ms. Gibbons before we finish checking out the pawnshops."

"You want to eat first?"

She laughed. "Since you already did, I'll grab a hot dog on the way out."

"I could handle another one."

Kerri shook her head. Maybe landing this new partner hadn't been such a bad thing after all.

Abbott Options
First Avenue South

Marcella Gibbons sank into the chair behind her desk. "It was months ago."

Her face had lost any semblance of color, and her hands shook as she fussed with the collar of her blouse.

"We need to know exactly when and for how long"—Kerri chose her words carefully—"you were involved with Mr. Ramsey."

"I met him on Saint Patrick's Day at that Irish pub between Eleventh and Twelfth. Brennan's. We . . ." She shrugged. "We hit it off, and we dated for a few weeks. I stopped going out with him last month."

"Were you aware he worked for Keith Bellemont?"

She shook her head. "He never told me that. He said he was a private security specialist. He told me all the things I needed to do to make my apartment safer."

"Why did you stop seeing him?" Kerri asked.

"He started asking me questions about work. Just the odd question here and there. Nothing too specific." She moistened her lips. "But then I got out of the shower one night and found him looking through my desk." She drew in a deep breath. "He said he was looking for a pen, but I didn't believe him."

Falco gave her a nod. "Understandable. Did the two of you ever go to his place, or did you always go to yours?"

She swallowed hard. "We always went to my place. He usually had some excuse why we couldn't go to his place. I realized later that the reason was because he wanted to go to my place. He was looking for *things*."

"Did you ever leave him alone in your apartment?" It was obvious Gibbons felt terrible about the potential security breach. Still, Kerri needed as much information as she could provide.

"No. Of course not."

"But you did shower," Falco countered, "maybe more than once. Basically leaving him with a few minutes to look wherever he wanted."

"That's true. But my phone and laptop—every device I use—is biometrically protected."

"So you don't keep anything in your apartment," Falco pressed, "like a badge for Abbott Options or a key to your boss's house."

There was the slightest hesitation before she answered. "No. Of course not. A retinal scan is required to get into secure areas at work."

Kerri wasn't satisfied with that answer. "Do you have a key to the Abbott home?"

She exhaled a breath. "Yes. I keep it in my purse with my own keys."

"So Ramsey could have taken your key and had a copy made," Falco suggested.

"No. It was never out of my possession. Never."

There were ways to make copies of keys without taking them anywhere. Molds that could be made on the spot and used for making a copy later. Kerri imagined the woman hadn't considered that possibility. Even highly intelligent people could succumb to denial.

"Think about all the times you were together," Kerri told her. "If anything at all comes to you that you feel might help with this case, please call me. I don't care if it's the middle of the night. I want to hear from you."

"I will." Her lips trembled. "Believe me. I want you to find the person who did this. I want Mrs. Abbott to be okay."

Tears spilled past her lashes. Kerri gave her a moment to compose herself before asking, "Will you allow us to have one of our technicians go through your home and look for any bugs Mr. Ramsey may have planted?"

Her eyes rounded in worry. "Of course. I checked my place after that last time we were together, but I didn't find anything."

"You were upset," Kerri suggested. "You may have missed something."

"Oh my God." She nodded. "Of course I'm more than happy to cooperate. What do I need to do?"

"Detective Falco will call for an evidence technician to come to your home. He or she will be accompanied by a uniformed officer. You meet them and allow them inside. The search won't take long."

She nodded. "Whatever I need to do."

While Falco made the call, Kerri thanked her and cautioned her not to have any contact with Ramsey. If he called or showed up at her door, she was to call Kerri or Falco immediately.

Once they were in Falco's car, he said, "We gonna bring Ramsey in?"

"If something's found in her apartment, we'll have him picked up." Kerri fastened her seat belt. "He's too savvy to be pressured into talking to us without some sort of evidence against him. If nothing is found, we'll wait a bit. Either way, we're going to demand some answers from Bellemont since he claims to be Ben Abbott's closest friend. Ramsey is supposed to be working for Bellemont, which would make him digging around in Abbott Options for another client a conflict of interest."

Falco sent her a sidelong glance. "Looks like he's playing both sides of the field. So who's the other client?"

A very good question.

33

4:00 p.m.

Law Office of Keith Bellemont
Third Avenue North

"If anyone calls or drops by," Keith said, "I am not here."

Martha looked at him skeptically. "You mean if those two detectives show up or call?"

He blinked. Wanted to say no, maybe even to chastise her for thinking such a thing, but his assistant was correct. "Yes."

"Don't worry," she promised. "I'll keep them at bay." Her gaze narrowed. "But I can only do that for so long."

"I'm aware."

Keith hurried beyond the lobby and into the side corridor. He ensured the alley exit was locked. He damned sure didn't want any surprises coming in from that direction. Devlin and Falco were determined. He didn't trust them not to climb in through the fire escape and drop down from above if the need arose. There was nothing on the second floor of this building but his files. Still, there were windows and that damned fire escape.

At this point he didn't trust anyone.

He closed his office door, locked it, too, and collapsed into the chair behind his desk. He withdrew his cell and called Ramsey. It was Monday. Keith needed something to warrant holding out any longer on telling the detectives what he knew.

He and Ramsey had to find a way to get things back under control. Abbott wouldn't stand for being left in the dark much longer. This thing was going to blow wide open any minute now.

The moment Ramsey answered, Keith demanded, "Have you heard from her today? I have to know something *now*."

"No," Ramsey said, "but I did speak to her last night."

Relief rushed through Keith. Thank God.

"What did she have to say?" His gut was in knots.

"She says she has no idea about anything. She swears she hasn't heard from Sela."

Oh God. "Were you firm with her? She may have lied, thinking she was protecting Sela."

"As firm as I could be. That detective's kid was watching out the window. I think she told her to watch."

The girl was too damned smart for her own good. "Was she visited by anyone else last night or this morning?"

He had given Ramsey explicit instructions to keep his eyes on that girl around the clock. At this point she was their only link to Sela.

"I wouldn't know. A police cruiser rolled through about half an hour later, stopped, and the officer asked what I was doing."

"She called the cops on you?" For the love of God.

"Evidently. I suppose it could have been coincidence."

No. Keith reached for calm. The girl had called the police. This was worse than he'd anticipated.

"Any luck on tracking down that car Sela purchased?" Keith did not understand what was going on. She had gone way off script. Everything had fallen apart, and Ben was dead.

Keith closed his eyes and pushed away the idea that, any way he looked at it, his friend's death was likely, at least in part, his fault.

"By the way," Ramsey said, "your two detective friends paid me a visit at lunch. I don't know how they tagged me, but they know I work for you."

"Jesus Christ." When he could breathe again, Keith warned, "Abbott is onto us. We have to get this under control before it's too late."

"Maybe it already is."

That was the part that scared Keith the most.

34

4:45 p.m.

"You want to swing by Bellemont's office again before five?"

Keith Bellemont's office officially closed at five, but Kerri wanted to finish this list first. "We have one more pawnshop."

Falco slowed and made the next left. "Heading that way."

Bellemont had not returned their calls, so it was doubtful they would catch him anyway. Each time Kerri called, his assistant said the same thing: *I already told you he's not in the rest of the day, Detective Devlin.* When Falco had called and pretended to be a prospective client, she had taken a message.

Kerri wanted to scream. What was wrong with these people? They had two homicide victims and a missing pregnant wife who might or might not be a victim. Either way, they needed to find her.

Damn it.

She shifted in her seat and stared out at the passing shops on Sixth Avenue. This case shouldn't have been so complicated. They'd had no hits on the prints lifted at the scene. Not a speck of trace evidence. There were the bodies and the blood. Nothing else. No witnesses, no one with truly useful information coming forward. They'd had to dig up every little trickle like searching for water in the desert. A damned needle in a haystack. It was sheer luck they'd learned about Keaton and his car deal with Sela. Or this Ramsey guy and his connection to Bellemont and Abbott Options.

"Last," Falco announced as he pulled to the curb in the middle of the block, "but hopefully not least."

He'd parked directly in front of the pawnshop. Kerri blinked, drew her mind back from the thoughts that had crowded out all else.

She climbed out, straightened her jacket, and started for the entrance. Falco came up behind her. She pushed through the glass door with its iron bars; the bell overhead jingled.

"Closing in five minutes," the man behind the counter announced without looking up from the device in his hand.

Kerri walked to his end of the counter and showed her badge. "Are you the owner?"

The man glanced at her. "I am."

The man was sixty-five or older. Reasonably tall, stooped shoulders, thin as a rail. Yet his voice was firm, unafraid. His eyes, on the other hand, were weary, cautious.

"You have a name?" Falco asked.

"Seth Byler."

"Mr. Byler," Kerri said, "we don't need much of your time. Just enough to ask a few questions."

Byler set aside the cell phone he'd been scrolling. "I don't buy stolen goods. I don't make illegal transactions, and I never remember the faces of customers. Otherwise, what can I do you for, Detectives?"

Kerri pulled up the photo of Sela Abbott on her cell and showed it to the man. "Has this woman—"

"I just told you I don't remember faces."

Falco leaned over the counter, put his face in the other man's. "Look at the photo," he ordered. "Tell me if she's been in your store."

"This is probably police brutality," Byler grumbled.

"No," Falco said with a fake smile. "This is me trying to get my point across to you. I can illustrate the difference if you're interested."

Byler shook his head. "Not necessary."

"Good." Falco hitched his thumb toward Kerri. "Look again."

"Have you seen her?" Kerri held up her phone once more.

Byler looked from the screen to Kerri. "She was in here week before last."

"And?" Falco prompted.

"She wanted to buy a gun."

Kerri stilled. "What did she leave your store with, Mr. Byler?"

"Ruger .22. Like new. Box of ammo."

"Did you run the necessary paperwork?" Falco inquired.

They knew he had not because they had checked the system. Sela Abbott had not legally purchased a handgun in the state of Alabama.

"Of course I did. I told you," he protested, "I don't make illegal transactions."

Falco leaned against the counter and shook his head. "Now that can't be true, Mr. Byler. You see, I checked. This woman did not legally purchase a handgun the week before last or any other time in the state of Alabama."

Byler swallowed; his Adam's apple bobbed. "She begged me to sell her the weapon without the paperwork. She said she was afraid. That someone was stalking her."

"We need to know the exact date, and"—Kerri glanced up at the camera—"we'd like to see the security video."

"The camera doesn't work. It's just for show."

Of course it didn't work. Frustrated, Kerri asked, "What day did she come in?"

Byler flipped through his ledger, his hands shaking. He knew he was in trouble; he just didn't know how bad.

"Friday, June first."

Falco turned the ledger around. He looked over the page, then glared at the man. "You charged her a thousand bucks?"

He shrugged. "She offered it to me."

"Find some paper, and write a statement for me," Falco ordered.

"But I—"

"You illegally sold a firearm," Kerri warned, "without checking to see if the person buying it had a record. That's a serious offense, Mr. Byler. A felony. You could lose your license and do time, particularly since that weapon may have been used to murder two people."

The man started to cry.

While Falco supervised the writing of the statement, Kerri called Bellemont's office yet again. This time there was no answer.

Keith Bellemont was now officially on her shit list.

Her cell vibrated, startling her. He might redeem himself if—not him. The number belonged to *her* attorney.

"Hey, Mac, what's up?" She walked out of the shop to get some privacy. Falco had things with Byler under control.

"Kerri, we have a problem."

The somber tone of Mike McGill's voice caused her heart to drop somewhere in the vicinity of the sidewalk. "Okay. What kind of problem?"

"Nick has petitioned the court for a hearing. He wants to become Tori's primary custodian."

Kerri couldn't breathe for a moment. Couldn't speak. Finally, she forced herself to deal with the situation. "Tell me what we have to do to stop this."

"Unfortunately, we can't stop it. We can only go to the hearing and show reason why the petition is unwarranted or unwanted."

"Tori wants to spend the summer with him in New York." Kerri rubbed a hand over her face. "I told her two weeks was enough. He warned me that if I didn't allow her to come for the whole summer, he would do this." But she hadn't believed him. She had assumed he wouldn't bother. He'd never been one to go to a lot of trouble for Kerri or for his daughter.

"I'm sorry you're having to deal with this, Kerri."

"So am I. It's just ridiculous. He's the one who wanted the new life. Why doesn't he leave ours alone?"

"The judge will most likely go with whatever Tori wants unless Nick can prove you're not taking proper care of her—and we both know that isn't true. It shouldn't be a problem. It'll just be a pain in the rump."

"I wish this was good news, Mac, but Tori's pretty upset with me right now. I'm not so sure I can count on her to want to stay with me."

"Talk to her, Kerri. We have perhaps a couple of weeks. Make things right with Tori, and most likely this will go away."

"Thanks, Mac." She drew in a deep breath despite the tight band around her chest. "I'll work on it."

Kerri tucked her phone into her pocket and resisted the urge to scream. Her life seemed to be spinning out of control, falling apart, and she couldn't stop it.

She turned to go back into the shop, but Falco came out. "This changes everything," he said. "You know that, right?"

It wasn't necessary for Kerri to respond. He was aware she understood.

Sela Abbott was no longer simply a potential suspect; she was their prime suspect.

Falco pulled his cell from his pocket and checked the screen. "It's the lab." He accepted the call. "Falco."

Kerri watched his face as he listened to the news. This case had just done a one-eighty. Bellemont obviously knew far more than he'd shared, since he was avoiding their calls. Sela might have contacted him for help. He was an old friend of her husband's, and since she had no close friends of her own—according to all their witnesses—Bellemont might be the person she turned to. And he was a lawyer. But would he represent the woman who had possibly murdered his best friend?

The call ended, and Falco rested his gaze on hers. "The blood in the bed with Ben Abbott was the mother's."

"Jesus Christ." Kerri had foolishly held out the tiniest bit of hope that this would not be the case.

Falco shrugged. "I told you. Vanishing wife. The woman hatched this elaborate scheme and executed it. Here we are thinking things have gone wrong, when the truth is maybe they've gone exactly the way she planned."

Kerri felt ready to explode. "I need a drink."

"There's a pub a couple blocks that way." He gestured to the left. "They have about fifty craft beers."

"I don't need a beer, Falco. I need a real drink."

"They got those too, Devlin."

————

The Derby
Sixth Avenue South

The pub had been around a few decades. Kerri had been in once back when she and Nick first married. Before she realized just how stupid she'd been, she had thought he was so handsome, so charming. He would be a wonderful husband, an ideal father. Boy, had she missed the mark.

"I know this case is going to hell in a hurry," Falco said as he sipped his beer. "But I'm sure you've been down a road like this before. Why is this one getting to you so hard? Is it because the wife is pregnant?"

"It's not the case. Not entirely, anyway." She tossed back the shot of tequila and tapped the glass so the bartender would bring her another.

"Better slow down, Devlin, or I'll be carrying you to the car."

"Ha ha." She took a breath, appreciated the nice buzz she had after downing two shots. "My ex is petitioning for primary custody of our daughter. Worse, she probably wants to go live with him."

"Oh hell. That sucks. I thought you said she wanted to spend the summer with him."

"That's how it started, and now it's out of control." *Like everything else*, she didn't mention.

He sipped his beer for a while. "Maybe you're missing the point here, Devlin."

The third shot landed in front of her, and she reached for it. His words kept her from immediately tossing it back. "What does that mean, Falco?"

"Maybe your daughter only wanted to have a summer adventure. Maybe the ex is the one taking the ball and running with it. If the daughter realized what he was planning, she might do an about-face."

Now there was a scenario she hadn't considered. She downed the shot, rode out the burn. Who was this guy? Luke Falco was supposed to be hotheaded and irreverent and sloppy and all that other stuff she had heard five days ago.

But he wasn't. He was smart. A savvy detective. A good guy.

The tequila had loosened her up, and she was having a hard time keeping things straight. Particularly whether she had responded to whatever he'd last said. "I don't want to like you." She bit her lips together at the realization that she'd said the words out loud.

"I know. Most people don't." He downed another swallow of his first and only beer.

"I mean"—she shook her head—"I had this whole idea of who you are. A don't-care kind of guy. A bullshitter. A guy who likes to skirt the fringes of trouble. A rule breaker."

He shrugged. "I've done all those things and more." He leaned forward, putting his face close to hers. "But I'm a good cop, Devlin. No matter how disrespectful and arrogant I can seem at times. I'm a damned good cop."

She dared to look him straight in the eyes. "You are. I admit it. I was wrong."

He smiled, drew back. "I should be recording this in case you change your mind when that buzz wears off."

"I won't change my mind. I'm glad you're my new partner."

He scoffed. "I'll ask you about that tomorrow for sure."

"I'm serious." She blew out a weary breath. "Now, take me home. I need to talk to my daughter."

"We could go by Bellemont's office one more time. Maybe bust the place up."

"You're a funny guy, Falco." She tossed a bill on the table that should cover both their tabs.

She didn't like misjudging people, but she was woman enough to admit when she was wrong.

Her cell vibrated in her pocket; she pulled it out as she followed Falco out of the pub. "Devlin."

"Detective, this is Officer Tanya Matthews."

Kerri paused outside on the sidewalk. "Hey, Matthews. You have something for me?"

"I do, but it may not be what you were looking for. The tech just completed the scan of Ms. Gibbons's home, and he found no hidden audio or video devices."

"Thanks. I appreciate the quick work."

She shoved the phone back into her pocket.

"Anything?" Falco asked.

She shook her head. Not what she was hoping for. The only thing the news meant when you got right down to it was that Ramsey was good enough not to get caught.

The man was a wild card in this case.

Maybe wilder than she had anticipated.

35

There is always one more thing.

No matter how carefully I plan. No matter the number of details that fall perfectly into place, there is always *one more thing*.

Exacting revenge is actually quite simple.

Far more complicated is the revealing of the whole truth while you do so.

Perhaps it would have been smarter to have the revenge and quietly walk away, but I want all of Birmingham to know the monsters who live among them. I want to expose the disgusting underbellies of all involved.

To do so requires evidence.

Conjecture and hearsay will not do. I must have tangible evidence.

When attempting to trap the devil, it is imperative to become acquainted with his behavior, his modus operandi, as the police would say. I now know that the devil at the core of this web of evil took certain steps to protect himself.

Insurance, so to speak. And now I have that insurance too. The insurance is evidence. Very good evidence.

I smile and press my hand to my belly as the baby inside me moves.

This evidence was an unexpected find and brought far more clarity to what must be done next. A fine-tuning. Of course, any changes require additional steps and time. Nothing I can't handle.

Very soon it will all be over.

36

Tuesday, June 12

10:30 a.m.

Kerri and Falco hadn't been able to avoid sitting in on the MID mandatory weekly briefing. Brooks didn't cut anyone slack on that one. Unless you were in the hospital or dead, you'd better be at the damned briefing.

From eight until nine they had listened to updates on every case in the division. Org changes and what have you.

When they had finally gotten back in their office, they'd gone over their case board again and made the necessary updates.

A quick call to Lieutenant Brown in San Diego had confirmed that Sela Rollins Abbott had been a regular at the firing range. She knew her way around a weapon. Then, they had headed to the scene of the crime. If Sela Abbott had purchased a handgun for the purpose of murdering her husband and her mother, what had she done with it after she did the deed? Had she taken the weapon with her or hidden it somewhere on the property?

Another long look around was in order.

Kerri scrubbed a hand over her face. What they really needed to do was find Sela Abbott. Whatever had happened, she was the key. "Our suspect had a car that couldn't be readily linked to her, and she had a weapon. It's clear she had been preparing for a while."

"No doubt," Falco agreed.

"If the woman went to all those lengths to prepare for whatever her endgame is, wouldn't she have a place to lay low as well?"

Falco nodded. "Damn straight she would."

"We need to know any other properties owned by the Abbotts in nearby areas. She could be holed up in a rental property or cabin by the lake."

"We could ask Ben Abbott's father," Falco suggested. "Personally, I think we'd have better luck going to his friend."

"Wouldn't that be nice." They had tried to reach Bellemont again this morning. A stop at his office had garnered the same as yesterday: *He's not in.*

Her cell vibrated. Kerri checked the screen. "Speak of the devil." She accepted the call, set it to speaker. "Devlin."

"Detective, I apologize for being unavailable yesterday. I'm hoping you're free right now. If so, please come to my office. Considering we're a week into this travesty, I think it's imperative that I share some additional information with you."

Well, it was about time. "We're on our way right now, Mr. Bellemont."

A pause went on for a beat too long before the attorney said what was on his mind. "I'd prefer to have this meeting with you, Detective Devlin. Alone."

Falco exchanged a look with her.

"I'm afraid that doesn't work for me, Mr. Bellemont. Falco and I are partners. We do this together."

His wearily exhaled breath rushed across the line. "Very well. I'll be waiting."

Falco executed a U-turn and headed back downtown. Kerri mentally listed the questions she had for the attorney.

As they reached their destination, Falco said, "I appreciate you keeping me in the loop, Devlin."

"That's what partners do."

He parked and turned his head to look at her. "So that wasn't the tequila talking last night?"

"It was not. But don't make me regret it."

Kerri got out and headed across the sidewalk. Last night she'd decided to explore Falco's theory about her daughter's motive for wanting to spend the summer in Manhattan. She and Tori had talked. They'd had a good long heart-to-heart. Falco had been right about Tori. She didn't want to move to Manhattan and leave her friends—or her mom, she'd tacked on lastly. What she wanted was a summer adventure to tell her friends about. Kerri had agreed to her staying four weeks. A damned good compromise in her opinion. This morning before heading to work, Kerri had called her ex and shared the news with him, and he'd told her it was too late for compromises. He would see her in court.

He was a bastard.

Falco caught up with her and opened the door to the attorney's office. The assistant, Martha, glanced up.

"He's waiting for you."

Kerri gave her a nod and headed back. There was something to be said for loyalty as long as it wasn't impeding a homicide investigation. She doubted telling the lady that protecting her boss in this situation had done so would make a difference in what she did in the future.

Bellemont stood behind his desk when they arrived at his door.

"Have a seat." He gestured to the chairs. To Falco he said, "Close the door behind you, please."

Anticipation had Kerri's nerves jumping. She was ready to hear something that would move this investigation substantially forward.

With the door closed and seats taken, Bellemont made the first move.

"I haven't been completely honest with you, Detectives. It is always my first obligation to protect my client."

"Understandable," Kerri agreed. "Unless that client is in imminent danger. And we have every reason to believe that Sela Abbott is in danger."

She made a conscious decision to keep the information about the gun out of the conversation for the moment. As he'd said, protecting his client was his first priority. He might feel different about talking if he learned his client had illegally purchased the very caliber of handgun used to murder her husband and mother.

"Ben came to me in February. Sela had revealed to him that she had an older sister who had gone missing here in Birmingham a decade and a half ago. She wanted his help in finding the truth about her disappearance. He was not happy at first. As you can imagine, he was concerned that she had used him to position herself for a personal vendetta of some sort. It took a bit of time for them to work it out, but he came to see that helping his wife would be the right thing. With that in mind, he approached me."

By this point, Kerri was beyond livid. "Six days have passed since we discovered the bodies of Ben Abbott and Jacqueline Rollins. You didn't feel like it was in your client's best interest to share this information before now?"

"As I said—"

Kerri waved him off. "What transpired after your meeting with Ben Abbott?"

"It is Sela's belief that Theo Thompson is somehow responsible for whatever happened to her sister."

"The Theo Thompson?" Falco feigned surprise. "Who's running for the Senate? I hope you've got serious evidence to back that up. Some might see your suggestion as an opportunity to damage his chances of taking over his father's legacy."

"As I said, this is what Sela believes. I warned Ben that we would need compelling evidence before making any sort of legal move against the man. Despite my warning, Ben and Sela were not prepared to let the theory go, evidence or no. So I agreed to do what I could to help."

"Since that initial meeting four months ago, what have you done toward that end?" Kerri watched him closely as he spoke. His expression was carefully closed. He looked at her from time to time but didn't maintain steady eye contact.

"First we started to dig into the events leading up to Janelle Stevens's disappearance. She was employed by Thompson's father, T. R., but only for a few months before she disappeared. There were no reports of trouble in the workplace or with any of her neighbors in the apartment complex where she lived. She was a bit of a loner and didn't have any friends outside work."

All the things Kerri already knew from reading the old case file. "Did you find any evidence that Thompson might have been involved in whatever happened to her?"

"I did find one woman who worked with Janelle who stated that she believed Janelle was having an affair with the son, Theo. She was adamant that she had told this to the police at the time of Janelle's disappearance, but no one ever came back to follow up. A few days later I returned to speak with her again, and she had fallen down the stairs of her home. She didn't survive the fall. I checked with a friend at the ME's office, and the death was ruled an accident. Still, it was quite the coincidence."

Kerri reserved judgment. Waited for him to go on.

"From that point forward, every step we've made in the investigation has sent us stumbling back two. Even with the help of my top investigator, Neal Ramsey, I'm no closer to the truth than I was the day Ben came to my office. It was the woman's sudden death, however, that convinced me Sela was onto something."

"You trust Ramsey?" Kerri asked without giving away what she knew of the investigator's activities.

"Implicitly."

"People fall and end up dead all the time," Falco argued. "Surely there was something more that convinced you Thompson was involved in the death of Stevens's former coworker."

Bellemont pressed his palms against his desk and stared at them for a moment, as if he wasn't sure he wanted to say more on the subject. When he looked up again, he gave a slight nod. "You're right, of course. I'm not one to jump to conclusions." He looked from Falco to Kerri. "If you're my age or older and you've lived and worked among the Birmingham hierarchy your entire adult life, you hear things. If you hear those same things enough, you begin to understand that there is likely some truth to the rumors."

"What rumors are we talking about?" Kerri asked, anticipation pushing her to the edge of her seat. "Does this have something to do with the property dispute Ben Abbott was having with Theo Thompson?"

Bellemont shook his head. "I don't believe so. I think the property was Ben indulging his wife and Sela wanting to twist the dagger into Suzanne's back. The two do not like each other."

"Back to the rumors," Kerri went on, satisfied on that score for now. "Tell us about the rumors."

"T. R. Thompson's wife died long ago," Bellemont began, "but even before her death there were rumors about certain personal proclivities the venerated senator had."

Kerri couldn't call to mind any particular rumors not related to his political office. "What sort of proclivities?"

"Ones involving women and bondage. It was said that he preferred a bit of extra titillation. Domination, that sort of thing. He was, of course, very careful, and not a single one of his paramours ever admitted to any such behavior. But my father, God rest his soul, believed T. R.

Thompson to be a womanizer of the highest order. If that is the case, I can only assume he paid the women involved very large sums of money since none has ever come forward against him."

"Maybe the only one who tried disappeared," Kerri suggested, a new kind of tension riffling through her.

"We—meaning Sela, Ben, and I—were exploring that possibility." Holy shit. Kerri's pulse started to race. "But you found no evidence?" Bellemont shook his head. "None."

"Has Thompson threatened, maybe pressured you or your family or Sela or her family?" Falco wanted to know.

"Not outright," Bellemont admitted, "but I've seen a decline in my client list. Particularly those in some way connected to the Thompsons."

"What you have, Mr. Bellemont," Kerri argued, "is an accusation made against one of the city's old money families, and that's it, an accusation. We can question the Thompsons and anyone who worked with Sela's sister, but you need to understand that we won't be able to waste resources on hearsay. I need something concrete."

If the man was holding anything back, he needed to give it up.

Bellemont turned up his hands. "And therein lies the rub. I told Ben the same thing. He understood this as well as I." Bellemont leaned forward. "This is what I know, Detectives. Sela was determined to find the truth. The Thompsons were aware we were actively looking into the case. Now Sela's family is dead, and she's missing. Whatever happened, Thompson had something to do with it. I can't prove it, but I know it."

"Did Ben Abbott believe the Thompsons, the father or the son, actually got their hands dirty by making Janelle Stevens disappear?" Kerri needed the answer to this question before she moved forward.

"He did not. He was convinced the disappearance would have been handled by Lewis York. Yorks have always been private counsel to the Thompsons. More than counsel, really. Again, these are rumors, but I've always heard that the Yorks were more fixers than attorneys. Ben never trusted the man. From a personal standpoint, I can tell you that you will not find a more arrogant, underhanded human being than Lewis York."

"York as in the partner in that big law firm?" Kerri was surprised Bellemont had thrown yet another big name into the pot. This was the firm where Amelia was interning.

"One of the most prestigious in the state, but also ruthless. York is the sort of man I wouldn't trust under any circumstances. He gives hardworking attorneys a bad name. He's far more dangerous, I believe, than his father was."

"Speaking of fathers," Falco said, "have you shared this information with Ben Abbott's father?"

"Absolutely not. Ben's parents know nothing of this. He wanted them protected. He insisted they not be involved at all in this ugly business."

"What would you say," Kerri began, "if I told you there is a chance that these murders were committed by Sela?"

"Outrageous." Bellemont shook his head. "How would you reach such a ridiculous conclusion?"

"She illegally purchased a Ruger SR22 a few days before the murder," Kerri said. "I'm sure you're aware a .22 is the weapon used to kill Ben Abbott and Jacqueline Rollins."

"She purchased a junker from the housekeeper's nephew and paid him more than what it was worth to keep his mouth shut," Falco added. "So she had transportation not readily tied to her and a weapon. All this adds up to trouble. We've got plenty of evidence on her. We have nothing on Thompson and York but accusations with no evidence to back them up."

"Whatever you do from this point forward, Detectives, is your decision," Bellemont insisted with an adamant shake of his head, "but believe me when I say that the only known threat to Sela and Ben was Theo Thompson and his hired lackey, Lewis York."

Bellemont locked down after that, said he had nothing more to share.

Kerri followed her partner out the side exit.

"You think he's telling us the whole story?" Falco asked.

"Not at all." Kerri was convinced there was more. "He's leaving out the parts that would put all the pieces together."

In her opinion, Bellemont was growing desperate, so he'd started to share, but he wasn't yet desperate enough to share anything that might implicate him or his staff in wrongdoing.

"Where to now, partner?"

"To see Theo Thompson, where else? We can search the house again later." If Sela Abbott had hidden the murder weapon there, they would find it.

Falco grinned. "I thought you might say that. I've got a feeling we'll be about as welcome there as fleas at a dog show."

When it came to a homicide investigation, Kerri had never cared much whether she was welcome.

As long as she got the job done.

Her cell started its frantic vibrating again. Kerri answered without checking the screen. "Devlin."

"Kerri, I need to see you. Right now."

Diana.

"Are you okay?" Kerri froze a few steps from the end of the alley. Falco waited at the sidewalk.

"It's about Amelia. It can't wait."

"On my way," Kerri promised her.

37

1:00 p.m.

Swanner Residence
Twenty-Third Avenue South

Kerri knocked on the door. Normally she would have knocked and gone on in, but Falco was with her. Diana might not appreciate her sister walking in with a stranger.

Diana opened the door, her face red from crying.

Kerri didn't hesitate. She hugged her sister. "Tell me what's going on."

Diana pulled herself together with visible effort. She stepped back and ushered them inside.

Tori stood in the middle of the room, her arms hugged around her slim body. She, too, had been crying.

Kerri rushed over to her. "What's going on? You okay?" The idea that something had happened and Tori had called Diana to come pick her up had Kerri's chest squeezing tightly. But she'd said it was about Amelia.

"I'm okay." She lifted one shoulder and let it fall. "It's Amelia I'm worried about."

Kerri turned back to Diana. "Somebody please tell me what's going on. Where's Robby?" If something was going on, he should be here.

Diana drew in a deep breath. "Robby's still at the shop. I didn't tell him anything yet. I didn't see any reason for both of us to be upset until after I spoke with you." She wilted down onto the sofa.

Tori sank down next to her aunt. "I should have told you, Mom. But I promised Amelia I wouldn't tell anyone."

Kerri took a breath. Told herself to stay calm. "It's okay." To Diana, she urged, "Just tell me what's happened."

Diana's hands were clasped around her cell phone, as if she expected it to keep her afloat in these rough waters. She took a breath and started to talk. "Amelia sent me a text saying she wouldn't be coming home for a few days because she needed to help a friend. She said her friend was in trouble and . . ." Tears welled in her eyes again; Diana handed her cell to Kerri. "Read the texts for yourself. I'll just bawl again if I repeat all of it out loud."

As Kerri read, her sister kept talking. "We all know Amelia is famous for going to the aid of anyone or thing who crosses her path. But . . ." Diana shrugged. "This feels different. Usually she tells me about these things. I had a feeling she was keeping something from me. I had been nudging her about my concerns, and then today she sent those." She shook her head. "Now she's not responding at all. Maybe I said too much. I even thought about going by the firm to see her, but I was afraid it would look as if I'm checking up on her. I don't want to do anything to make her look bad."

When she finally paused for a breath, Kerri passed her sister's cell phone back to her. Admittedly, the messages were troubling. Diana had begged her daughter for more information and for her to come home, and she had refused; then she had stopped replying at all.

Kerri chose her words carefully. "Amelia's eighteen. She could be feeling the need for more independence. I recognize this is out of character for her, but it may not be as bad as it seems."

Diana and Tori exchanged a look.

Well, hell. Kerri held up her hands stop-sign fashion. "All right, now tell me the rest." She looked to her daughter. "The part you feel bad about not telling me already."

"When Aunt Diana called"—Tori balled her hands together in her lap—"and started asking questions, I realized I couldn't keep Amelia's secret any longer."

Kerri held her tongue, waited for her daughter to continue.

"Sunday night while Aunt Diana was in the tub," Tori explained, "this guy kept calling Amelia. She wouldn't answer, but then he drove up outside. She finally went out to talk to him. She told me to watch and that if I got worried about whatever was happening to call 911."

Kerri bit back the *oh my God* she wanted to launch at her daughter.

"He didn't touch her or anything, but I could see they were arguing, and he stuck his face right in hers. I got scared and used Amelia's cell to call 911. But then Amelia came inside, and everything was okay. Still, that guy hung around until the police drove up. When he'd driven away, Amelia went out there and told the officers that everything was okay."

Kerri waited a full five seconds before she spoke. "Did Amelia tell you what this man wanted?"

Tori shook her head no. "She said he was trying to find a friend of hers, and she was afraid her friend was in trouble, so she didn't want to tell him anything." A lone tear rolled down her cheek. "She made me promise not to tell."

"Did she say who the guy was?" Kerri pressed, barely restraining the need to hold her daughter and promise her that all would be well.

Tori shook her head. "She said she couldn't tell me."

Diana swiped at her own tears. "I took a long hot bath, had a couple of glasses of wine. With the music on I had no idea any of this was happening. I should have been paying attention."

"Hey," Falco said to her, "we all need a break now and then." He shifted his attention to Tori. "What did this guy look like?"

"It was dark, so I didn't get a real good look at him. He was tall, kind of"—she moved her shoulders up and down—"muscled up. Like he worked out. His hair was really short, and he was dressed like your old partner." Tori looked to her mom. "You know, like a detective."

Kerri and Falco shared a look. They'd both obviously just thought of the man they'd spoken to at Pop's diner—Neal Ramsey. The same man who worked for Bellemont to help Sela Abbott—and for an unnamed client to spy on Ben Abbott. A new kind of worry gnawed at Kerri. She asked her daughter, "What color was his hair?"

"I couldn't really tell, but it wasn't dark. It was lighter, maybe blond."

Falco pulled out his cell and opened a screen. "Was it this guy?"

Tori studied the image on the phone for a bit; then she shrugged and handed it back to Falco. "I can't be positive, but it looks like him. You know, he had that tough-guy detective look."

Definitely sounded like Ramsey.

"Do you know who he is?" Diana asked, her eyes wide with worry.

"Maybe," Kerri said. "If it's who we believe it is, he's a private investigator who works for a local attorney."

Why would he be talking to Amelia? Kerri wondered again if Bellemont knew his oh-so-trustworthy investigator was moonlighting—maybe against him. Kerri had a feeling Ramsey was not at all the dedicated employee Bellemont believed him to be.

"Could he have something to do with Amelia not coming home?" A new kind of fear claimed Diana's face.

"I don't know," Kerri admitted, "but we'll find out. For now, you keep trying to get Amelia to respond, and Falco and I will go see some of her friends." Whatever Amelia was doing and whomever she was with might not have anything to do with Ramsey or Sela Abbott. Before Kerri went there, she wanted to be sure this wasn't some post–high school drama playing out.

"It's possible she might be staying with one of her friends from school for a couple of days," Kerri offered. "Does she still have that boyfriend? He may have heard from her. Sometimes kids will tell their friends things they won't tell their parents."

Tori stared at her hands as Kerri said this. No surprise there. Most kids felt that need eventually. Her daughter wouldn't be any different. And this thing with Amelia was likely the same—normal teenage stuff.

Kerri recognized a bit of denial might be at play here.

Only one way to find out. To do that, she had to stay focused and keep her personal feelings in check. Not always easy to do.

Diana chewed at her nails, something Kerri hadn't seen her do since grade school. "Katie Jo Spencer is her best friend. They've been friends since kindergarten. Her boyfriend is Thad Gaines, but that relationship is a little fragile right now. She's leaving for school; he's not. They have different visions for their futures. I don't think she would go to him."

"Text me cell numbers and addresses, and we'll talk with them." Kerri pushed to her feet. She would feel better when she had this sorted out. "Tori, why don't you stay here until I get home tonight? With the twins away at camp, I'm sure Diana could use the company."

Tori nodded. "Sure."

Diana stood. "Kerri, I know you don't have time for this. I've already called Katie Jo, and she said she and Amelia have hardly seen each other since school was out. She's busy with a summer job and readying to go off to college too. I don't think she would lie to me."

"Did Katie Jo know anything about this friend who's in trouble?"

"She said she's completely out of the loop. Had no idea or suggestions of who Amelia might be hanging out with." Diana's arms went around her waist. "It's like I don't even know what my daughter's doing or who her friends are anymore." She shook her head. "I've always trusted her. Maybe I should have gotten that tracking software on her cell ages ago like all those other mothers."

Kerri produced what she hoped was a decent smile. "Let us talk to Gaines, see what he has to say. We'll go from there. Meanwhile, you keep nudging Amelia to tell you where she is. The more information we have, the easier our job will be. Bottom line, she's a smart girl. She'll do the right thing. I'll call as soon as I've spoken to Gaines."

Diana reached for her. "Thanks, sis."

Kerri hugged her hard. "Hang in there." Then she hugged Tori. "Love you."

Tori nodded. "Love you too."

"Nice to meet you, Diana," Falco said when he and Kerri would have turned to go.

Kerri squeezed her eyes shut for a moment. Shit. "By the way, this is my partner, Luke Falco."

Diana pressed her palms to her cheeks and shook her head. "I'm so sorry." She extended her hand toward Falco.

He gave her hand a quick shake. "Really, you don't have to be sorry. It isn't so bad working with your sister."

Diana laughed, a pathetically unfunny sound. "No." She exhaled a big breath. "I meant I'm sorry for ignoring you."

"No problem. I'm used to it."

"Let's go, Falco," Kerri ordered.

Falco gave Diana and Tori a little salute.

Outside, Kerri checked her cell and called out the street and house number for Thad Gaines. She and Falco would nudge the kid for whatever he did or didn't know first.

When they had loaded up and pulled out of the drive, Falco asked, "Have you considered that Amelia works for the firm where Lewis York is a senior partner? The same Lewis York that Bellemont says is a fixer for the Thompsons?"

"I have." From the moment Bellemont had dumped that load of information, Amelia's employment there had been hanging around the fringes of Kerri's thoughts. "She worked for the firm one afternoon a week after school all spring, and she's done nothing but rave about how impressed she is with all they do."

Falco slowed for a turn. "They would never let an intern see the ugly side of the operation. She would only see the pretty parts."

Kerri closed her eyes for a moment. "Having kids is scary as hell."

"Yeah, I know."

Kerri bit her lips together. Reminded herself that Falco's personal life was not her business. Didn't stop her mouth from overriding her reasoning. "People change. Circumstances change. Have you considered talking to your ex about getting to know your kid?"

"He has a dad. He's happy. I'm not going to disrupt the life they've built for him."

If only her ex would be so thoughtful.

"What're you going to do about your ex?" He glanced at her as he braked for a traffic light.

How was it possible he could already read her so well? "My lawyer's working on it. At this point the only thing I can do is wait."

And lose my mind.

"By the way, you were right," she told him. "About Tori wanting a summer adventure, I mean."

He shot her a grin. "Told you."

"I called Nick and offered a compromise, but he didn't go for it."

"Your ex is a selfish asshole."

"He is."

"Have you given any thought to putting a hit out on him?"

Kerri laughed. "I wish I could say the idea hadn't crossed my mind, but that would be a lie."

Falco laughed. He didn't do that often. Then again, there wasn't a lot to laugh about when working homicide.

———

Red Mountain Terrace South

Thad Gaines and his family lived only a few neighborhoods over from Amelia and her family. The Mustang registered to him sat in the driveway, so hopefully he was home.

Kerri knocked, and Falco scanned the yard, as if he expected Gaines to make a run for his car any second. The door opened, and the eighteen-year-old stared out at them, looking like he'd only just awakened and crawled out of the bed. In fact, based on his attire—a tee and boxers—he probably had.

"Thad Gaines?" Kerri had no doubt it was him; Diana had sent along a pic. But she asked the question and showed her badge to him anyway.

"Yeah." He looked from Kerri to Falco and back.

"I'm Detective Devlin, and this is Detective Falco."

"Are your parents home, Mr. Gaines?" Falco asked.

Kerri mentally high-fived him for that one.

Gaines was nervous now. "No. They're at work. What's going on, Detectives?"

"Why don't we step inside, Mr. Gaines?" Falco sounded dead serious.

"Sure. Okay."

The kid backed into the house; Kerri and Falco followed. Falco closed the door behind him.

"So . . . what's this about?"

"Amelia Swanner," Kerri said. "When was the last time you saw her?"

He blinked, obviously confused or surprised by the question. "A week ago maybe." He shrugged. "It's been a while."

"Have you spoken to her or exchanged texts?" Falco asked.

"I text her, but she doesn't answer half the time. She blows me off, like every day."

Falco cocked his head. "I thought you two had a thing."

"I don't know . . . I guess we broke up. She works all the time. Apparently I'm too boring for her. We haven't hung out in over two weeks."

"The last time you spoke, did she mention someone in trouble that she might need to help?"

He shook his head at Kerri's question. "She doesn't tell me anything anymore. I'm out. Some other guy is in."

"Other guy?" Falco echoed. "Who is this other guy?"

"I don't know. She just said she was working on some special project with a guy."

"Can you describe this man to us?" Kerri asked.

"I never saw him."

"She didn't say anything else about this special project?"

"Nope. I told you she doesn't talk to me anymore."

"You don't know any of her friends who might be in trouble?" Kerri repeated the question. She was so hoping the answer would be a simple one. She needed this to be simple.

He shook his head. "No. I don't know what else to tell you. Like I keep saying, she isn't talking to me."

Falco offered him one of his cards. "Call me if you hear from her or anything about her. Okay, champ?"

The kid took the card. "Okay. Sure."

"This is important, Thad," Kerri reiterated. "Call if you hear anything."

He nodded. "I will."

Outside, Kerri waited until they were in Falco's car. "I didn't get the impression he was hiding anything."

"Me either."

"We need to find Ramsey. If he's the other guy—and that's a good possibility, considering he fits the description of the guy who showed up at her house on Sunday night—we need to talk to him."

"Heading to his last known address now."

As much as Kerri wanted to believe this couldn't be connected, there was only one logical reason Ramsey would be talking to Amelia.

Sela Abbott.

———

There was no answer at Ramsey's condo. If the abundance of mail jammed into his box was any indication, he hadn't been there in a while. From the deserted condo they headed to Bellemont's office.

"There he is," Falco said as he eased to the curb in front of the attorney's office. He had just exited the side door.

Kerri was out of the car before it stopped rocking at the curb. She met Bellemont just inside the alley. "Headed home?" she asked, noting his briefcase.

The attorney exhaled a beleaguered breath. "Yes, Detective, I am headed home."

Falco moved up beside her. "We have a problem, Bellemont. Your man Ramsey has been harassing young girls."

Bellemont looked from Falco to Kerri. "I've already told you that Neal Ramsey is completely trustworthy. Whatever he's done, I can assure you it's not only legal but ethical."

"You call stalking and harassing my eighteen-year-old niece ethical and legal?"

The attorney sighed, his shoulders slumped. "Amelia." He shook his head. "You're blowing this out of proportion."

The idea that Bellemont spoke not only as if he knew Amelia but as if he knew her well had a volatile mixture of worry and outrage twisting through Kerri. "How the hell do you know my niece?"

Bellemont shook his head adamantly. "It's not what you think."

Falco moved a step closer to him. "I'm reasonably confident you can't read minds, Bellemont. So since you have no clue what she's thinking, why don't you just give us the skinny? Why was your man talking to Amelia on Sunday night? Harassing her to the point that 911 had to be called."

Bellemont glanced beyond them, as if he feared being overheard. "We needed to ask Amelia a few questions," he admitted.

"About what?" Kerri demanded, rather than the litany of other things she wanted to hurl at the man. What the hell was he thinking? Amelia was barely eighteen. She was a kid. And this—*this* was a fucking homicide investigation.

"Some months ago Amelia befriended Sela Abbott. It was after working with her on one of the fundraisers. Sela was impressed with Amelia, so she indulged the girl's adoration."

Kerri crossed her arms over her chest. "That doesn't sound like Amelia. People are usually drawn to her rather than vice versa."

"Whatever the case," Bellemont relented, "the two began spending time together. Once we started the preliminary investigation into Sela's accusations against Thompson, we felt it necessary to keep an eye on her, so to speak. Ben is my friend, and I felt compelled to see that his wife remained safe. To that end, we needed to understand the nature of Amelia's relationship with Sela."

Fury kicked Kerri in the gut all over again. "You're suggesting she was spying on Sela. Reporting to who? York?" She shook her head. "Jesus Christ. Amelia wouldn't do that. Not to anyone and not to the firm where she worked." The idea was outrageous.

"I didn't say that," Bellemont argued. "Those are your words. All I'm saying is that we were concerned about the relationship, considering Amelia's employer, and I relayed those concerns to Sela. Like you, she disagreed adamantly, and that was the end of it. Until . . . the murders. We started watching Amelia again at that point. Hoping she might lead us to Sela."

Kerri stepped in toe to toe with him. Every instinct she possessed warned that Amelia could be in over her head. That this friend in need was Sela Abbott. Goddamn it! "If you're keeping anything from me that puts my niece at risk, you will regret it, Bellemont."

He moved his head wearily from side to side. "I would never do that, Detective."

"Just to be clear," Falco said, "you and Ramsey have no idea where Amelia or Sela are?"

"I wish we did."

It bugged the hell out of Kerri, but she believed him. At least on that one point. As much as she wanted to punch the guy for keeping this from her for days now, she turned around and walked back to Falco's car. He followed.

As her partner drove away, Kerri stared at Bellemont. He stood in that alley looking utterly lost. Whatever *this* was, it wasn't going the way he had anticipated either.

Falco asked, "Who's up next, partner?"

"Thompson—for the good it will do to try and catch him." Kerri hesitated for a moment. "Then York."

She couldn't tell Diana about this . . . not until she was sure. Fear snaked around her chest and squeezed. It was bad enough this case was all over the place . . . but this was personal.

"You know what the problem is with those three? Bellemont, Thompson, and York?"

The adrenaline suddenly bled out of her, leaving Kerri exhausted. "Why don't you tell me?"

"They're lawyers. No matter how good or nice you think one is, you can never really, completely trust one of them."

She laughed, a half-hearted sound. "Ain't that the truth."

While her partner drove, Kerri sent a text to Amelia.

We need to know you're ok. Now, pls.

To Kerri's surprise a response came right away.

I'm fine. Everyone needs to chill. I have to do this, Aunt Kerri. My
friend needs me.

Is your friend Sela Abbott?

No answer.

Kerri sighed. This is not a game. It's dangerous. Be careful.

A thumbs-up and then a heart appeared on the screen.

Kerri wanted to feel better about the situation after reading Amelia's
texts. But she didn't. She was terrified that all this—the murders, the
deceptions, the betrayal—all somehow tied together, and Amelia was
tangled up right in the middle of it.

38

6:00 p.m.

Swanner Auto Repair
Richard Arrington Junior Boulevard South

Robby stared at the news on the television mounted on the wall in his shop. Photos of murder victim Ben Abbott, his missing wife, and his dead mother-in-law flashed on the screen.

"According to the Birmingham Police Department," the anchor said in his perfectly modulated voice, "this investigation is ongoing, but there are still no firm leads in the case."

Robby shut off the damned television. He couldn't stand to watch any more of it. The story about the home invasion seemed to be on every channel twenty-four seven. It was driving him crazy.

This wasn't his fault.

He suddenly realized he was standing in the middle of his shop, and his mechanics were staring at him. They were all working late, again.

"Too depressing," he offered with a nod to the dark screen.

Agreements were mumbled as the men went back to work. Robby walked into the break room and shut the door. He pressed his head against the door and swallowed back the screams that rose in his throat.

He'd made a mistake all those years ago.

His father had almost lost this place before his heart attack. When he'd died nearly sixteen years ago, Robby had been twenty-four with a wife and kid and a shop that was going under fast because of the bad decisions his father had made.

But everything had turned around that one night.

Robby had been at the shop alone. Another of the mechanics had quit. Robby hadn't blamed him. He couldn't pay him what he'd deserved. Just before he'd decided to call it a night, a man had knocked on the door, needing assistance. He'd claimed that he'd heard Robby could work magic—that he was the best, and only the best would do.

What he'd really heard was that Robby was desperate.

Even as he'd agreed to do the job, Robby had recognized the price he was being paid was hush money. But the man had promised that if he did this right and kept quiet, he would never have to worry again.

Robby had been a fool.

And now that night was back to haunt him.

He walked to the freezer and dug out the box Jen had discovered. Maybe he was a fool, but he wasn't stupid.

All these years he had kept a little memento from that night.

Just in case.

39

7:00 p.m.

York Residence
Saddle Creek Drive

Falco did the knocking at Lewis York's door. The man lived on a private estate in one of Birmingham's premiere neighborhoods. The enormous colonial revival–style house was as grand as the address suggested. But Kerri wasn't impressed.

She surveyed the property. The meticulous landscaping, the abundance of space between the homes. Five-car garage. Each probably filled with something that cost more than a full year, maybe two, of her salary.

Didn't mean the guy inside wasn't capable of all manner of bad things.

There were certain things money definitely could not buy. Honesty. Integrity. Ethics.

The door opened, and Lewis York himself greeted them. Kerri had looked him up on the way over here. Closer to fifty than forty. Dark hair with a peppering of gray. Medium height, medium build. Not much of a chin, but a hell of a nose. Not classically handsome like his friend Theodore Thompson Jr. She had done a hell of a lot of research on the wannabe senator as well. She really, really had wanted to talk to him. But since Thompson was not available at his office or at his home, this guy had been next up on Kerri's list.

"I'm Detective Devlin." She showed her badge. "This is my partner, Detective Falco. We have a few questions about a double homicide case we're investigating."

Without inquiring as to what case or why they would need to speak with him, York opened the door wider in welcome. "Come in, Detectives."

Kerri and Falco followed him into the grand entry hall.

"Let's talk in my study."

With that he turned and strode deeper into the house, made a left, and paused to slide apart elaborate wood-and-glass pocket doors. He entered the office and settled behind the desk.

"Please have a seat." He gestured to the lushly upholstered chairs that stood before his desk. When they had complied, he said, "How can I help you?" His gaze lingered on Falco before he shifted back to Kerri.

"I'm sure you've seen the news about Ben Abbott and his family," she said. She wouldn't start with Amelia. She had made her mind up on the way here to let York do the leading. Sometimes a suspect's need to prove his innocence helped to show his guilt. York was an attorney. If he was half as good as the prestigious firm would have her believe, he would never allow Kerri to lead him anyway.

"I have. It's a terrible tragedy. My family and his are well acquainted."

"Did you know Mr. Abbott or his wife personally?" Falco asked.

"Not really. Ben was several years younger than me, and he has been away for a good number of years. Frankly, I never really knew him beyond social events. I'm more acquainted with Ben's father and his wife. I'm sure you know that everyone who is anyone is involved with DATACO on some level. Daniel has ensured that his company touches all of our lives in one way or another. He's a brilliant strategist when it comes to business. His son obviously inherited that ability."

It wasn't necessary to be much of an investigator to know this. His waxing on was interesting, though. Kerri asked, "What about Ben's wife, Sela?"

York shook his head. "I really don't know her at all. As I told you, I've seen her in social settings. Nothing more."

"Any rumors in your social circles as to what happened? Known enemies of the Abbotts? Talk of trouble?" she asked.

York turned his hands up. "None at all. I wish I could help you, Detectives, but I'm afraid I really know nothing about the situation other than what a somber tragedy it is. All of us at York, Hammond & Goldman are keeping the family in our prayers."

"Beyond your staff that's shown on the firm's website"—Falco took the conversation in the next direction—"do you have other employees who aren't in the photograph?"

"I'm not sure why you would ask in this context," York qualified, "but the answer is we have custodial personnel and a few others who aren't a part of the staff photograph. The ones in the photo are the members who interact with clients. When a new client arrives at our office, we want that client to recognize the faces he encounters."

"You have how many investigators?" Falco pushed. "Five? Six?"

"Four," he corrected. "The clientele to which we cater rarely requires those sorts of services."

"We'd like the names of those investigators," Kerri said, hoping he would answer without overanalyzing the question.

He held her gaze a moment. "Don't doubt my desire to help in any way possible, but why are you interested in my firm's staff?"

It had been worth a try.

"We have a witness," Falco said, "who stated that a member of your staff was seen coming out of the Abbott home the day before the bodies were found."

Kerri kept her gaze steady on York. She didn't have a problem with the straight-up lie her partner had just told. Particularly if it got the job done.

"I tell you what, Detective. You stop by my office tomorrow during regular business hours, and I'll have my secretary provide you with a list of the firm's employees—as well as photos. If your witness identifies one of my people, I will personally escort that person to your office."

"We may take you up on that offer," Falco said.

"I wouldn't have made it if I weren't prepared to follow through."

"Is it your firm's policy to spy on people? Perhaps someone conducting some activity against one of your clients?" Kerri watched him closely as she waited for his response.

He shrugged. "To some extent—and within the law, of course—what my investigators do might at times be deemed as spying. But it's no different than the things you do in the course of an investigation."

"When this sort of situation arises," Kerri went on since she'd gotten this far, "I assume you select someone who presumably would be able to get close to the target." Her pulse was hammering now.

"That is a reasonable assumption." He'd settled deeper into his chair, seemed to be enjoying this dance on the edge.

"Would you use another staff member if necessary rather than one of your investigators? An assistant, maybe?"

His gaze narrowed. "Possibly."

"What about an intern?" She held his gaze, didn't even blink.

He shook his head resolutely. "Absolutely not. Interns are basically children. I would never use a child in such a way. I have a child of my own. The idea is unconscionable."

Before she could decide if he was telling the truth or just a really good liar, he stood, signaling the meeting was over.

Kerri and Falco did the same. She said, "Thank you for your time, Mr. York."

"Always happy to help the Birmingham PD." York led the way back to the front door. "Good evening, Detectives."

Falco turned to him once more before walking away. "I'm sure if we have more questions, you'll be available."

"Of course." York's face remained clean of tells.

They had stepped out onto the veranda when his voice stopped them once more. "Detective Devlin, you're Amelia's aunt, aren't you?"

Kerri shifted back to him, held her breath. "I am."

He smiled. "She speaks of you often. At the firm we're very proud to have her on staff. She is a brilliant young lady. I predict she has a bright future ahead of her."

Kerri forced her lips into a smile. "Thank you."

When they were in the car driving away, Falco asked, "Pick up any vibes?"

"Only that Bellemont was right. He's arrogant, for sure. Unafraid. He wasn't the slightest bit worried about talking to us. He probably saw it as a challenge. Whatever he knows about Sela Abbott, he will never tell."

"He wanted you to know he was aware you were talking about Amelia when you mentioned an intern."

Kerri blocked the dozens of scenarios—all related to Amelia—that bombarded her. "He did."

If he'd thought that being so accommodating would take him off Kerri's bad-guy radar, he was dead wrong.

"You mind stopping by Diana's so I can pick up Tori?"

"Sure thing, Devlin."

"I was thinking of ordering pizza," she ventured. "You could stay for dinner if you'd like."

Falco shot her a grin. "I knew it. You like me, don't you, Devlin?"

She shook her head. "You're growing on me."

40

Leaving exactly the right number of bread crumbs is crucial.

People are so often oblivious.

It's true. They are selective about what they see. It's easier to see things through that narrow view of only what they want to see. The concept makes life more comfortable. No one wants to believe a woman might actually murder her husband and her mother or that she would destroy the baby she carried. Or that someone you trust—someone you know well—might betray you . . . hurt you . . . perhaps kill you.

No one wants to think about it. It's too hard.

Too painful.

So they don't look. They block it from their minds. Allow the news to scroll past unnoticed. They wear their blinders to protect their sensibilities.

But I need them to look.

It's time to lead them to the truth. The first move in that direction starts today.

I climb into the back seat of the Uber and watch the blue car that served my purposes fade into nothing behind me as the driver speeds away.

The utterly unmemorable relic is now going to play the most important role of its pathetic life.

I didn't forget the detectives. I left little clues for them as well. I am confident Detective Devlin will appreciate the effort.

It's strange, but I like her. I'm betting she is everything I've heard she is.

She will put the pieces together.

Most important, by leaving the car at this remote cabin, I am sending the property owner a message.

I'm coming for you.

When he gets the message, I hope he warns his friends.

They are next.

41

Wednesday, June 13

9:00 a.m.

Abbott Lake House
Great Pine Lake

Only a family as wealthy as the Abbotts would call a multimillion-dollar, seven-thousand-plus-square-foot mansion their lake house. The house sat in the woods on nearly two acres. The water and mountain views were spectacular. Natural beauty and utter serenity only twenty minutes from the city's most upscale lifestyle center (a.k.a. mall).

"Too bad we can't go inside," Falco noted as he surveyed the three-story house.

Asking the Abbotts for permission would have given a heads-up that they were checking out the family's numerous properties.

"No rule says we can't look in the windows." Kerri climbed the steps to the large porch. It was impossible to see through the stained glass of the front door. She walked from window to window and peered inside. The plantation shutters were open. The rooms beyond were fully and elegantly furnished. No lights on. No sign of occupancy. Falco was right: too bad they couldn't go inside.

"No one has gone through this door in weeks," he said, drawing her attention to him.

She joined him at the door, and he pointed to the knob. "See all that pollen? We haven't had a high enough pollen count to do that since the last week of May. I'm guessing the cleaning service only comes out every month when the house is empty."

The guy was full of surprises. "You keep a watch on the pollen count?"

He tapped the side of the nose. "Plays hell with my allergies."

"Let's check out the other doors."

"Good idea, Devlin." He grinned. "I wish I'd thought of it."

Kerri ignored his dig.

It was the same at the other four entrances to the house. A heavy layer of dust and pollen sat on the antique bronze knobs or handles. No sign that anything had been disturbed beyond the windows through which they could see.

After a walk around the property, they loaded into his Charger once more and headed back to the city. They had already checked the offices and rental properties owned by the Abbotts. All were occupied.

"It's possible there's something under a different name," Kerri said, more to herself than to her partner.

"We could check under Ben Abbott's mother's maiden name." Falco pulled out his cell phone. "I'll have my contact in property records check it out."

Kerri scanned the passing landscape. Sela Abbott was laying low somewhere. She had resources, and Birmingham was a big town. She could be anywhere. "Where are we headed?"

"We didn't get back to the Abbott house to look for that weapon."

They'd meant to get back there yesterday, but then Diana had called. Another look around the crime scene was essential with the discovery that Sela Abbott had purchased a handgun.

"I should finish going through the rooms upstairs as well." Kerri hadn't gotten past the mother-in-law's room on Sunday. Sometimes the most complex answers were found in the simplest of places.

Diana had called first thing this morning to let Kerri know Amelia hadn't come home last night. She had, however, sent a text this morning saying she was okay and at work.

Kerri wanted to be grateful for that, but mostly she wanted to shake her niece. What the hell was she doing? Everyone who loved her was walking around on eggshells for fear of wrecking her future by showing up at the firm in person to demand some sort of explanation for her out-of-character behavior. Their calls to Bellemont's investigator, Neal Ramsey, had gone unreturned. Who the hell knew what was going on with that guy? Bellemont insisted he was completely trustworthy, but Kerri wasn't convinced.

It would be so easy to set the whole issue aside and just call it Amelia attempting to prove she was an adult now. But the connection to Sela Abbott prevented Kerri from being able to let it go so easily.

Why the hell did daughters have to be so nerve racking?

———

Abbott Crime Scene
Botanical Place, Mountain Brook

The Abbott home smelled of death. It had been closed up for a week now, and the odors related to the killings had seeped into the walls and the upholstery. The air was thick with it. Part of it was the idea of knowing what took place within these walls. The images that replayed instantly triggered memories of the smells from that first visit.

So far no one had pushed for release of the property, which was a good thing. Generally, every attempt was made to release a residence as quickly as possible, but since no one who had resided in this house was still around, there was no hurry.

They started outside, checking behind, under, and between shrubs before going inside. The garage was easy enough. Ben Abbott hadn't been a DIY kind of guy when it came to maintenance around the house, so there was little to sort through. The downstairs living areas took additional time.

Finally, they moved upstairs. Kerri took the mother-in-law's space while Falco checked the nursery.

Jacqueline Rollins had liked pink. Most of the clothes hanging in her closet were either pink or had pink somewhere in the fabric. She preferred shoes with practical flat heels. She owned only two handbags: a white one and a brown one. At the time of her death, she had been using the white one.

Her wallet contained a photo of her and Sela—the first one they'd found of the two together. Some cash but no credit cards. An insurance card and a state ID card. No driver's license.

Kerri checked every shelf and drawer once again. Between the mattress and box springs and beneath the bed. She moved to the first of the two bedside tables. Nothing in the drawers beyond the usual tissues, flashlight, and typical personal items. She checked the bottoms of drawers and beneath the table itself just as she had last time.

So far nothing had been overlooked in previous searches, certainly not a handgun. She moved on to the table on the other side of the bed.

Nothing helpful in the drawers.

She shifted the lamp and clock radio from the top and settled both on the floor, then removed the drawers. Nothing under either.

She peered into the empty cavities of the table. When she would have called it done, she looked up again. Something caught her attention. A notebook or book was taped to the underside of the tabletop. How had she missed that last time?

Kerri reached inside and pulled it out. Not a book. A small scrapbook or mini-album. Maybe six inches by ten.

She sat down cross-legged on the floor and opened it.

The first pages showed a young woman in various places. One appeared to be an apartment; others were outside. A yard. Trees. Nothing unusual. Kerri studied the woman's face. The younger woman appeared to be Sela's mother at what looked like twenty or twenty-five years of age. She frowned, looked more closely. Maybe not. The features weren't right somehow.

Kerri moved to the next page in the mini-album. Some of the areas where shots were taken looked vaguely familiar. Judging by the cars in one photo, the time frame would have been in the late seventies, maybe early eighties. If she could see a license plate—

"Devlin!"

Clutching the album, Kerri got to her feet and went in search of her partner. "Where are you?"

"The kid's room."

Nursery. She headed in that direction. The smell of death was stronger here. The crimson stains on the carpet reminded anyone who looked that a life-and-death struggle had played out in that spot, culminating in the death of Jacqueline Rollins.

"What'd you find?"

Standing at the crib, he gestured inside it. "Did you do this?"

Kerri moved to his side and peered at the white bedding with its pink unicorns. The quilt had been drawn back and the stuffed unicorn, along with the pillow, pushed out of place. She shook her head. "I looked each time we walked through the scene, but I didn't touch anything. I didn't see any reason to."

"Me either," Falco confirmed. "So unless one of the other cops did this after we left, someone else has been in the house."

"You check with the security company, and I'll call Officer Matthews. She was here when the house was locked up that night." Beyond the second pass by the crime scene investigators—and Matthews would have been with them—no one else had been in the house except her and Falco. Well, and Gibbons, but Kerri had been with her at the time.

Matthews answered on the first ring. Her response to Kerri's question was exactly what she had expected. Nothing in the crib had been disturbed. The struggle had taken place on the other side of the room, and the crib had appeared untouched. No reason to go there.

In truth, no one wanted to poke around in the crib, knowing that the pregnant mother was missing.

Falco walked back in the room. "Someone was in the house Sunday night. If it wasn't Tanya or you, then we need to find out if one of the parents was here, because it damned sure wasn't me."

As far as anyone knew, the only other person who had the code and wasn't confirmed dead was Sela Abbott.

Except, in view of Marcella Gibbons's little fling, maybe Neal Ramsey.

"We need the crime scene folks to come dust this room and the security pads for prints." Kerri's heart started to pound. "Damn it. We need to know what was hidden under this pillow and comforter." She wanted to kick herself for not looking. She'd done this long enough to know better than to ignore the most innocent of situations.

Falco made the call. Kerri backed away from the crib for fear of accidently depositing some trace evidence.

"They'll be here in half an hour," her partner announced.

Kerri nodded. "Good."

"What've you got there?"

Kerri held up the mini-album she'd completely forgotten she was clutching. "I found this stashed beneath the bedside table in the mother's room. I can't believe I missed it before, but apparently I did."

Falco took the album and flipped through the pages.

"I think that's Jacqueline when she was maybe in her twenties. She looks a lot different, but that was a long time ago." Kerri shrugged.

"There's not enough recognizable background in the photos for me to determine where she is."

Falco studied photo after photo. "She's here."

Kerri leaned toward him and looked at the photo that had stopped him. "How can you be sure?"

"You see that shop right there?"

"I do, but I don't recognize it."

"That's over in Irondale. It was a pharmacy. Had a soda fountain where you could get ice cream cones."

"You can't really see the name of the place. It's behind her."

"I grew up in that area. I know this place."

"I thought you grew up in Montgomery."

He shook his head. "We didn't move there until high school." He tapped the photo. "This is Irondale."

"So the mother lived here first." Her gaze connected with Falco's. "Maybe that's why Janelle came to Birmingham. There could have been family friends. Distant relatives."

"It would sure as hell help if we could find someone who remembers Janelle coming back."

If only, Kerri mused.

Falco flipped a few more pages. He stopped and tapped another photo. "That's the missing wife."

Kerri studied the photo. He was right. She hadn't gotten that far before he'd called her to the nursery. "This must be her older sister, Janelle, and the mother, I think." It was the first photo of the three women together they had found. Again, the mother looked so *different* it was difficult to say for sure. Time and poor health changed people.

When Falco turned to the next page, something fell to the floor. Kerri bent down and picked up a small envelope. The kind purchased in a set with matching stationery. She turned it over. The envelope was addressed to Jacqueline Rollins in San Diego. Postmarked in

Birmingham. Janelle had been the sender. The return address was the apartment complex where she'd lived.

Kerri opened the envelope and pulled out the letter. It was a single page folded in half. In the fold was a small photograph of Janelle and a man who appeared a few years older than her. Instinct nudged Kerri, but it was difficult to say for sure if she'd ever seen him. He wasn't looking directly into the camera lens. "Does he look familiar to you?"

Falco shook his head. "You?"

"A little. I've seen him, I think." Recognition sucker punched her. "Holy shit, I think this is Theo Thompson."

Falco took the photo from her.

"Bear in mind," she reminded him, "this was—what—at least fifteen years ago? And that's a pretty small photo with him looking away from the camera." She shrugged. "Maybe someone said something to him." Or he was uncomfortable having his photograph taken with a woman who wasn't his wife.

Son of a bitch. Sela Abbott had been right when she'd told Bellemont this was about her sister and Theo Thompson.

"Well, I'll be damned," he said. "I think you might be right."

Kerri turned her attention to the letter.

Momma & Sela,

He is the one! We're still keeping the news a secret from his father—he worries he won't approve. Whether he does or not we're getting married. Maybe we'll come to San Diego so the two of you can be a part of the celebration!

Love,

J

Fire lit in Kerri's belly. "We need to confirm this is him." She tucked the photo into her jacket pocket. "This might just go a long way in gaining a little cooperation from Thompson."

He'd sure as hell evaded their every attempt to interview him so far.

"Since Bellemont has fessed up about knowing the older sister, maybe he can confirm what we suspect." Falco shrugged. "It would definitely help if the guy was looking at the camera."

"It's him." But they had to be sure. "We can start with Bellemont," Kerri agreed, "assuming we can catch him."

Her cell vibrated with an incoming text, and Kerri checked the screen. *Amelia.* Kerri couldn't decide if she was relieved or pissed off at hearing from her.

Do you believe the top level of Birmingham PD can be trusted?

Kerri made a face. What kind of question was that?

Yes. You know you can talk to me. Your mom is worried. I'm worried. I'm calling you.

Can't. In meeting at work. I'm good, I promise. The subject came up in the meeting. I was curious. Gotta go!

If Amelia was at work, then she was okay, wasn't she?

Kerri sent Diana a text and let her know about the exchange; then she decided to check in with Tori on the way to Bellemont's office.

Not with a text. A call. She needed to hear her daughter's voice.

42

12:30 p.m.

The Country Club
Country Club Road, Mountain Brook

Keith climbed out of his car, leaving the door open for the valet. Meetings at the country club were his least favorite ones. No one came here anymore except members of the old Birmingham guard. The ones like the man he was to meet, who had run things for so long he couldn't grasp the concept that his reign was nearing an end.

Younger men, the next generation, like Lewis York and Theo Thompson, were taking over. Ben would have been one of those coming up. He had possessed the power of the family name and the old money as well as lots of new. He could have been governor. He could have been anything he wanted.

But he had wanted his freedom. He had wanted the challenge of creating something no one else had. The funny thing was—Keith stared at the aging building representing power in this city—Ben had never cared about the money or the power. When his software development company had skyrocketed, he had been pleased, of course, but it had never been his priority.

No matter that he had left years ago, landing on the other side of the country, this place, the unescapable pull of the family umbilical cord, had dragged him back.

Now he was dead.

Keith walked through the double doors, where he was greeted by the coat check attendee. Keith didn't slow his forward momentum since he didn't have a coat to check—or a hat or anything else.

What he would more than anything like to check was the guilt weighing down on his shoulders.

He should never have allowed this to start. He should have found a way to stop it.

There was no way as far as he could see to make this right. The only thing he could do at this point was keep trying to find her . . . and let this damned nightmare play out.

Daniel Abbott waited for him at his usual table. Men like Daniel had a table in this hallowed place. There were no designated tables for people like Keith. Not that he cared. He hated this political part of the world in which he was forced to operate. In a place like Birmingham, you were either in or you were out. To be in, you had to play especially nice with the folks in power.

Like the Abbotts and the Thompsons and the scumbag Yorks.

Keith pulled out the only other chair at the table for two. "Traffic was heavy," he mentioned since he was fairly certain he was a minute or so late.

"I'm glad you had the time to see me. What will you have?"

The old man was already nursing a scotch on the rocks.

"Water for me," Keith said. Though he would love nothing more than to drown the guilty voices nagging at him, that could not happen right now. Not in this place or in the presence of this man. Rare was the day he dared to imbibe. Too many things could go wrong. A client could need him.

There was never a good time for him to be anything less than stone-cold sober.

Daniel gestured to the waiter standing by, and Keith's glass was quickly filled with icy water. He doubted he would ever understand the subtle sign language in which these waiters and waitresses were obviously versed.

"I genuinely hope you have an update for me." Daniel sipped his scotch and waited.

Keith wished he had the sort of update Daniel wanted. What he had was more bad news. "I've had no response from any of my sources. As for Sela, it's as if she has dropped off the face of the earth."

"Except we know she hasn't. She is out there somewhere."

Keith took a long swallow of the water, hoping the cold liquid would moisten his dry throat. "I genuinely feel we're in over our heads, sir. We need to let the police handle this, and there is only one way that can happen. Those detectives must have all the information we can give them; otherwise they'll continue to operate blindly."

Daniel shook his head adamantly. "We've already shared too much. I do not want this to go any further down that path. Ben is dead. Nothing we do will bring him back. I will not have his name sullied by the bloodthirsty media. They're still showing up at my office and my home. But if *she* had anything to do with his death, I want to know."

"I don't believe Sela was involved." The man was stuck on that idea, and Keith couldn't adequately convince him otherwise.

"Your misplaced loyalty has not persuaded me, Keith. Unless you can prove this scenario to me, then we must continue to operate under the assumption that her involvement is not only possible but probable."

Keith wanted to argue, but he couldn't. The police had discovered her purchase of a car. They had also uncovered her illegal purchase of a handgun—one the same caliber as the murder weapon. No doubt Sela now fell firmly into the suspect category. What a mess.

"I'll do all I can. But I'll tell you now, I don't expect to find anything new."

"Hire another investigator, for God's sake."

For men like Daniel Abbott, this was a simple matter. But in the real world, trusted investigators were hard to find. Right now Keith would love to hear from the one on his payroll. Ramsey had gone dark on him. Keith didn't know what was going on with the man, but he had a very, very bad feeling.

"We've talked about this before," Keith ventured, "and you said Ben had not spoken to you about any concerns or worries he had in regard to Sela. Have you remembered something that you had perhaps forgotten?"

Daniel drained his glass, then leveled a glare at Keith. "Are you asking me if I conveniently forgot a discussion with my son about his wife?"

Keith met his glare without wavering. "Yes. That's what I'm asking."

Another of those subtle hand signals, and the waiter whisked the empty glass away and quickly returned with another sporting more of that expensive liquid sunshine.

The older man indulged in a long swallow, then placed his glass back on the white-linen-covered table. "Two weeks ago we had a short discourse regarding Sela and my concerns."

Keith had known the old bastard had been lying to him when he'd denied such a conversation.

"Ben said that he had everything under control and that I should not trouble myself with worries about his wife."

"He was right," Keith announced, renewed fury blazing inside him. "Obviously, Ben was the one who should have been worried."

"Find her," Daniel said. "She's out there. I feel it in my gut. Find her, and bring her to me. I will know why my son had to die. Bear in mind, Mr. Bellemont, that I always have a backup plan—it is one I hate to use, but if you fail, I will not hesitate."

Keith gave him a nod; then he stood. There was nothing more to say. He was afraid the old fool had already set that backup plan in motion, which was in all likelihood the very reason the entire situation had gone to hell.

He turned and walked out of the house of cards that had stood as a symbol of greatness in the city for far too long.

It was all about to come crashing down.

43

1:00 p.m.

York, Hammond & Goldman Law Firm
North Twentieth Street

Amelia had sent a text to Diana saying that she was at work. She'd said the same to Kerri. But Diana could not take it anymore. She needed to see her daughter with her own eyes. She hadn't seen her since Sunday night.

Downtown parking was always at a premium. Luckily, she found a spot on the same block as the firm. Not that she minded a nice walk, especially in this pleasant weather, but she didn't want to get all sweaty. She already felt a little embarrassed by her jazz pants and tee. She should have taken time to change rather than taking off on impulse.

She had been here once before. The lobby always threw her off balance. The marble floors and towering ceiling. It really was a beautiful place. She had asked Amelia if the offices upstairs were as pretty, and she had raved about how luxurious the entire place was. The conference rooms. The law library. Diana drew in a deep breath. This was the life her daughter would have. Elegance and affluence. Not struggling from paycheck to paycheck like her parents had most of their twenty-year marriage.

The receptionist looked up as Diana approached. "May I help you?"

Diana smiled. "I'm here to see my daughter, Amelia Swanner. She's an intern with the firm."

The receptionist frowned. "I don't think she's here today. Let me check." She picked up the phone and pressed a series of keys.

There had to be a mistake. Amelia had said she was here. Surely she wouldn't fail to show up for work and risk the future she so badly wanted.

When the receptionist placed the receiver back in its cradle, she said, "Mrs. Swanner, please have a seat. Miriam Foster, our personnel director, will be down in just a moment to speak with you."

Fear welled inside Diana. "Is something wrong?"

"I'm sorry, Mrs. Swanner, I'm afraid I don't know."

"I'd like to see Mr. York," Diana blurted, desperation rising inside her. He could help her. They had been friends for all those years she'd given his daughter private dance classes. He'd stopped by her house just the other day.

"I'm afraid Mr. York isn't in the office just now."

Diana's heart sank.

An elevator on the other side of the lobby dinged, and the doors opened.

"There's Ms. Foster now. I'm sure she can explain everything."

Diana couldn't move. She told herself to walk toward the other woman to find out what was going on, but her body refused to cooperate. As the woman approached Diana, the words *everything is fine* echoed in her head. Of course everything was fine.

"Mrs. Swanner." Foster smiled one of those polite, not real smiles. "Let's step over here"—she gestured to the seating area—"a moment so we have some privacy."

Diana glanced at the receptionist and then did as the other woman asked. "What's going on?" she finally found the wherewithal to ask. "Amelia should be here. I—"

"Frankly, Mrs. Swanner, we don't know where Amelia is, but she isn't here. We thought she had quit, which as you know will not look good on her resume."

The woman was still talking, but Diana interrupted her. "What do you mean you thought she quit?"

"Mrs. Swanner, Amelia hasn't been here since last Friday."

44

2:30 p.m.

York, Hammond & Goldman Law Firm
North Twentieth Street

"You can't go in there half-cocked, Devlin."

Kerri stared at her partner. When had she become the one on the edge and her partner the steadying force?

"All I want to do is find out what's going on. We were at his house last night. He asked me if I was Amelia's aunt. He could have told me something was wrong. That she hadn't shown up for work all week."

Saying the words out loud only made her angrier. When Diana had called and then calmed down enough to explain what was going on, Kerri had been cool and levelheaded. There had to be a reasonable explanation.

But sometime between hearing the news from Diana and the fifth time her call to Amelia had gone unanswered, Kerri had lost control.

Diana was right. Something was wrong. Really wrong.

Maybe York, despite his claims, had used his charm and intellect to convince Amelia it was okay to spy on Sela. That it wasn't wrong—and now Amelia was in trouble.

Didn't make sense. Amelia was not that naive.

"Let's go over what we know, Devlin."

They were sitting here in his damned car parked at the curb halfway down the block from the law office, and he wouldn't shut up.

"We've been over this before."

"We have, yes," he said calmly, so calmly she wanted to punch him. "But," he argued, "we're under a lot of pressure to solve this case. Your ex is giving you hell about custody. Your daughter is pushing for her independence. Now you've got your niece going rogue. There's a lot happening, and some of those things intersect. Like your niece working for York. Bellemont telling us that York might be involved in this homicide case. Ramsey stalking Amelia and then disappearing. But you just have to back away from all that and go after this one thing. Did something happen at work to cause Amelia to quit?"

"You're right. I need to cool down and look at this one thing. Leave all the rest out of it for now." Kerri took a breath. She could do that.

"Good. All right." He reached for his door. "We'll go in together and talk to York."

"No. I want to do this alone. He might say more with only me in the room. No matter how calmly I present myself, he'll know my emotions are in a knot. If he's as overconfident as I suspect, he may try pushing my buttons if I'm alone."

Falco started to argue, but she held up her hands. "I'll be calm. Don't worry. You keep prodding the crime scene folks to give us something from the unauthorized access of the Abbott home."

"Okay, but if sirens start blazing and I see SWAT barreling down the street, I'm coming in."

He almost made her smile. *Almost.* "Deal."

Kerri climbed out of his car and headed for the law office. She focused on deep, steadying breaths. At the entrance to the lobby, she cleared her head once more and walked in.

The receptionist looked up as she approached her desk. "Welcome to York, Hammond & Goldman. How may I help you?"

Kerri showed her badge. "I'm here to see Mr. York. It's urgent police business."

"Please have a seat, and I'll call his office and see if he's available."

Kerri couldn't sit. Containing the wild mixture of worry and adrenaline long enough to be still was impossible. She wandered to the grouping of sofas and chairs and waited. She watched as the receptionist made the call and then placed the handset back in its cradle. The woman rose from her chair and walked over to where Kerri waited. She couldn't help holding her breath.

"Mr. York can see you now. Take the elevator to the eighth floor, and his assistant will be waiting for you."

"Thank you."

While she waited for the elevator, Kerri studied the numerous cameras installed for security. She imagined no one entered or left these offices without being captured on camera.

The doors opened, and she stepped into the car and selected the floor number. When the doors opened once more, another young, attractive woman waited for her.

"Right this way, Detective Devlin."

Kerri followed her along the lushly carpeted corridor, left into another corridor, and to the fourth door on the right. The woman opened the door and waited for Kerri to enter, then closed the door behind her.

"Detective Devlin." York stood behind his desk. "To what do I owe the pleasure of a second visit in the same twenty-four-hour period? I feel like Mr. Popular. Please, sit." He held up a hand. "Of course, yes. You're here about the employee roster."

"No. I'm here about my niece, Amelia."

He frowned. "Yes, we talked about her last night. At the time I wasn't aware she hadn't been in this week. Can you tell me if there was a problem with someone here at the office? I can assure you if there was, I will personally take care of the problem."

How generous. The offer almost seemed genuine.

Kerri reminded herself of all that Bellemont had told her about this man; then she softened her voice and settled into a chair. "I honestly don't know what happened. I was hoping you could tell me."

York lowered into his own chair. "I spoke with Ms. Foster, our personnel director. She talked with Amelia's colleagues here, and no one is aware of any sort of problem. They're all quite shocked that she stopped showing up. We thought she was very happy to be a part of the team."

"Is there anyone who was particularly close to her that I might be able to speak with?"

He seemed to consider the question for a moment. "Ms. Foster didn't mention anyone, but I have to say that I saw Amelia a couple of times in the lounge with Finn. Would you like me to have him come to the office? I'm sure he would be happy to speak with you. He's our intern from my old high school. He's heading off to Harvard, his father's alma mater, this fall."

"I would appreciate the opportunity to speak with him."

"Let me round him up." He stood. "Would you like coffee or water while you wait? Perhaps something stronger?"

Kerri shook her head. "No thanks."

York walked out of his office, leaving the door open. Kerri didn't have to look to know there would be cameras in all the offices as well. A minute, then two, elapsed, and she couldn't help feeling restless. She pushed out of her chair and walked to the man's extensive praise wall. His credentials and too many honors to count lined the wall. Amid all the acclamations were a few framed photos. She surveyed each. York and the mayor. York and the chief of police. York and the governor. York and Senator T. R. Thompson. York and Daniel Abbott. Anyone who was someone in Birmingham was photographed with York, shaking his hand or passing along some award.

She turned to his desk. Spotted the framed photo of the man with a young woman who looked to be around Amelia's age, most likely his daughter. Another framed photo sat next to it. In this one York was considerably younger, maybe in his early twenties. Kerri's gaze narrowed as she moved closer. She picked up the photo and stared at the second man.

A new shot of adrenaline fired in her veins. The second man in the photo looked very much like the one in the photo with Janelle Stevens . . . the one in Kerri's pocket. He was younger in this photo, but she was certain it was Theo Thompson.

When she would have replaced the framed photo where she'd found it, York walked in. He looked surprised to find her at his desk.

"I was admiring your wall of fame." She mustered up a smile. "Then I spotted this photo. Who is the man with you? He looks so familiar."

York accepted the photo from her and smiled down at it, as if remembering the day it was taken. "This is back in my college days, and that is my old friend and frat brother Theo Thompson. I'm sure you've seen him all over the news. He's following in his father's footsteps to the Alabama State Senate. Of course, he's a wee bit older now, like myself."

"That's probably why he looks familiar." Barely able to restrain the need to rush out to tell Falco she had confirmation, Kerri surveyed the wall once more. "You have quite a number of impressive awards, Mr. York."

"Just doing my job, Detective. Like you."

A young man entered the office, almost stumbling over his own feet. Tall, thin. Dressed impeccably. Dark hair. "Sorry." He righted his glasses and then extended his hand toward Kerri. "I'm Finn Garrett. You're here about Amelia? I was wondering why she hadn't come back to work. Is she all right?"

"This is actually my nephew," York said. "We're very proud of him."

Kerri shook the boy's hand, noting the two had the same nose. She should have noticed that already. "Thanks for talking to me, Finn. We actually don't know where Amelia is, and we're very worried about her.

She's been out of pocket for a few days, and now we've learned that she hasn't been coming to work. That was quite a shock to us all."

He blinked twice, three times. "Amelia did mention that she had a friend who was experiencing a bit of trouble. Maybe she's helping her."

Since he referred to the friend as *her*, Kerri asked, "Do you know which friend it is?"

He shook his head. "Sorry, I don't. We're always busy at work, so we don't have a lot of time for social conversations. I really hope she's all right. Amelia is a great intern and a really nice person. Everyone loves her."

That was Amelia. Everyone always loved her.

Kerri withdrew one of her business cards and handed it to Finn. "Could you call me if you remember anything at all she might have said that would give us some idea what's going on with her?"

"Of course." He tucked the card into the pocket of his button-down shirt. "When you find her, please tell her that we miss her."

Kerri thanked Finn and York for their help and got out of the building as quickly as possible. Falco was leaning against his car, waiting for her. He didn't ask any questions until they were inside and driving away.

"York and the others insist they don't know what happened. She just stopped coming to work. I did speak to another intern, and he said the same thing." Kerri leaned back against the headrest. "I don't like this, Falco." Her gut was in knots. This was wrong, wrong, wrong.

"We'll find her." Her partner glanced at her. "While you were in York's office, we got a callback from the crime scene tech."

"Any hits on the prints?" She doubted they would get so lucky, but she could hope. She rubbed at her temples, wished away the headache forming there.

"Sela's, Ben's, the mother's, and some others that didn't match anything in the system."

"Damn it. I was hoping for more."

He glanced at her, a grin cutting across his face. "The rushed analysis we asked for on the crib linens was a different story. They found traces of mineral oil, alkaline salts, and some kind of acid that I can't remember the name of as well as a couple different alcohols along with benzyl acetate and a vegetable oil of some type."

She groaned. "Is there something more specific all that tells us?"

He braked at a red light and turned to her. "Gun cleaner and lubricant."

"Well, I'll be damned." She shook her head. "There was a gun hidden in the crib."

"Yep, and we missed it."

"We just . . . shit."

"Yeah. We just gave the crib a pass. Like everyone else."

Kerri shook her head. "Of all the dumb-ass bad moves." She turned to her partner with her own news flash. "One good thing did come of my visit with York."

"Don't keep me in suspense, Devlin." He glanced at her as he slowed for the next intersection.

"The guy in the photo with the older sister is Theo Thompson. No question."

"You showed him the photo?"

"I didn't have to." She explained about the photo on his desk.

Falco's grin was back. "Well, kiss my ass. Maybe Bellemont isn't trying to lead us down the wrong path. He said whatever happened to Sela had something to do with Thompson and York."

"Which makes this photo evidence—sort of," she qualified. "We should take this and talk to Bellemont. Maybe if he realizes we're taking him seriously, he'll give us more. I'm certain he knows more than he's sharing."

"There's someone else we need to talk to first."

Falco didn't look at her as he rolled away from the intersection. "Who?"

"She's a friend of mine. We did some undercover work together once. She's my contact that does a little PI work on the side. You know, the one I told you had heard some things about Abbott."

She remembered. "Why do we need to talk to this person?"

"Because she knows things, Devlin."

Well, that really explained everything. "You said that before."

"Trust me."

That was the thing—she did trust him.

———

Corner of Sixth Avenue, Twenty-Seventh Street

"Her name is Sadie Cross. Her friends call her Cross because if you cross her—"

"I get the picture," Kerri grumbled. She'd lost track of the details he'd spouted off about the woman on the drive over here. What was it about this Sadie Cross that made him nervous? Maybe he and she had a thing?

Whatever the case, his friend lived in a not-so-hot neighborhood with a higher-than-average crime rate—above a pub, no less. The perfect combination for trouble. To access her place, the fire escape stairs in the alley had to be utilized. The entrance from inside the pub had been closed off long ago, according to Falco.

"So this Sadie Cross is a cop," Kerri said as they climbed the stairs.

"That's right. She doesn't talk about her work in the department, so don't bring it up."

"What's the deal with the PI gig?"

"She took over for a friend after he died."

It didn't really matter who Cross was or what she did. Kerri was desperate. She needed to find her niece, and she needed this case solved.

To that end, she waited on the landing while Falco knocked on the woman's door.

The pop of one, two, three, no wait . . . four dead bolts turning in succession sounded before the door opened. Judging by the two cameras Kerri had spotted—one at the bottom of the stairs and another at the landing—the woman knew who was coming before they knocked on the door.

In the pub, folks were already piling in for the posted four o'clock happy hour.

Falco walked through the door; Kerri followed. The place was one massive space. Very urban with exposed ductwork and a ceiling that went all the way to the roof. Metal-framed windows on three sides looked out over everything but the alley between this building and the next.

The woman, presumably Sadie Cross, closed the door and looked from Falco to Kerri.

"I said I'd talk to you." This she directed at Falco. Her voice was raspy like she'd smoked cigarettes for too many years. "Why is she here?"

Maybe Kerri should ask herself the same question. Just how desperate was she?

She thought of Amelia. Pretty damned desperate.

"You can trust her," Falco said.

Cross made a sound, a sort of disgruntled rumble. Kerri estimated her to be a couple of years older—thirty-eight, maybe. She was about the same height as Kerri, five-five or five-six, but leaner. Her hair was black, eyes were gray, and the clothes she wore were as dark as her hair. With her too-pale skin she looked like one of those anime characters who could be a hero or a criminal.

Kerri was leaning toward the criminal possibility.

"Whatever you say." Cross cut Falco a look that warned it was his head if he was wrong.

"I mentioned we're working the Abbott homicide case," he said.

"Sucks to be you." Cross wandered to a table and picked up a pack of cigarettes, tapped one out, and lit up.

"We think the wife is still alive and hiding out, but we haven't been able to find her."

"It's always best to start with the most obvious places," Cross suggested before taking a long draw from her cigarette.

If this was her expert advice, Kerri wasn't impressed. Did she think they were idiots?

"We checked all the properties owned by the Abbotts," Falco said. "We haven't located anything owned by Sela or her mother. Though we do have reason to believe the mother lived in Birmingham maybe forty or so years ago. We also think the mother may have been treated for some sort of health issue in Mexico City. This may or may not be relevant, but we're missing two years in Sela Abbott's life right after college. It's possible she and her mother were south of the border for a while, which might clear up the missing years."

Cross cut a look between them. "Sounds like there's a lot you don't know."

Falco shrugged. "Can you ever know enough?"

Kerri kept her mouth shut, but she imagined her face spoke loudly of how she felt about the woman's smart-ass retorts. How was this helpful? She and Falco would be talking about this in the car.

"Send me a text with the mother's details," Cross announced with an exaggerated sigh. "If she owned any property around here, I'll find it. I'll look into the south-of-the-border thing too."

"We already checked with the property records office," Kerri interjected. She was well versed in how to track down the details on property. In this case, the *we* was actually Falco and his friend in property records.

Cross laughed, the sound rusty, as if she rarely made it. "Look, Detective, you've done this long enough to know things aren't always where they're supposed to be."

How the hell did she know how long Kerri had done *this*?

"Whatever you can find will be useful, I'm sure," Kerri said instead of telling her to screw off.

Cross blew out a lungful of smoke. "Like I told Falco, you better watch your step. You're dealing with people who are accustomed to making whatever they want happen, no matter the cost."

"Powerful people, for sure," Kerri agreed with a fake smile.

"Scary people," Cross corrected. "Thompson and York are part of the untouchables. You mess with them, you end up dead or worse—wishing you were dead."

"Are you suggesting," Kerri countered, her hands settling on her hips in challenge, "that Sela Abbott and her family are dead because of Thompson and York?" If the woman had a point, she needed to make it instead of throwing out accusations. They needed evidence, not more theories.

Cross tapped out her cigarette in the pot of a dead plant. "I'm not suggesting anything, Detective. I'm telling you that if the murders were what they wanted, that's what happened. Making the connection to that desire or need or whatever-the-hell motive prompted the decision is your job, not mine. It's your case." She shrugged. "I'm just *suggesting* you be careful so you don't end up dead too."

Wow. "Well, okay. Thanks for the warning." She turned to Falco. She was ready to go. "Anything else you want to ask?"

More of that rusty laughter. "I told you not to waste your time or mine, Falco. She's one of them. She sees what she expects to see."

Kerri turned to the other woman, took a couple of steps in her direction. "What exactly does that mean, Cross?"

"Devlin," Falco warned.

Cross took the final step between them, putting her nose to nose with Kerri. "It means, Devlin, that you were raised up among the good working folks who never got into trouble or had really bad things happen to them. You went to school and church like a good girl, trained to be a cop under the tutelage of the old regimen. You've worked as a cop for well over a decade, been a detective for the better part of that. You see what they trained you to see. That's all I'm saying."

Kerri turned to Falco. "This has certainly been illuminating, but I think that's my cue to go."

Before Kerri could turn away, Cross gave her one more piece of advice. "Open your eyes, Devlin. You'll be surprised what you see."

45

5:00 p.m.

Thompson Building
Richard Arrington Boulevard

"Cross seems like a burnout," Kerri said frankly. She glanced over at the reception desk and the woman seated behind it who had been on the phone since Kerri announced that she and Falco needed to see Mr. Thompson. "How long does it take to determine if the guy is available?"

Falco leaned his head toward Kerri. "She's waiting for someone to tell her what to say."

"Guess so." She'd suggested they have a seat in the plush seating area, but Kerri had decided to stand as a reminder that her time was short.

"Cross is complicated," Falco said. "Not exactly a burnout."

"How does she stay in good graces with the department with an attitude like that?" The woman was seriously jaded.

"I think maybe they're afraid to cut her loose."

Kerri turned to him. "Afraid?"

He shrugged in that guy sort of nonchalant way. "Like I said, she knows stuff."

"Detectives." The receptionist smiled in their direction.

Kerri headed for her desk, hopeful their luck with interviewing Theo Thompson was about to change.

The woman's smile faded as they reached her. "I'm afraid Mr. Thompson is still in a meeting across town. Would you like to leave a message for his assistant?"

"No," Kerri said with a faux smile. "We'll wait." She turned around and marched back to the seating area. Falco did the same.

The receptionist got back on the phone.

"Some senator he's going to make," Falco said. "You can't ever talk to him."

"It's scary how much we think alike," Kerri noted.

Falco chuckled. "Great minds."

The receptionist stood, and this time she walked over to where they waited. "Mr. Thompson's chief of staff, Mrs. Thompson, is in. She is happy to speak with you. She's waiting in the small conference room, if you're agreeable."

"We can do that," Kerri said without hesitation. Of course, she'd already spoken to the wife and come away with the idea that the woman didn't like Sela Abbott. Maybe Kerri would give her something to really dislike this time.

The receptionist led the way across the lobby and to the left beyond the open doors to a large meeting or conference room. The final door at the end of the corridor stood open, and she paused and gestured for them to go in.

Falco thanked the receptionist and followed Kerri inside. Mrs. Thompson waited at the table that held court in the center of the room. Like everything else in the building, the room had an air of vintage elegance, not unlike the lady who stood as they approached.

"What a surprise to see you again. How can I help you today, Detectives?"

Kerri said, "We still have questions about the Abbott case."

"Of course. Please sit. If you'd like water or some other refreshment, let me know. The Thompsons have always been supportive of the BPD. We like to help anyway we can. We donate generously every year."

Kerri took the nearest chair as Mrs. Thompson resumed her own. Falco pulled out a chair next to Kerri.

"Has Ben's wife been found? We've all been praying for her safe return."

Kerri would just bet she had been praying. Apparently the lady had changed her tune about Sela, or maybe she'd decided that sharing her disdain was not in her best interest. "Not yet, I'm afraid."

"We've tried several times to meet with Mr. Thompson," Falco interjected. "We have questions for him specifically."

Suzanne Thompson nodded. "I hope you understand that my husband is very busy just now. But I'm happy to answer whatever questions you have. You may not be aware, but I'm his chief of staff. I spent the past two decades serving as his father's chief of staff. I can assure you I'm qualified to speak on his behalf."

Kerri decided to play her ace right at the start. She removed the photo from her jacket pocket and placed it on the table in front of Thompson. "Do you know the woman in the photo?"

She didn't have to look at Falco to know he would be surprised by her move. But not nearly as surprised as Suzanne Thompson. Her face drained of color, and she looked exactly as if she'd seen a ghost.

"I'm . . . I'm not sure." She reorganized her face into one of intense concentration. "She looks vaguely familiar."

"That is your husband with her," Falco pointed out.

"Yes." The single word was like an icicle, cold, brittle, ready to slip from its precious grip on whatever edge was holding it and shatter into a million pieces.

"Perhaps she was someone from his office," Kerri suggested.

The wife continued to stare at the photograph. Her husband's arm was draped over the woman's shoulder; the woman's was wound around his waist. The scene was an obviously intimate one.

"We found it going through some old case files," Falco ad-libbed. "We thought Mr. Thompson might be able to help us identify her."

Thompson looked from Falco to Kerri. "You don't know who she is?"

"We'd really like to find out about her," Kerri said. "Do you think your husband could help us?"

"You have to understand that my husband has always been a very public figure. Simply being T. R.'s son ensured a sort of celebrity status. People are always taking their pictures with him. He probably won't recall, but I can ask him." She gestured to the photo. "May I take a picture to show him?"

"Of course."

She picked up her cell and snapped a photo, then presented a smile to Kerri. "I believe I have your card. I'll let you know what he says as soon as I've had a chance to speak with him."

Kerri stood. "Thank you, Mrs. Thompson. We appreciate your cooperation."

She rose, her face still frozen in that smile. "Always a pleasure, Detectives."

When they turned to go, Falco paused. "We drove by the house on Whisper Lake Circle. Beautiful place. It's a shame it's being torn down. There's a big old excavator sitting there, all ready to go."

Before she could stop the reaction, surprise and confusion flashed across Suzanne Thompson's face. "I think the work there has been put on hold. My husband and I still hope to purchase it from the Abbotts."

"You mean," Falco countered, "from Ben Abbott's parents? Since he's dead and his wife probably is too."

Her cheeks stained a light pink. "Let's hope that isn't the case. But we do hope to reacquire the property from whoever is in possession of it when this is over."

"Thank you again," Kerri said.

She scarcely contained herself until they were outside and across the street. "Did you see her face when she looked at that photo?"

Falco rounded the hood and met her gaze across the top of the car. "I did. That was a hell of a move, Devlin."

She opened the passenger door and slid into the seat. "I would love to be a fly on the wall and hear how Theo Thompson explains that photo."

"She's still determined to get that property back." Falco eased out into the flow of traffic.

"Let's drive by there again. There's something about that place. Something that's bigger than it being the house her mother loved."

"We need to know more about it for sure," he agreed.

"Maybe your contact at property records can do a little digging," she suggested.

"I might have to take her to dinner to make that happen."

"You free tonight?"

Falco glanced at her. "We having pizza again?"

Kerri laughed. "After we drive by Whisper Lake Circle, I'm going home. My daughter and I are making dinner to take over to Diana and Robby. They're beside themselves with worry about Amelia."

"Understandable. Can I help?"

"Yes." Kerri turned to him. "You can take your contact to dinner and get the deets on Whisper Lake Circle."

"You have my word, Devlin. I will find out everything she knows."

"I'm counting on it."

Kerri felt fairly certain the property wasn't motive for murder, but it was part of the puzzle. She just needed to know where it fit.

Maybe if she figured out this puzzle, she would find Amelia.

Sela Abbott, too, hopefully.

46

9:00 p.m.

Thirty-Third Avenue West, Ensley

"Where the hell are we going?" Jen twisted around in the seat and peered through the darkness.

This was not the kind of neighborhood you wanted to be lost in after dark. They were supposed to stay at the hotel and have room service. He'd promised her a five-star experience tonight. Then that call had come, and now they were barreling toward west Birmingham.

"This will only take a few minutes," Theo assured her. "The night is still young."

But we're not, she wanted to snap. Her biological clock and every other sort of clock she had were ticking louder with each passing day. She was tired of the games. Tired of the promises.

He slowed down considerably, as if they were approaching their destination. She scanned what she could see with the aid of the sparse moonlight. If this was his idea of keeping a low profile from now until the election was over, she was out. This was not happening. No way.

"Why couldn't you drop me off at the hotel?" She could be soaking in a glorious whirlpool tub and drinking champagne.

"I've explained already. There was no time."

This end of the street was totally dark. Not a single streetlight—at least not one that was working. He braked and turned right. The headlights flashed over a derelict house surrounded by massive trees that towered over the yard, giving the property a truly creepy feel. Another car sat next to the house. Jen couldn't tell if the car was black or dark blue.

"I am not getting out of this car." She shivered at the idea.

"No need." He patted her bare thigh. "This won't take long. Sit tight."

He climbed out, and she exhaled an impatient sigh as she watched him walk up to the house, his form cutting through the headlights. Obviously the place was abandoned. Then again, maybe not. There was that other car parked next to the house. She wasn't exactly an expert, but the car looked far too expensive to belong to anyone who lived here—unless that person was a drug dealer.

What the hell were they doing here?

Another man appeared from the side of the house where the car was parked. It wasn't until he walked through the beam of the headlights to catch up with Theo at the porch steps that Jen recognized him.

Lewis York.

Apparently, this was business.

Jen dropped her head back against the seat. "Great." She was starved. She hadn't eaten tonight. She'd wanted to save her appetite for room service.

If York dragged this out, she was going to be pissed.

Theo abruptly raised his hands and held them out stop-sign fashion. York, his face twisted in anger, pointed toward the house and said something to Theo. Were the two arguing? Just enough light reflected off the house for her to make out their faces. Holding her breath and hoping they wouldn't hear, she powered down her window and listened.

"I am always the one," York growled, "who has to clean up the messes. Your first mistake was on me, but this"—he pointed to the house again—"you are going to take care of this one. This one is on you."

"You know I can't do that," Theo argued.

"You will do it." York shook his finger in Theo's face. "Or you can kiss this election and everything else that matters to you goodbye."

Jen reminded herself to breathe while the two continued to stare at each other as if they might come to blows.

"This," Theo warned, his voice a nasty growl, "is what you do. What we pay *you* to do! Now do it!" He turned away and strode back to the car. York stared after him.

Jen powered her window up and prayed Theo wouldn't hear.

He climbed into the car and backed out of the drive. The headlights flashed over a beat-up mailbox. The reflective numbers, 1528, seared into Jen's brain. Whatever had happened back there, it was something she wasn't supposed to have seen.

She wished she could unsee it . . . unhear those words.

"Now," Theo said, his voice a little hoarse from all the shouting, "let's get back to our evening."

He glanced toward her, and she forced herself to smile. "It's about time."

He reached into her lap and took her hand into his. "We have until midnight."

And then he would run back to his wife.

Suddenly the idea of a long hot bath and champagne held no appeal. She almost asked him to take her home. But he might think it had something to do with what happened back at that house.

Deep inside she understood that calling attention to what she'd seen and heard would be a mistake.

47

9:30 p.m.

Thirty-Third Avenue West, Ensley

Mad as hell, Lewis roved his flashlight over the form huddled in the corner.

The dirty work was always left to him. He—and his father before him—had made a fortune cleaning up behind the city's elite. The work afforded Lewis the pleasure of being one of them.

But it also infuriated him at the same time. His lips tightened with that anger now.

It wasn't enough that he'd graduated alongside Theo, had taken far higher honors. No, it wasn't enough at all. His family was not as wealthy as the Thompsons or the Abbotts, but they were far more than comfortable.

Because of *this*.

Tidying up the shit the bastards left in their wake.

He crouched to a squat and peered at the current mess. Despite being bound and gagged, she was quite beautiful. Infinitely smart as well. More than a little resourceful.

Unfortunately, the latter had been her undoing.

"You took something from me."

She shook her head, sobbed, the sounds muffled by the tightly secured gag. Terror and tears glistened like diamonds in her eyes.

She was so very afraid. As she well should be. She had made a fatal mistake.

"If you tell me exactly what you did after you took it, I'll make this easier on you. Death doesn't have to be painful."

A pitiful stifled wail issued from her parched lips.

"Shhh," he soothed. "Your tears have no effect on me. They are a complete waste of energy."

He watched her for a moment longer. Her eyes blinked and spilled more of that pathetic emotion. Finally, he said, "Last chance. Tell me what I want to know so we can end this in a civil manner."

She closed her eyes and leaned her head against the wall.

He sighed. "Very well."

Lewis stood and walked to the back door. He retrieved the container he'd brought with him. He crossed the kitchen and stepped into the adjoining living room. A small sofa and an upholstered chair were perfect targets. He dashed the accelerant over both. Then he moved on to the first of two bedrooms, making a trail, dousing curtains and any other piece of furniture he found. As he made his way back to the kitchen, her grunts and wails grew louder. She understood what he was doing and that she was about to die. She could smell what was coming.

He felt no sympathy.

The bitch should have realized she couldn't get away with this ridiculous plan.

In the kitchen he pushed a mound of trash and an old blanket no doubt left by a squatter over to where she huddled. He pressed the piles in close to her before picking up his container and dousing the whole lot, including her, with the remainder of the accelerant. He dumped the plastic container onto the pile.

He backed to the door, picked up the newspaper he'd saved for this final step, and took his time wadding page after page into a nice firm ball. She wiggled and tried to scream. Sobbed frantically.

He lit the ball of paper and tossed it onto the pile mounded around her.

Then he walked away.

Another loose end tied up.

48

Thursday, June 14

8:30 a.m.

Birmingham Police Department
First Avenue North
Major Investigations Division

"I know my niece." Kerri had gone over this with the LT once already. "Amelia wouldn't do this. Something is wrong. The only way she would drop out of sight is if she was in trouble or she was protecting someone in trouble. Either way, under the circumstances, she could be in danger."

Brooks raised his hands in a sort of surrender. "I get what you're saying, Devlin."

She halted her pacing and faced him. How could he just sit there behind that desk and insist a young girl wasn't in trouble? How did she make him see this wasn't the usual ungrateful-teenager scenario?

He would not be happy if he discovered she had taken Amelia's laptop to the lab. The tech, a friend of hers, had promised to keep it off the books.

"But you know the way these things work. There is no suggestion of foul play. The only thing we know for sure is that she doesn't want to come home right now." When she would have interrupted, he held up his hands again. "On top of that, she has recently been in contact with you. Give it twenty-four more hours. If she hasn't come home, we'll move forward."

Fury rolled through her. "She could be dead in twenty-four hours."

Brooks shook his head. "What do you want me to say to that, Devlin?"

Despite her misgivings about sharing this part, she had no choice at this point. If he tried to take her off the investigation, she would fight him tooth and nail. "Amelia is an intern at York, Hammond & Goldman. Before Abbott's murder there was some animosity between him and Theo Thompson. York is Thompson's go-to guy for clearing up issues. We have reason to believe Sela Abbott befriended my niece because of her position at the firm. We're worried that's why Amelia has suddenly gone dark on us."

"You have any evidence of this conspiracy theory?"

She was wasting her time. "Tomorrow morning," she relented. "We make it official then."

"Unless she shows up," he agreed. "We will make it official tomorrow morning."

"Thanks." She didn't feel the least bit thankful, but she forced herself to say the word.

"Speaking of people who've been out of pocket, the two of you don't seem too worried about reporting in with any sort of regularity."

"You know how these investigations can be," she reminded him. "They can consume your whole life."

"Be that as it may," he cautioned, "you and Falco need to watch yourselves, Devlin. There are people who are definitely watching you. Meanwhile, I'll pass along this morning's update to the chief and the mayor."

"Yes, sir." Kerri wondered if one of the Thompsons had complained to the chief about her persistence.

You see what they trained you to see.

Cross's words of warning echoed in her brain.

She hesitated before leaving the LT's office. "Do you know a detective named Sadie Cross?"

"Now there's a name I haven't heard in a while." Brooks leaned back in his chair and studied her a moment. "Seems an odd question out of the blue. Why do you ask?"

"I heard one of the guys mention her."

He nodded. "Sadie Cross is one of those detectives no one talks about. Spent a lot of years under deep cover. Her record is like Falco's: most of it's redacted. But I do know she went a little crazy and ended up in the psych ward for a time. She's still around. I think she reviews cold cases."

"Thanks." Kerri shrugged. "I was just curious."

Brooks looked past her to the glass wall that made up the front of his office. "Your partner is out there pacing around like a caged lion. Go on. But in the future, I want to hear about new discoveries while they're still new."

"Understood."

Kerri exited the LT's office, and Falco hurried over to her. "We have to go."

"Where are we going?" She had every intention of finding a way to talk to Theo Thompson today—assuming his wife hadn't killed him. Just because he was running for senator didn't exempt him from necessary questioning.

"A house over on Thirty-Third Avenue was torched last night. There's a body."

Dread blasted her. She wanted to find Sela Abbott alive for a growing number of reasons, one being her niece. "Is it Abbott?"

"Don't know. The vic's a crispy critter, Devlin. We're on the list for calls about any unidentified female vics, so we got a call."

"Right." She followed him toward the stairwell. Until this one—the *crispy critter*, as Falco called it—was identified, it fell into the call-list category. "The victim is a woman, then?"

He shrugged. "The body's burned too badly to be sure."

Damn. "Did you learn anything about the property on Whisper Lake Circle?"

"The house was built twenty years ago. A pool was added five years later. A new roof ten years ago. Theo's old lady's parents built it. Her mother died four years ago, and it was sold. Then Abbott bought it from the most recent owners, as we know."

"I want to talk to Theo Thompson." She lowered her voice when she said the name. "He's put us off far too long already."

Falco opened the stairwell door. "I was thinking the same thing. I'm sure his wife has shown him that photo by now."

Oh yes, she and her new partner were on the same page.

Thirty-Third Avenue West

The house had stood amid a copse of trees with no close neighbors. The Ensley address was low rent for sure. According to the officers and the detective on the scene, Steve Russo, the house was a rental property, but it hadn't been lived in for months. Which made it ripe for squatters and the homeless. ID'ing the victim in a timely manner might be damned difficult without dental records.

The remnants of the house still smoldered, but the firefighters had been able to get the body out since it had only been a few feet from the back door.

"We've walked the area around the driveway and what used to be the house, but we haven't found anything that might be related to or useful in ID'ing the vic," Russo said. "We've canvassed the few neighbors down the block. Several of the houses you see are vacant. The shipping business down the street doesn't operate at night and has no video surveillance in the parking area that points in this direction. So there's no witnesses." Russo glanced at Kerri. "Maybe this is your missing person. If she was trying to lay low, this is about as low as you can go."

Kerri watched as the duo from the medical examiner's office struggled to get the bowed body into the bag. Muscles contracted in the fire, causing a curling of the body. There was no way of visually ID'ing the charred body. "Maybe. We appreciate the call, Russo."

He gave her a nod, and Kerri headed in Falco's direction. When she reached him, she suggested, "We should drive around the neighborhood and see if that blue junker Abbott bought is parked around here somewhere."

"Sure." He surveyed the ongoing activity around the property. "I'll call Daniel Abbott and see if he knows what dentist Sela used in the Birmingham area."

Kerri's brow furrowed as another thought occurred to her. "A preliminary exam by the ME will tell us if the vic is female. If that's the case and he could go a step further and determine if this victim was pregnant, that would certainly narrow things down."

"Maybe the ME can check on that ASAP so we're not wasting time."

"I'll call him," Kerri offered.

"I'll go back to Russo and see if he found anything on the owner of the house."

Kerri nodded as she put through the call to the medical examiner's office.

When she'd convinced Dr. Moore to have a look at the body as quickly as possible—which still might be Monday—she walked around the yard and considered why Sela would have been here.

Had someone been holding her in this off-the-beaten-path location? Or was she hiding here? Was this a property the Abbotts owned that hadn't shown up in the property records search?

Or had Sela Abbott bought this place the way she had the car and the gun?

Her cell phone records hadn't shown any contact with York or Thompson. No cell towers in this area had been pinged. Would she have anticipated those records would be subpoenaed? Of course she would have. Sela had been preparing for this—whatever this was—for a long time. Kerri thought of what the folks from Sela's past had told her. Solving the mystery of what had happened to her sister was her primary goal in life.

Why hadn't learning that she was pregnant tempered her desire for revenge or whatever she had planned? Pregnancy usually changed people.

Sela Abbott had hidden a handgun in the baby's crib.

Something was fundamentally wrong with that scenario.

49

1:00 p.m.

Fear trickled through Jen as she drove past the house on Thirty-Third Avenue.

It was the one from last night. The numbers 1528 were on the dilapidated old mailbox.

Official vehicles were parked in front of the burned-out house. Yellow crime scene tape was draped around it. She had heard the news. A body had been recovered from the ashes and rubble.

Someone had died in that house.

She sucked in a breath.

The house where Theo and his buddy York had argued. The one at which York had pointed and said the mess was Theo's and that he could clean it up or deal with it or something like that.

Had Theo burned the house, killing the person inside?

A choking sensation tightened inside her. She didn't want to believe he would do such a thing . . . but she had seen the two of them arguing. She had heard the heated exchange. There was no mistaking the situation. Someone or something had been in the house, and it was a problem. A big problem. York had demanded that Theo take care of it. Was it possible some homeless person had been inside—someone they hadn't known about—and that all of this was a mistake?

She didn't think so.

She turned on the next street and drove away from her new nightmare.

Life was full of coincidences. Strange things happened all the time.

But this was no coincidence. Even her need to continue believing in Theo didn't make her that blind.

She couldn't worry about that right now. She had taken the afternoon off to be with Diana. She might take tomorrow off too. Diana needed her. She was going through the worst kind of nightmare.

Jen was barely aware of the miles as she drove to Diana's house. All she could think about was the very strong possibility that Theo was the one who had set fire to that house.

The news hadn't mentioned who owned the house or the name of the victim. The victim had burned inside the house. It was very possible that they didn't know who he or she was. Wasn't it nearly impossible to identify a burned body?

She couldn't remember.

Relief flooded her when she reached Diana's house. She needed to do something to keep all this out of her head.

When Diana answered the door, Jen's heart broke. She had been crying again.

Jen hugged her. "Tell me what I can do. Anything. Name it."

Diana drew back, wrapped her arm around Jen's. "Just be with me."

They curled up on the couch, and Diana told her about how she and Robby had searched Amelia's room. Kerri and Tori had brought dinner to them last night, and Kerri had agreed to take Amelia's laptop to the lab since none of them could get beyond her password.

Jen hated to ask, but it was a reasonable question. "Did they find anything that gave you some idea of what's going on?"

Diana shook her head. "Kerri just called me. She heard from her friend at the lab. Whatever Amelia has been doing, she was really careful. Nothing on her Facebook. No weird emails or files or photos. I swear, I just don't get it. How could I have been so blind to what was happening?"

"Hey, hey, now." Jen wrapped her arm around Diana's shoulders. "You are a fantastic mother. This isn't about what you did or didn't do; this is about a choice Amelia made."

Diana nodded, but she looked far from convinced.

Jen searched her friend's face. "Have you eaten today?"

Diana looked away. "I can't eat."

"You have to eat. Come on." Jen got up and offered her hand. "You always have ice cream for the boys. Let's have ice cream, and we'll put all the ooey-gooey shit on it we can find."

Jen found the ice cream and chocolate syrup. It took some searching in the twins' room for their hidden stash of M&M's, but she found them. Pecans and sprinkles added the finishing touch.

"Oh my God." Diana stared at her concoction. "This is like a million calories."

"Maybe a million and a half," Jen teased. She dug her spoon into her bowl and brought a hunk of the amazing combination to her lips. She moaned. "I haven't eaten anything like this in twenty years."

Diana laughed sadly, chocolate rolling down her chin. "You've deprived yourself that long? Not even one lapse in willpower?"

"Never," Jen declared. She had tortured herself with exercise and starved herself of all the goodness that contained sugar or fat. And for what? So some asshole could treat her like a whore? "But that's changing today."

"Really?" Diana ate another bite. "You're going to stop being so worried about how you look?"

Jen stilled, spoon halfway to her mouth. Was she? Could she be someone different? "Yes. Yes, I am." She stuffed another spoonful in her mouth.

Diana set her spoon down. "Amelia should be here with us."

Jen covered her friend's hand with her own. "I know. It's going to be all right."

Just because Amelia worked at York's firm didn't mean she was involved in whatever Theo and Lewis were doing. And just because she had helped Sela Abbott with a fundraiser didn't mean she was missing the way the Abbott woman was.

This was all probably just some teenage bullshit.

Even as Jen told herself these things, fear tightened around her throat. She forced out the rest of the words that needed to be said to reassure her friend. "Kerri will find her."

50

2:30 p.m.

Second Time Around Auto Salvage
Ninth Avenue North

Joey Keaton didn't intend to waste his life working in a scrapyard. As soon as he paid off the loan he'd taken out to pimp out his 944, he was out of here. He'd never been a delayed-gratification kind of guy. He liked his now.

Maybe he should spend more time hanging around his aunt and those rich folks she worked for. Who knew if the Abbott woman was coming back, but that was no problem: his aunt would just move to the next big house in Mountain Brook. And even if she decided to go back into retirement, she had contacts with all those big shots.

He'd done a little landscaping for the Abbotts and a few of their neighbors. Maybe he'd start his own business. At least that way he didn't have to worry about anybody bossing him around. There was money to be made doing shit for people who were too rich, lazy, or busy to do it themselves.

George Sanders, the salvage yard's driver, barreled through the gate in the rollback. He drove straight past the office and into the back of the yard. Joey watched him go.

He did a double take. "Well, I'll be damned."

That crappy blue Plymouth Breeze was nestled on the rollback, as if she had wanted to come back home to Daddy. The car didn't look damaged. Maybe it had broken down. He wouldn't be surprised. It was basically a piece of shit. He'd told Mrs. Abbott that, but she'd said she didn't care.

Whatever. Ten K was ten K. He was happy to take the rich lady's excess cash.

He tossed aside the broom he'd been pushing around the shop and headed for the back of the yard. Usually cars that were in reasonably good condition were left behind the shop for repairs. Old Man Tate made big money flipping cars that people either didn't have the money to fix or didn't know how.

As Joey strolled past the rows and rows of crushed cars waiting for pickup, he lit a smoke and pretended he wasn't supposed to be cleaning the shop. If Tate saw him, he'd be pissed. All the more reason to have a smoke. He would just say he'd needed a break. Smoking wasn't allowed in the shop.

George had parked the rollback next to the cars lined up for crushing and unloaded the Plymouth. Damn, they were going to recycle her. Maybe the engine was kaput.

"George, my man," he said, announcing his presence. George was seventy if he was a day, and he didn't like anybody sneaking up on him. He carried a .9 mm in his coveralls. No way Joey was sneaking up on the old dude. "What's up with this one? Doesn't look like it was in a crash."

"Who knows?" He hopped down from the cab. "Somebody abandoned it in front of a guy's house. He wanted it removed."

"Damn. Maybe the engine blew or something."

"Maybe. Gotta take a leak."

George hustled toward the shop. Joey circled the Plymouth. The keys were in the ignition. He glanced around, then opened the driver's-side door. He settled into the seat. Curious, he twisted the key. The engine started.

What the hell?

He shut it off and got out. George would tell the boss if he caught Joey messing around with anything other than a damned broom. Since they were going to crush the car anyway, he yanked the keys from the ignition and stuffed them into his pocket. As he withdrew from the car the second time, he spotted something on the floorboard. Shiny. Slender.

He picked up the chain . . . no, *bracelet*. Shoved it into his pocket too.

He pushed the door closed just in time. George came around the end of the row of compacted cars.

"Tate's looking for you," he said, the air huffing and puffing out of him.

Damn, it was hell getting old. Joey did not want to turn into that.

"On my way. Just needed a smoke break." He started toward the shop but paused. "Where'd you say you picked up this piece of shit?"

"Canyon Lane off Shades Crest Road. Up on the mountain. Number fourteen. Way off the beaten path. I guess that's why they dumped it there. People are stupid. Could've brought it here and made a few bucks."

"Yeah," Joey agreed. "People are stupid."

Especially people with money.

Joey walked back to the shop.

His boss was waiting for him. "Where the hell you been? You were supposed to have this place cleaned up before three."

Tate was older than George and as mean as hell. Joey was reasonably sure if you looked in the dictionary for *junkyard dog*, you'd find Tate's picture.

"I was asking George about the Plymouth he just brought in. It's just like the one I used to have. Can't believe somebody just dumped it. Especially in the middle of nowhere. Talk about weird."

"Let me tell you something, boy," Tate said, moving closer. "In this business you learn fast to keep your nose out of other people's business. You don't ask questions. You don't talk about what we do here. You got that?"

"Yeah, yeah, I got it." Old bastard.

He swept the floor and cleaned the bathroom in under twenty minutes, and then he was out of there.

He was still cussing under his breath as he spun out of the lot. The old turd stood at the door, watching him go. He was probably cussing Joey too.

He stopped for gas and entered the address into the navigation app on his phone. Once he was back on the road, he relaxed. He thought of that detective and the card she'd given him. Maybe he'd impress his aunt for once and call this shit in. The bracelet he'd snagged out of the car had looked a little rusty, but now that he thought about it, maybe it was blood dried into the tiny links. That could be evidence. His pulse rate shot into high gear right along with the 944.

Yeah, he could be like a hero or something if he helped the police figure out this case. Angie would really be after him then.

———

3:30 p.m.

The drive took half an hour. The mountain road was curvy as hell, but that wasn't a problem for the 944. This baby hung with those curves. The road dead-ended at an old cabin. He raised up his sunglasses and peered at the number on the mailbox.

"Damn it." He'd passed the address.

The other turn was half a mile back, and it was hard to see until you'd already driven past. Since he hadn't seen any other houses and that was the only side road he'd gone by, that had to be it.

He turned around and drove back in the direction he'd come, this time a hell of a lot slower. He made the left turn, and there was the mailbox. He glanced at the numbers painted on. Yep. This was the place. He drove along the narrow gravel road. The cabin sat a quarter of a mile back in the woods. This one was an upgrade from the one at the end of the road.

He parked and got out of the car. The place was damned quiet. He climbed the steps and crossed to the front door. He peered through the door and then the windows lining the porch. No lights on inside, but it was furnished and clean. Somebody lived here at least part time. He knocked hard on the door just in case someone was in there. No answer.

Worked for him. He wanted to have a look around. Maybe the chick was here. Or maybe her body was here. He shuddered. Damn, that was cold.

When he'd walked the yard and the tree line, he approached the only other structure, a shed. Nothing there either.

He didn't find anything with a name on it. Shit. He should have checked the mailbox. There might have been mail inside.

As he walked back to the front of the cabin, he fished out his wallet and retrieved the detective's card. He called her cell. The call went to her voice mail.

"Hey, Detective Devlin. I think I might have some information that would be useful to your investigation."

He left the details as he headed for his car. "I'll be waiting to hear from you."

He'd been watching the news. There was a reward involved. This would probably be the first big break in the case.

By this time tomorrow his handsome mug might be on the news.

51

4:00 p.m.

"Just be really careful," Kerri urged her daughter. "Keep the fire extinguisher close to the stove. When I get home, we'll go see Diana."

As she ended the call with her daughter, a chime told her she had a voice mail. She hadn't heard the notification for an incoming call.

"Tori's cooking tonight?" her partner wanted to know.

"Yes," Kerri admitted, "and I'm terrified." She pressed the phone to her ear and listened to the voice mail.

She hoped the call was something useful. This day had given them shit, and the situation with Amelia had made bad matters worse.

The voice that drifted from her phone had her heart beating faster. Of all the people she'd anticipated would come through with useful information, this guy was at the bottom of her list. "That was Keaton." She turned to Falco. "He says the blue Plymouth showed up at the salvage yard this afternoon. He knows where it was picked up."

"Did he say where?"

"He didn't. I'm calling him back."

The call went to voice mail. She tried once more before moving on. "Let's go to the salvage yard. If the car is there, we'll call the CSI folks to do their thing."

Falco took the next exit and turned around. If the salvage yard was closed before they arrived, the owner would just have to come back and open up for them. They knew Sela had purchased the car. There could be evidence inside of where she'd been and who might be with her.

By the time they were across town, Kerri's nerves were frayed, and Second Time Around was indeed closed, but the owner was still in the office. He opened the gate and ushered them inside before closing it once more.

Kerri introduced herself and Falco; they showed their badges.

"What can I do for you, Detectives?"

"We're looking for Joey Keaton," Falco said. "Is he available?"

"He left at three, lazy little shit."

Falco raised his eyebrows at Kerri. She moved on to the part that really mattered. "A 1996 Plymouth Breeze, blue in color, was brought to your yard this afternoon. We need to see that vehicle. It may be part of an ongoing investigation."

Tate shook his head. "Don't have a Plymouth Breeze. Didn't have no blue car come in today."

Though he met her gaze with no fear, he was lying. The subtle shift of his attention to the right as he spoke told the tale.

"Are you sure?" Kerri countered. "Maybe you were out or busy and didn't notice."

Tate folded his arms over his chest. "I know everything that happens here. That's why I'm the boss."

"I'm sure you won't mind allowing us to have a look around, boss," Falco spoke up.

"Actually, I would mind. I'm going home. I'm already closed. I told you we don't have one, but if you think you need to see for yourself, you can come back in the morning and have a look."

"I'm afraid this won't wait until morning, Mr. Tate." Kerri folded her arms over her chest, matching his stance.

"I guess you'll have to get yourself one of them warrants, then."

Well, hell. Her mind instantly calculated the time required to do so. "We can do that if you insist."

"I do." He gestured to the gate. "You'll need to wait outside until then. We're closed."

Frustrated but with no other choice, they climbed back into the Charger and parked outside the gate. Tate locked up once more and walked back to his shop.

"Asshole," Kerri muttered.

She tried Keaton again. Voice mail. Damn it. "He said he'd be waiting to hear from me. Something must have happened."

"Maybe the *boss* ran him off so he could close up," Falco suggested. "We might as well get some food while we wait for this thing to happen. There's a Jack's across the street."

"Whatever you want." She couldn't care less about food at the moment. "I'll hang around here and call in the request. Maybe Keaton will come back."

"I can do that while you go, if you'd prefer."

Kerri shook her head. "I'm not moving until I search this place."

"I'll be back in five." He climbed out of the car and headed across the street.

Kerri climbed out as well. She wanted to make the call standing in plain sight of the office beyond the chain-link fence and gate. While she waited for the callback about the warrant, she surveyed what she could see of the salvage yard. Keaton had absolutely no reason to make that call to her unless what he said was true.

The car was here, and she wasn't going anywhere until they were allowed to have a look.

Falco returned with burgers, fries, and colas. The lunch of hero cops everywhere. He ate his fast and completely. She nibbled. Sipped at her drink. She wasn't really hungry. She hadn't been since school let out and Tori started being mad at her all the time. Then her ex had launched the legal stuff. With the Amelia situation added to that and this case, food wasn't a priority.

"How's your sister?" he asked.

Kerri nibbled on a fry. "She's hanging in there, trying to get right with the idea that Amelia would just disappear like this." It felt wrong. And terrifying.

"I passed off tracking down the history on the house that burned to Cross since my girl at property records is out sick today."

"Whatever it takes," Kerri said. She wasn't going to complain about his tactics as long as no laws were broken and they got the answers they needed.

They ate in silence. The minutes crept by like hours. Whatever Old Man Tate was doing in there, he hadn't left his office, at least not beyond the view of the front window.

A ping from her cell signaled a text had arrived. She checked the screen. It was the warrant. Two unis were en route with the paper.

"We got it." Kerri called Tate. He answered, but he took his time, allowing the phone to ring three times. "We have the warrant, sir. Open the gate, please."

Within five minutes they were walking the salvage yard, which was a good deal larger than she'd estimated. This was going to take a while. Backup arrived, and they split up and moved in a grid pattern to ensure they didn't miss anything.

Just over an hour later it was clear the blue Plymouth in question was not on the lot.

Kerri looked for a rear exit. Maybe he'd had the vehicle moved while they waited for the paper. Falco was giving Tate hell. Kerri surveyed the area again, looking for anything they had missed.

Her gaze landed on the compacting machine. She walked the twenty or so yards to the machine and did some looking. Sure enough, beyond the bars that prevented a person from accidentally getting caught in the process was something blue.

She strode back to where she'd left Falco questioning Tate.

"What's in the compactor, Mr. Tate?"

He looked surprised that she had thought to ask. "I have no idea. My employee George Sanders does the crushing."

"Then I guess you'd better get Mr. Sanders over here, because there's something blue in that crusher, and my money is on the Plymouth."

Two hours were required to round up Sanders. The Plymouth was in the crusher, and both men claimed Keaton had brought it in.

Kerri needed to find Joey Keaton.

52

Friday, June 15

9:00 a.m.

Birmingham Police Department
First Avenue North
Major Investigations Division

Kerri collapsed into the chair behind her desk.

It was done.

Amelia was officially listed as missing . . . an endangered-adult alert had gone out.

"They're going to the carrier with a warrant for Amelia's cell phone records," Kerri announced. "We need some idea of where she is. We needed it yesterday, damn it."

Falco nodded. "That's a step in the right direction, but the problem is it'll take even more time to get those phone records the usual way. It might be Monday or Tuesday before that happens."

Kerri closed her eyes. "Damn it, Falco, tell me something new, will you?" Then she looked at her partner, hope daring to swell inside her. "You have a better option?"

"Cross can go a different route and have those cell phone records as early as tomorrow."

Of course she could. Cross obviously didn't play by the rules. At the moment, Kerri didn't care how they got them as long as they got them. "Make it happen."

"You got it."

Kerri listened to the low rumble of Falco's voice as he made the call. This morning she felt as if she were in a black tunnel and couldn't find her way to the light. The murders at the Abbott home had taken place nine days ago, and they still had nothing concrete. No true suspects, though they did now have a plethora of persons of interest and fragments of information and leads that all appeared to circle around and come back to the same place.

Sela Rollins Abbott.

Kerri rubbed at her forehead. She'd gotten home really late last night, and she'd barely had a minute with Tori this morning. Her daughter had gone to breakfast with the family of a friend, and then they were heading to the mall. Kerri had watched out the window as her little girl had loaded up with Sarah Talley and her mother.

The good news was that Tori had completely understood Kerri's need to ask a slew of questions. They had both watched how Amelia's MIA status was affecting her parents. On top of that, Kerri's attorney had called and said that the hearing regarding Tori's custody was on Tuesday. Evidently, Nick was dead serious about going after primary custody. His own attorney had pulled some strings to get such an early date on a typically crowded docket.

Great. Just great. But Kerri wasn't so worried about the hearing now. Tori wasn't trying to escape her mother. She would speak the truth to the judge and with the innocent impartiality of a child who loved both her parents. As Kerri's attorney had suggested, the whole thing was just a pain in the ass.

Her cell vibrated. She picked it up without even looking at the screen. "Devlin."

"Detective, this is Officer John Brashier. We have a gunshot victim over here on Shades Crest Road. The victim is male, but I thought I should call you anyway because your card is in the man's wallet. Name's Joseph Keaton."

"Is he alive?" Hope dared to make an appearance.

"No, ma'am. Looks like he's been dead a little while."

Son of a bitch! "I'll be right there."

His own call finished now, Falco looked to her. "Where we going?"

Kerri stood. "Shades Crest Road. Joey Keaton is dead."

Well, now she understood why he hadn't answered her calls.

———

Keaton's red Porsche sat behind a long-closed gas station. He was in the driver's seat, his body slumped forward. He had one bullet wound to the left temple. No exit wound. Probably a small-caliber pistol not unlike the one used on Ben Abbott and Jacqueline Rollins. The scene might have passed for a suicide except the weapon used was missing, and Joey Keaton had been right handed. She had watched him write out his statement the first time they met.

Kerri thought of the gun that had been hidden in the Abbott nursery and how it had disappeared on Sunday night.

"If Sela Abbott is still alive and we indulge the theory that she killed her husband and mother," Kerri said to her partner, "this would seem to indicate she's trying to tie up loose ends."

Frankly, Kerri still had an issue with the idea of her killing her mother. Then again, maybe Sela was just tired of taking care of her. The ME's call about finding no cancer or anything else wrong with the woman nudged Kerri. There was something more to that chapter in this story.

The same went for the husband. If he was helping Sela with her search for the truth, as Bellemont had suggested, why would she kill him?

"If that's what's going on, she's a little behind the curve," Falco commented as he surveyed the area around the defunct gas station. "Keaton gave us a heads-up about the car. Why kill him now?"

"Maybe he was blackmailing her for more money?" Kerri could see Keaton pushing the envelope that way.

There were no operating businesses on either side of the station or across the street. The chance that anyone had witnessed the shooting was about zero.

Kerri went around to the passenger side of the vehicle and opened the door. With her gloved fingers she picked up a key from the console. She held up the single key on the clasp, the Chrysler logo impossible to miss. "What you want to bet this belonged to the car flattened in that compactor?"

The car was now at the lab in hopes of finding some damned clue about what Sela Abbott had been doing while the vehicle was in her possession. The expectations for results were dim, but they had to try.

"That's a bet you would win."

"Let's check his pockets."

The two front pockets of his jeans had the usual. Loose change and a lighter. Nothing in the back pockets since Officer Brashier had already removed the wallet. Falco pulled a pack of Marlboros from the shirt pocket, tucked his fingers deeper inside.

"Wait. Got something here."

He fished out what looked like a gold chain of some sort. He spread it in the palm of his gloved hand. "Bracelet."

The S charm on the bracelet had Kerri's anticipation climbing to the next level. There was dirt or something on part of the chain. "What's that? Dirt or blood?"

They both looked closer.

"Looks like blood to me," Falco said, confirming her suspicions.

While Falco bagged the bracelet, Kerri checked Keaton's cell phone. He or the shooter had meticulously erased his call and text logs. She checked the map app in hopes it would give her something. Bingo.

"When he called me," she said to her partner, "he had just taken a trip to this location." She held the screen up where Falco could see it. "Maybe that's where the Plymouth was picked up."

She sure as hell didn't believe the story the old men at the salvage yard had given her. Keaton would not have called to tell her about the car if he'd been trying to hide it.

"I say we take a ride, Devlin."

"Maybe we'll get lucky." She wasn't holding her breath, but she could hope.

The crime scene investigator arrived and started his work. As soon as the ME—not Moore, but another of his associates—was on the scene, Kerri asked about time of death. He estimated time of death at between five and eight last evening, which meant he had taken the bullet not long after leaving that voice mail for Kerri.

Once the ME had taken the body away, she and Falco left the scene in the hands of Brashier and the forensic investigator.

They dropped the bracelet at the lab and headed for Canyon Lane. The shooter hadn't bothered going very far to drop his victim. Shades Crest Road snaked its way up the mountain and right past Canyon Lane.

The address led to a cabin in the woods. The long narrow drive cut through the trees as if it had been designed to disappear. The cabin was not your run-of-the-mill rustic getaway either. This was a nice cabin.

Best of all, according to county records, the property belonged to one Lewis York. Kerri resisted the urge to jump for joy. That news was like Christmas and her birthday all rolled into one. They were getting closer.

Since no one was home, Kerri and her partner did some looking around. The doors were locked. The windows weren't shuttered or curtained, making seeing inside as simple as pressing her face to the glass. Nothing inside looked suspicious, taking the possibility of exigent circumstances off the table.

There was a shed in back. It wasn't locked, but there was nothing inside, not even a lawn mower. Odds were, York had a service that took care of that sort of thing.

"Keaton came here, looked around," she said, "and that put him on York's radar."

"The question is"—Falco turned all the way around, surveying the yard—"unless York was home, how did he know Keaton was here?"

"There have to be cameras somewhere."

A new search began. This one to find any sort of surveillance York might have installed.

It took a few minutes, but they found them. The cameras were well hidden—camouflaged, really.

It wasn't until the air suddenly surged into her lungs that Kerri realized she had been holding her breath. She got it now. "He was here." She turned to Falco.

"What do you mean? Who was here?"

"When Keaton called me, he said he would be waiting to hear from me." She surveyed the property. "I thought he meant at the salvage yard, but I was wrong. He was waiting here. That's how York got to him before I could respond to his voice mail. When he drove onto the property, York probably got some sort of notification on his cell or something."

"I'll check for a camera close to the road." Falco hustled off down the driveway.

Kerri stared directly at the camera they'd found at the front of the house. She smiled and then mouthed two words: "Got you."

Falco found the camera at the Canyon Lane end of the driveway. Kerri's scenario for what had happened to Keaton was right, even if they couldn't prove it.

When they loaded up in the Charger, Falco asked, "We going to see York or Thompson?"

"Both, but Thompson is first. He's scheduled to do a lunch thing at his office, so we know he'll be there. He's too hard to catch to risk missing this opportunity to trap him."

When they reached the end of the driveway, Falco stopped and fished his cell phone from his pocket. He checked the screen and then glanced at Kerri. "It's Cross."

"Put it on speaker." Kerri hoped the woman was as good as Falco thought. They needed something that would push this investigation over the hurdle that had been stalling it for days.

"Hey, Cross, got you on speaker. Devlin is in the car with me, so be nice."

The woman grumbled something unintelligible, then: "I heard back from my contact in Mexico City."

Obviously Cross had contacts everywhere. Kerri couldn't help wondering how she'd managed that feat.

"Did he find anything on Sela Rollins and her mother?"

"Oh yeah," Cross said. "You were right about Sela taking her mother to Mexico for treatment. The clinic treating her in San Diego said there was nothing more they could do. Sent her home with a bagful of pain meds to die. Sela heard about this so-called miracle clinic, which, according to my contact, is just one of those places that takes money from desperate people."

"The mother was terminal?" Kerri needed her to get to the point. Adrenaline was pumping through her heart with enough force to launch it out of her chest.

"Yeah," Cross said. "She died six months later. I don't know who got shot in the Abbott house, but it wasn't Sela Rollins Abbott's mother."

Holy shit. Kerri asked, "Your contact confirmed this information?"

"I'm looking at the death certificate. He snapped pics of a bunch of records and sent them to me."

"Damn, Cross, I really appreciate this." Falco looked to Kerri. "I don't see how we can view Sela Abbott as anything other than a straight-up suspect now."

"That ain't all, Falco." Cross spoke up.

Kerri braced for more startling news.

"Your MIA vic went a little crazy after her mother died. Ended up spending a few months in a Mexican psychiatric hospital. While she was there, she became good friends with a guy named Oliver Wilmington. He was this big West Coast tech whiz who flamed out early in the game. Mental health issues—bipolar or some such shit. When she finished her gig in the crazy house," Cross went on, "she moved in with this guy for a while before returning to California and going to work for a law firm."

"Is there any way to get in touch with this tech wizard?" Falco asked the question on the tip of Kerri's tongue.

"Nope. He was found dead the day after your missing vic's departure. Apparently, he decided he couldn't live without her and took a dive off the third-story balcony of his Mexican palace. The authorities ruled it a suicide, but the autopsy shows his time of death as the day before Sela left Mexico. So maybe he had a little help taking that dive."

Falco was right. Sela Rollins Abbott couldn't be called a victim anymore. But would she really kill her husband? The father of her child? Or a former lover? She might not be a victim, but somehow, she had set all this in motion.

The other glaring question was, Who the hell was the woman posing as her mother?

"Did you find anything on the property on Thirty-Third?" Falco asked.

"It's your lucky day, Falco," Cross said. "I found something I think your partner is going to love."

A new wave of tension rolled through Kerri. "What's that?" Maybe the house belonged to Thompson or York. That news she would love.

"Forty-two years ago Jacqueline Rollins lived in that house, only she wasn't a Rollins then, and she went by Jackie. Her real last name was Carter. She changed her name to Stevens when she moved to California."

"So this does go back to the mother." Kerri wasn't actually surprised. It made sense now. She had found that photo album that proved the mother had lived in Birmingham when she was young.

How was it that Ben Abbott knew about Janelle and her involvement with Theo Thompson and didn't know the rest? Not logical. Why would Sela keep that from her husband?

"I'll give you three guesses who she worked for, and the first two don't count."

Jesus Christ. Kerri offered, "The Thompsons."

"And we have a winner. Jacqueline worked for Theo's old man back when he was a young state senator. But she only worked for him a few months, and then she disappeared. Six months later she pops up in San Diego with a newborn baby girl. Five years later she married a Rollins, Sela's father."

Janelle was the baby girl. That could mean T. R. Thompson was Janelle's father. But why would Janelle want to marry a man who could very well have been her own brother?

"So Old Man Thompson knocked her up," Falco suggested, voicing Kerri's thought, "and then sent her away."

"Maybe," Cross agreed. "But he isn't the one who set her up in that house while she was working in Birmingham. The one that got torched, I mean."

"Wait." Anticipation zinged Kerri. "If it wasn't Thompson, who was it?"

"DATACO."

Falco turned to Kerri as she asked the question Cross had already answered. "*Daniel Abbott* set her up in the house?"

"The one and only. The property still belongs to his company. A year ago it was rented by an S. Carter. Still is."

S. Carter. Sela had used her mother's maiden name to rent the house.

And now they knew. "That's where she's been hiding." Kerri drew in a tight breath.

Falco's eyes told her he'd just realized the same thing. The vic pulled out of that burned house was likely Sela Abbott. Damn it! They needed some word back from the ME on that body.

Falco cleared his throat. "Anything else?"

"That's it. You owe me big time, Falco."

"Yeah, yeah. I got you covered, Cross."

Falco ended the call and dropped his phone onto the console. "We need to talk to Daniel Abbott."

"Oh yeah," Kerri agreed. "Sela didn't come here just looking for the truth about what happened to her sister. She had a second agenda. To get back at the man who got her mother pregnant and then threw her away. What better way than to marry his only son?"

"I have to give the lady credit," Falco said. "That was a hell of a move."

"Let's just hope she didn't kill him as part of that revenge." Or that she didn't burn in that fucking house.

Falco laughed a dry sound. "The best part in all this is that the bastard had to know it all along. He could see the woman posing as Sela's mother was an imposter. How the hell many secrets have these people been keeping?"

"We'll probably never know."

Falco started his car. "I assume we're heading to pay Abbott a visit now."

"First, I have to go to that big luncheon Theo Thompson is hosting. It may be my only chance to catch him in a situation where he can't ignore me. We'll hit the Abbotts right after." Kerri fastened her seat belt. "Daniel Abbott may have gotten Sela's mother pregnant and sent her away, but Theo Thompson may have killed her sister."

"Gotcha." Falco pulled out onto the road. "Murder trumps being an asshole."

53

12:15 p.m.

Thompson Building
Richard Arrington Boulevard

By the time Kerri arrived at the Thompson Building, the closed-door luncheon had already started in the main conference room. Though patience had never been one of her virtues, she had no choice but to sit it out.

The Thompson Building was actually the historic Harris Building built in 1910. T. R. Thompson had purchased it right out of college and decided this would be his primary business office—right downtown for all to see. The building had been in the family for half a century. This was in all likelihood where Sela Abbott's mother had worked when she'd lived in Birmingham. Like some ill-fated legacy, her sister, Janelle, had worked here as well. Kerri wondered how many times Sela had walked these halls and considered those bizarre facts?

How had she sat at the table with Daniel Abbott for a family meal knowing how he had hurt her mother?

During the half hour or so that had passed since hearing from Cross, Kerri had mulled over the shocking information. No question the woman who'd died along with Ben Abbott was an imposter. Sela's mother had died in Mexico. Based on the history of the Thirty-Third Avenue house, they were assuming Daniel Abbott had been involved with Sela's mother, but it was possible they had jumped too quickly to that conclusion. Maybe he had been trying to help her. Maybe it was his buddy T. R. who'd gotten her pregnant.

Every new piece of information came with multiple questions— and new potential holes in the puzzle.

Kerri pushed the troubling thoughts aside for the moment. She needed a clear head for this meeting with Thompson. Falco had taken her to get her Wagoneer since she would be hanging around the Thompson Building for a while. No point in both of them being stuck waiting. He had gone back to the house—the one where Sela's mother had lived all those years ago—to have another look in light of what they now knew. He intended to show Sela's photo as well as one of a similar blue Plymouth to the few neighbors along the street. Maybe someone had seen her or the car. The cops canvassing the neighbors the day of the fire wouldn't have known to ask about the car.

The investigator, Neal Ramsey, had dropped out of sight. He wasn't returning her calls or Bellemont's. The attorney was still standing by the man. Kerri wasn't. She'd issued an APB on the vehicle registered to Ramsey. For all she knew, he could be holding Amelia hostage some-where for this unnamed client.

Kerri wasn't taking any chances. The worry and fear she had com-partmentalized for the past thirty or so hours attempted to break loose, but she pushed it back. She couldn't help Amelia if she lost control.

She put her hand on her right knee to stop its impatient bouncing. She sent a text to Diana to see how she was doing. Kerri's heart twisted with the need to fix this for her. Then she sent a text to Tori to see how her day at the mall was going. Her response was a photo of multiple shopping bags. Kerri hoped she wasn't going to regret sending her credit card with her daughter.

She glanced at the reception desk. It would have been nice if she had arrived before the luncheon started, but the call had come in about Keaton, and then they'd heard from Cross. Exhaling a big breath, she resituated herself and checked her messages again.

———

It was nearly one o'clock before the luncheon was over. Kerri had already warned Thompson's personal assistant that if he didn't see her in his office, she would ask her questions right out here in the corridor, where anyone could hear. Particularly the media, who had all decided the Abbott murders were no longer as interesting as their next senator and governor.

Kerri watched Thompson as his assistant passed along the message.

He promptly exchanged his final handshakes and thank-yous and departed the group. He didn't look at Kerri as he walked hurriedly past.

The assistant appeared next. "This way, Detective."

Unlike Thompson, the assistant took her time showing Kerri down the main corridor and off to the left to an even larger corridor that ended at a set of towering double doors. "He's waiting for you just beyond those doors."

Kerri thanked her and walked into the man's office.

His office was far more lavish than the small conference room where she and Falco had met with his wife. Thompson sat behind an extravagant mahogany desk, his hands resting on the leather-bound blotter pad.

"Please have a seat." He gestured to a chair in front of his desk. "To what do I owe this pleasure, Detective?"

His voice was strained, but the smile on his face was pure politician. Not surprising. The man was born to be exactly who he was.

"Mr. Thompson, you're aware of the double homicide involving Ben Abbott and his mother-in-law, Jacqueline Rollins."

"I am. A tragedy. I understand there are still no suspects. Is that true?"

"Actually," Kerri said, "we have two prime suspects."

"Really?" Surprise flared briefly on his face.

"One of them is you, Mr. Thompson." Kerri smiled, enjoying far too much his initial reaction to the announcement. The startled look was priceless. She would likely take a raking over the coals for that statement, but it had been worth it.

He laughed, the sound more a scoff than a laugh. "You can't be serious, and please don't tell me this has anything to do with that photograph you showed my wife."

Kerri held her smile in place. "I'm glad you mentioned the photo. We're also reopening the case of Sela Abbott's missing sister. You remember her, don't you? Janelle Stevens? The two of you had an affair when she worked for your father."

The pallor that fell over the man's face was confession enough for Kerri.

The door burst open, and Lewis York strode in. Behind him were two members of Thompson's security staff, judging by their uniforms. The two men remained by the open doors as York stormed all the way to Thompson's desk. "Don't say another word, Theo."

Theo snapped shut his sagging jaw, but it was far too late to recover from what his evolving expressions of shock and fear had revealed.

The would-be senator had an affair with Janelle Stevens. He was clearly stunned and perhaps more than a little terrified that the case was being reopened. Kerri had accomplished at least part of her goal.

York rounded the desk to stand next to his client. "If you'll excuse us, Detective, I need to confer with my client."

Thompson looked up at him, as if he had no idea what was going on.

Kerri stood. "Actually, I'm glad you're here, Mr. York. I have questions for you as well."

"Leave. Now, Detective," York commanded, his face so tense his jaw throbbed.

He was probably pissed about her discovering his little cabin in the woods.

"Were you surprised that the car Joey Keaton sold Sela was left at a property you own?"

York glared at her and motioned at the guards standing by.

As the two men moved toward Kerri, she said, "Don't forget what I told you, Mr. Thompson. We know what happened."

She'd said all she had to say. For now. She walked out; the guards marched right behind her until she was out of the building.

Kerri had kicked that hornet's nest but good. If she was lucky, they would now go into swarm mode to cover their asses. Desperation led to mistakes.

All she needed was one mistake.

She crossed the lot to her Wagoneer and climbed in. Her cell vibrated. She hoped it was a text from Tori letting her know she'd made it back home.

The call was from her attorney. Her heart pounding, she answered. "What's going on, Mac?"

"Well, you're not going to believe this."

She swallowed the massive lump of worry in her throat. "Try me."

"Nick's attorney just canceled the hearing. He's withdrawn his petition to modify custody. For now, Kerri, it's over. Enjoy your weekend."

Stunned, relieved, overwhelmed . . . she struggled to find her voice. "Thanks."

After the call ended, she stared at the screen for a moment and let the news set in; then she called Falco and told him.

"That's great, Devlin. We could celebrate if we had time."

But they didn't. As thrilled as she was at Mac's call, the pieces of this puzzle were slowly but surely coming together. They couldn't stop until this was finished.

Thompson and York weren't getting away with what they'd done. Neither was Daniel Abbott.

"Did you find anything?" she asked.

"Nada. You want to rendezvous at the Abbotts'?"

"Sounds good."

A BPD cruiser rolled up beside her. The uni behind the wheel powered his window down.

"Hang on, Falco." The rhythm of Kerri's heart instantly changed as the glut of possibilities for trouble whirred through her mind.

"Have to let you go, Devlin. I just got blue lighted."

She frowned. What the hell was going on? She set her phone aside and rolled her window down.

"Detective Devlin?" the officer asked.

"That's me." She told her heart to slow its pounding. Tori was fine. Diana was fine.

Shit. What about Amelia?

"I have orders to escort you to the chief's office."

Well, that certainly hadn't taken long. She glanced at the building she'd exited just minutes ago.

The hornets were swarming.

54

1:00 p.m.

Abbott Residence
Saint Charles Drive, Hoover

Tempest Abbott perched on the edge of the sofa in the family room. She'd dismissed the staff early. Daniel was on his way home. She had called him, which she rarely did, and told him she needed him. He would be here any moment. She had prepared his favorite drink, scotch on the rocks, as well as a lovely glass of white wine for herself. The elegant glasses, handmade in Italy, stood on the silver tray resting on the cocktail table in front of her.

She glanced around the enormous room and recalled the day construction had begun on this beautiful house. Ben hadn't been born yet. She couldn't wait to fill the rooms with children. But sometime during her pregnancy with Ben, Daniel had taken steps to ensure that didn't happen.

He'd never told her, of course. She'd discovered his secret all on her own, just as she had so many of his other indiscretions.

His decision to have a vasectomy had stolen her dream from her. Ben was her only child, and she had poured everything into that sweet boy.

Now he was gone.

Emotion would have engulfed her, but she'd prepared well for the occasion. She had taken a nice dose of the Valium the doctor had prescribed after Ben's murder.

She had hoped if Sela were found, perhaps the grandchild could help fill the crack left in her heart by Ben's death. But that was not going to happen. She would never have the opportunity to know her grandchild.

It was over.

Ben's life.

Their lives.

No amount of money . . . no home . . . nothing could make her want to live another day. Another minute, for that matter.

Except she had something to take care of first.

Daniel had chosen to have the vasectomy because he'd wanted to enjoy his little indiscretions without the worry that some woman would try and trap him with an unexpected pregnancy.

Tempest smirked. His decision had been a little like closing the barn door after the cows got out. But he was so very selfish that he stole her dream for the sole purpose of continuing his.

She had known he was selfish. She shouldn't have been surprised. Since the chief of police had come to their home and told her about Ben, she had been contemplating taking this step. Alone, of course. She'd even purchased a hefty dose of what she would need to do the job. But then, when she'd learned the rest, she had known the two of them had to do this together.

Over the voices from the past clamoring in her head, Tempest heard the front door open and then close.

He was here.

She sat perfectly still, waited for him to enter the room.

He stood there, staring at her. "Dear God, woman, I thought something terrible had happened."

Selfish, selfish man. Something terrible had happened . . . to their *son*. Had he put the tragedy behind him so soon? Of course he had.

She patted the sofa beside her. "Sit down, Daniel. Have a drink with me. There is something we need to discuss."

Outrage washed across his face. "Did you actually summon me here for no other reason than to have a drink and some frivolous chitchat?"

"I did. You go to the country club with your friends quite often. Why not have a drink and chat with me?"

He took a breath, seemed to remind himself that his wife had suffered a great loss and had not yet put it behind her. The rage drained away, and he crossed the room and sat down next to her.

She picked up the tumbler of scotch and handed it to him. She even managed to smile. Then she reached for her stemmed glass of wine. She touched her glass to his. "To moving on."

His eyebrows lifted in surprise. "Have you decided to try and move on beyond this horrible tragedy?"

"Yes." She sipped her wine, the tiniest little sip.

"Good." He knocked back a long deep slug of his own libation.

Tempest had known he would. He always drank scotch with enthusiasm.

She indulged in another sip of wine. "I had a visitor today."

He downed the last of the scotch in the glass. "I certainly hope it wasn't those damned detectives again."

"No." Tempest took a larger swallow of her wine. She moistened her lips. "It was Sela."

He slammed the empty tumbler onto the tray. "What the hell? Are you hallucinating again?"

Tempest wanted to slap his face, but she lacked the energy. On Tuesday, she had gone into Ben's bedroom—the one he'd grown up in—and had a talk with him. It had made her feel better to get everything off her chest . . . to say the words out loud. Daniel happened to walk past the door and hear her talking. He'd accused her of having lost her mind. Perhaps she had. Whatever the case, it hadn't helped with the crushing pain that filled her every waking moment.

There was only one way to end that pain.

"Believe what you will," she offered. It was almost over, in any event.

"If she was here, why didn't you call me?" he demanded with a smirk—the sort that expressed how little respect he had for her even after all these years together.

"She needed to speak with me privately."

His gaze narrowed with faked suspicion. "What did she want?"

Tempest shook her head. "She wants nothing from us, Daniel."

"Well," he said, "that's a relief."

Tempest finished her wine and set the glass aside. She turned slightly to look her husband in the eye. "Tell me she was lying, Daniel. Tell me," she pressed, "that you didn't force her mother to agree to weekend after weekend of sexual favors. I would have expected such a thing from T. R. Everyone knows how he is—how his father was. But you? How could you do such a thing?"

Daniel blinked, but not before she saw the shock in his eyes. She almost smiled. She had his attention now.

"Who concocted this ridiculous story?"

"Does it really matter?" All that mattered was that she knew. She knew everything. "You and T. R. took advantage of her mother, and then the two of you threatened to make her regret it if she dared to tell anyone. She ran away. Changed her name. Then she discovered she was pregnant."

He puffed out a breath. "This is preposterous." He grabbed his glass and stood. "I need another drink."

"Sit down, Daniel," she demanded.

"Who do you think you are?" He glared at her before walking toward the bar. He poured the scotch and turned to face her, leaning against the counter. "What if we did? We were young and stupid. We drank too much. But we didn't force her. She wanted it. She was like that. Ready. Willing."

Disgust hardened in her stomach. "Tell me," Tempest managed to say despite the thickening of her tongue, "how many other women you used in that way."

"That was more than forty years ago. Things were different then." He shrugged. "Women were different then. Office relationships weren't as complicated and saddled with rules. There was none of that me-me-me nonsense. Everyone understood their place. It was fun and games, not criminal activity. Those women knew what they wanted, and we gave it to them."

"She was carrying *your* child."

He waved her off. "Don't be ridiculous. She couldn't possibly have known whose child she was carrying. T. R. was with her every bit as often as I was."

The urge to vomit was nearly overwhelming, but Tempest could not do that. "That girl who went missing, Janelle Stevens? She was here, at that party we had for Ben's twenty-fifth birthday. Do you remember?"

He stared at her without saying a word.

"During the party, she went into our bathroom and took your toothbrush and razor. She used them for DNA. She was your daughter, not T. R.'s. Did you kill her after she told you? Is that why she disappeared?"

"Are you insane?" He started toward her, staggered. Almost fell. "What the hell?"

Tempest was glad it was finally kicking in. "Don't worry. It'll be over quickly."

"What the hell have you done?" He staggered closer, fell this time.

Tempest watched as he clambered to his hands and knees. "You," she snarled, "are the reason our son is dead. What have I done? Just a little something to put us both out of our misery. Goodbye, Daniel."

55

2:00 p.m.

York, Hammond & Goldman Law Firm
North Twentieth Street

"We have to do something," Theo urged. He had no idea what, but he understood there was no more assuming this would just go away . . . like before.

"Sit down, Theo," Lewis demanded.

Theo glared at his old friend. How could he be so calm? "I cannot just sit down. This is out of control. They know about my affair with Janelle. If Sela Abbott shows up, she will ruin me."

"You have no reason to be concerned. All is under control. Trust me."

Theo shook his head. He was nearly afraid to mention the other, but he had no choice. Lewis was going to—

"What?" Lewis demanded. "What are you not telling me?"

The bastard had always read him like a book. "It's Jen. She's angry with me. She called a little while ago. She's threatening to go to the police about Wednesday night."

Lewis shot to his feet, braced his hands on his desk, and leaned forward. "What errant brain cell prompted you to bring that whore with you? Have you lost your damned mind?"

"I had no idea a command performance was going to be expected of me that night. My God, man, you should have given me a goddamned clue what you were planning, and I would have dropped her off. You said come immediately, and that's what I did!"

Lewis dropped back into his chair. "It's nothing that can't be neutralized. You'll just have to take care of the situation."

"I believe we've established that I can't do that. I'm not like you," Theo snarled.

He had known this man since he was old enough to walk. He would never have dreamed in a million years how very ruthless he could be. Admittedly, Theo had issues with staying faithful to his wife, but he'd never had the sick sexual proclivities his father had. And he damned sure had never killed anyone. Dear God, what the man had done. Scenes from the news coverage of the fire flashed before his eyes.

"How easy for you to say," Lewis sneered. "Of course you're not like me. You've never had to be. You've always had either your father or me to clean up your messes. Don't you dare look down your nose at me, you fucking coward. I only do what needs to be done because you aren't man enough."

Fury whipped through Theo. "There must have been another way then and now."

"Certainly, there was and is. You could learn to keep your dick in your pants."

He spat the words at Theo. He felt the force like a slap to his face.

"What?" Lewis demanded. "You have nothing to say to that?"

There was plenty he wanted to say, but now wasn't the time. This thing had to be handled, and Lewis was the only person who could do the job right.

"That's what I thought," Lewis mused. "Now, listen to me, and this time do as I say. First, the situation is under control. Those detectives won't be bothering you anymore. You have nothing to worry about.

Now, go back to your office, or go home. No getting agitated or nervous. This will all be over soon."

The phone on his desk buzzed, and Lewis picked up the receiver. "Yes."

Theo tried to calm himself. Lewis wasn't the enemy. Theo was his own worst enemy. He needed Lewis if he hoped to get through this. God knew he would never manage alone. He'd never been good at this sort of thing.

"Give me five minutes before you send him back," Lewis instructed the caller. When he replaced the receiver in its cradle, he stared at Theo for a long moment. "We will survive this, just as we have survived all other hurdles before this one."

Theo managed a nod. "It's just that with the election, this is not a good time for trouble."

"Trust me," Lewis said. "It's all under control, and I will take care of that whore you've been playing with."

"What do you want me to do?" Really Theo wasn't a coward. He just wasn't built like Lewis.

"Do not go near your whore again, and whatever you do, don't get cornered by those detectives. Just stay calm, and carry on with whatever events you have scheduled this weekend. We'll talk again tomorrow."

Theo nodded stiffly. "And what are you going to do?"

"You don't need to know anything beyond the fact that I will get this done. Do we understand each other?"

Theo blinked away the image of Jen dead. "All right."

"You should go. I have another appointment."

Theo stood.

"I'll talk to you tomorrow," Lewis assured him, "and we'll finish this."

Theo gave another of those stiff nods and walked out.

He was halfway to the elevator when the doors glided open, and Robert Swanner emerged. Theo slowed his pace, pretended to check his phone until the other man had passed him. Then Theo turned around and followed him at a safe distance. The man practically twisted the knob off the door and walked right into Lewis's office, slamming the door behind him. This could only be more trouble.

Theo moved close enough to the door to hear the man's raised voice.

"Where is my daughter?"

"Your daughter has not been to work all week. I have no idea where she is. I would think a good father would have that answer."

"You think I don't know what's going on here, you bastard?"

"Control yourself, or I will call security and have you removed, Mr. Swanner."

"Call them," Swanner dared. "Go ahead and call the police while you're at it. Let's tell them about that night fifteen years ago when you came to me, begging for help with the repairs to your car."

Lewis laughed. Theo flinched. What the hell was Swanner talking about?

"I came to you, but I don't recall begging. I believe you were the one only too happy to accept a payoff of your defaulted loan. Shall we share that with the police as well?"

Theo leaned against the wall, his heart thundering. How many others knew?

"I swear to God," Swanner said, "if you have harmed my daughter—"

"Whatever has happened to your daughter," Lewis said, cutting him off, "is as much your doing as anyone else's, Mr. Swanner. Before you dare to come in here threatening me, remember that you have two other children and a wife. Perhaps you will do a better job taking care of them."

For a single moment Theo could not move, even as his instincts screamed at him to go. Fifteen years ago . . . after *she* had vanished, he recalled distinctly a car having to be repaired after hitting a deer. But it wasn't Lewis's car.

Theo pushed away from the wall and hurried as fast as he could without breaking into a run. He stabbed the call button for the elevator and prayed it would arrive and take him away before Swanner left Lewis's office and caught up with him.

The bell dinged, and the doors opened. He relaxed a fraction as he stepped inside and pushed the button for the lobby. He moved to the back of the car and leaned against the wall as the doors started to close.

Thank God.

At the last possible second, an arm suddenly thrust between the doors, and they slid apart. Swanner stepped inside and glanced at the keypad. As the doors closed again, he moved to the opposite back corner and leaned against the wall.

Theo stared straight ahead.

He practically held his breath until the car bumped to a stop at the lobby level.

Rather than wait for the doors to open, he moved forward and waited so close to the doors that his nose nearly touched the cool steel.

When the doors slid apart, Theo shot out like a racehorse exiting the gate. He walked straight up to the reception desk and fished for his phone to give Swanner time to exit the building.

He was not cut out for this kind of shit.

The receptionist smiled at him. "May I help you, Mr. Thompson?"

He shook his head and spoke the most truthful words he had ever uttered. "I don't think anyone can help me."

He left the building and considered the consequences of simply running away . . . or exiting this nightmare some other more permanent way.

Lewis was right. He was a coward. He'd always been one.

56

3:30 p.m.

Birmingham Police Department
First Avenue North

They stood on the street. Kerri and this new partner of hers. She glanced at him. His hands tucked into the pockets of his jeans, his shoulders slumped like someone had kicked his dog.

He turned to her. "What're you thinking?"

"I'm thinking we were escorted here like a couple of common criminals." She glanced up at the revered building that had been her second home for better than a decade. Fury ignited anew inside her. "We were forced to wait a half hour while the chief did whatever he did."

Seriously. They had been dragged to his office, and the man had them twiddling their thumbs for thirty damned minutes.

She reached for calm. Falco waited patiently for her to find it and continue.

"Then he rakes us over the coals about how we've made the whole department look bad by bullying esteemed citizens like Thompson and York."

Breathe.

"He didn't mince words, partner," Falco pointed out. "If we even breathe close to Thompson or York, we get suspended or worse. We can't talk to them. We can't . . ." He blew out a big breath. "Do shit."

The part that pissed Kerri off the most was that the LT hadn't said a word. He had simply sat there, deferring to the boss.

Kerri shook her head. She couldn't blame him. Why should he jeopardize his career for two detectives going rogue on him without any real evidence to back up their accusations?

"I know what I have to do." There was no question in Kerri's mind. There was a very strong possibility that her niece was tangled up in this somehow. She could not—would not—back off. They were too close to finding the truth. She turned to her partner. "I have to finish this, Falco. I don't want you to do anything to risk your career. Just because I'm willing to gamble with mine doesn't mean you have to do the same. I'll understand if you're out. I've got this."

He stared at her as she spoke. "Miss By-the-Book-We-Have-Protocols is going to buck the chief of police?"

"I am. You can go back in there and write up your report saying Sela Abbott killed her husband and some woman posing as her mother if you want to. Hell, she's probably dead anyway. But I can't do that." She squared her shoulders. "It's up to you. What do you say?"

He shrugged. "I say fuck 'em. Let's do this thing, Devlin."

She smiled. "Good."

"But I'm driving. You're too damned slow."

They had just climbed into his Charger when her cell vibrated. Kerri reached for it. *Dispatch.* "Devlin."

She listened as the officer on the other end of the line listed the location of a possible murder-suicide scene. "On my way," she cut in without hearing the rest.

She didn't need any other details.

She knew the victims.

Abbott Residence
Saint Charles Drive, Hoover

The ME was already on the scene when Kerri and Falco arrived.

Two police cruisers and the crime scene unit van were in the driveway. Yellow tape was being reeled along the front yard from one immaculately manicured shrub to the next.

Officer Ted Olson met them at the door. "The bodies are in the family room."

Kerri and Falco donned shoe covers and gloves and headed to the room where they had met with Daniel and Tempest Abbott on two occasions. Dr. Moore was stooped over Mrs. Abbott's body where she lay on the sofa. Daniel Abbott was sprawled facedown on the Persian rug.

One step forward, two steps back. Damn.

As Falco walked around the room, Kerri joined the ME. "Anything yet on cause of death?"

"No visible injuries." He pursed his lips a moment. "Considering the wineglass on the coffee table and the glass on the floor near the male victim, I'll be testing for various poisons."

"What about time of death?" Kerri wondered if they searched the house if they'd find one damned thing to explain the connection between Daniel Abbott and Jacqueline Carter/Stevens/Rollins beyond what Cross had given them about the house.

Probably not.

"They haven't been dead long. An hour, hour and a half. I'd estimate time of death somewhere between noon and two."

If they'd come here first—before the Thompson fiasco. Damn it!

"Devlin!" Falco sent her a look.

"Thanks, Dr. Moore." Kerri pushed to her feet and went to the bar, where Falco waited. "You find something?"

He pointed to a drawer he had opened beneath the bar top. Two small vials lay next to the hand towels folded there.

"Looks like we have our answer." She scanned the room, looking for any indication the couple had had company when their drinks had been served. "The only question is, Did one of them take this step, or was it someone else?"

Despite her best efforts, Kerri's mind went immediately to York, Thompson, and Sela Abbott—in that order.

"Detectives."

Officer Olson joined them at the bar. "I spoke to Mr. Abbott's receptionist at his office. She said his wife called at twelve thirty and asked him to come home."

Kerri looked to Falco, then said to Olson, "Call the security-monitoring company and find out if the Abbotts have cameras. We need to know if there was anyone here besides the wife when Mr. Abbott arrived. If they don't, check with neighbors. Call in backup. We need at least two more officers interviewing the neighbors. If someone besides the Abbotts was at this house this afternoon, we need to know."

"Yes, ma'am."

When Olson had walked away, Falco said, "I can't decide if someone is tying up loose ends or taking out targets."

He was right. Particularly considering what they knew about Daniel Abbott's obvious connection to Sela's mother. Ramsey was still MIA. Keaton was dead. Maybe Sela was as well. Now these two. Who was next?

The idea that Amelia could be on that list terrified Kerri.

"Either way," she decided, "I think we should be keeping an eye on the only other two suspects we have before they disappear or end up dead too."

"York and Thompson," Falco agreed.

Falco leaned his head toward hers and spoke quietly. "Those two will either be *doing* more of this"—he nodded to the room at large—"or ending up like this."

And if Amelia was involved in this, one or both likely knew where she was.

She and Falco were out the door when Kerri's cell went off again. She checked the screen.

Jen.

A new wave of worry washed over Kerri.

———

O'Malley's
Morris Avenue

At barely five o'clock O'Malley's was already crowded. It was Friday; folks were ready to get their weekend started. Kerri scanned the bar and tables looking for Jen's red hair.

Jen had called and asked Kerri to meet her here. She'd insisted it was urgent. Couldn't wait. It wasn't like she and Falco had anything else to do. They were ten days in, and though they had gleaned a great number of details and had numerous theories, they basically had nothing that would push them to the next step—arrests.

And the chief had just told them to stay clear of their prime suspects.

They had both promptly decided to ignore the order.

There was an upside to Jen's call—it wasn't about Diana or Amelia. No change there. As much as Kerri was desperate to find her niece, she was grateful there was no bad news just yet. Like the old saying, sometimes no news was good news.

Just not for a homicide investigation.

Kerri finally spotted Jen. She waited at a table in the darkest corner of the establishment and appeared to be halfway through a Long Island Iced Tea. She threw up her hand in a half-hearted wave. No matter what else was happening around her, Jen always looked expertly put together. From her hair to the sexy green stilettoes she wore, she could be a celebrity right here in Birmingham.

As Kerri reached the table, Jen stood and leaned in for a hug. When they'd dropped into their chairs, Falco followed suit.

"Jen, this is my partner, Luke Falco. Falco, Jen Whitten."

The woman who had been a part of her family for as long as Kerri could remember flashed one of her trademark bombshell smiles. "Very nice to meet you, Detective Falco." She offered her hand.

Falco gave it a shake. "Back at you, Jen."

"Kerri, there's something . . ." Jen suddenly looked ready to crumble. Tears slipped down her cheeks.

"What's going on?" Kerri reached for her hand and held it tightly in hers. She was just about maxed out with trouble.

The waitress appeared, and Falco ordered a couple of beers.

"I've been struggling with this since yesterday morning. I've had a bad feeling for days now, but I didn't know how to tell you. Now I have no choice."

"Just tell me, Jen. Whatever's going on, we'll work it out."

Jen moistened her lips and took a breath. "It's about Theo Thompson."

Kerri frowned. Of all the potential issues that had gone through her mind, that wasn't one of them. "How do you know Thompson other than on the news? Is this something you overheard at work?"

Jen downed the last of her drink, then hugged her arms around her waist. "Theo and I have been involved for two years."

Kerri drew back slightly at the idea. Jen? A woman Kerri knew as well as her own sister was somehow involved with the prime suspect in this investigation. She didn't understand. "Involved how?"

Her gaze downcast, Jen said, "An affair."

Kerri absorbed the impact of her words, the meaning quaking all the way through her. "Go on."

"For the past week or two, he's been acting strange. At first I thought it was just stress about the campaign, but then I overheard a couple of phone conversations that made me uncomfortable."

"Were they from his wife?" Kerri tasted the bitterness of her sharply spoken words. Of all people, Jen understood what Kerri had gone through with her cheating ex. She mentally blocked the thought. She had to hear her out, for more reasons than one.

Jen shook her head, swiped at her eyes. "I don't know who he was talking to, but there was trouble. Something bad."

Disappointment pulsed through Kerri. "Unless you have something criminal to share, I'm not sure I'm the person you should be talking to."

When she would have pushed out of her chair, Jen blurted, "He was at that house on Wednesday night. The one that burned."

Kerri froze. "How do you know this?"

"I was with him." Jen moistened her lips again, twiddled with the straw in her empty glass. "We were going out that night, and he got a call. He was extremely upset by the caller. He told me he had to meet someone to take care of a problem. When we got to the house"—she drew in a deep breath—"he told me to wait in the car."

"Who was he meeting?" Kerri waited for her answer, the thundering in her chest refusing to quiet.

Jen stared directly at her then. "Lewis York."

Son of a bitch. "Why the hell didn't you tell me this before now?"

"I meant to," Jen cried. "I started to call you a dozen times, but I couldn't bring myself to do it."

Kerri restrained the emotional words she wanted to hurl across the table. She reached deep inside herself and grabbed on to the training and experience that made her a damned good detective. "Tell me exactly what happened and every word you heard the two of them say."

This could be crucial to their case.

Through bouts of tears and with the aid of another drink, Jen explained what she had seen and heard that night. When she stopped talking, she dropped her gaze to the table once more.

Deep, deep breath. Kerri looked to her partner. "We need to take this to the LT."

"Like he's going to listen, especially since it's her word against theirs," Falco pointed out. "Thompson would likely say she was a jilted lover trying to get back at him."

"But he hasn't dumped me," Jen interjected. "I'm dumping him."

"Your word against his. We need evidence, Jen. Something we can use to physically link them to that house on that night."

Kerri rubbed her hands over her face. She was tired. So damned tired. "We have to find a way to use this. This could make all the difference."

Falco looked at Jen a moment before turning back to Kerri. "She could confront Thompson about that night while wearing a wire."

Kerri shook her head. "It's too risky." She looked at her lifelong friend. "As much as I want that bastard, I don't want to put her in danger."

"I'll do it," Jen asserted. "I'll do whatever you need me to do. I swear. Anything."

Kerri stared pointedly at her. "You feel guilty. You want to somehow make this right. What Falco is suggesting isn't going—"

"I'll do it." Jen nodded frantically. "I'm so sorry. I'm an idiot, but I can do this."

"No." Kerri shook her head. "I will not let you get yourself hurt or maybe killed. I'm not sure you understand how ruthless these people are."

Tears filled the other woman's eyes again. "Please, let me help. For Amelia and her friend—that Sela Abbott."

"This could make the chief and the LT see this case the way we need them to," Falco reminded her.

As much as Kerri didn't want to admit it, he was right. "When are you supposed to see him again?" Kerri's tone was harsher than she'd intended. Calm and cool wasn't exactly handy right now.

"We haven't made plans, but I can call him." Jen looked from Kerri to Falco and back. "I can do this. He trusts me."

Kerri's cell vibrated in her pocket. She checked the screen, couldn't identify the caller. "Devlin."

"Kerri Devlin?"

Kerri put a hand over her ear in an effort to hear the caller better above the noise in the pub. "Yes."

"Ma'am, my name is Eleanor Gonzalez. I'm at the Delta counter here at Birmingham-Shuttlesworth. Your daughter, Victoria, is here."

"I'm sorry, I don't understand. Why is my daughter at the airport?" Uncertainty washed over Kerri.

"She's attempting to exchange an airline ticket to New York from her scheduled flight on Monday to one today. Unfortunately, since she's only thirteen and not the purchaser of the ticket, we can't make the change for her. I called Nicholas Jackman, the purchaser of the ticket. He asked me to cancel the ticket and to call you to pick up Victoria."

Outrage bolted through Kerri. "I'll be right there." She slid her phone into her pocket as she stood. "I have to pick up Tori."

"Call him," Falco said to Jen as he pushed back his chair. "Try to see him tonight if possible. As soon as you have a time and place, let us know. We'll help you prepare."

Jen nodded. "Okay. I can do this. I really can."

Kerri still didn't like this. Not one bit.

"Is Tori okay?" Jen asked, worry and fear and no small amount of pain etched on her face.

"I don't know. She's at the airport, trying to leave for New York."

Jen's hand went to her mouth.

"I have to go." Kerri hesitated. "Do not do anything without talking to one of us first. Got it?"

Jen nodded. "Got it."

Kerri hurried for the door. She had to get to Tori.

———

Birmingham-Shuttlesworth International Airport

Kerri stood just beyond the automatic doors for a long moment. Her daughter sat in a seat directly across from the airline desk. Her backpack and a small suitcase sat at her feet.

Kerri had no idea why the son of a bitch had canceled the hearing—though she was glad he had. But she had a feeling something more had gone down. Tori wouldn't have come to the airport trying to use the ticket he'd emailed her otherwise. Something had happened to upset her.

Deep breath.

Kerri walked over to the row of chairs. "Tori, what's going on?"

She wouldn't look at Kerri; she kept her gaze glued to her phone and her scroll of Instagram.

Kerri moved around to the other side of her and sat down. "I'm really sorry, but your father canceled the tickets, so you're going to need to come home with me now."

"You're not sorry. You're glad. Don't pretend to be something you're not." She shoved her phone into a pocket on her backpack.

Kerri leaned forward and braced her forearms on her thighs. "It's true I don't want you to spend the entire summer away. I'll admit that much, but I was okay with four weeks, remember? I would never have wanted anything to happen to hurt you. I'm sure we can call your father and work out a new schedule for you to visit. Whatever is going on—"

"She's pregnant," Tori cried. She swiped at her eyes. "She found out today she's having a baby, and Dad said they would be too busy this summer for me to come."

The dirty rotten bastard.

Kerri pulled her daughter into her arms. "Baby, I am so very sorry. I don't even know what to say."

"I thought if I just showed up, he would change his mind. I could help them get the baby's room ready. I could do lots of things."

Her thin body quaked in Kerri's arms, and her heart fractured.

"He'll never have time for me now."

Tori cried for a while, and Kerri let her. She said nothing more. To say anything more was unnecessary. Her daughter had just learned the hard way what a dick her father could be. Kerri wished she could have protected her from this. Nick should have called her and explained the situation. He should never have just canceled on their daughter.

"I want to go home," Tori whispered between sobs.

"Come on. We'll stop for ice cream on the way."

She grabbed the small suitcase, and Tori shouldered her backpack. Kerri draped an arm around her, and they exited the airport. Falco's car sat at the curb. He was leaning against it, waiting for them.

"Hey, pretty girl."

Tori stopped and faced her mother. "Can Falco stay with us for a while and play video games with me? We could order pizza like last time."

Kerri laughed and looked to her partner. "I don't know. Can he?"

"Sure thing, girlie. But I have to warn you"—he opened the rear passenger door—"I'm the best at just about any game you name, so prepare for a beatdown."

"It's on," Tori said as she launched into the back seat.

As they prepared to get in, Kerri mouthed the words *thank you* across the top of the car to her partner. He gave her a wink and slid behind the wheel.

She wasn't always a great mom, but Falco was wrong. He would make a good dad.

57

6:30 p.m.

Devlin Residence
Twenty-First Avenue South

Tori and Falco had just gotten settled in front of the television with their ice cream and a fierce game Kerri couldn't name, much less understand, when the doorbell rang. She hoped it was Jen with news of a rendezvous with Thompson. Falco was right. With Jen's help they could tie both York and Thompson to that murder scene . . . *maybe*.

The sooner they finished this and found Amelia, the better. If she was in hiding and her cell was dead, Kerri wasn't sure how they would get in touch with her.

As long as she was safe, the rest would work out.

In the meantime, Kerri had decided to talk to Tori about staying the night at Diana's so she and Falco could move forward with their plan to surveil Thompson and York tonight. Whatever was going down with this case, it was starting to move faster. They couldn't risk following orders. Not tonight for sure. Kerri's instincts were humming.

She walked to the door and checked the peephole. Diana and Robby.

Kerri's heart rocketed into her throat. She almost ripped the door off its hinges getting it open. "Have you heard from Amelia?"

Diana shook her head, the weariness in the move squeezing Kerri's chest.

"We need to talk to you, Kerri." Robby glanced at the racket on the television, then at Tori and Falco on the sofa.

"Sure. Come on in. We can talk in the kitchen."

Tori shouted "Hey!" to Diana and Robby but never took her eyes off the game. Falco gave one of those jerks of his head that guys used as a form of greeting.

In the kitchen, Kerri gestured to the island. "Pull up a stool, and I'll get the beer. So not even a text from Amelia?"

"No." This from Diana. The icy fear in the single syllable tore at Kerri's soul.

Robby didn't say anything; he just stood there staring at Kerri.

She grabbed two beers and walked back to the island, set both on the counter. "You guys are making me nervous. What's going on?"

The two looked at each other before turning back to Kerri. Robby swallowed hard and seemed to struggle drawing in a breath. "We think something bad has happened to Amelia, and it's my fault."

"No." Diana shook her head. "It's *our* fault."

Kerri put the brakes on the emotions that started to twist inside her. "Have you heard something from one of her friends?"

There had been nothing on Amelia's laptop or social media. Her friends claimed not to have heard from her. Bellemont claimed Ramsey had only been watching her to see if she would lead him to Sela. Though Kerri didn't trust the guy to be telling the whole truth, they damned sure couldn't find Ramsey to question him.

Diana and Robby shook their heads in answer to her question about Amelia's friends.

"Okay," Kerri said. "Sit down. Drink the beer, and tell me what you mean."

Robby waited for his wife to sit, then pulled out a stool for himself. He opened a beer and downed it. Kerri glanced at Diana; she shook her head, then pushed the other beer to her husband.

"Take it a little slower this time," Kerri suggested.

Robby sipped the beer, then took a big breath. "You remember when my dad died?"

Kerri nodded. "Of course. It was rough for you guys for a while." His father had left the books at the shop in a mess. But Robby had turned it around.

"There's a reason I was able to turn it around so quickly."

"You're good at what you do." Kerri eased up onto a stool on her side of the island.

He shook his head. "The bank was foreclosing. I had no idea what I was going to do. All I could think about was how Di and I would lose everything. Amelia was only three and . . ." He shook his head again. "I was desperate."

"Been there, done that," Kerri assured him. Most everyone experienced hard times at one point or another.

"No." His gaze collided with hers. "You would never do what I did."

"Now you're really freaking me out. What did you do?" When he hesitated, she said, "Robby, this is just me, you, and Diana. Whatever you say, I'm not telling anyone."

His face crumpled, and for a second she thought he would cry. "You have to, Kerri. There's no way around it. I should have done this a long time ago and maybe . . ." He closed his eyes and shook his head.

Kerri looked to Diana, who seemed to have drifted into a coma. She shifted her attention back to Robby. "Okay. Why don't you start at the beginning?"

He downed the rest of his second beer. "I think you should probably get your partner in here for this."

Oh hell. "If you're sure that's what you want."

He nodded. "I'm sure."

Kerri went into the living room. It took her a moment to convince Tori to release Falco from his promise. He swore he would make it up to her. Kerri decided her daughter sensed something was wrong when she said, "No problem. I have new clothes to hang up."

She turned off the game and headed for the stairs.

Back in the kitchen, Kerri introduced Falco to Robby; then he took a seat on a stool at the end of the island. Kerri brought a round of beers.

"Right after my dad died," Robby started again, "the bank had sent the loan to foreclosure. I had done all I could do." He exhaled a big breath. "A few days later I was working late—"

"You worked late all the time," Kerri reminded him. Poor guy. "Still do."

He nodded. "Yeah. Well, this one night a man knocked on the door. It was maybe nine o'clock. He said he had a proposition for me. He showed me his car, where he'd had what he called a fender bender. It was a company car, he said, and he didn't want any trouble. When I hesitated, he told me he could help with my loan problems if I could fix the car then and there. When I still hesitated—to tell you the truth, I thought the guy was nuts—he said if I made the repairs and kept my mouth shut that he'd make the whole loan problem go away. I laughed because it was a hell of a lot of money, so I knew he was pulling my leg. I was a little rattled since I wasn't sure how he knew about my loan."

Kerri refrained from asking questions. She didn't want to stop his momentum. This was obviously difficult enough without her interjecting her thoughts. Questions or comments could come when he was done. Falco apparently had decided the same.

"He told me he was a lawyer at the firm who was working the foreclosure. He kept telling me he could make it go away. Finally, I said okay. He sat down in my office to wait. It took me hours because I couldn't go for parts or paint. I had to use what I had on hand and mix colors to make it match." He shrugged. "But I was really good at that kind of thing, so I kept at it until I got it just right."

He scrubbed his hands over his face. Kerri had never seen him so exhausted and shaken. Diana looked lost, defeated. Kerri's chest hurt. She hated seeing her sister suffer so. Amelia couldn't possibly understand how she was hurting her parents, or she would come home.

Unless someone wouldn't allow her to do so.

"Before he left," Robby continued, "he gave me his card and said that as long as I kept my end of the bargain, he would keep his. I figured I had just been screwed, but what the hell—I had been screwed before. The next day one of those messenger guys stopped by the shop and delivered the paperwork on my loan. It was stamped 'Paid in Full.' I thought it was a joke, so I called the bank. But it was true. The loan was paid in full."

Robby's gaze shifted full on to Kerri's. "In fifteen years, not a day or a night has gone by that I haven't worried that he'd come back and want something else. I knew what I'd done—whatever he had done—was bad. Really bad."

Falco asked, "Did this man ever approach you again?"

"Before you say more," Diana said to Robby, her hands up in a sort of surrender, "let me talk."

Robby didn't look happy about it, but he nodded for her to go ahead.

She cleared her throat. "Around that same time, maybe a few months later, a man approached me at the little studio I leased when I first started out."

"I remember the one," Kerri said. *Little* was a generous description. Her sister had worked really hard to move up from there.

Diana nodded, drew in a shaky breath. "He was widowed and had a little girl. She was four at the time. She was very shy. He said she just hadn't been the same since her mother died. He wanted me to give her private classes. At first I refused because honestly I couldn't afford to spend the time with just one child. I needed at least ten students in each class to make it financially feasible."

She looked to Robby, and he took her hand in his before she continued. "He offered me two hundred dollars per session. All I had to do was work with her one on one for one hour each week."

Kerri made a surprised face. "Wow."

Diana shook her head slowly from side to side. "He was so nice, and his little girl was so sad. God knows I needed the money, so I said yes." She moistened her lips. "These private lessons continued for the next several years, and I put aside most of it. I really wanted to be able to one day buy a studio of my own. As luck would have it, the place I'm in now came available. But I didn't have enough for a proper down payment, and the interest rate was insane. This man offered to give me an interest-free loan. I refused, of course." She drew in a big breath. "The next thing I knew, he'd bought the studio and handed me the deed. He said I could pay him back in whatever way worked for me." She turned to her husband. "I never told Robby. I didn't want him to worry that I was getting in over my head or that there was something else going on."

Robby put his arm around her. "Because I had kept my mouth shut, she had no idea that the man who'd been bringing his daughter to her all that time was the same one who showed up at my shop late that night wanting his car repaired."

Kerri suddenly felt sick to her stomach. She knew where this was going.

"Have you," Falco asked Robby again, "heard from him since that first time?"

"Not until just over two weeks ago. He came to my shop and said he had another job for me. This time he was going to give me cash. All I had to do was damage the braking system on a car so that the brakes would fail. He would see that the car was brought to me, and I would never know who it belonged to or anything."

Kerri held her breath. But she knew Robby. He wouldn't do anything to hurt another human. Neither would Diana.

"I told him no way. I couldn't do it. He reminded me that I owed him a big debt of gratitude. That I still had my business, and it was flourishing because of what he did for me. I told him that was payment for a service I provided. He said it was more than that; it was tampering with evidence, and if I didn't do what he needed me to do, the police might find out. I figured he had as much to lose as I did, so I stood my ground."

"Did he let it go at that?" Kerri had to ask. Deep down she knew there was more. What Robby had said about Amelia when he and Diana first arrived kept echoing in her head.

"He said okay, if that's the way I wanted to do things, but he warned I would regret turning him down. Then he left."

"But that wasn't the end of it," Falco suggested.

Robby shook his head. "A few minutes after he left, another man came in demanding to know if I was working for the first guy. I told him no and made up a story about why he'd stopped by. This guy was livid. But I couldn't tell him what he really wanted to know. I was already scared shitless of what the bastard would do to me for saying no. This other guy finally left, and then a few days later he was all over the news." Robby dropped his head. "He was Ben Abbott, and the next time I saw his face, he had been murdered."

His words seemed to echo in the abrupt silence for five or so seconds.

Kerri took a moment to absorb what he'd just said. "Who was the other man—the first one?" She glanced at Falco. They both already knew the answer.

"Lewis York."

Another look passed between Kerri and her partner, but neither of them reacted. No matter that she had a million questions and her heart was pounding, she needed to hear whatever else Diana and Robby had to say.

"Then," Diana said, "on Sunday he stopped by my house. I haven't given his daughter a lesson since she went off to college, and I repaid the loan before that, but suddenly there he was at my door. He'd never come to my house before. He said he just wanted to tell me how much they loved Amelia at the firm and how they planned to donate generously for any needs beyond her scholarship."

Kerri's lips tightened. Arrogance personified. The bastard. "Did he pressure you in any way?"

Diana shook her head. "No, but it felt *strange* . . . as if he wanted to remind me of who he was and all he'd done for our family."

"He called me that same day," Robby put in, "just to remind me that I owed him and that he was still planning to collect. After all that's happened this week with Amelia, I'd had enough. I went to his office this afternoon." The big guy took a moment to compose himself. "I told him if he'd done anything to hurt Amelia, I would make him pay. I didn't like it when she went to work there, but she was so happy. I didn't want to do anything to ruin it for her."

"What did York say?" Kerri prompted, ushering him back on track, dread thickening in her throat.

"He told me to go home and remember that I still have two kids and a wife and that I should take better care of them." Robby stood. "I saw it in his eyes. He did something to my girl. I know he did."

"Robby," Kerri said, adrenaline burning through her, "before you say anything else, you need to know your rights." This was skirting into dangerous territory, and she did not want to risk Robby incriminating himself further.

"I don't give a damn about my rights, Kerri. Amelia is missing, and that son of a bitch did something to her. I know it!"

"First," Falco said, "I need you to think about what York asked you to do. Did he mention Abbott's name or what kind of car he wanted you to sabotage?"

Robby shook his head. "No. He didn't. I assumed since Abbott stormed in right after his visit and then turned up dead a few days later that it was about him. Why else would he have been following York around? He knew the guy was up to something that involved him and his family." Robby swore. "I let that happen."

"You're right about Abbott," Kerri said, drawing him from that guilt-ridden path for now. "I just don't know if that conclusion will be enough to get the powers that be to allow us to move on York. I know you're telling the truth, Robby, but in the court's eyes this will be your word against his, and he's a very powerful man."

Robby stared at the ceiling and expelled every profane word in his vocabulary, all directed at York.

"What kind of damage was done to the car you repaired for him fifteen years ago?" Falco asked.

"Front bumper. He said he hit a deer, but I didn't believe him. I think it was a person. This was a sedan. You hit a full-grown deer straight on in a sedan, the animal is coming up on the hood. Deer are top heavy. You hit a person straight on, it's a little different. They're most likely going down. Whatever he hit went down. I looked under the car, and there was . . ." He took a breath. "A hunk of meat trapped . . ." He shook his head, as if trying to clear the image from his mind. "Whoever he hit, they didn't survive. Couldn't have."

Diana covered her mouth with her hands, her eyes filling with tears.

"We need the exact date this happened," Falco pressed.

"August first, fifteen years ago."

"Jesus," Kerri said. "That's the last day anyone saw Janelle Stevens."

"If we could tie him to this," Falco said, "we could take the son of a bitch down."

Kerri reminded her partner of their current reality. "Robby's word against York's. We all know how that will go. Hell, the LT will remind me that all these people—Jen included—are my family."

"Jen talked to you too?" Diana asked, regret filling her dark eyes.

"She did." These bastards had hurt this family and too many others to count.

Falco shook his head. "We can't just let this go."

Kerri wanted to scream, but she refrained. "What do you suggest we do beyond what we've planned?"

"I have evidence."

Both Kerri and Falco, even Diana, looked at Robby and simultaneously asked, "What?"

"I might have been desperate, but I wasn't stupid. I always took pictures of every car I did bodywork on. I posted the befores and afters on the bulletin board to show customers. I took a photo of the damage to the front end and of the license plate. I wrote down the VIN, and"—he took another breath—"I kept that hunk of meat."

Anticipation walloped Kerri. "Please," she said, her voice quivering, "please tell me you're serious."

He nodded. "As a damn heart attack."

"What did you do with it?" Falco asked, on his feet now.

"It's in a box inside a plastic bag tucked into the freezer part of the fridge at my shop."

Kerri could hardly breathe. "Falco, take Robby to his shop, and get that evidence to the lab. I'm calling the LT."

Falco patted Robby on the back. "Let's go, buddy. You may have just solved two cases."

Robby's gaze held Kerri's for a moment. "Find my girl for me." He shook his head. "If . . . whatever has happened—"

Kerri held up her hand to stop him. "It's not. Go. Get the evidence."

Diana hugged him, her face burrowed into his broad chest. "We'll get him," she murmured.

When the two were out the door, Kerri ushered Diana into the living room. She called Tori downstairs to sit with her while she went into the kitchen and called Brooks. She filled him in on all that she and Falco had just learned, though she opted to not identify her sources for now. His response was not the one she had wanted to hear. She and Falco were already on thin ice. The chief had ordered them to stay away from Thompson and York. They would talk about this tomorrow.

End of story.

As frustrated and furious as she was, she didn't bother arguing. It was pointless. Sadie Cross's comment reverberated through her. *Thompson and York are part of the untouchables.*

The notification of a new text chimed. Kerri checked it. Jen was still trying to get in touch with Theo. So far, he wasn't taking her calls. She promised to keep trying until she made it happen.

Before she could answer, another text from Jen appeared.

I'm so sorry, Kerri. I never meant to hurt you.

Kerri smiled sadly and sent her a response. I know you didn't. Keep trying. Let me know ASAP if you reach him.

She hit send and started to put her phone away but sent one more message first.

Be careful. Do not try this alone.

A thumbs-up was Jen's response.

Kerri stood in the middle of her kitchen for a long moment. She thought of what Amelia had asked her just a few days ago.

Do you believe the top level of Birmingham PD can be trusted?

Kerri had been so sure the answer was yes.

Maybe not.

This was the first time in her career that she felt as if the chain of command had let her down.

When she wandered back into the living room, Tori was brushing her aunt's hair and telling her how pretty she was. Kerri had never been so proud of her daughter. *Please, please, please let Amelia be okay.*

As soon as Falco and Robby returned, Robby gave Diana a kiss and went to pick up the boys from camp. He would come back for Diana and Tori. Kerri didn't want her daughter alone. Particularly not since she had made it abundantly clear to Thompson and York that she intended to get them both.

Falco ushered Kerri into the kitchen, out of earshot of Tori and Diana. "The lab is crazy busy, but they're going to put us at the front of the line." He studied her face, then frowned. "What did the LT say?"

"Brooks says we have our orders."

"Are you fucking kidding me?"

Kerri shook her head. "One or both of those two bastards got away with killing Janelle Stevens fifteen years ago. We're this close"—she held her thumb and forefinger about an inch apart—"to connecting them to that one and the Abbott case. I'm not letting them get away with murder this time."

With every fiber of her being, she hoped Amelia was not part of this. Kerri prayed she actually was with a totally unrelated friend. Safe and lying low.

"We should prepare for an all-nighter," she said. "I don't know if Ben Abbott's parents are dead because they knew too much, or one or both couldn't live with what they knew anymore. God only knows who killed Ben or the woman posing as Sela's mother or Joey Keaton. But like we talked about before, it feels like cleanup. We need to keep an eye on Thompson and York until we can take them down."

"The sooner, the better," Falco agreed.

"I'll take York," Kerri offered. If he had anything to do with Amelia going into hiding, she intended to make him pay.

"I'll stake out the Thompson place." He gave her a warning look. "If anything goes down, I want to hear from you right then. No moving on your own."

"Same goes, partner," she shot back.

If York or Thompson made a move or had a visitor, she and Falco would be there, ready to pounce.

58

8:00 p.m.

T. R. Thompson Residence
Briarcliff Road, Mountain Brook

His cell phone buzzed. T. R. slipped into his robe, tied the belt, and enjoyed the soft feel as the fabric snugged against his well-toned body. He reached for the phone. How many reporters had mentioned during interviews that he and Theo could be brothers?

He grinned. Enough for him to know his hard work in the gym all these years still paid off. A frown tugged at his brow as he viewed the screen. He didn't recognize the number. Rather than answer with his name as he generally would, he said, "Hello."

"T. R., how have you been?"

Shock rumbled through him at the sound of *her* voice. "Why are you calling me?"

"Why wouldn't I call you? You and I have been such good friends. Look at all that money I raised in your name for those poor children. The hospital is naming that wing after you because of me."

"What do you want?"

"I need to see you."

He laughed as he exited his bath and strolled across his bedroom. A nice nightcap was in order. That was another of his antiaging secrets. Early to bed and early to rise. Since he had no one to answer to other than himself and his constituents, he could damn well do as he pleased. That was the way he liked it.

"I'm afraid I'm quite busy these days. You're aware I'm sure to be elected governor. I'm afraid I simply have no time. Besides, the way I hear it, you're a fugitive. Frankly, I thought you were dead."

He ended the call and dropped his phone into the pocket of his robe. How dare that gold-digging slut call him? His bare feet were silent on the long carpeted corridor that led to the landing. He should notify Lewis. Let him handle the . . .

The thought slipped from his head when his gaze landed on the woman standing at the bottom of the staircase.

"How did you get into my house?" His hand tightened on the railing. He should call the police. Lewis, he should call Lewis now.

"Don't you remember?"

She walked to the bottom of the stairs, the bulge of her belly far too visible with her tight clothing. What the hell was she wearing? Black leggings and some tight-fitting black top that covered all of her save her face and neck. Even the shoes she wore were black, as were the damned gloves. What was she up to? She looked like a burglar. He almost laughed out loud. She'd certainly separated him from a few of his millions.

Well, if she was after more of his money, she could forget about it. He was onto what she was really after. Revenge.

"You gave me a key and the passcode to your gate back in January after the New Year's party. You may have been a little tipsy. You urged me to come some Friday evening when your staff was off duty."

Fury tightened his lips. Teasing bitch. "But you never came." He walked down a step and then another. He had forgotten about giving her the key and the passcode until just this moment. "What do you want?" he demanded once more.

"Come down, and we'll talk about it. I promise it will be worth your while. And then I'll be on my way. You'll never see me again."

She was clearly unarmed. She certainly couldn't be hiding anything in that getup. He descended another step. "What do we have to talk about?"

"All I want to know is who killed my sister. One name. That's all."

He laughed as he moved down another step. What a fool. Her trollop sister had gotten exactly what she'd deserved. Who did she think she was, trying to worm her way into places she did not belong? "You actually went to all this trouble for revenge? How sad for you." He took another step down, feeling bolder. "I have no idea—"

His foot caught against something. He pitched forward.

Falling.

Fear hurtled through him.

His body slammed against unforgiving marble treads over and over until he fell flat on his back at the bottom of the staircase.

Pain seared through him. He cried out. Tried to move. More pain. He needed his phone. Tried to drag his arm down to his pocket.

"Looking for this?" She waved his phone in front of his face.

How had she taken it from him so quickly? Had it fallen from his pocket?

"Call an ambulance." He moaned with the rising agony.

"I'll call an ambulance," she promised, "as soon as you tell me who killed my sister."

Why would he tell her anything? He wouldn't. Dear God, the pain was unbearable. His body was on fire with it.

To hell with it. "She did," he hissed. Better for her to suffer than him.

"Who is *she*?"

His son might never forgive him . . . but he couldn't hold out. He needed help . . . he was in such pain and so afraid of dying. "Suzanne."

"Why?" the bitch demanded.

A roar of agony wailed from his throat before he could answer. "Theo," he moaned, "told her he was leaving her for Janelle. He was willing to give up everything. Suzanne followed her until she found the right opportunity. She ran her over and then buried her body."

Dear God! He couldn't bear this pain any longer. His entire being radiated with the force of it. His heart was pounding. The pressure in his chest was horrendous. "Please. I told you what you wanted to know. Make the call!"

"Where did she bury her?"

He wailed again with the rising agony.

She moved. He managed to turn his head the slightest bit to watch her. Was she calling for help?

Taking her time, she climbed the stairs. Midway up, she paused and bent down. "What're you doing?" He howled with another flood of misery.

When he looked again, she was coming down the stairs, wrapping something around her hand as she moved toward him. Then he knew. She had put something in his path. A wire or string of some sort. That was why he had tripped.

Fucking bitch!

She crouched next to him. "Where was she buried?"

"You won't get away with this," he snarled.

She smiled. "I already have. Now tell me what she did with my sister's body, and then I'll make the call for an ambulance."

He suddenly saw two of her. Her two faces swam in front of him.

"Tell me," she whispered, her faces suddenly close to his.

He thought of that night. Of how Suzanne had come to him with the girl in her trunk. He'd called Lewis, and they had . . .

His mind drifted back to those frantic moments. Dear God, what they had done . . .

He stared up at the two faces peering down at him. A voice was speaking . . . was it his voice or hers? But her lips weren't moving.

Oh, what they had done . . .

59

9:30 p.m.

Whisper Lake Circle

Suzanne parked next to T. R.'s car. What on earth was he thinking, coming here at this time of night? She shook her head. He must have some reason. She hoped it was a good one.

"I swear, I think you're getting senile, old man." How did he expect to be governor if he kept forgetting things and making little mistakes? Perhaps he would see that he needed her more than ever.

Suzanne had decided long ago to make herself invaluable to T. R. God only knew if she would be able to count on Theo. He was far too weak.

She climbed out of her car, hit the fob to lock it, and then dropped it back into her purse. She hurried to the front door. She assumed he was inside since the downstairs lights all appeared to be on. The door was unlocked. Did he have a key?

"T. R.?" She called his name repeatedly as she roamed through the empty house. "Where are you? Are you all right?"

Her cell vibrated. She noted the name on the screen, then answered. "What do you want, Lewis?" The idiot should be babysitting Theo tonight just to make sure he didn't do anything stupid.

"Stay close to your husband, Suzanne. The next twenty-four hours are crucial to getting through this."

She rolled her eyes. "You should be babysitting Theo. The two of you are the reason this all started." She had other things to do, like see after T. R.

"You have my word. By lunch tomorrow, this will all be behind us."

"How the hell do you know when this will end? If you had paid better attention, you could have ended this before it started." *Fool.*

"I'm meeting her at the cabin in the morning at nine sharp," Lewis insisted. "She's told me what she wants. We're going to end this. Just the two of us."

Suzanne laughed. "I'd be careful if I were you, Lewis. She's a cunning little bitch."

"Trust me, Suz. I've got this. I'll be waiting when she arrives, and when it's done, I'll expect a very nice bonus for cleaning up this enormous clusterfuck."

She ended the call. T. R. was right. Lewis York greatly overestimated his worth.

Speaking of T. R., where the hell was he? "T. R.? It's late. Where are you?"

Once she reached the far side of the great room, she stalled. The french doors were open. There were no exterior lights on. Had he gone outside? What was he doing out there? She stepped through the door and onto the patio.

Suddenly the exterior lights blared to life.

An excavator still stood next to the pool. Rubble lay in massive piles.

The air trapped in her throat. She'd thought they had this under control.

"Fuck."

Someone had dug up the pool. "What the hell?"

She ventured across the patio and to the edge of the former pool. Some pieces still lay in the pit that had once been her mother's beloved oasis. Another piece of equipment sat next to the excavator. It wasn't so large and looked like a metal barrel on legs.

"T. R.?"

She should call the police. Something was very wrong.

The lights went out.

Suzanne jumped. Dropped her phone and her purse. Damn it! She couldn't see a thing. She reached down and scratched around on the ground. Where was her phone? Couldn't find it.

"T. R.! What the hell is going on?" She straightened and peered into the darkness, willing her eyes to adjust faster.

Something slammed into the back of her head. Pain shattered through her skull. The blow sent her pitching forward. She twisted to grab on to something, but there was nothing except air. She fell into the pool, landing on her back atop a pile of rubble. Pain exploded in her body. Her head throbbed and spun. Her eyes wouldn't focus.

She . . . she . . .

"Hello, Suzanne."

The bright beam of a flashlight shone in her eyes. She blinked. Wanted to shield her eyes from the brightness but couldn't seem to initiate the necessary action.

Who . . . ? The voice sounded familiar.

"Isn't it amazing what the right contractor will do for the right price? It was so easy to hire him to show up this afternoon and rip out this lovely pool your mother built for your children to use when they visited her." She laughed. "If she was anything like you, she needed some sort of bribe to woo them here." She sighed. "Anyway, I digress. The contractor even left his nifty concrete mixer loaded with the dry mix I would require. All I have to do is add water."

Suzanne tried to get up. Why couldn't she move? The sound of water pouring into metal brushed her dulling senses. Something started to hum. The hum soon became a growl. Fear shattered in her chest. She needed to move, but she couldn't. Her body would not cooperate.

The pain was overwhelming. She couldn't keep her thoughts together.

"There we go." The growling stopped. "I think we're ready now."

The organ in Suzanne's chest flopped wildly. *Sela Abbott.* The voice belonged to that disgusting gold digger. "What . . . what the hell are you doing?"

Suzanne's words sounded strange. Her voice was frail, and her head was spinning again. "What've you done to T. R.?"

"Oh, I'm afraid he's going to have to drop out of the race for governor."

"You will not get away with this," Suzanne said with as much force as she could muster. Her body began to shudder and quake, and she couldn't stop it.

She needed help. "H-help me."

"I know everything, Suzanne," Sela warned. "T. R. told me what you did to my sister. If you want my help with the pain, you only need tell me one thing first."

Suzanne tried to scream, but her throat wouldn't form the sound. She couldn't stop shaking. "An-anything."

"Who killed my husband?"

60

11:45 p.m.

Neal watched for headlights in the darkness.

Suzanne had ordered him to meet her. Keith Bellemont was hounding him. The police had put out an APB on his vehicle. At this point, he wasn't sure how much longer he could make himself available, period.

Amelia was MIA. He hadn't been able to reach her in days.

His fingers tightened on the steering wheel. He had a bad, bad feeling.

The police didn't have anything on him. He'd cleaned up too carefully behind himself. He smirked. None of it had been complicated. Marcella Gibbons had been an easy target. She'd spent years mooning over her boss only to watch him marry and start a family with someone else. Neal had used her neediness to achieve his goal. The code to the Abbott home and a copy of the key. On his last visit to her place, he'd removed his bugs. Then he'd moved on to the Abbott home. He'd planted nearly a dozen cameras and listening devices in the big house. He'd known every move they'd made for weeks. He had known where Sela had hidden the weapon she'd bought. When he'd finished with it that fateful morning, he'd tucked it right back where she'd hidden it.

Too bad the cops hadn't found it, or this might have all been over days ago. At this point, he had no idea where the gun was. He'd dared to go back into the house on Wednesday, but it was gone. Either the police were holding back the find, or that bitch had found a way to get her hands on it. He couldn't see her going into the house to get it. She wouldn't risk coming out of hiding.

If the police had done their job, he wouldn't have had to endure Bellemont ranting that everything had gone to shit. The man needn't worry. Neal had most of his assignment under control. Amelia was the only variable, and she had disappeared. Not that he would be worried if she reappeared. She knew nothing about him or what he'd done that Bellemont hadn't already told the police.

Chances were, Amelia was the one who'd sneaked into the house and taken the gun for her friend. Naive kid.

Headlights bobbed into his rearview mirror.

He waited until Suzanne had pulled to the curb in front of him. When the headlights darkened, he got out of his car.

As he moved toward the front of his car, he wondered why she had turned the headlights off but not the engine. She generally did both. Then again it was muggy as hell tonight. Knowing how vain she was, she wouldn't want to shut off the air-conditioning even for a few moments. He would join her in the car and learn the reason for this hastily scheduled rendezvous.

He cut between their vehicles.

Backup lights flickered, and the engine roared. What the . . . ?

The rear bumper of her car rammed into him, pinning him to the front of his own.

Pain seared through him, stealing his breath. He needed to . . . he tried to reach his gun. He always carried his gun, but his right hand was trapped between his body and the hood. He attempted to reach into the shoulder holster with his left.

Her car accelerated.

His own vehicle rocked with the force of her car pressing into it.

A new flood of pain exploded, racing through him. Was excruciating. He had to . . .

His upper body fell forward. His face pressed into the warm metal of her trunk.

And then he felt nothing at all.

61

TODAY

Saturday, June 16

8:30 a.m.

"Go ahead. Shoot me."

The bastard had called her bluff. He'd lunged at her . . . they'd struggled.

Her weapon had fired.

He was dead.

Kerri had left him there—lying on the floor—and driven away from that damned cabin. Hurrying to the crime scene Falco had called about, she'd missed a curve and spun off the road, slamming into the mountainside. She'd had to climb out the passenger's-side door. Pain throbbed in her skull from where he had banged her head against the floor over and over. She touched the left side above her temple and the new ache hammering there. She had apparently hit the driver's-side door window during the crash.

She leaned against the rear bumper of her Wagoneer and squeezed her eyes shut. She had killed him. All she'd wanted was the truth. Where was Amelia? Where was Sela Abbott . . . had she been the one who died in that fire?

"Shit!"

Her scream echoed around her, bouncing off the snaky highway that uncoiled down this godforsaken mountain. She opened her eyes. Squinted at the bright sun. She wished she had her sunglasses, but the idea of climbing back into her wrecked vehicle to search for them was more than she could handle at the moment.

She should have called Falco when she'd followed the son of a bitch from his home to the cabin. Going on her own was stupid. Truly stupid.

Too late now.

She was in way over her head, and she still had no idea if Amelia was okay. Damn it!

Holding an unsteady hand over her eyes, she scanned the road. As much as she hadn't wanted to involve her partner in this, she'd had no choice. Asking him to come get her had been her only option. He would have questions she couldn't answer.

He had been at the new crime scene when she'd called. Another body had been found. Possibly female. Wasn't that what he'd said?

At *Whisper Lake Circle.*

"Oh God." If it was *her* . . . the pounding in Kerri's skull had her stomach churning. She felt confused and unsteady.

What the hell had she done?

Her throat thickened, and nausea roiled in her gut.

How had she let something so damned irresponsible happen? She should have realized he wouldn't be bullied into telling her anything. What she hadn't expected was him charging toward her and the weapon she'd held.

If she'd had any question at all of his guilt, there was certainly none now. An innocent man would never have charged someone holding a loaded weapon—especially someone trained to use that weapon.

Guilty or innocent, dead was dead.

She squeezed her eyes shut again as the world around her started to twirl like a drunken ballerina. She should have called it in instead of driving away.

The sound of Falco's Charger forced her eyes to open. He pulled over to the side of the road and climbed out.

"What the hell happened, Devlin?"

"I was reaching for my cell, and I missed the curve."

The long assessment that followed warned he wasn't convinced of her explanation.

He checked the driver's side, where she feared there might be substantial damage. "Doesn't look too bad. I'll call a wrecker."

Kerri wanted to feel relieved, but what she felt was ill. "Thanks."

Falco looked her up and down. "So what really happened, Devlin?" He glanced up the road. "And what the hell are you doing here? I thought we agreed to—"

"*He* came here. I followed him. That's what I was supposed to do, right? What about you?" She turned the question on him. "Weren't you supposed to be keeping an eye on—"

"Dispatch called me because they couldn't reach you. We have a body, Devlin. That takes priority over our surveillance plans. And I seem to recall we were supposed to notify each other if something came up."

He stared at her. She couldn't hold his gaze. Her head hurt too damned bad. And the guilt . . .

She looked away.

"What is it you're not telling me?"

She struggled to gather her wits about her. "We can talk about it later; let's go. Like you said, we have a body."

"Okay, okay," he allowed.

Kerri forced herself to meet his suspicious glare once more. "Is it her?"

"The vic hasn't been ID'd yet. I did hear back from the lab on the bracelet. Blood type matches Sela Abbott's."

Not what she'd hoped for. "What are we waiting for?" The energy required to make the demand weakened her knees. "Let's go."

For a moment she worried that he would interrogate her further, and she didn't have it in her to hold up to any more questions.

"We'll come back to this," he warned.

Kerri followed him to his car, her mind reeling with another shocking reality. Yes, she was glad the bastard was dead, but if she was charged with murder and went to prison . . .

Her daughter needed her.

She collapsed into the passenger seat of Falco's car.

What the hell was she going to do?

———

Whisper Lake Circle

Kerri's head throbbed relentlessly. She felt as if she might throw up any second. Her mouth was dry, and she was craving water, but she didn't dare take a swallow for fear of setting off a nasty chain of events.

She had killed a man. She stared at her swollen hand.

An unarmed man.

No matter that the piece of shit had deserved something worse than death.

She should have let Falco watch York last night . . . she should have taken Thompson. Then she wouldn't have ended up following the bastard to that damned cabin this morning. And he wouldn't have caught her sneaking a look through the window to see what the hell he was doing.

She pushed the thoughts aside and scanned the area as Falco parked in front of the house, joining the array of other official vehicles. The

ME's van and two other BPD cruisers along with the van sporting the department's crime scene logo. Yellow tape swung in the slight breeze, warning that something bad had happened here.

She climbed out of the car and trailed after Falco. She had been so certain she could end this—force the son of a bitch to give her what she needed, and maybe, just maybe, he would tell her where Amelia was.

Not at all how things had turned out.

Falco led the way around to the back of the house. An excavator still stood near the pool—or where it had been. The pool was now nothing more than a big gaping hole and a number of piles of rubble. The ME's gurney sat next to . . . she squinted . . . a cement mixer. What the hell?

She wanted to ask Falco what had happened, but her stomach roiled, and she barely restrained the urge to puke. She couldn't remember when she'd last gotten sick at a crime scene.

But this wasn't about this scene. This was about the one she'd left on that mountain.

Dr. Moore appeared from behind the cement mixer. "Detective Devlin," he said to Kerri, his knowing gaze roving over her. "You feeling all right this morning?"

"Not particularly," she admitted. "Have you ID'd this victim?"

He shook his head. "Female, we think, based on the nail polish and the shoes we found." He pointed to a single stiletto pump in a brazen red color abandoned on the ground. "The fingernails of the one visible hand are a similar red," Moore went on.

A memory of red nails flashed in Kerri's aching brain. "Where's the body?"

"Down there." The ME pointed into the area that had been the deep end of a luxurious pool.

As she stared into the hole, Kerri swayed. A firm hand gripped her arm and steadied her. Falco was standing next to her.

"We're assuming," her partner explained, "the vic was pushed from about where we stand; then freshly mixed concrete was dumped on top of her. The only part of the body visible is the one hand."

Kerri stared at the hand that extended out of the hardened concrete, as if reaching for help. The nails weren't particularly long, but they were that deep red.

Did Sela Abbott wear nail polish? Kerri tried to call to mind the numerous pictures of the woman she had seen. If this was her, then who was the victim in the house that had burned?

Kerri swayed again. God, her head was pounding. The likelihood that she had a concussion was becoming clearer and clearer. Damn it.

"I need to sit down," she admitted.

Kerri pushed away Falco's attempt to help and staggered from the pool. She left him with the ME and moved toward the steps that led down to a lower terrace with the intention of sitting down.

She didn't make it.

Before she could stop herself, she had fallen to her hands and knees, and vomit spewed from her mouth.

"You okay, Detective?" one of the crime scene investigators called out.

She couldn't answer. Didn't want to look up. The idea that the unis and the crime scene investigators were witnessing her crash and burn had her heaving even harder.

And there was no way to escape what was coming.

That memory of red nails flashed again, and then she remembered. She closed her eyes. Oh hell.

Falco's boots appeared in her line of sight. He crouched down. "There's something I need to show you, Devlin."

She struggled to her feet and dusted off her knees and hands, then swiped at her mouth. "I think the woman in the concrete is Suzanne Thompson. She wore nail polish like that."

"I'll let the ME know, but there's someplace we need to go right now."

"Have you heard from Jen?" She'd stopped returning Kerri's texts about three this morning. The last one had said she still hadn't reached Theo.

Falco shook his head. "I tried calling her but got her voice mail. We'll deal with that in a minute. There's something we have to do first."

———

Thirty-Third Avenue West

The car stopped moving, and Kerri opened her eyes.

The small house that had stood in this spot was nothing but charred rubble now. A few bricks and cinder blocks. But if all that charred rubble could talk, the tales it would tell. This house was connected to decades of pain and at least one murder.

"What're we doing here?" Kerri held her head, wished the pain away. The urge to vomit rushed into her throat, and she twisted, shoved the car door open just in time to heave. Those damned dry heaves went on and on.

When her stomach stopped spasming, Falco waited outside her door. "You need water or something?"

"No." She wiped her mouth with her forearm.

"Come on. We need to talk."

Kerri dropped her feet to the ground and forced herself into a standing position. Deep breath. "So talk. I feel like hell."

"First, I need you to tell me what happened at that cabin." He held her gaze. "All of it."

She drew in a steadying breath. She might as well get this over with. Falco was her partner. He deserved to hear it from her. "Like I said, I followed York there. He went inside, and I needed to know what he was doing." Her body trembled with the images that tumbled one after the other through her mind. "He caught me. We argued, and I drew my weapon."

"Son of a . . ." Falco shook his head. "Did you kill him?"

Kerri nodded.

"Fuck!" Falco walked a few steps away. Hands on hips, he took a long deep breath.

And she'd been worried about him screwing up. Emotion burned her eyes. What the hell was she going to do? This was her mistake; she didn't have a problem with owning it. But Tori would be the one to pay the most for what she had done.

Falco turned back to her, recovered the ground he'd put between them. "Was it self-defense?"

Kerri allowed those moments to replay once more. "He charged me. We struggled. The weapon discharged."

"Okay." Falco reached out, gave her arm a squeeze. "We'll figure this out. For now, there's something you need to know."

It wasn't his words as much as the regret in his eyes that had a new kind of fear chilling her blood. "What?"

"I came back here yesterday after Cross called with what she'd discovered about the history on this place."

She steadied herself, swallowed at the bitter taste lingering in her mouth. "I know this already." He'd come here while she'd waited to see Theo Thompson. It felt like a lifetime ago.

He shrugged. "While I was here, I got this hunch. So I walked this property over and over, and I found something the others missed." He reached into his shirt pocket. He extended his hand to her, a small piece of what looked like jewelry in his palm.

A tiger. Like a charm from a bracelet or the dangly part of an earring. "What does this prove?" She shrugged even as some latent instinct stirred. The tiger was the mascot of the University of Alabama's number one rival, Auburn. "Someone is an Auburn fan."

Definitely wasn't Amelia. Their whole clan was hard-core Alabama Crimson Tide fans. She didn't recall seeing either team logo in the Abbott home. This didn't prove anything. Anyone could have walked across this property and lost . . . whatever it was.

"That was my first thought too. But then Cross called me back and said she had the location where Amelia's cell phone last pinged a tower."

Since they still didn't have anything from the carrier, Cross had agreed to go through a contact of hers to get Amelia's phone records. The woman was just full of resources. Kerri should be grateful. She was. But just now, she was so damned tired and so damned worried that she couldn't think straight.

"What does Amelia have to do with this place?" Kerri reminded herself to breathe. Some instinct deep inside warned she did not want to hear this.

"I checked, and Princeton has a tiger mascot too."

"Why are you doing this?" Fresh hot tears stung her eyes, but she would not buy into his insinuations. Denial shrouded itself firmly around her. She recognized it. "Just say it," she demanded despite the fact that she didn't want to hear any more. The intellectual part of her brain wouldn't stop. "*Say* it!"

"I asked Moore to check her dental records," Falco said gently. "Since most doctors and dentists in the area have digital file sharing, it wasn't difficult."

She stared at the burned-out house, and the earth shifted beneath her. "No." The word erupted from Kerri in a long wail.

Falco pulled her against him and held her tight. "I'm sorry, Devlin."

62

11:00 a.m.

Swanner Residence
Twenty-Third Avenue South

Falco parked in front of Diana's home. Kerri stared at the house. Tori had spent the night, so she would be inside already. Robby had picked up the twins last evening. Everyone was here.

Everyone except Amelia.

And Jen. Where the hell was Jen? A strange mixture of outrage and fear churned inside Kerri. Jen had been at that house. Had Amelia been in there already? Alive?

Kerri closed her eyes for a moment. This wasn't about her feelings or what Jen had done. It wasn't about Diana and Robby's anniversary. The cake and balloons no longer mattered. There wasn't going to be a celebration today. Her heart twisted in her chest. Her gut churned violently.

Amelia was the victim who had died in that burned-out house. Anger and hurt ripped through Kerri all over again, making her tremble.

Nothing in this world would bring her back.

Falco was suddenly at her door, opening it. Kerri climbed out, her mind and body numb. They walked together to the front door. Falco knocked.

Robby came to the door, but he didn't say anything, just opened it and returned to the sofa to sit next to Diana.

The defeat they both wore warned that they understood; deep in their hearts they knew Amelia wasn't coming home.

"Where are the kids?" Kerri asked, her voice hollow.

"Upstairs playing video games in the twins' room," Robby said.

"We should go to the kitchen."

Robby nodded his understanding.

Kerri's cell vibrated. She ignored it as they all moved into the other room. They gathered around the table, though no one sat down. "There's something I need to say."

Falco touched her shoulder. "Dispatch is calling. I need to take this."

She nodded, and he went outside.

Diana and Robby stared at her, waiting for the news that would change everything.

"I don't even know what to say." Kerri closed her eyes, reached deep inside for the courage to do this. To tell her sister that her daughter wasn't coming home.

"Amelia's dead, isn't she?"

Kerri met her sister's gaze. She looked so tired, so hurt, as if she could just melt away into nothing. "Yes. The body that was found in the house that burned was identified through dental records. It was Amelia."

Diana covered her mouth with both hands to hold in her sobs. Robby hugged her close and wept like a child.

"It was York, wasn't it?" Robby demanded. As if her face gave him the answer, his entire body shook as he asked, "Do you have enough evidence to get him?"

Kerri held his gaze a moment. "I already got him. He's dead." More hurt welled inside her. For that she would likely go to prison, and still she was glad the bastard was dead. But now she wanted the ones who had ordered him to do what he'd done.

Robby's gaze held hers. "Thank you."

Tori and the boys appeared in the doorway between the living room and the kitchen, but Kerri herded them back up the stairs. That challenge would have to be handled later.

By the time Kerri returned to the kitchen, Falco had come back inside. He pulled her aside.

"That was dispatch. One of the crime scene guys found human bones in the rubble at Whisper Lake Circle. Bones that have been there since the pool was put in. *Fifteen* years ago, Devlin."

Son of a bitch. The Thompsons had wanted the property back so badly because the only known evidence of Janelle Stevens's murder was buried there.

"Looks like you were right about Suzanne Thompson," he went on. "Her car was found in the garage there. There's a big dent in the rear end, like she backed into another vehicle or a telephone pole or something."

"We need to round up Theo Thompson," Kerri said, grateful at the moment for how numb she felt.

"You know he'll lawyer up. He's not going to talk to us."

Kerri shrugged. "Maybe not, but we can at least pick him up, considering he needs to identify his wife." The chief couldn't suspend them for that.

Kerri went over to her sister. "I will make sure that everyone responsible for what happened to Amelia pays. Do you hear me?"

Diana nodded. Her violent sobs made speech impossible. Kerri hugged her hard and promised her she would be back as soon as possible. Nothing would ever be the same. Amelia was gone. Kerri pulled herself away from her sister and gave Robby a hug next.

She wanted to rush upstairs and hold her daughter tighter than she'd ever held her before. But she had to do this first.

For Amelia.

When Kerri and Falco were in his car driving away, she said, "I'll have to come clean with the LT." She couldn't keep what she had done a secret. There had been too many secrets already.

Falco, one hand on the wheel, fished his phone from his pocket. "We'll figure that out later. I have some ideas." He took the incoming call.

Kerri closed her eyes and rested her head against the seat. She had never felt so tired in her life. The idea that Amelia was dead ripped her in two, and yet somehow she felt empty and numb.

When she opened her eyes again, Falco was turning onto Augusta Way. Maybe Thompson would fall apart and give them the whole story.

Falco parked in front of the piece of shit's multimillion-dollar mansion. "That was dispatch again. They located Ramsey's car."

Kerri forced her mind to focus on the investigation. "Is he in custody? We need to talk to him. He could fill in some of the blanks in all this."

Falco shook his head as he shut off the engine. "He's dead. Hit and run." He looked Kerri in the eyes. "First officers on the scene found a Ruger SR22 hidden under the driver's seat."

"Ramsey is our shooter in the Abbott case?" What the hell? Bellemont's investigator had killed his best friend? Ramsey's relationship with Gibbons had likely given him the access he'd needed. The question was, Who had hired him to do the job?

The idea that the weapon Sela Abbott had illegally purchased had been a Ruger SR22 as well wasn't lost on Kerri. This case had been this way from the beginning. Each step forward, each piece of the puzzle, took them backward or added more questions and holes.

"The Thompsons don't get their hands dirty," Falco pointed out. "Maybe Theo Thompson is the other client Ramsey mentioned."

How the hell had Bellemont not known that his own man was working against him?

Somehow, maybe with the help of adrenaline, Kerri managed to keep up with Falco's long strides as they approached the Thompson home. The front door stood slightly ajar. They drew their weapons, paused, and listened.

Silence.

Falco pushed the door inward and stepped inside.

Kerri moved in right behind him.

A faint sound brushed her senses. A sob? A moan?

On the left.

Falco pointed to himself and then the left. He pointed to Kerri and made a circling motion. She nodded her understanding.

As Falco moved deeper into the entry hall, Kerri went right, checking the front parlor. Clear. Then she moved through a doorway into the massive kitchen, then to the dining room. Clear. As she reached the great room from the kitchen side, a voice stopped her at the doorway.

"I've been waiting for you to get here."

Theo Thompson.

But he wasn't speaking to Kerri. His back was to her.

Someone screamed, the sound muffled. A woman. Kerri moved quickly through the opening between the kitchen and the great room. With Thompson facing the other direction and holding the woman in front of him, she couldn't see who it was. Maybe she'd been wrong. Maybe his wife was here with him. Kerri could see nothing but the woman's legs. Thompson wore trousers and an untucked shirt. Judging by how wrinkled they were, he'd been wearing them since this time yesterday. Now that she thought about it, the pin-striped trousers did look familiar.

"Nice to see you too, Mr. T." Falco now stood face to face maybe four yards from Thompson and the woman. He'd approached from the other side of the room. "How you doing, Jen?"

Jen? Trepidation pierced Kerri. Then she spotted the shoes . . . green. Spiked heels. The same ones Jen had been wearing yesterday at O'Malley's. Kerri's fingers tightened on her weapon.

"Why don't you put down the weapon and let your lady friend go?" Falco suggested.

He had a gun? The air evacuated Kerri's lungs.

Thompson said nothing. Jen sobbed. Kerri's gut twisted. She needed to think! Did she move closer? Give Falco time to talk Thompson down?

"She's not part of this," Falco said. "This is just between you and me."

Thompson raised the weapon. Kerri froze. He planted the muzzle against his right temple.

"It doesn't matter now," Thompson muttered. "Nothing does."

A new tension slid through Kerri. With the weapon no longer aimed at or near Jen, Kerri had an opportunity here. She could move up behind him as long as Falco kept his attention focused forward.

"I think we found your wife," Falco said. "Someone pushed her into that swimming pool at your in-laws' old house and poured a little concrete over her."

More sobbing from Jen. Her feet twisted, and Thompson's upper body jerked, as if she had tried to wrench away from him. He pulled her harder against him; her stiletto-clad feet lifted slightly off the floor. One shiny shoe dropped onto the hardwood.

Kerri moved a step closer. Then two. Her pulse hammered in her brain. She had to be oh so careful. No room for error.

"Oh yeah," Falco said, "they found what was left of your girlfriend too. You remember Janelle? Janelle Stevens."

Thompson's body twitched the slightest bit. Jen whimpered.

Kerri extended her arms and readied to press the barrel of her weapon to the back of his head. All she had to do was take one last step.

Thompson suddenly twisted around, shoved the barrel of his weapon in her face. "You!" he snarled. "I knew you'd be here too."

Jen's eyes rounded with renewed fear. Thompson's arm was around her, his hand clasped over her mouth. Her muffled sobs grew more frantic.

Kerri held perfectly still. Her weapon aimed at his face too. A familiar calmness spread through her. All she had to do was keep her focus on Thompson.

Do not look at Jen.

"How many people have to die to keep your secrets?" Kerri asked, her voice amazingly steady. "You didn't really think your pal York could fix all this, did you?"

Fury flared in his eyes. "It wasn't even me. It was my father. He was the one who started this. He and his buddy Daniel Abbott. They were the ones who loved toying with their female employees. This day and time they'd both be burned at the stake."

"If you despised what he did so much, why did you do the same thing?" Kerri asked. She zeroed her aim in on his forehead.

"I didn't." The hand holding his weapon shook the tiniest bit. "Janelle and I were in love. We were going to get married as soon as I could file for divorce. But my father intervened on Suzanne's behalf, and Janelle disappeared. They were going to kill Jen too. They've always taken whatever I wanted away from me."

Jen cried out, tried to speak around his hand. The arm wrapped around her tightened; his hand clutched harder at her face and mouth.

"But she betrayed me too." He glared down at Jen. "Showing up here in the middle of the night, trying to console me. She was recording the whole thing on her cell phone."

Jen's body rocked with sobs.

Over his shoulder, Falco came into view. He was almost on Thompson now.

Keep him talking.

"I know what you did to Amelia." Fury so hot it scorched her from the inside out roared through her. "I'm going to see to it that you spend the rest of your life regretting that, you son of a bitch."

"Believe me, Detective, I do regret my part in that, but it had to be done."

Something changed in Jen's eyes. She suddenly fell slack against him. Thompson glanced down at her.

Kerri moved.

His attention whipped back to her, and he steadied his aim.

A mournful, gut-wrenching scream filled the room. Jen jerked free of his hold and shoved at his right arm, forcing it upward.

The weapon discharged into the air above Kerri's head. She rushed him before he could attempt to get off another shot.

Falco grabbed him from behind, twisted his arm, and wrenched the weapon from his hand.

Kerri took the weapon, and Falco secured his hands behind his back, all the while reciting the bastard his rights. He ordered him onto his knees. Thompson complied.

Sobbing, Jen collapsed to the floor. Kerri sat down with her and pulled her into her arms. They cried together. They cried for Amelia and all the others who had given their lives for no other reason than to satisfy the wants of greedy, selfish bastards like the Thompsons.

Somewhere beyond the agony consuming her, Kerri heard Falco calling for the crime scene investigators and backup for preserving the scene.

Her cell vibrated. She swiped at her eyes and nose and dug the damned thing from her pocket. It could be Tori. She didn't bother checking the screen. "Devlin."

"Detective Devlin, this is dispatch. Two officers just reported picking up a pregnant woman wandering along Shades Crest Road. She identified herself as Sela Abbott."

63

1:30 p.m.

UAB Hospital
Sixth Avenue

After suffering through a scan to ensure there was no serious damage to her head, Kerri dropped by the vending machine and grabbed a coffee. She didn't trust herself to eat anything yet, but she needed some sort of fortification.

Since they couldn't interview Sela Abbott until after the doctors were finished examining her and Bellemont had spoken with her, Falco had left to take care of something. He wouldn't say what, only that he would be right back.

Kerri hadn't possessed the mental fortitude to question him. She'd checked her voice mail and found a message from the lab confirming that the *meat* Robby had saved all those years was human. The tissue would be compared with the bones found beneath the pool at Whisper Lake Circle to determine if they belonged to the same person. Kerri didn't need any sort of analysis to tell her this. The remains belonged to Janelle Stevens, Sela's sister.

A few minutes ago the doctors had finished with Sela Abbott and pronounced her in reasonably good condition. She was slightly dehydrated and had a number of minor injuries, but otherwise she and the baby were stable.

Now Bellemont was in the room with her. When he gave the word, Kerri would be able to question her. She was all too ready. But she would really like her partner to be here for this. She glanced back down the corridor. Where the hell was he?

She thought of Jen and was grateful all over again that she hadn't gotten herself killed showing up at Thompson's house early this morning. Falco had already been called to the scene at Whisper Lake Circle. Since Jen had parked on the street behind Thompson's house, Kerri and Falco hadn't spotted her car when they'd arrived. An officer had taken her to Diana's house. Kerri wasn't sure how her sister would take what Jen had to tell her about being at the house the night it burned, but that issue would have to be worked out eventually. The pain might just be too raw now.

Kerri leaned against the wall. Too damned tired to hold up her weight on her own anymore. She glanced at the room down the hall where the two unis stood on either side of the door. Around-the-clock protection had been ordered for Sela Abbott.

How long did Bellemont expect to put off the questioning? Kerri finished off her cold coffee. What the hell was taking Falco so long?

As if her thought had summoned him, Falco rounded the corner and strode toward her. She had never been so glad to see anyone in her life.

"Are the doctors still with her?" he asked with a glance at the door of Abbott's room.

"They finished, said she was in good condition. Bellemont is with her now."

Falco glanced around. "We need to talk."

They moved down the hall a few yards. "What's up?" Kerri wasn't sure she could handle any more. Her niece was dead, along with a whole slew of other people.

And she had killed a man.

She closed her eyes. Shit.

"Falco." She looked up at him. "I'm not sure I should even go in there for the questioning. At this point, my involvement could jeopardize the case. After what I did—"

"Stop."

She frowned, waited for him to continue.

"There was no body."

"What?" She stared at him, too weary and confused to follow, obviously.

"I went to the cabin, and the living room area was clean. I'm talking spotless. No body. No blood. Nada. I walked through the kitchen and out the back door and around the yard. Nothing."

"That's impossible. I killed him. He was dead. There was a lot of blood. Do you hear me? The bastard was *dead* dead."

"Doesn't matter if there's no body."

Oh hell. "Did you clean it up?" Irrational anger bolted through her. "Did you?" She did not want to drag Falco down with her. Damn it. It was bad enough Tori would suffer for her sins.

"Devlin, I'm telling you it was clean when I got there."

She wasn't sure she believed him. "I still need to make my statement. If what you're saying is true, I don't know what the hell happened, but I know a dead man when I see one. I killed him." If she was smart, she would back off, let Falco finish this. But she couldn't, she suddenly understood. Whatever mistakes she had made, she had to see this all the way through. For Amelia.

"Just wait," Falco said. "We need to see how this all shakes down first."

Kerri couldn't comprehend how that would matter. Eventually someone was going to report York as missing. He had a daughter. Partners at the firm.

She closed her eyes again. This case had exploded in the past thirty-six hours.

Her family was devastated. She was devastated.

At least eight people related to this case, besides York, were dead.

Suzanne Thompson and Neal Ramsey in addition to Daniel and Tempest Abbott along with Joey Keaton.

And Amelia. Sweet Amelia. The crack in Kerri's heart widened.

They'd found out since reaching the hospital that there was at least one more casualty.

When Theo Thompson had been arrested, he had insisted his father be called since he couldn't reach his attorney, Lewis York. T. R. Thompson hadn't answered his phone, either, so a uniform had gone to his house to round him up, only to find the front door ajar and the man dead at the bottom of his staircase.

The ME believed Neal Ramsey had been crushed between two vehicles. There was rear-end damage to the Lexus belonging to Suzanne Thompson. Paint transfer indicated her vehicle and Ramsey's had possibly been in contact. Further testing would confirm. The last text message Ramsey received had been from Suzanne requesting a meeting. For now, Kerri and Falco were thinking that someone—maybe Theo Thompson or Keith Bellemont or Sela Abbott—had decided to tie up all the loose ends of this case.

Had to be one of them. Everyone else was dead.

The problem was, Bellemont had an airtight alibi, Sela was thirty-one weeks pregnant, and Thompson wasn't talking yet.

"I think we can safely say," Falco murmured, "that anyone who had anything to do with what happened to Amelia, Sela's mom and sister got what was coming to them. Except maybe for Theo."

"He'll get his," Kerri said. She would make sure the guy did not walk.

The door to Abbott's room opened, and Bellemont stuck his head out. "You may come in now," he announced, "but we are not to overtax her. Doctor's orders."

Kerri didn't bother answering him; she walked in, and Falco followed. She tossed her empty coffee cup into the trash can near the bathroom door.

Sela Abbott's bed had been raised, allowing her to sit in a relaxed position. Her face was pale against the green nightgown. Both wrists were bandaged. The linens were smoothed neatly around her.

"Sela"—Bellemont stepped close to the bed—"as I told you, any question that makes you uncomfortable can be skipped. You've been through a lot, so don't try to say too much all at once."

She nodded. "I'm ready to make my statement."

Kerri pushed the tray-top table across her bed and set the audio recorder there. She turned it on, identified everyone in the room, and reminded Sela of her rights before turning the floor over to her.

"State your name, and then begin telling us whatever you'd like to say. We may have questions as we go along."

She nodded. "My name is Sela Abbott. Very early in the morning on Wednesday, June sixth, a man came into our house. I don't know how he knew the passcode to our security system, but he did. He shot my husband and then shot my friend Carol Lofland."

"The woman claiming to be Jacqueline Rollins," Kerri said for clarification.

"Yes. She was a very dear friend of my mother's, and basically, she became my surrogate mother after her death. I became reliant upon her. I needed her with me, so it was simply easier to introduce her as my mother."

Not exactly normal, but whatever. Sela waited to see if Kerri had more questions; then she went on.

"The man dragged me from my house and took me to a cabin in the woods. He restrained me and left me there." She held up her arms to show her bandages. "Another man came to the cabin daily and gave me food and water. He occasionally emptied the bucket I used as a bathroom."

"Did you recognize either of these men?" Falco asked.

She nodded. "I wasn't sure about the first one. But the one who brought me food, yes. His name is Lewis York."

Ice chilled in Kerri's veins. "From the moment the intruder broke into your house, did you at any time see anyone besides these two men?"

Sela looked at her a moment. "No. But early this morning before I was able to escape, I did hear voices and a sort of struggle. At one point I thought I heard a gunshot. It was very loud. After that the house was quiet again; that's when I was able to escape. I had been working on the ropes the whole time, trying to get loose."

How convenient. Kerri would have laughed outright if she weren't terrified there might be a slice of truth in the woman's words. She must have been there. If she hadn't heard the voices, struggle, and gunshot . . . how would she know?

"When you were able to get loose," Kerri asked cautiously, "did you see anyone? A vehicle? Anything?"

Sela shook her head. "The place was quiet. It was like the man holding me captive just disappeared. I walked all the way down Canyon Lane and onto Shades Crest before someone stopped to help me."

Another of those eerie sensations slid through Kerri. No question about it. Sela was referring to the cabin belonging to Lewis York . . . the one where Kerri had shot and killed him.

"What about the other man?" Falco asked. "The one who took you from your house."

"I don't know his name, but I have seen him before." She glanced at Bellemont. "In your office. It was that investigator you said could help us find the truth. He was using my friend Amelia Swanner too."

Hearing her niece's name pierced Kerri's heart all over again.

Bellemont appeared horrified by the news but kept any comments to himself.

"How did you and Amelia become friends?" Kerri wanted to know. Needed to know the whole story.

"When Mr. Bellemont agreed to help Ben and me figure out what really happened to my sister, I was so thankful. The investigator suggested Amelia might be able to help since she was working at York's firm. I made it a point to involve her in one of my fundraisers, and we became friends. Eventually I told her my story, and she wanted to help. She was so excited." A tear slipped down Sela's cheek. "I should never have allowed her to be involved."

Kerri's lips tightened to hold back the angry words roiling in her throat.

Since the lawyer hadn't said a word, Kerri turned to him, outrage blazing inside her. "Is this true, Mr. Bellemont?"

"As you can see, I have not been privy to all of Mr. Ramsey's activities."

It wasn't a yes or a no. Kerri wanted to kick his ass. He had children of his own! How could he do this to someone else's child?

Sela said, "He must have been working for someone besides you. You loved Ben like a brother." Tears welled in her eyes. "This man, he . . . he shot my husband. The sound woke me up. Then he brutalized and shot my friend." Sela put her hands to her face. "She tried to help me. She came into the room. He shot her there first."

This could be accurate, Kerri reasoned, as long as the woman was on or near the bed.

"I screamed for her to run. She took off, but he chased after her." She closed her eyes a moment. "That's when I should have run, but all I could do was try to wake up Ben. When I realized the bad man was coming back, I tried to call 911. He took the phone away from me and knocked me out."

Falco asked several questions. Kerri asked her share as well. No matter how they asked the questions, Sela Abbott never changed her story. But there were holes. Like the fact that there was no blood trail suggesting the woman who'd been shot in the house ran from the master bedroom up the stairs to the nursery after being wounded. She admitted to having purchased a weapon, claiming she'd noticed someone following her on several occasions. She'd hidden the weapon in the baby's crib, which was why her friend had rushed to the nursery when Ramsey was after her. The car she'd bought from Keaton, she insisted, was a way to prevent her stalker from knowing every move she made. In hindsight, she admitted, she should have told her husband.

Kerri was blown away by how carefully she had planned every step—how easily she explained every little thing. Unbelievable.

When they had been over the woman's story at least three times, Bellemont ended the interview.

In the corridor outside, Kerri said to the lawyer, "We will have additional questions for both of you."

He shrugged. "I wish I could give you more or better answers. I'm afraid I'm as in the dark as the two of you. I had no idea Ramsey . . ." He shook his head. "I would have trusted the man with my own children's lives."

"Good thing you didn't," Kerri said, allowing him to see and hear her fury.

When he'd walked away, she turned to her partner. "We need to go to that cabin now—ahead of the crime scene unit."

"You read my mind, Devlin."

York Cabin
Canyon Lane

Sure enough, in the bedroom at the back of the house stood a five-gallon bucket containing urine and feces. A rope was attached to the bed. More pieces of rope lay on the floor. The knob from a drawer in the bedside table had been removed, and the decorative metal plate that went with it had apparently been used as a sort of knife to cut through the ropes. Since it wasn't exactly sharp, it would have taken days.

Exactly as Sela Abbott wanted them to believe.

An abandoned food tray sat on the floor.

Scanning the bed, Kerri spotted a dark hair that was very likely Sela's.

"She's good," Falco said. "I'll give her that."

Just like her professor had said.

Kerri took a breath. "We should go outside and call the crime scene folks." Putting it off any longer would only look suspicious.

They had gone over the front room to make sure nothing of Kerri's scuffle with York had been missed. Whoever had done the cleanup and removed the body had done a hell of a job.

Once they were outside, she turned to her partner. "It's do-or-die time, Falco. Are we really going to try and pull this off? We both know she's lying. She was not in this house when I was here this morning. But she somehow knows I was here."

Falco rubbed his jaw. "The cameras. Maybe she figured out how to use them."

Without another word, they went back inside and checked the computer that sat on the small desk in the corner of the living room. There was no log-on, which seemed odd to Kerri. Even odder, she didn't remember seeing the computer this morning when she had been peeking inside to see what York was up to.

The memory of him catching her rushed into her brain. She blinked it away. If the laptop was there, why hadn't she noticed it? Maybe she'd been too focused on forcing the truth out of a man who didn't know how to tell the truth.

"I'm not seeing anything that suggests he has a surveillance program on here," Falco muttered as he continued tapping keys.

"Maybe there's nothing there. He could have it stored on some cloud."

"We can't take the risk." Falco pulled out his cell and made a call.

Kerri listened as he asked Cross to bring her geek.

Even with all the known players dead or accounted for, this was getting more complicated all the time.

———

Half an hour later Cross and her friend arrived. He looked like a homeless drunk she'd picked up from under a bridge. Kerri's heart sank. This was a total waste of time. She should just call the LT and do what needed to be done.

Falco provided both Cross and her friend with gloves and shoe covers. Kerri paced the room while the man who'd come with Cross sat down behind the computer and went to work.

She thought of Tori and what would happen to her when this all came out. Could she plead temporary insanity? Would the new baby her ex was having with his fiancée cause him to ignore Tori even more? If Kerri went to prison, Tori would end up with him.

Damn it.

"Found it."

Kerri whipped around and stared at the guy.

Falco was looking over his shoulder. "All right. Now we're cooking with gas."

Kerri wandered over, her curiosity and no small amount of hope overtaking her.

"He has a state-of-the-art surveillance program on here. It's the bomb, man."

"Can we see the footage?" Kerri asked.

"You could." The guy looked at her. "Except someone deleted all of it. Every stinking pixel."

"Can you tell when this happened?" Falco asked.

"This morning. Time stamp is nine forty-five a.m."

Kerri had already been out of here by then. She'd wrecked her car, and Falco had picked her up. Someone else had shown up after she'd left. But who? The one person they could definitely rule out was Lewis York. He had been dead before that. Jen had been with Thompson. Suzanne, T. R., and Ramsey were already dead by then. Daniel and Tempest Abbott too.

Who the hell did that leave? Only Sela Abbott.

"Does the FBI or someone like that have people who can recover the deleted files?" Falco glanced at Kerri as he asked the question.

"Not if you don't want them to," Cross's friend said.

"I don't want them to."

Everyone in the room looked at Kerri. She hadn't realized she was going to say the words until she did.

The guy tapped a few keys, then a few more. This went on for what felt like forever. Finally, he looked over at Kerri and said, "Done."

"Thanks, Cross," Falco said. "I'll square this with you."

Sadie Cross nodded, then glanced at Kerri. "See you around."

Kerri managed a vague nod.

Cross and her geek left. Kerri wasn't sure if she was relieved or undone.

"We should call in the crime scene guys now," Falco said as he dug out his phone.

"Yeah. We should." Kerri felt as weak as a kitten.

"Don't think about it," Falco said as he waited for the call to go through. "That's the best way to get past it."

She wondered how many times he'd had to do that. Maybe she didn't want to know. He was her partner, and she trusted him.

The past didn't matter.

Within an hour four other cops and the crime scene investigators were on the scene. Kerri stayed out of the way. Falco drifted between the goings-on and her. He was worried about her.

She was worried about her.

The work was wrapping up when Lieutenant Brooks showed up. Kerri was actually surprised he didn't have the chief with him.

Falco moved close to her as Brooks approached them. He shook his head. "This is stunning. You two have brought down some damn big names. You're going to be in the spotlight for a while."

"We were just doing our job," Kerri said. She wished she sounded more enthusiastic, but she just couldn't summon the energy.

"I was very sorry to hear about your niece, Devlin. I don't know how you're even still here."

He had no idea.

"I should probably take her home," Falco said.

"That's a good idea," the LT confirmed. "As soon as your final reports are wrapped up, you two need to take some time off. You've earned it. The department is very proud of you both. You make a damned good team."

At least she could agree with that last part.

"Thank you, sir," she offered, somehow managing to almost make it sound sincere.

"Thanks," Falco mumbled.

Kerri got the feeling he was not accustomed to praise.

Brooks nodded. "Carry on." When he would have turned away, he hesitated. "Just so you know, Thompson is cooperating fully. He's spilling his guts on his cronies. I have a feeling he's going to take a deal."

As her boss walked away, Kerri wanted to kick something. Thompson didn't deserve a deal.

"I guess we're big news now, Devlin. Heroes."

She let out a dry laugh. "I don't know if I'd go that far, Falco."

His face turned serious, and he looked around before saying, "What're you thinking about our vanishing wife who suddenly reappeared?" He glanced around again. "You think she made all those murders happen last night? She is pregnant."

Kerri thought of what Sela Abbott's professor had said. She was his best student. He predicted she would either become a great detective or a clever criminal.

"I don't know how much of what happened was her personal doing," Kerri allowed, "but I know she made it all happen." She thought about what she wanted to say next for a moment. "I'm a cop. I've dedicated my entire adult life to taking down the bad guys."

"You see her as the bad guy, then?"

Kerri shook her head. "No. I see her as someone who did what she had to do. Sometimes we just have to do that."

"And what you did? Can you live with that?"

She thought about the question for a moment. "Yes. Someone once told me I should open my eyes. That I would be surprised at what I could see. My eyes are wide open, Falco."

"Come on." He tugged her by the arm. "I should get you home. I'll wrap up things here."

At his car she hesitated before getting in. "Do me a favor, would you?"

"What's that, Devlin?"

"Don't change. Not one thing. I want you to stay exactly the way you are."

He grinned. "I can do that."

64

It is done.

They have all paid for their evil, selfish deeds. The one who survived was only guilty of loving my sister . . . and being a coward.

He will pay a high price for both.

A celebration is in order. I am understandably proud of myself. I successfully lined up all the players in a neat little row, like ducks in a shooting gallery.

I studied and analyzed each of them long before I came here. I schooled myself in where they lived, what they ate, when they slept . . . what they did with their time and money. By the time I arrived in Birmingham, I knew everything. But they didn't see the real me until the time was right.

Fifteen years of preparation culminated quite nicely.

Surprisingly, despite the elaborateness of my plan, there really was only one true glitch beyond the unexpected pregnancy. No one was more startled than I.

You see, all this time I felt certain no one could touch me . . . hurt me.

I was wrong. Perhaps I am not as dead inside as I thought.

When they took my one remaining friend, I realized simple revenge would never be enough. I wanted more.

I wanted to be the last thought on each of their minds before they took their final breaths.

My hands rest on my protruding belly as the nurse fusses over me. She's going to help me with a shower soon. She thinks I'll feel much better then. She's placed a printout of the ultrasound on the bedside table so I can look at my little girl as I lie here resting.

I feel sad for the man who loved me and gave me this baby. He shouldn't have had to pay for the sins of his father. For that, I feel a great deal of regret—far more than I expected.

I will make sure our daughter knows what a good man her father was. I will also make sure she is strong and learns to protect herself from the ugliness of this world. Knowledge is so very powerful, and I have armed myself with every bit of knowledge I could glean from the many, many sources I have encountered in my life.

I suspect Detective Devlin has learned a good deal during this investigation. I respect her. She is one of the good ones, which is why I felt compelled in the end to see that she was protected from what she was forced to do. Actually, she saved me the trouble. Cleaning up her little problem was nothing. It was the least I could do after her family sacrificed so much.

My heart aches for the loss of Amelia. She only wanted to help. She searched relentlessly until she found and took the key I needed from York's office. That key, a simple brass object, allowed me access to the place in that damned cabin where York kept his laptop locked away. The laptop that held all the details of all the dirty little deeds.

For that key, Amelia gave her life.

I walked her through the steps necessary for shutting down the cameras in the building. Just long enough to do what she had to do. It was simple. I am somewhat of an expert when it comes to security systems. If only York's nephew hadn't seen her coming out of his office . . . perhaps the bastard would never have known about my sweet little spy.

Dear Finn won't get away without a little payback. I've heard fraternity hazing at Harvard can be hell. I'm counting on him suffering, just a little.

I have changed my mind about my baby's name. She will be named Amelia. I will send a photo and a note to Detective Devlin. She really did do me a great favor, putting that bullet through a very black heart. She needn't worry about her future where that part of all this is concerned.

Her secret will always be safe with me.

ACKNOWLEDGMENTS

Birmingham, Alabama, holds a very special place in my heart. When my older daughter was born with multiple and life-threatening issues, she was rushed to Birmingham's Children's Hospital. After major surgery, months of hospitalization as an infant, and multiple additional surgeries over the years, my girl is happy and healthy and the mother of two daughters of her own. Most recently my younger daughter, who has two sweet boys, was faced with her youngest needing surgery. He was taken to this same hospital and is doing fantastically well. I am so incredibly thankful for this amazing place. For me and my family, Birmingham truly is the Magic City.

I have immense respect for Birmingham and its prestigious police department. Any negativity about either portrayed in this novel is strictly a product of my vivid imagination and is in no way based on real people or events.

ABOUT THE AUTHOR

Photo © 2019 Jenni M Photography

Debra Webb is the *USA Today* bestselling author of more than 150 novels. She is the recipient of the prestigious Romantic Times Career Achievement Award for Romantic Suspense as well as numerous Reviewers' Choice Awards. In 2012 Webb was honored as the first recipient of the esteemed L. A. Banks Warrior Woman Award for courage, strength, and grace in the face of adversity. Webb was also recently awarded the distinguished Centennial Award for having published her hundredth novel. She has more than four million books in print in many languages and countries.

Webb's love of storytelling goes back to her childhood, when her mother bought her an old typewriter at a tag sale. Born in Alabama, Webb grew up on a farm. She spent every available hour exploring the world around her and creating her stories. Visit her at www.debrawebb.com.